Praise for

"This striking fiction debu~~~~~~~ ~~~~ter-rich story of connection and political awakening in a dystopian future New York where Manhattan and Brooklyn are behind seawalls and the Earth has been ravaged by climate change and resource scarcity." —*BookLife*

"At the heart of this thought-provoking novel are two damaged people trying to build a relationship while working at cross purposes to help society amid dealing with a broken system's inequities... An engrossing book that holds out hope despite all the mistakes made by humans." —*Kirkus Reviews*

"A compelling near-future dystopia about climate collapse and helping the vulnerable survive." —*Independent Book Review*

"Weik von Mossner's gripping novel hits the target on the most urgent problems of scale that come with climate change. *Fragile* takes climate fiction to a new level: a fast-paced, suspenseful must-read for anyone interested in our planet's future." —Ursula K. Heise, Author of *Imagining Extinction*

"Written in the tradition of genre-defying page-turners like Ray Bradbury's *Fahrenheit 451*, Emily St. John Mandel's *Station Eleven*, and Lawrence Wright's *The End of October*, Alexa Weik von Mossner's debut novel is, by turns, thrilling, thoughtful, romantic, terrifying, and imaginative. Pick *Fragile* up at your own peril—I promise that you won't want to put it down." —Kareem Tayyar, Author of *The Prince of Orange County*

"One of the most exciting elements is how visual this near-future version of New York is, split between being greener, with less cars and gardens and plants everywhere, while also half the city has been swept under water." —*The Black List*

FRAGILE

FRAGILE

a novel

ALEXA WEIK VON MOSSNER

ELZWHERE

Weik von Mossner, Alexa.
Fragile: A Novel/Alexa Weik von Mossner.

Published by Elzwhere Press
Burgstrasse 4
79312 Emmendingen
Germany
www.elzwherepress.com

First edition

Cover design by Dane Low

Paperback 978-3-9824969-1-7
Hardcover 978-3-9824969-0-0
Ebook 978-3-9824969-2-4

For Michael

ONE

How do you get used to being a raider—a thief and plunderer—so you can save lives? Shavir couldn't help wondering as they sped eastward on the 495 into Queens. Wearing black pants and a turtleneck, she sat on the floor of an unmarked e-van with fake license plates, her body motionless, face frozen, blood pounding.

Four other inert figures, equally clad in black, huddled next to and opposite her, the space between them filled with duffle bags and large lidded plastic crates. In the front seats, Finn's bright blond hair shone next to Troy's shimmering brown as the city lights washed over them.

It was all familiar, their normal routine, but how could you ever get used to that kind of thing?

They took the Van Wyck Expressway toward the coast, right into the permanent evacuation zone, the world turning pitch-black once they reached Belt Parkway. The city no longer provided electricity for anything east or south of here. Where JFK Airport's big pool of light used to be, broken terminals and flooded runways lay hidden in the hot night. Shavir tried to picture what it had looked like when she'd taken her last flight out of there six years ago, but all she could see was the epic disaster of Hurricane Shelby that had washed it all away.

Finn slowed the van as they reached the closed exit ramp for Cross Bay Boulevard, curving carefully around the warning signs and roadblocks before heading into the nothingness of Howard Beach.

They slid past long rows of abandoned houses, the broken facades adorned with elaborate patterns of flood marks.

"Turn left and then make a right," Troy directed from the passenger seat with the authority of the guy responsible for scouting it all out.

Finn turned the van toward the oceanfront, the dimmed headlights grazing over piles of debris and a shadowy thicket of overgrown yards.

"Stop right here," Troy said into the silence. "That's it."

The van came to a halt.

Lenny cracked the side door, and they waited. Seven people, motionless in the black night, listened to the racing songs of the cicadas and the slow wash of the surf below the van. Wafts of air came seeping in, so hot and humid Shavir felt them through the fabric of her turtleneck. She tasted salt and realized she was panting.

"All clear. Let's go!" Tara hissed from behind, and then Lenny pushed open the door.

Shavir switched on her night-vision goggles and grabbed a crate before stepping into the unreal greenish world outside. Reality came lapping against her shins and gurgling into her rubber boots as she sank into the muddy mix of seawater, dirt, and trash that covered the streets. They'd never gone this far into the evacuation zone before. Troy had told them to prepare for some wading in the Atlantic, but this was deeper than expected. The green froth of breakers crashed against the remains of beachfront houses just a few blocks down the street.

Troy took the lead, and the rest of them followed single file, walking upright with their crates and bags since, aside from the cicadas, no one else was around. They slipped along the side of an old storage building, its narrow windows boarded up against the onslaught of the elements. Someone had taken the trouble to elevate the path with concrete, so they now stepped on dry ground even though it was high tide.

At the back entrance, they waited for Nacho to snap the lock.

Sweat collected under Shavir's mask, along the edges of her goggles and below her chin. Adrenaline bled into exhilaration and a strong sense of fear as she followed the others into the derelict building, leaving Lenny and Zeno behind at the door. Up a narrow staircase to the second floor, and through another door, this one fortified with soundproofing rubber and an additional lock and metal bolt. Nacho and Troy worked in tandem on those, and the door sprang open.

They all held their breath. No alarm.

The men stayed behind while Shavir followed Tara into the dim room, muted whimpers pervading the foul air. It was at this point, usually, that her fear subsided and the anger set in, propelling her into the methodical mode of action she now needed. She counted the cages, twelve of them—old, decrepit, too small as they always were—and, reliably, the wrath came. She snatched the bolt cutter from her belt and sliced through the padlock of the first cage.

The puppies were much bigger than expected, at least sixteen weeks, and predictably chubby, overstuffed with cheap, fatty food. They were jumping up and cowering down, torn between dread and delight that someone had broken into their crowded cage.

Shavir grabbed the first squirming mass of life and pressed the warm shivering body to her chest. A little tongue found its way between her ski mask and turtleneck, excitedly licking her salty skin.

"It's okay, baby," she whispered. "I'm gonna get you out of here."

She lifted the lid off her crate and placed the puppy inside, grabbing the next one and putting it down beside the first in a single movement, working swiftly until they all tumbled over each other. She closed the lid, yanked up the load, and carried it to the door where Troy was waiting, offering his empty crate in exchange. Tara was right behind her, placing her crate into the hands of Nacho, who followed Troy down the stairs.

The stink of decay was getting more intense, and it was when she opened the third cage that Shavir found the body. The other pups were still alive, but this one little thing was cold, lifeless, already decomposing and poisoning its siblings.

She knew what to do. *Don't freeze. Keep moving. Grab a puppy. Ignore the body. Don't lose time.* But despite herself, tears blurred her vision, soaking the goggles, the mask. She looked up, around at the room—the soundproofed walls, the broken cages, the rotting dog food, the dirty floor laced with excrement and maggots. She inhaled the putrid air and started gagging.

"You okay?" Tara asked, suddenly next to her.

Shavir wasn't okay. Nothing in this room, in this whole damn city, was okay, and all she wanted to do right now was sit down in the muck and grime and cry. But she nodded without stopping her momentum, not allowing the slightest break in her routine, doing what she had to do until the cage was almost empty. Only the one little dead body was left, like so many other dead bodies they'd had to leave behind.

It took her and Tara less than ten minutes to clear everything out. They received two empty bags in exchange for the last couple full crates and turned to check the walls for doors. The first was locked, but there was a second one at the back of the room.

The way Tara's body grew rigid when the door gave way told Shavir they'd found what they were looking for. She pushed past her friend into a tiled space, the floor sticky against her boots. She recoiled from the greenish outlines of the tools, but, stepping forward, she put everything in reach into her bag: meat hooks, knives, hatchets, and all the electrified stuff that ran on batteries. The nausea was so bad by now she was just grabbing things, paying as little attention as possible to what they were or were meant to do. A mistake.

A meat hook caught the hem of her sleeve and pulled it back, ripping her skin. She saw a dark line well up along the underside of her exposed forearm and yanked at the sleeve, covering the wound before her blood dripped on the floor. Bending down for a precious thirty seconds, she frantically scanned the floor for anything allowing for DNA recognition. Tara told her to get out, twice, her voice uncharacteristically urgent, and so she finally zipped up her bag, and they ran down the stairs and out the back door.

Lenny's dark shape was waiting for them outside, his right arm gesturing to duck down into the water immediately.

Obeying, Shavir stepped off the path and sank into the muddy ocean, the cut on her arm screaming at contact. She crouched down and looked up at the black sky.

The high pitch of a surveillance drone whirred above the cicadas and the surf. It had both ears and infrared eyes, so the thing to do was to duck deep down into the rancid water and remain absolutely still.

Shavir tried to keep herself from breathing, from thinking, even, aware only of Tara's body next to her own and the menacing drone above.

It didn't pause, nor did it turn or descend. But if the van got into its vision range, they were screwed.

The drone flew on to the back of the building, its whir dying away into the perverse soundtrack of the neighborhood. When it was gone, they emerged from the ocean and waded back to the van, where Nacho swung open the side door for them, on his face shock and relief.

Shavir ripped off her goggles and mask as she jumped in, gulping for air. She dropped her bag on the wet floor and collapsed next to it as the van started moving. A whiplash of pain shot up her arm when her knee bounced against the cut, and this time she cried out.

Finn turned around from the driver's seat. "You got hurt?"

It baffled her, that question, coming from him at that moment. A rare display of care so sudden and so misplaced in the grand scheme of things, it made her want to laugh out loud. She stared at the milky oval of Finn's face across the dark van filled with dripping activists and terrified dogs. "I'm fine."

Without another word, he turned back around.

One of the rescues started whimpering in a crate stacked close to Shavir's ear. "It's okay, baby," she breathed. "We're safe now."

She leaned back against the crates and wondered if that was true. That dark line of blood on her skin. The stained floor that had made it impossible to tell apart her own blood from whatever had dripped from the tools over the months these fuckers had been running their illegal meat farm. Hopefully, she'd been fast enough covering the wound. But really, what was she doing out here, doing this job, if she couldn't ever get used to it or do it right?

Across from her in the dark, Tara laughed as she peeled off her soaked turtleneck, exuding confidence as she always did. But Shavir was still obsessing about her mistake and what it might mean when they passed the roadblock again and the van sped up in the direction from where it had come, back to the distant lights of Brooklyn.

TWO

NOTHING RUINS A DAY quite like waking up to another round of disasters and knowing you must take your pick. Jake wasn't fully awake yet, his mind still spread out wide and flat under the dampening blanket of the three sleeping pills he'd swallowed only a few hours earlier. But like every morning he had made the mistake of pouring himself a glass of water and booting his Spine before he was ready. Now he was slumped against the kitchen table in the dim solitude of what he called his apartment, glass in hand, head against the wall, eyes glued to the holographic projection of a Cambodian news feed in front of him.

The rage and fear were palpable in the workers' faces. They were young, most of them. The men stood in front, arms reaching up toward the sky, fists clenched in a furious gesture of protest. The women huddled behind them, chanting in support, keeping their children pressed close like chicks underneath the protective wings of their mothers. Angry voices rose, toppled, and broke, sweaty features hyperreal and way too close, contorted by despair.

To Jake's right, at the far edge of the Spine projection, a long row of bulldozers stood trembling, waiting, ready to attack and devour the slum at the center of this confrontation. The workers' shanties had to make room for the construction of a seawall to protect the sweatshops that employed them—that was the logic of the day. But there was nowhere for them to go.

The riots had started in the late morning. Late morning in Cambodia, that was, so they'd been going on for almost four hours. By now, the workers were outnumbered by security forces in riot gear that looked evil next to the colorful assemblage of cotton pants, skirts, and *kramas*. Had it not been for the drone cameras swirling around the fighting parties, the whole thing would have found its bloody ending hours ago. But the workers in Koh Kong knew their images were being projected by millions of Spines across the globe. They shouted their rage and despair not at the armed forces in front of them but upward into the drone cameras, fixing their gazes on the people elsewhere in the world who were responsible for their plight.

Jake stared back and knew two things.

One, this would end very badly for the Cambodian workers. And two, it was his job to find alternative suppliers for the drugs now stuck in the embattled export processing zone: several tons of antibiotics, antivirals, and anticoagulants, along with other critical-supply meds, all of them needed urgently in New York. It was a matter of minutes before scarcity alerts would start pouring out of the NY SAFE, and every other SAFE center across the country would follow. He had to stop wallowing in his guilt and get to work.

The Spine was still on voice recognition, and his data gloves on the induction charger next to his bed, so he pressed his sternum against the cold curve of the kitchen table to quell the nausea and asked for a list of the drugs they'd just lost in Koh Kong. His voice sounded off, parched by five hours of chemically induced sleep, but as he reached for his water, a dragon zipped into the translucent riot scene and whipped the glass right out of his hand.

Diving forward into the sea of angry faces, Jake caught the glass midair. He felt its surface for an instant, smooth and cold and perfect against his palm. Then it burst into pieces, slicing his skin.

"Standby!" he screamed into the perfect quiet of his apartment.

The hologram collapsed in on itself, the Cambodian workers and their roaring voices gone, leaving an unobstructed view of the broken glass on the floor and the long red shape of the bearded dragon resting next to it like she had never moved.

"Goddamnit, Lucy!"

Lucy spun her head around, puffing her crimson throat as if mocking the scale of human ineptitude. Surfacing from the virtual world of the Spine, Jake had trouble finding focus, his gaze sliding past her reptile stare, unable to hold on. She hissed at him, the sound echoing back from the bare walls. Then she scurried away into the darkness below the kitchen counter, leaving him alone with the mess.

There was a moment of suspension, a quiet break from reality in which doing nothing seemed like an actual possibility. Jake closed his eyes, his body perfectly still, his mind awash with the wave of pain surging upward from his hand and the mental afterglow of the riot. The seconds slipped by as he sat doing absolutely nothing and seeing no necessity to ever do anything again. Then his Spine self-activated with an emergency call that overrode the standby mode.

The tense face of his boss popped up in front of him, eyes red-rimmed like they hadn't seen much sleep. "What a great fucking morning," David blared without a greeting. "You've seen the news?"

"Yes," Jake said. "Cambodia."

"Fucking bastards," David barked, leaving it unclear whether he meant the workers or the armed security forces. "I'm trying to get our meds out. I need you to find a way to move them."

For a second, Jake forgot his pain. "You wanna go in there?"

"Our security says they've got contacts to a local militia."

"A *militia*? I thought we were doing logistics, not war."

"Got a better idea?"

Jake's gaze was stuck on the puddle of blood below his hand on the table, growing brighter and redder by the second. The sun was coming up outside the big bay window in the living area. Soon, it would heat Manhattan's skyscraper canyons and set fire to his already sore eyes.

"You still there?" David asked into the silence.

"I'm thinking."

"Where's your goddamn camera?"

Jake looked up. "I can't wear my glove. Don't ask."

"Not asking. When can you be here?"

"You're at SAFE already?"

"Never left. When will you be here?"

Jake looked at the glass shard sticking out of the slick surface of his palm, his stomach curling at the metallic scent of blood.

"About an hour."

"Can't you take a car for once?"

"I'm on it," Jake snarled. "Will you please relax?"

But David had already hung up, his face vanished.

With a frantic jerk, Jake dislodged the shard from his hand and pressed the back of his head against the wall again, fighting the dizziness. David not leaving SAFE was a bad sign. It meant they were in deep shit with the pharmaceuticals and that his boss was once again going without sleep because he had overdosed on pep pills. The irony of that seemed lost on him.

A shuffling to his right told Jake that Lucy had reemerged from under the kitchen counter. He looked at the dragon he'd brought into his life: a twenty-two-inch *Pogona vitticeps* that took naps on his bed and sunbaths on his sill, behaving in no way like the quiet vermin exterminator he'd expected when ordering her online on a whim after witnessing a roach infestation under his kitchen sink. He'd begun to realize his mistake when the accompanying reptile starter setup kit included a fifty-gallon glass terrarium equipped with a twenty-six-watt desert UVB bulb and everything else necessary to keep a dragon comfortable. But since she was supposed to help with the roaches, Lucy freely roamed the house during the day, meaning the apartment's temperature control system was now also set to her liking.

When he'd made the mistake of mentioning Lucy to Shavir the other day, she'd called the dragon a pet with that suggestive smile of hers, but that label struck him as absurd. His job didn't leave much time to yearn for company, and the last thing he needed was a pet.

He'd even considered returning Lucy to the farm that produced her kind once it became clear how vastly she outmatched him in laying down the ground rules for their coexistence. But the breeder seemed oddly evasive about what exactly they did with returns, and so Lucy ended up staying and had tripled in size since then, reminding Jake daily that he didn't always pay enough attention to detail when making rushed and far-reaching decisions, which was what he did all day long. Most of those decisions were life-or-death, so it was almost refreshing that this one had resulted only in a roommate that was much more of a presence than anticipated. For once, bad judgment hadn't been deadly—not yet, anyway.

"See what you did?" He turned his bloody palm in Lucy's direction as he got up and walked to the kitchen cabinet that contained his own high-priority medical supply, among it several bottles of the sophisticated uppers, downers, and sleepers that kept him functional at all times of day. He dug into the depth of the cabinet and found a bottle of healing accelerant and an assortment of antibiotics, half-hidden behind the truckload of asthma medications he stockpiled for his niece. He poured the accelerant over his wound and swallowed some cephalexin along with his two usual pep pills.

Fixed for the day, he turned to the hollow space of his apartment, its most prominent features—a bed, a couch, and Lucy's terrarium—on full display in the sunlight now gushing through the window. The spectacular vista of green facades and rooftop gardens outside was one of the perks of living on the seventh floor in one of the most exclusive parts of Manhattan. From up here, Chelsea was overtaken by a benevolent army of grasses, shrubs, and vertiginous climbers devouring brick, concrete, glass, and steel alike, protecting buildings and people from the heat, and slowly perishing in the process.

His bionic lenses dimmed down to shield his eyes as he walked to the window, but he could still make out the two trees on the roof of the neighboring building that he'd grown fond of for reasons he couldn't explain. Scratching an itch along the fine scars that covered the implant processor in his neck, he paused while the Spine babbled in his ears, the familiar mix of news, logistical data, and scarcity alerts. He didn't know what kind of trees they were, but they stood tall and close like lovers, clad in shades of yellow in mid-July, leaning against each other's fragile frames. His eyes had trouble finding focus, making the lovers seem to twist their branches around each other in mutual support, swaying back and forth in a precarious dance against the elements.

Tearing his gaze from the trees, he forced his injured hand into the smart fabric of his data glove, working steadily through the pain. Then he grabbed his bag and said goodbye to Lucy, who had relocated to the windowsill, her scales sparkling bright red in the blazing morning sun.

The city pounced on him when Jake opened the front door of the building. Even at this early hour, people were on the move, a fraction of them in the city's decrepit subway trains, the rest above ground, pushing forward with determination below long rows of trees recently planted along what used to be parking lanes. It hit him every time he opened the door—how the street had shrunk, how the sidewalks and bike lanes had expanded, and how these rearranged proportions had changed the atmosphere into something radically new, an entirely different city. He squeezed through the squirming masses, brushing against arms, legs, bags, and bicycle tires, their owners oblivious to him, gazes glued to their Spine feeds. Then he darted across the narrow street in a well-practiced slalom around the sleek podcar trains that had replaced most conventional traffic in Manhattan, their bright yellow color reminiscent of the city's once-iconic cabs, the quiet hum of their electric engines not so much.

Given the pressing Koh Kong situation and his aversion to podcars, the most sensible thing to do was walk the High Line all the way down to SAFE's headquarters in the West Village. Or, slightly less sensible, he could turn right toward the even longer stretch of green along the Manhattan seawall, his favorite place on earth and the second-fastest way to reach SAFE on foot. But even with David on high alert, there was no way Jake would start his day without coffee. It was the one luxury he allowed himself, the one break in his daily routine that itself had become a habit because it made everything else bearable.

He reawakened his Spine as he turned left, away from the seawall and past the stairs leading up to the old trail park, onto 7th Avenue. The pep pills kicked in when he paced along the wide sidewalk of 17th Street, but he knew they weren't what was causing the cacophony in his ribcage by the time he pushed open the door to Soma, Chelsea's finest vegan coffee shop and eatery.

Shavir shot him a glance and a smile while she served another customer. She wasn't wearing an apron yet, only jeans and a tank top. The dark flood of her hair followed her fluid movements, exposing with each turn the tattooed ring of interwoven roots around her biceps and a thin line along the inside of her right forearm he'd never seen before.

The sight was too overwhelming for the still-unstable state of his visceral system. He forced his gaze back onto his Spine projection until it was his turn, zapping randomly through local news feeds. Another furious protest against the worsening hospital crisis in Queens. Another illegal meat farm raided in the coastal evacuation zone. Another squad of Frontline officers soaking their uniforms in the Atlantic. And more of the same. Filled in on the latest round of local calamities, he returned to the map of Southeast Asia he already knew by heart.

"Hey, Jake, you're early." Shavir turned around from the espresso machine. There was still a smile in her dark eyes, shining through the coastline of Cambodia.

Jake put his Spine on standby. Cambodia folded and faded, giving the woman in front of him a shocking immediacy. The other customer was gone; they were alone in the small room.

"Latte's on its way," Shavir said, hesitating. "Is oat milk okay? We're out of almond. And out of soy."

Feeling overwhelmed by her unfiltered gaze, Jake just nodded and walked to the display case. Only now did he notice how overstuffed it was with salads and sandwiches. "That's a lot of food, though."

"Yeah." Shavir brushed back a strand of hair, looking uncomfortable. "We're doing emergency harvesting at the Roots farm. Our veggies are rotting on the plants in this crazy heat." She paused, another palpable moment of hesitation. "But we're almost out of coffee," she then added, gazing directly at him again. Only people without a Spine could look at you like that. Calm. Steady. Penetrating.

Jake's eyes escaped to the display case, and he ordered a random crunch wrap he didn't plan on eating. He rarely ate anything anymore.

Shavir passed the food across the counter but shook her head when he put his glove on the scanner to pay. "It's on the house," she said slowly. "Hector's treat."

Jake finally caught on. "Don't tell me the 4Flow's broken again."

She nodded wearily. "He's in the back room trying to fix it."

So that was what was going on. Jake didn't know how many times he had told Shavir's boss that he would never get SAFE's sophisticated scarcity app to work properly on the ancient laptop he kept in that room. But Hector was as immune to advice as he was tenacious. A short, wiry man with an exuberant temperament and a deep tangle of scars along his neck that looked like someone had bitten off a chunk of it. There used to be a Spine processor underneath all that mangled tissue, and until Hector plucked up the courage to get a new one, Soma would always be in trouble with its supply.

"Could you perhaps take another look?" Shavir's voice was soft, pleading. "Hector has no talent at this and he's pretty desperate."

Jake felt himself relax as they were moving onto familiar territory. "See," he said with a smile, "if you weren't even more freaked than your boss, you could at least run our app on your Spine and he—"

"I'm hardly the freak in the room," Shavir shot back, the usual spark returning to her eyes. "And you know perfectly well why he's so scared of getting a new one."

Jake did know that perfectly well. He dropped his eyes from Shavir's steady stare, to her lips and down to the counter, only to realize that the unfamiliar line on her forearm was in fact a nasty cut, welled up on both sides and colored an alarming shade of pink.

"That looks bad," he said. "You should worry about that instead."

Shavir turned her arm to hide the injury, blood rising to her cheeks. "It's nothing. I got it harvesting at Roots. Just need to put something on to not gross people out."

Roots was the rooftop farm in Brooklyn where she seemed to spend most of the time she wasn't working at Soma, but adding a bunch of agricultural germs to the picture only made it more alarming.

"Wait," Jake said and reached over the counter for her wrist before she could bend to get her hoodie, acting on impulse as he did every so often, sometimes leading to success and sometimes to utter disaster.

"I've got something for you," he added, conscious of his transgression. But her life was more important.

His left hand dropped into his bag and produced the bottle of healing accelerant he'd brought from home.

Shavir's eyes widened. "No, Jake, that stuff's really expensive, and I've taken some pills."

"What kind?" he asked, unimpressed. One of the things his job required was a near-encyclopedic knowledge of antibiotics, along with the understanding that most of them were now useless.

"What kind?" she echoed. "I don't remember. I'm good, really."

Jake finally managed to steady his gaze, his right hand still holding her wrist in a painful embrace that was shockingly unfamiliar.

"What did you take?" he repeated. "Please tell me."

"I don't *know*," Shavir snapped, defiance seeping into her eyes. "Amoxy-something."

"I hope that's not true. That shit stopped working years ago."

"Well," she returned, "it's the best we can do on *our* side of the river. Homeland makes sure all the good stuff goes to Manhattan."

"I happen to know that's not true either," he said matter-of-factly to cut short another familiar argument, this one about his work and SAFE's complicated relationship to Homeland Security. "But regardless of what you actually took, please let me do this."

Shavir hesitated for another second, then her arm finally slackened, allowing him to turn it around and trace the cut with a thin jet of healing accelerant.

"It kills the bacteria, and you won't get a scar," he explained, acutely aware of his wet palm within the thin fabric of the data glove against Shavir's slender wrist. "We use it for our Spine implants."

"I know," she said as he let go of her arm.

And then her eyes widened again, this time because of the bright red blood that covered the skin on her wrist where he had touched it. With equal surprise, they both looked at the large stain on his glove, glistening in the LED light.

"It's me, not you," he said needlessly, and now it was his turn to hide a wound. "I had a little accident myself this morning."

"Do you want me to get you—"

"No! I'm good." His face felt hot.

"Accident, huh?" Amusement crept into Shavir's voice as she turned to the sink and turned on the faucet to wash off his blood. "Was that a... pet-related accident?"

"She's no pet," he said too quickly.

Her grin widened. "Yeah, you keep saying that."

Another customer opened the door, flooding the room with a wave of hot air. Shavir stopped the water and leaned across the counter toward Jake, twisting her hair up into the familiar bun at the back of her head. "Can you *please* take another look at Hector's 4Flow?" she asked, barely audible.

How could he say no with her face inches away from his, close enough for him to catch the scent of her hair? "Sure," he squeezed out. "But not now. We've got an emergency at SAFE. I can come back in the evening if he's around."

"He will be."

"What about you?"

She nodded. "Double shift." The weariness crept back into her eyes.

"Alright." Jake tried to keep his voice even. "I'll see you later then."

He turned away from her in a haze and almost walked into the guy behind him, a business suit with twitching eyes, too engrossed in whatever was playing on his Spine to even notice him. Jake regained control of his body and curved around the man toward the door.

"Hey, Jake," Shavir called when he had almost reached it.

He turned around and into another smile that very nearly made him drop his coffee.

"Thank you."

"No problem," he managed to return, and then he was outside.

Pacing down the crowded sidewalk of 7th Avenue, Jake moved in what little shade he could get from the spare canopies of yet another long line of newly planted trees, all part of an ambitious urban-heat-control program that would make Manhattan the greenest it had ever been. He was wide awake now, smiling at the translucent wall of data that had reemerged before his eyes and zigzagging around human shapes that were too slow or moving in the wrong direction. His palm pulsated in step with his heartbeat, a physical reminder of the unfamiliar touch, the bizarre sight of his blood on Shavir's wrist, that smile he never knew what to make of.

The daily detour to Soma had become a morning ritual more invigorating than any amount of pep pills since he'd wandered into the place by accident one day and stood in front of that stunning woman, too mesmerized to articulate an order. But after several months of daily lattes, he still didn't know much about Shavir, and what he knew suggested it would be wise to stay away from her.

Behind that elusive smile she was utterly unapproachable and deeply suspicious of what she called "government types," a category that included him. He also knew that she was involved in Roots, a counterculture group that had emerged during the long nightmare of the Global Supply Crisis in the early 2050s and now ran a community farm in Brooklyn. Both her parents were dead, just like his own, but she had a bunch of half-siblings in California.

That was about as far as he had abused his security clearance at Homeland. Turned out they had a pretty big file on Shavir, but he'd told himself it didn't matter. Just like it didn't matter that she wasn't on social media, on or off the Spine, a choice typical for government types but rarely for average citizens unless they had something to hide. None of these things really mattered since Shavir had shown no interest in him, anyway. And so their interaction had never gone beyond him being mesmerized and her making coffee, sprinkled with the occasional half a dozen times he had fixed Hector's 4Flow so Soma wouldn't have to close.

But today had been different. He could still feel the aftershock of the collapsed distance between them. He wondered if they really had functioning antibiotics on their farm. Given the supply situation, it seemed unlikely. *Amoxy-something* was what she'd said, so if she had taken anything at all, it had probably been a bunch of expired fish meds. That was what people took when they couldn't get their hands on the stuff made for humans, as he was painfully aware.

The thought made him shudder and reminded him to call Masao.

"Already tried that" was his assistant's placid response when Jake presented him with an alternative supplier for one of the antibiotics that was stuck in Koh Kong. "Richard Becker was faster than us, so that stuff's all on its way to Berlin now."

Becker, of course. Always faster than anyone else on the planet, with the possible exception of David. Another man who never slept.

Jake crossed 12th Street without looking, forcing four podcar trains to a soundless stop on the scorching asphalt, then leaped into the delicious coolness of Abingdon Square Park. Unlike the struggling newbies along the streets, the majestic old trees in the park had been around long enough to develop deep roots and large, dense canopies, their millions of leaves breathing a freshness onto the paths below that allowed him to slow down and listen to his assistant's extraordinarily long list of bad news.

"The good news," Masao said finally, "is a start-up in Ohio can deliver about ten percent of the antivirals we need. You won't like the price though. But I'm in touch with Bangkok, and I've sent a message to Cristina, though it's still too early in LA. We haven't yet managed to replace all the stuff we lost last week, so the first rationings will hit our hospitals in five days."

"How's David doing?"

"Hovering right below the ceiling."

As usual, Masao's voice was supremely tranquil, a hint of irony hiding in the corners of his words. Barely thirty years old, he had this rare gift of sardonic calm that didn't seem to depend on any chemical interventions to his system but instead sprang from a relatively intact personal life. Unperturbed by the commotion around him, Masao was laser-focused on the essentials. It was an admirable quality in any human being, but in their line of work, with their boss, it was invaluable.

"Let's get him some meds then," Jake said, smiling.

"He still wants our stuff from Koh Kong."

"I know. Can you get us surveillance of the Cambodian west coast? If David manages to perform a miracle, we'll have to run this thing through the port of Laem Chabang."

The sun hit hard when Jake stepped out of the park and jogged toward the white glare of the SAFE building, which was smack in the middle of what used to be a residential neighborhood. Everything was mixed up now in Manhattan. There were condos in what used to be a small continent of office space, and for some reason, the city had decided SAFE's headquarters needed to be in the West Village. Jake stopped next to the entrance below a sign announcing New York's *Special Agency for Essentials*, crowned by the Homeland Security seal. He dipped his fingers into a wall-mounted Delphi scanner for fingerprint and DNA recognition. The bulletproof glass door fell into a gap below, and he stepped into the territory of the four heavily armed men who guarded the upper levels of the building.

After the usual ritual of security checks, he walked to the elevator and soared up to SAFE's epicenter on the seventh floor: the Critical Supply Room, CSR for short.

Everything that mattered in his life came together in this windowless space: every bit of information on the planet's web of economic activity and its ruptures; every seismic disturbance, storm, flood, wildfire, epidemic, war, or incident of civil unrest; anything that could interrupt the flow of high-priority supply into New York City. Most of the enormous array of goods streaming into the city every day of the week was monitored on the lower levels of the building. The CSR was only invested in medical drugs and supplies and certain foods and industrial goods—things that not only saved lives but had also proven a pressing security issue. The CSR was what kept the city running and alive at its most existential level. It was also the only place where Jake had ever felt at home since losing his real home at the age of twelve. The man who had given it to him seemed to be regretting that right now.

"Next time, you get a fucking car!" David yelled from inside the CSR. "And can you tell me how the fuck we're gonna get ten tons of temp-sensitive meds overland from southern Cambodia all the way up to Laem Chabang in Thailand? *Donkeys?*"

"I don't think they actually have donkeys in Cambodia," Jake returned, looking past David at the screen walls pulsing with animated figures, graphs, supply alerts, weather reports, and news coverage of the riots from three dozen stations around the world. "I was more thinking trucks or boats—if we can get our cargo out. Can we?"

David shrugged his bony shoulders. "We don't know yet."

Unlike most people, David looked more translucent in real life than on the Spine, his eyes pale gray, his hair washed-out brown, his worn features covered in sweat despite the chilled air of the CSR. He had been more substantial when Jake first met him at his job interview six years ago, a few months after the Global Supply Crisis—Jake, a newly minted supply chain PhD from NYU, and David, a legend in the field tasked with building a team that would keep New York stocked in a broken world running out of everything. David had interviewed him across an empty desk, encircled by data streaming down screen walls. Then he'd hired him on the spot before getting up and walking right out of his own office. The next day, he'd waited impatiently by the elevators to give Jake an on-the-job training that ended fifteen hours later in a bar with two terrible drinks and a string of recall questions he seemed to make up on the spot. Apparently, Jake had managed to answer them. David made him first his assistant and then the number-one troubleshooter on his team because, as David liked to put it, they were two of a kind.

The latter hopefully wasn't true since David wasn't known for his social skills. "What the fuck did you do to your hand?" he demanded.

Jake looked at the gooey mess of high-tech fiber and half-dried blood that was his right glove. "Don't ask. It won't be a problem."

"You got something to put on it?"

Jake pulled out the bottle of healing accelerant.

"Every two hours," David snarled. "You gotta put that stuff on every two hours, or it won't work. That's what Lisa says, and she's got kids. And take some pills, I can't have you crippled!"

Jake ignored that outburst. He exchanged a look with Masao, who shrugged his shoulders ever so slightly, then focused his attention on the satellite images that covered part of the screen wall next to his and Masao's desks. "So how does it look?"

"Not too bad." Masao flicked through a series of satellite images covering the overland route from Koh Kong on Cambodia's west coast to Laem Chabang, Thailand's most important port. He sounded like someone speaking in the presence of a frantic child, his long pale face accentuated by a frame of black hair and a red sweater, a typical specimen from a wardrobe consisting only of prime colors. "If we can get our cargo out—," Masao made a point of not looking at David, "—and if we have transport, we're good to go."

David ignored the first *if*. "So where do we get those trucks, Jake?"

"I've got no fucking clue," Jake admitted when he saw no answer on Masao's face, "but we'll figure something out."

And it would have to be figured out soon, he thought as he slumped down on his chair. Every two hours meant Shavir needed her own bottle of accelerant, and she would need proper antibiotics, too.

He called the pharmacy on Hudson Street and put in an order, making a mental calculation of how many hours he had left to solve the Cambodia problem before Shavir would leave Soma. Then he dialed Cristina at the LA SAFE.

THREE

She couldn't believe the heat. Air so heavy and humid it could be cut into slices. Shavir pulled Soma's front door shut, nodding back to Hector, who had taken her place behind the counter, face glowing like a Christmas tree while he served one of their peskiest customers. He had been outright giddy when she'd told him Jake would come back in the evening to give his 4Flow another try, willfully ignoring the part where she'd said it was unlikely to work without a new Spine. Hector was good at ignoring things, and over the years, he'd become quite resourceful in dealing with the constant shortages.

Soma now produced its own plant milks, vegan cheese, and range of cookies and breads, and much of its menu featured veggies that Roots grew across the river. Ironically, its reputation had soared because of these homemade emergency measures, but it was still dependent on some things that couldn't be grown or made in New York, things that had to travel to the city from elsewhere. Without coffee and tea, without spices, almonds, and maize, they would have to close Soma's doors again. Hector had looked frightened when Shavir said this, reliving the dread of past closures, maybe going all the way back to the horror of the Crisis. Then he'd said that Jake would fix things—he worked for SAFE after all. It was as simple as Hector needed it to be.

It took her a moment to adjust to the physical challenge of being outside after 11 a.m. There were now official warnings and recommendations on how to adapt one's personal schedule to the necessities of a heat wave. But her personal schedule said that Sam was waiting for her, so she walked to a podcar that sat underneath one of the newly planted trees. Already dying, she decided after a quick glance at the thin layer of speckled leaves that had collected on the roof and windshield of the car. It was beyond her why they kept replanting maples in this town. This one would die of a heatstroke like so many others before it. The car had already recognized her phone and took less than three seconds to unlock its door, but she still found herself yanking at the handle in her urgency to get out of the sun. The door slid backward, and she dove into the cool air and onto a comfortable seat that had the chemical stink of newness.

Like most sensible people she knew, she hated Manhattan's new Personal Rapid Transit system, which allowed less sensible people to step into a fully automated podcar on the ground floor of their apartment building and out again on the ground floor of their destination without ever breathing unfiltered air during the relocation process. It was as alienating from the world as things could get, but it was also the quickest way to move around the city without getting cooked in the subway or fried by the sun.

A soft female voice asked for her destination, and Shavir gave Finn's address in the East Village. As the vehicle slid into the moving traffic and attached itself to the next available car train, she braced herself for the sensual assault she knew was coming.

The windshield lost its transparency and promptly inundated her with the latest commercial for Emovia, the most popular emotion regulator in town. She stared at the impossibly white teeth, golden hair, and beaming faces floating on silver clouds, aware she was missing out on the fully personalized experience of the car's 5DX entertainment system because she didn't have a Spine to hook it up to. But even this impoverished version invaded her senses, engulfing her in whispered promises of instant calm and hyperconcentration that resonated with a sweet low hum in the deepest corners of her being. Sweet to the point that you almost forgot the bitter.

The next ad was sponsored by the art-meat industry and brought back the bitter with a bang. Grazing cattle were herded by cowboys into an epic sunset, Marlboro style, never mind that cattle were all but extinct, as were Marlboros. Cut to close-ups of sizzling steaks on red charcoals in an all-clean, all-white lab and the art-meat industry's battle cry, "Better than Nature." Shavir recoiled from the reddish glow of the synthetic meat juices and looked down at her cell phone display instead, plugging in her headphones to check for local news.

The third channel had what she was looking for: heavily armed Frontline men in a room full of empty broken cages. It looked even dirtier and more disturbing in bright daylight. The rusty wire floors were caked with blood and excrement, surrounded by buckets of rotting dog food. Which made the illegal meat produced there an unsavory and unhealthy meal, the reporter patiently explained, his flat voice suggesting he was practicing the same shallow breathing that had allowed her to do her job last night without puking all over the place. He reminded viewers dutifully that though the US government had had to shut down all legal industrial meat production to save the last functioning antibiotics and curb carbon emissions, they should never buy meat of uncertain origin on the black market, adding that all black-market meat was of uncertain origin. And that, against common conception, most people couldn't tell the difference between the pork they paid for and the dog meat they got instead, so it was better to be safe than sorry.

"Here in New York," he explained, "where keeping big animals like cattle and pigs isn't feasible for an illegal farm, the reality behind black-market meat often looks like *this*." The news camera zoomed in on the dead puppy from last night.

"Assholes!" Shavir cried, wondering, as she often did, whether guys like him were on payroll for the art-meat industry. Hopefully, it would at least deter people from buying animal meat.

But now he was finally getting to the point, shoving his mic into the face of the heavyset Frontline man standing next to him, a typical exemplar of the special police force Homeland Security had hired to take over law enforcement in the eastern boroughs in the aftermath of the Crisis. He was wearing riot gear, as they always did, signaling that he was expecting the worst when, really, he was only standing in a room full of broken cages and dog remains.

"The owners of the place have been arrested for illegal livestock farming after an anonymous report," he explained with a voice slow and sluggish from the heat, going on to say the illegal livestock in question had vanished into thin air, as was always the case when they got these anonymous calls.

"This keeps happening in Queens," the reporter explained into the camera, "the prime suspects being activists—"

"Terrorists," the cop said. "They're terrorists, legally speaking."

"—the prime suspects being *terrorists*," the reporter corrected himself dutifully, "who are stealing these animals before they can get illegally slaughtered in a place like this or legally euthanized by the police. Do you already have a lead on these criminals?"

Shavir held her breath as the cop looked around, perhaps at his boss, a colleague, or nothing at all. "Frontline investigations are proceeding aggressively," he then declared, which was Frontline's way of saying the case had already gone cold. She looked up and smiled, just in time for the next Emovia ad.

Of course, she'd known all along that was what Frontline would say. It had been unreasonable to think they might properly analyze the place, with all the dried blood and poop and whatnot, and with the real bad guys right in front of their noses, a ready-made arrest. She'd gotten scared again that morning when Jake saw the cut on her arm, as if by his sheer association with Homeland, he could have made connections. But that made no sense, either—she could see that now and should have seen it all along. Jake was no risk. Not really.

A waft of hot air smacked her in the face as the car stopped and its door slid back, revealing another sizzling sidewalk and more distressed trees. She got out and sprinted to the entrance of an ivy-clad brownstone. From the top spilled the overhanging branches of a garden.

This is not just 110 degrees, she thought as she dipped her hands into the Delphi scanner next to the door. They were too sweaty for recognition, so she wiped them on her jeans and tried again, the sun burning holes into her back. At the third try, a beep and a checkmark on the scanner screen accompanied the sound of the retracting deadbolt. She slipped into the nineteenth-century opulence of the entrance hall, brightly lit and ridiculously cold. Catching her breath, she rode the elevator all the way up to the top floor, which only had two doors, one belonging to the sprawling apartment of an Iranian antiques dealer, the other one to the lower floor of Finn's penthouse loft. After having her hands read again, she set foot into significantly warmer air.

Sam appeared before she reached the upper floor. Taking four steps in each leap, he flew down the stairs, almost causing her to fall as he tried to stop his momentum, all wagging tail and moist dog nose.

She laughed as she grabbed his hot fur. "Easy, boy, easy! You're too big for that, how many times do I have to tell you? Sit!"

The mastiff sat down, balancing his enormous weight on the narrow step, his face furrowed, his soft ear flaps straining with an attempted perk. He was a natural.

Shavir started laughing again as her sit-down comedian got all jiggly, bursting with desire to move *somehow.* "Okay, goofy, you clearly got more sleep last night than me." She turned toward the upper floor. "Let's get your leash, I'm late already."

She followed the dog up the stairs into the living area, a sparsely furnished space that was airy and light-suffused though the wood shutters in front of the long row of windows to her left were almost closed, the sun painting patterned shadows across the white couch and the shiny hardwood floors. Behind the French doors to her right, she caught glimpses of bamboo and blossoming yuccas whenever the billowing curtains allowed her an unobstructed view of Finn's rambunctious rooftop garden—which explained why it was so hot in the apartment. Apparently, he had forgotten to close the doors when he left.

She walked over to close them herself but stopped short when she passed the doorway to the adjacent studio. For a few seconds, she stared at the tanned skin and defined back muscles of the tall blond figure standing shirtless and utterly oblivious to her presence.

"Why are you here?"

His body moved rhythmically to whatever was playing on his Spine.

"Finn!" She walked to him, Sam by her side.

He turned before she had reached him, sensing her presence. "Oh, hey, Shav. You're picking him up already?"

Again, she stared, this time into the vacant blue of his eyes. He looked at her through a translucent projection of what was probably the model for his latest garden project, but it wasn't just a matter of dislocated visual focus. She peered around for the Emovia bottle, and there it was, sitting right next to her on the Japanese sideboard. Within seconds, her stomach curled into a tiny ball of rage.

"No, I'm not picking him up already," she snapped. "I told you I'm working a double shift today because we're taking the puppies to New Jersey tomorrow."

"That's what I thought," Finn said, unmoved. The black of his pupils seemed to vibrate as his eyes shifted focus between her face and the projection of his Spine.

Shavir hesitated, torn between her rising anger and her residual glee. "Have you seen the news?" she asked, succumbing to the glee. "Frontline's got *nothing* on us. But they totally busted those fuckers after our call. And we've saved another sixty-seven souls. Tara's already found homes for some of them, she's that fast."

Finn nodded, his gaze fully gone now. His index finger brushed ever so slightly along the fabric of his glove, moving the holographic cursor to wherever he needed it. He hadn't even heard what she'd said, or he simply didn't give a shit that they'd almost gotten caught last night.

"Can you please switch it off?" she asked. "It drives me nuts."

"No, I can't. I'm working overtime because I spent most of last night giving sixty-seven souls a tour around the evacuation zone. And Sam's already been outside." He turned back to the screen wall with its long rows of perfect trees in all shapes and sizes—the building blocks of the virtual rooftop garden he was designing.

"Finn!" she yelled at his back. "I'm only here because you said you wouldn't be and because I thought Sam desperately needed to pee. Hector's furious because I'm leaving him alone in the middle of the day." That last part wasn't exactly true since Hector probably was still in a state of bliss anticipating the wonders he expected from Jake, but any other boss would have been furious. "What happened to your appointment?"

"They decided to cancel when I was halfway there," Finn said without turning. "Found out it's too hot for walking around their roof at noon. I believe I mentioned that fact when they came up with the brilliant idea."

"So Sam's already been outside?"

Now Finn did turn, features frozen. "I just said that, didn't I?"

Shavir stared at his eyes, so brilliantly blue in the reflecting light yet so utterly dead, all empathy shut down by the drug. Sam was fine, she told herself, Hector was waiting for her, and Finn was high as a kite. She had to let this go and get out before it went any further. "You said you're not taking that shit anymore," she hissed in spite of herself.

"What can I do when I have people in my life who keep yelling at me for no reason?" Finn asked coolly. "Especially when such people are no longer in my life at all but park their dog at my home after a busy night for the sake of convenience."

And there she lost it. "You *offered*!"

"I always offer things. But only some people take advantage."

Screw him. "Come on, Sam." She turned toward the stairs.

"And where exactly are you taking him?" Finn asked.

Shavir had no idea as she looked around for Sam's leash, trying to make herself leave. The tears pressing against her eyelids told her she and Finn were sliding into their familiar pattern of call-and-response: Finn's call cold and controlled, like a scientist stimulating a lab rat; her response livid, out of proportion. Before long, she'd wriggle and writhe as he dropped words on her with surgical precision, words loaded with two years of bait and rejection.

"This is what ended us," she shrieked. "You wanted to know? *This* is precisely the reason. I'm done with this shit!"

Annoyance rippled across Finn's face, suggesting the Emovia hadn't yet fully kicked in. "Good," he said, turning away. "Because I really need to work."

She stared at his bare back that was moving again to the soundtrack he had never stopped. Behind him, the screen wall showed more of the roof garden project he was working on, already bearing some of his signature traits: stormwater fountains, cream-colored yucca blossoms, a spiraling tent roof, and the windbreaker wall made of intertwined steel arabesques and living wood that had won him a chest full of environmental awards and design prizes.

She stood for another moment, her eyes glued to the screen wall so she wouldn't tear the goddamn Spine out of Finn's neck.

Then, Sam trailing her closely, she returned to the living room.

When she passed the French doors to the terrace, she stopped, overcome by almost physical pain. After the breakup, Finn had offered to continue taking care of Sam while she was at work. She knew he would offer again; it was some kind of fucked-up vicious cycle, like everything else between them. But she wouldn't—couldn't—play along anymore, no matter how convenient it was or how much she loved this place, his place.

She'd been so overwhelmed when she first stood here, in almost exactly this spot, dwarfed by the immense beauty, wealth, and privilege. Finn had been throwing one of his lavish parties, and for some unfathomable reason, he'd invited Roots to it. Not Lenny or Judy, not anyone in particular, just Roots, as if unconcerned that the whole farm might show up and crash the thing. Lenny had been disinclined, as he'd put it, to spend an evening with a bunch of supercilious Manhattanites, and Judy would probably have bombed the place given the chance. But they all knew going to the party might allow them to learn more about the patented shading-and-cooling system that had made Finn famous and his rooftop gardens sustainable. They were under no illusions that they could ever afford the system for their farm, but the party seemed like a one-time chance to learn enough to build a poor man's version of it and keep their veggies from dying.

Tara, of course, was up for it, and, as usual, she'd convinced Shavir to tag along. They would infiltrate the party—sort of, since they had actually been invited—and have some fun along the way. But then they started doing research on this guy, Finn Larsen, award-winning urban landscape architect, born and raised on the Upper East Side, son of an even more famous architect who had designed some of the most prominent landmarks of East River Park and other highlights along the eastern part of the enormous seawall that now protected Manhattan. The father was best buddies with the mayor, apparently, and the son swung back and forth between rebelling against his famous old man and following right in his footsteps.

They'd processed all this information, she and Tara, and for the first time, Tara folded. The woman who wasn't afraid of getting beaten, bitten, arrested, or shot had lost her nerve at the prospect of going to a party and mingling with the upper crust. Outrageously, she did so while hinting that, as a poor climate refugee from India, she wasn't equipped with the right social skills and Shavir was much better suited for the task because of her rich father, displaying her usual lack of tact and willful ignorance of facts. Not only was it Tara who had enjoyed an upper-middle-class upbringing before she and her dad had to flee Kolkata and embark on that harrowing journey that ended first in a refugee camp in Texas and then in Brooklyn, but Tara was also perfectly aware that Shavir had seen the renowned heart surgeon who happened to be her father exactly two times and that both of those meetings had been disastrous. Plus, the man had died a few years after the second meeting, crashing his car into a San Francisco bridge pier on his way home from the hospital. Neither her father's life nor his death had had any impact on Shavir's ability to navigate a party in Manhattan, so it looked like no one was going to go.

But on the night of the party, something had pulled her across the East River. Whether it was curiosity, idiocy, or a mixture of both, she'd borrowed an ill-fitting dress and asked Lenny for the invitation. She instantly regretted her decision when, after climbing the stairs, she was introduced to Finn's swanky East Village world. The Asian antiques, the ageless crowd, the fifty-foot gourmet buffet with the towering arrangement of white orchids, everything had screamed at her that she didn't belong here, that she had come from the wrong side of the East River. But knowing she had a job to do, she'd downed a glass of the ubiquitous champagne, put her insecurities aside, and headed straight to the rooftop garden.

Now, a little over two years later, it was time to say goodbye.

Finn was utterly absorbed by his screen wall or deliberately ignoring her continued presence, so Shavir stepped outside. It was hot up here but not so hot that plants and humans couldn't survive. The fanned-out triangles of the giant tent roof gave much-needed shade while their photovoltaic fabric provided the solar power fueling the engines of the outdoor aircon and misting system that allowed this impossible paradise to withstand the trying climate of New York.

It had been a shock, the night of the party, seeing all this for the first time. The bamboos and yucca trees, lit from below, glowing in fantastic shades of green. Oleander, hibiscus, and bougainvillea blossoms popping out in yellow, pink, and purple. A slight breeze from the hidden aircon units had ruffled the leaves, the sound mixing with the murmur of the Moroccan fountain that had since become Sam's favorite drinking spot. She'd promptly headed for the trees that night and hiked up her dress to climb the central mast of the shading system, which looked like a giant sailing vessel, only the photovoltaic sails were horizontal and they could tip and tilt so they *wouldn't* catch the wind. By the time she'd reached the first joint and started inspecting its mechanics, Finn was standing below her, looking up at her undies.

It had started from there. He invited her into his studio—never mind the couple hundred party guests in the main room—and shared the details of his patented shading system with her. He was witty and charming and genuinely interested in their work at Roots in a way she'd never have expected from a guy who by any count was too smart, too hot, and too fucking rich to be messing around with a communal farming project. He drove her back across the East River that night, past the military checkpoints and home to the farm, and ended up seeing not only their veggies in the moonlight but also her undies again.

She fell for him, hard, and he joined Roots, helping them in ways no one else could have, for reasons still mostly unclear to her. After learning about their nocturnal activities, he joined that group, too, seemingly unconcerned about what it would mean for him, or his family, should he get arrested on charges of domestic ecoterrorism. He'd been a mystery to her back then, the kind of mystery that makes you wanna know. He was still a mystery to her now, the main difference being that she had learned enough to finally keep her distance.

She looked at the table surrounding the wooden mast of the roof construction that had been her climbing pole back then. There was nothing on it but Sam's cotton leash and the two antique candleholders she'd given Finn for his thirty-fifth birthday. The guy at the flea market had told her they were from the drowned city of Venice, which in hindsight was very fitting. Their gracefully twisted forms were made of copper, stained by age to a blackish green, and formed what looked like two upside-down question marks. Whether that was a comment on their relationship or on humankind in general, she didn't know. Whichever it was, the answer was negative.

"What are you doing?" The chill in Finn's voice cut through the heat. He'd come outside, finally aware she was still here.

"What does it look like?" She grabbed the dog leash.

"Looks like you're being impulsive again, making stupid decisions."

Finn's drug-frozen features had an ugliness to them in this harsh light, their symmetry too perfect, his eyes too blue. She'd never noticed it before, the ugliness. But now it hit her, and it hurt more than all the hurtful things he'd said and done to her over the years. It wasn't the drug, as much as she loathed it. The ugliness lurked behind and below the drug, springing from a void at the very core of Finn's being. Every time he'd asked her to come back to him, she'd poured herself into that void and disappeared in it without making so much as a sound. She didn't know whether it could be filled or what substance was needed for the filling, only that nothing Finn did for Roots or the animals seemed to have done the trick and that she couldn't ever plunge into that void again or face the ugliness of this stunning iceman who was staring at her in the heat without any sign of melting.

A soft, wet swipe across her right hand reminded her why she was here. "Let's go, boy," she said to Sam without looking at Finn again. An elevator ride later, she was outside in the blazing sunlight, looking for a dog-friendly podcar.

FOUR

SOMA'S FRONT DOOR WAS locked when Jake reached it shortly after 9 p.m. He hesitated, his knuckles suspended inches away from the glass, torn between his fear that Shavir had already left and his doubts that he'd be able to interact with another human.

It had been a rough day in the CSR, rougher than most, and his long walk up here hadn't been long enough to shake it off. David's illegally hired militia had blasted its way into the Cambodian EPZ in the late morning and seized what New York so desperately needed: several tons of antibiotics and antivirals, along with other critical-supply meds, all of them their very own drugs, ordered months ago by New York hospitals. For hours, their precious cargo had sat in the middle of what was swiftly turning into a war zone. For hours, it had looked like they wouldn't be able to get any of it out because there were no trucks, boats, or drones, not even donkeys. By now, the Cambodian army had taken control, seizing everything in sight. But David's militia had managed to get their meds out just minutes before the Cambodian seizure. They were on their way up the coast now, to Laem Chabang, and at least some of them were coming to New York.

Jake didn't regret his decision. By the late afternoon, he and Cristina from LA SAFE had been in what Cristina called an "interesting situation." After spending the day working frantically in parallel and against each other, he still hadn't managed to find appropriate transportation while Cristina had somehow unearthed two cooler trucks in Koh Kong but hadn't been able to put anything on them because her meds were stuck in the EPZ. It either hadn't occurred to her to hire a militia, or her guys simply weren't as good as David's. Either way, at 5 p.m., Jake had cargo without transportation and Cristina the opposite. She was a tough woman, a supply troubleshooter like him, as inventive and ruthless as one had to be in this job, but at that point she was exhausted, worn out by the atrocities she had witnessed all day, and herself under fire for the failed operation. It was much the same for Jake, with no way left for either of them to succeed alone.

So they'd made a deal.

David did not take it well. His tension had risen all afternoon, and this served as his reason to finally explode. He scolded Jake in front of the entire CSR team for making the decision without prior consultation. Behind him on the screen walls, the EPZ suddenly popped up again—new footage from an illegal camera drone, its uncensored live images of the army's brutal takeover sold to news stations around the world: tear gas, smoke, and explosions swelling skyward; men, women, and children running, screaming, and stumbling over one another, fire raining down on them. Standing right in front of it all was David, oblivious to the horrendous spectacle at his back, complaining about losing half their meds to LA. Jake couldn't remember his response very clearly, but it hadn't been what David called professional.

Even now, standing in front of Soma, he couldn't stop shaking. His Spine was on standby, but the bloodied faces, missing limbs, and endless explosions kept replaying themselves in his mind, more visceral than any Spine projection could ever be. He jerked up his head and knocked on the door, his fingers numb against the glass, the sound too loud in a city that had become eerily quiet since the introduction of podcars. An unreasonable amount of relief washed over him when Shavir's slim figure emerged from behind the counter.

"Hey," she said when she opened the door. "You look terrible."

"I'm alright."

He saw her face and realized she, too, was exhausted. It took the last of his self-control to resist the urge to take her in his arms for comfort and support, foggy as he was about which one of them needed it more. She seemed so much stronger than he felt.

"You sure you're okay?" There was concern in her voice.

The images in his mind began to fade and recede as he strained his eyes to focus on hers in the semidarkness. He let go of the half-open door he didn't know he'd grabbed for balance.

"Yeah. I just need a beer to wash down my day."

She locked the door behind him. "Thanks for coming back. Hector's waiting for you, but there's something I need to explain to you first." She turned in the direction of the kitchen.

"Wait," he said, reaching for her arm for the second time that day, his bare fingers touching the tattoo around her biceps. "I've got something for you." He reached into his bag and pulled out the bottle of healing accelerant he'd picked up from the pharmacy on his way here. "Every two hours," he inadvertently parroted David's words, "or it won't work."

Shavir hesitated, which gave him time to become acutely aware of the fact that they were completely alone in the room. "You really shouldn't have," she said. "I'm fine."

"I honestly don't think so. But you hopefully will be if you take this. And this, too." He pulled out a bottle of ciprofloxacin from his bag, his hand still trembling.

She stared at the antibiotics. Her eyes flew up to his, black in this light. Then, to his relief, she took both bottles from him without further resistance.

"I will. Thanks, Jake."

He couldn't retain focus and, embarrassed, let his gaze wander around the room. "Will you still be here when I'm done?"

"Well," she said, "since Hector pays the cleaning people only to mop the floors, I'll be busy for a while. And given how I feel right now, there's a good chance you'll find me sleeping on a stack of kitchen towels when you get back."

The thought made him smile. "Alright, but don't disappear on me, okay?"

"I can't, actually. That's what I wanted to show you. Or, rather, explain to you. Come." She led him past the kitchen door to Soma's small back room. "It's not Hector's fault," she said, "so please don't give him trouble."

Jake wanted to remind her again that he wasn't working for NYPD or even for Homeland in the way she seemed to imagine, but the thought got stuck in his brain when he looked past her into the room. "What's that?" was all he could think to say, in part because he truly didn't understand what he was looking at.

It looked like a dog, for sure, but it had little to do with the silky creatures he encountered during his walks along the Manhattan seawall, and it also bore no resemblance to Farley, the dog he'd had as a boy. This one weighed at least two hundred pounds with a chest wider than his own, a yellow coat like the extinct mountain lions he'd seen in Spine features, and a massive dark face covered in furrows. Its tail made loud thumping sounds every time it bounced against the armrest of the couch Hector used for his naps during the quieter hours of the day. *Thump, thump, thump, thump.*

"That," Shavir said, "is Sam."

Jake nodded stupidly, as if the name meant anything to him.

"Is it yours?"

"Yes, he's mine." Pride swung in her voice. "Come here, boy."

The hellhound sprang forward, bridging the distance to them in one giant leap. Jake didn't have time to step back or steady himself against the door frame. The next thing he felt was the animal's prickly fur against his left hand and the soft wetness of its tongue.

"Stop it, Sam!" Shavir commanded, and the dog stopped, looking up at her with a grotesquely wide dog smile while placing itself on its behind. "Are you afraid of dogs?" she asked Jake, a sensible question he would have appreciated earlier.

"Not... really," he stammered. "I just didn't realize that... Sam... classifies as one."

Shavir laughed. "I know. You don't see his kind much around here."

He nodded, still in awe before the unfamiliar animal. "What *is* his kind?"

"English mastiff. They're usually bred for their meat."

He nodded again, unable to follow up on this. He wiped his palm against his jeans. Farley had done that sometimes, lick his hand. He remembered that now. And how his mother used to scold him because Farley was licking all kinds of things, and he was supposed to keep his hands to himself. The memory was making him dizzy.

"Jake!" Hector popped up between them, his voice too loud. "Thanks so much for coming. I'm sorry about the dog. It was an emergency." He glared at Shavir. "Can you please tie him somewhere outside in the alley? It's dark now, so no one will see."

"No!" Jake said. "He can stay. I don't mind, I grew up with a dog."

Shavir smiled and led the dog into a niche behind the couch where it lay down and vanished from view. "Thanks, Jake," she murmured as she returned and walked past him. "He's going to be good," she snapped in Hector's direction. "Call if you need me."

"I don't know what she was thinking," Hector said when they were alone. "They can close my restaurant for this. Please don't mention it to anyone."

Jake gave him a look and changed the subject. "So when will you finally get a new Spine? Why don't you ever listen to me?"

"I *do* listen, Jake," Hector protested, waving his wiry arms for emphasis. "I really do. But I can't let them touch my neck again. It's just... I can't, you know?"

Jake did know. Hector couldn't seem to forget the infection that had turned him from a slim man into a very thin one, as he would say. Jake hadn't known him back then, when the idiots at one of the Spine Stores had somehow managed to butcher Hector's neck during a routine processor change in the middle of the Global Supply Crisis. He'd been living in Queens then with his wife, right before the riots broke out, and for a man of his means and social standing, it had been impossible to get antibiotics. The unhappy coincidence of personal and global emergency had almost killed him.

"Hector, please." Jake dropped his bag on the floor. "You need a new Spine. And we do have antibiotics at the moment."

"I know," Hector returned with a sheepish smile, "but the laptop's still working fine. It's just the 4Flow that's giving me trouble because my license is for the Spine."

"And because the app is way too big for your old processor. It was designed for the Spine. I've told you this—" Jake stopped, knowing he sounded irritated. He wasn't in the mood for another round of this nonsense. His gaze wandered to where the dog had disappeared behind the couch. It had barely moved since Shavir had left, but one of its enormous paws was stretching out of the shadow, dark at the bottom and yellow on top, with long, sturdy claws in between.

"Does it bother you?" Hector asked.

"No." Jake tore his eyes away from the paw. "I just didn't know Shavir had a dog. So are you gonna get a new Spine?" Shavir was all by herself in the front room, and he was trapped back here, feeling the minutes go by. He wanted this to be over.

No such luck.

Hector pointed to his laptop. "Can you try one more time?"

Ten minutes later, Jake took a sip from the beer Hector had brought him before retreating to his kitchen and slowly sat down on the office chair that had nearly killed him last time. Its broken backrest gave way when weight was thrust against it, a detail Hector had forgotten to mention before leaving Jake alone with it. Now, the lower part of it was wrapped with bright yellow tape that had no effect on its stability but at least served as a visual reminder of its treachery.

Jake called up the 4Flow app and started the download process on Hector's laptop, his fingers producing awkward clicking sounds on the old physical keyboard.

He glanced over at the dog again. How could he have missed it? There had been no dog registration in Shavir's Homeland file, but she wouldn't bring a dog to Manhattan illegally, would she? Apparently, it had been an emergency, but that didn't explain the missing registration unless it wasn't actually her dog. Perhaps she hadn't told the truth, or he had overlooked something in her file. Not an easy animal to overlook, though. The municipal fees for a dog of that size were hideous, several thousand dollars per year. It was the city's pathetic attempt to make the illegal meat market unprofitable, by hiking up the fees for keeping any type of animal so only the people with serious money to spare could afford them. How could Shavir pay those fees on the money she made here?

Once again, he'd reached the point where he needed to stop asking questions. It didn't matter whose dog it was or if it was legal, and he wasn't the police. He resisted the urge to search Shavir's Homeland file for the dog registration and instead stared at the laptop, where the 4Flow had discovered it wasn't being downloaded onto Hector's nonexistent Spine and aborted the process. After one brief call with Niya Taylor, SAFE's designated IT genius and the app's creator, it was downloading again. Niya was a master of creative problem-solving, and she rarely asked questions when Jake had problems to solve.

Shavir's dog was extremely well-behaved, lying in the same spot behind the couch but now presenting both paws. Jake wanted to walk over but was unsure how it would react, so instead he inspected the paraphernalia that decorated Hector's walls: old certificates, restaurant reviews, and images of cooking crews, all of them featuring Hector in different positions like a culinary spot-the-mouse game in which the mouse grew progressively older. Right above the desk was a faded picture of Hector as a boy with his parents, all of them smiling with their eyes pinched together against the glare of the afternoon sun. Behind them was the weather-beaten welcome sign of Papago Park. Hector had moved to New York two decades ago, just like Jake had, but at a different age and for different reasons. It had been a hurricane that had swept Jake up the coast when he was a boy while Hector had left Arizona because he'd become sick of the dust storms in Phoenix, where he had buried both his parents before they'd turned sixty.

But New York hadn't been able to give Hector shelter from a different kind of storm that would sweep the entire nation fifteen years later, leaving no American life untouched. After working for years in one of Manhattan's Mexican restaurants, he and his wife had opened their own eatery in Queens only to be shaken to their core by the Crisis. Hector had dedicated an entire wall to that part of his life; it featured images of a *Closed Until Further Notice* sign on his old restaurant's front door, the empty shelves in the superstores, the tear-gassing of protesters, and his late wife, Maria, a vibrant young woman who'd died of pneumonia because no hospital in Queens had the meds to treat her, and it had been impossible to leave the borough.

Jake shuddered at the thought of doing the same with his own history. There was a reason he liked his walls bare.

"What are you looking at?" Hector asked, balancing a plate of tacos.

"Your little wall of horrors. Might wanna see a therapist about that."

Hector shrugged. "I like to be reminded."

"Yeah," Jake said. "I really don't."

"Here. You gotta eat." Hector put the plate on his desk. "She saved my life back then, you know?" He nodded to the picture of his dead wife. "I didn't tell her, but she knew I'd gone out to the evacuation zone during curfew. I was trying to find the black market. There were rumors that somewhere out there in the zone you could still get antibiotics if you had the cash. I didn't want them for me, but for her, you know? Even though my neck was all pink and gooey and infected from those Spine Store butchers, and I probably would have died just like her before long. But she saved me."

Jake tried to push the image of the laughing young woman, along with the reason why she had to die, out of his mind. "I thought the National Guard saved you."

Hector nodded. "They saw me, a patrol or something, and arrested me before I even got to the market, if it ever existed. I still don't know. But it wasn't a coincidence that they picked me up. Maria reported me to them for breaking curfew."

"To the National Guard?" Jake asked, staggered. "Your own wife?"

"She knew they had antibiotics." There was a tremor in Hector's voice that belied the lightness of his tone. "She'd heard it somewhere and told me about it, too, but it wasn't like you could walk up to one of those guards and ask them for some pills. When they arrest you, though, they gotta treat you, that's what the law said, still says. And that's what happened to me. I was in some jail clinic for a week, and when I got back home, Maria had died." He paused to collect himself. "That's why I like to be reminded."

"I'm really sorry." Jake could barely hear his own voice.

"Yeah," Hector said. "We all got those stories, right?" He raised his eyebrows like he expected some story in return, but Jake just nodded. There was no way he would talk about his own losses, certainly not now and certainly not with Hector.

Hector looked at the plate. "Your food's getting cold."

Jake nodded again, knowing he wouldn't be able to get anything down, and then Hector left him alone with his own memories of the Crisis. He'd been a graduate student then and didn't yet have his bionic lenses. He'd nearly gone blind from the sheer wear and tear of his old data contacts as he tried to figure out from a logistical perspective the interlocking disasters that fed off one another. Countries prescient enough to build strategic reserves had been better off for a while, but few were able to prevent violent conflicts. The US certainly wasn't. The day Hector had stumbled into Queens's permanent evacuation zone in the hope of finding antibiotics on the black market, only to be arrested and effectively saved by the Guard, was the day on which the 51st president finally declared the supply crisis a national state of emergency. It was the birthday of the SAFE centers and the end of a great many things Americans had taken for granted. For Jake, it was the beginning of a career that tied him to Homeland Security in a way that, to this day, he resented. But back then, it had looked like a chance to do something useful with his life, a chance to alleviate the guilt he'd been lugging around since childhood. Little had he known that all it would do for him was add new layers of guilt on top of the old ones.

The dog was still watching him, its massive head resting on its paws. It reminded him so much of Farley, the way the dark eyes followed every movement and the ears picked up every word. It unnerved him, that resemblance. He'd forgotten how much he had loved that dog, and now it felt like some distant echo of something powerful was resonating in him. He got up and walked to the couch. He never touched any of the dogs on the boardwalk, but this one had touched him first, and it belonged to Shavir.

"It's Sam, right?" he asked, and then, more softly, "Hi, Sam."

He reached out his hand and jumped back when the dog lifted his head, accompanied by the familiar rhythm—*thump, thump, thump.*

Farley had had the same rhythm, lying sprawled out on Jake's bed, wagging his tail against the mattress because he knew he wasn't supposed to be there, and Jake, instead of telling Farley to leave, had flung himself next to his dog and buried his face in the black-and-golden fur.

Now he reached out again, and this time he touched Sam. His fur felt different, shorter and less soft than Farley's, a deficit he made up for by a much louder tail and a deep guttural sound as he rolled over, offering his belly for a rub. Jake swallowed hard and got up to finish his work on the 4Flow. There were too many memories in this room.

The lights were still dimmed when he returned to Soma's front room, looking for Shavir. It was empty, the only sound the electric buzz of the display case. A soft grunt made him look behind the counter, and there she was, sitting on the floor, her knees covered by a towel and drawn up to her chest, her back resting against the door of the fridge, her head slumped forward onto her crossed arms. She hadn't been kidding about going to sleep.

He stood there for a moment, looking at her huddled figure with a directness he normally didn't allow himself. Then he walked around the counter and crouched next to her. Her back was rising and falling with long, slow breaths, enviable for their evenness. He lifted his hand, uncertain what to do. Then he touched her hair, a slow stroke in rhythm with her breathing. The intimacy of it was overwhelming.

"Hey," he murmured. "Shavir."

She winced and lifted her head, disoriented. She looked at him, glanced around. "Shit!" She made an uncoordinated gesture to rub her eyes before she fully regained consciousness. "Oh, shit," she said again, letting her head fall backward against the fridge. "I was so tired, I thought I needed to sit down for a minute. What time is it?"

"Quarter past ten."

"Shit," she said for the third time. "Where's Sam?"

"Still behind the couch. Amazing resolve, that dog. Didn't even get up for a taco."

She smiled. "What about the 4Flow? Is it working again?"

"Yeah, for now," Jake returned with a grunt as he sat down next to her. "Hector's back in his room with Sam, watching the scarcity alerts come in like it's actual good news."

"Thanks, Jake," Shavir said in a voice still sleepy. "Thanks for helping us out again."

He turned to her, their faces inches apart. He wanted to say something, but the urge got drowned out by the hormonal rush. Plus, he was coming down from pep pills, which took some of the jittering out of his eyes and the tension out of his body but also left him cracked and brittle, much more vulnerable than at any other time of the day. He didn't like being around other people during this time, at least not people he knew. It was the time when he would go out to the seawall for his long walks home, ignoring everybody else on the boardwalk.

But today was different. This was different. If only he could figure out what to say.

"Is it still on?" Shavir asked. "Your Spine?"

"On standby." Wasn't he always.

Her face was serious now, scrutinizing. "Do you ever switch it off?"

"Not really. They have to be able to reach me if something comes up."

"What a nightmare."

He laughed. "I call it my job."

Shavir laughed with him. She couldn't possibly know she'd just summed up the essence of not only his job, but his entire life. His eyes were watering from the stress of the day like they always did at this time, but it might as well have been tears of despair.

She raised her hand and caught the next forming tear with her index finger, her touch so light it made him shudder. "How did it go today?"

"Well... I don't know." The images welled up in him again, bodies convulsing, falling, screaming. "There's not much to tell," he said helplessly, pushing the images to the back of his mind.

"You mean you aren't allowed to tell," Shavir suggested, her finger floating out of sight.

He nodded, although that was only part of the problem.

"I should get going," she said abruptly.

As she got up, Jake pushed himself off the floor, aware he had just ruined something he hadn't meant to ruin. "Can we talk sometime, you and I?" he spilled out. "Not like this," he added when he saw her questioning face. "I mean really talk. Over dinner, perhaps?"

Her expression was unreadable. "Like... a date?"

"Yes. Like a date." He was terrible at this. "I can't do lunch with my crazy schedule, but evenings I get off sometimes. We could grab a bite."

She dropped the towel onto the counter. "Please, Jake, don't. You know we can't do this."

"Why not?" He found it difficult to breathe. "Because of my job or because of me?"

"Neither," she said, staring right at him, sounding exasperated. "I like you, Jake, and whatever it is you guys are doing over there at SAFE, I'm sure it's helping some people in this city."

"It helps everyone in this city."

"Right." She looked down, marking her disagreement. "And it's so top secret you can't even tell me what you did today or why you look like you ran into a bulldozer."

"Not so unusual if you're working for the government."

She faced him again, her tense features reminding him that she didn't like government types. "Why are you doing this, Jake?" she erupted. "What do you expect me to say? We're like... from opposite ends of the universe, can't you see that? Hell, I'm even from the other side of the *fucking river*. Can you imagine us out on a date? We wouldn't even make it to the appetizers before arguing about, well, everything."

"That's bullshit," he said roughly. "I'm not what you think."

She inhaled, her face a blurry shape behind the steady waterfall of his sore eyes. "Maybe. But I really can't do this, Jake. I'm sorry."

"Alright." He steadied himself against the counter. "I understand."

"No, I don't think you do."

Her eyes flew up to him one more time, and then she turned away and left the room. "Bye, Hector!" he heard her yelling a minute later from the back door. Then she was gone.

Jake closed his eyes, the emptiness inside him filling with the buzzing wave of sound still emanating from the display case until there was nothing left but the resonance of that droning electric song that seemed to rise and fall with his heartbeat.

Instinctively, he searched his pockets for pep pills.

Hector came in from the kitchen, two beers in his hand, face vacillating between pity and amusement. "Don't worry," he said, "you're not the only guy she's turned down."

Jake erupted in a hoarse laugh. "Thanks, Hector."

"Beer?" Hector asked, raising one of the bottles.

Jake shook his head. "I gotta go back to SAFE. Do the good deed."

There was a faint beeping sound, and the front door opened a crack.

Shavir stuck her head in, looked at him. "How about tomorrow at seven?" she asked. "Buddha's Kitchen. Can you make it?"

Jake stared at her across the room.

The crack in the door widened as Sam pushed his big head through it, smiling his dog smile.

"Sure," Jake said, though he wasn't even sure Shavir and her dog were actually there.

"Great." A smile scurried across Shavir's face. "See you tomorrow."

She pushed Sam's head back, closed the door, and was gone again.

Dumbfounded, Jake turned around and was met by Hector's wide grin.

FIVE

SAM TOOK THREE STEPS at once as they ran down the stairs to the L-train. He never seemed to mind the long, noisy train ride underneath the East River, knowing that the adventures of the Brooklyn boardwalk were waiting for him on the other side. Shavir had trouble keeping up, but they managed to board the train at the exact same time, sitting down with the synchronized precision that sprang from countless repetitions, she on one of the shabby plastic seats, and Sam, with a thud, on the floor next to her, the car swinging with his weight.

A woman sitting three seats away got up and sat down again at the very end of the car, a mix of fear and disapproval in her eyes. It happened all the time. People weren't used to big dogs around here. Shavir bent down and caressed the inside of Sam's ears, knowing he'd make the low cooing sounds that some people mistook for growling. It was hard to resist teasing Manhattanites, and, clearly, today wasn't one of her best days when it came to resistance of any kind.

Her pathological lack of restraint, combined with her penchant for impulsive decision-making, was the only explanation for what she'd just done—why she had stopped in the middle of the street and walked back to say yes to Jake when no had been a perfectly good answer. There was no sane reason for it and about a million suggesting insanity. She let go of Sam and leaned back against the window as she tried, once again, to figure out her own decisions.

She had always liked Jake, that much was true, but it was also true that she could never date him, not even for one night. Working at SAFE meant he worked for Homeland Security, no matter how he tried to spin it or how much he needed to delude himself so he felt a little less shitty about it. And he did feel shitty, that much she could tell whenever she raised the topic, which was whenever she saw an opportunity. She just couldn't wrap her head around someone like Jake working for something like Homeland, and yet that seemed to be the only thing he did, a thing that gnawed at him, consumed him. She'd watched him get thinner and wearier over the months, and he'd been pretty thin and weary to begin with when he first walked into Soma one morning about half a year ago.

He'd worn a big, puffy jacket against one of that winter's blizzards, his face half-hidden in the oversized hood, his eyes transfixed by whatever he was watching on his Spine. Soma had been hot and damp as it always was on early winter mornings, the heating working overtime to drive out the night's chill. But Jake had been so insulated against the world, he didn't notice the change in temperature or scenery. Upon finally registering he stood in front of a coffee counter, he'd cracked a smile that was a surprise because, in its self-mockery, it was charming.

And he'd kept coming back. On the day she learned what it was that got him up so early every morning, she'd nearly dropped the almond latte that had already become his regular thing. It was such an epic mismatch, this smart, somber, sensitive man working for something as brute and barbaric as Homeland. It made no sense to her, and she'd told Jake so a few times more than strictly necessary in the faint hope, perhaps, that he would go do something else instead.

He hadn't been very receptive, of course, because in his book, and in those of most people in Manhattan, he worked for this amazing agency that kept the city alive and running. The problem with that pretty picture was it was a lie, and deep down, Jake knew it as well as she did. She could see it every time it took him five seconds too long to assure her that he *really* was just a logistics guy managing supply chains.

He made his job seem as boring and mundane as he possibly could, which was about as honest as the related lie that SAFE tried its best to ensure critical supply got distributed equally within the city. No matter how often he repeated those lies, though, he had to know how ludicrous it all sounded to someone living in Brooklyn or to anyone, really, who bothered to look at him whenever he was too raw or too overdosed to hide the horror he was witnessing and inflicting all day. Whether Jake liked it or not, SAFE was part of Homeland Security, and that department wasn't known for its altruism.

As if she needed another reminder, two Frontline cops were standing near the escalator when she came up from the subway in what was left of Williamsburg. There were no green buildings or podcars here, no fancy biophilia projects or even the most basic municipal efforts to keep things sustainable and above water. Instead, it was all plywood and flood marks, a few old, electrified cars, and people fending for themselves as well as they could, swarming around the hawker stalls, pop-up restaurants, and makeshift stores. A group of men wolfing down their dinner looked on as she sank to her knees to muzzle Sam as the cops approached, steps heavy from their usual riot gear. Their faces were half-hidden behind visors, but she recognized them from previous encounters, and she knew they must have recognized her, or, at the very least, Sam. But if they had, they didn't let on.

"Evening, ma'am," one of the cops said. "We need to check your dog registration."

Reluctantly, she offered Sam's neck to their scanner and then her own fingers, avoiding their eyes and biting her lips the entire time to keep herself from saying something that might provoke them.

When it was over, Sam's legality once more ascertained, she got up without looking at the cops and led him to the Brooklyn seawall along the East River. It was only once they had walked past Hurricane Point, and Sam was sniffing the brown grass and the corroded sheet metal piles for dog news, that she started to relax again.

No matter how often she went through these checks, each time there was a part of her that waited for the Frontline cops to tell her she was arrested, that they knew what she was doing at night, that she would get tried as a terrorist and go to prison for it. They were a trigger-happy gang with military training, people you didn't want to run into even if you hadn't just cleaned out a dog-fattening station out in the evacuation zones. Supposedly, they reported to the mayor as well as the feds, but fact was they did whatever the fuck they wanted. And they got their intel from Homeland. Their fucking drones, too.

So regardless of what Jake had said, and regardless of what she had said, there was no way she could have dinner with him. It would mean inviting trouble to a degree excessive even by her standards. And that wasn't even considering what the others would say about a date with an overworked, overdosed Homeland guy. Or the fact that her two years with Finn had drained all charm from the idea of a romantic dinner date. If there was one lesson she'd learned, it was that such dates came at a hefty price even if you weren't the one paying the check.

Jake hadn't tried to be romantic though. He hadn't even tried to flirt. Instead, he had given her antibiotics. The cynic in her wanted to know if they had that kind of stuff lying around in the office, stuff that half the city would kill for, literally. But it was the bottomless sincerity with which Jake did these things that she didn't know how to place or handle. The way he looked at her like he cared.

Maybe it was all made up. Maybe he was spying on her, on the group, helping Frontline bust them. She knew that was what Lenny would say. And Tara. And perhaps it was true. Perhaps Jake's dark, dancing eyes had confused her radar. Those eyes were what had propelled her back to Soma and made her say words that would force her to come up with new words, words of apology and evasion, words to somehow undo what she'd done.

Perhaps she didn't have to keep beating herself up about this, she realized as the group of broken office buildings that was home to Roots came into sight. She would spend most of tomorrow with Tara and the dogs in New Jersey, and that likely was the solution to her problem right there. Tara was notorious for her ambitious planning skills, so there was a decent chance they wouldn't be back in Manhattan by dinnertime, giving her the perfect excuse for a last-minute cancelation of her date with Jake. Not that she could explain any of it to him.

There was light on top of the first building, unusual at this late hour. Shavir walked up to the roof and pushed open the old metal door still warm to the touch from the heat of the day. A few scattered floodlights threw their pale beams on long rows of veggie beds where some of the Roots people were harvesting in the warm glow of their headlamps. The lamps looked like fireflies against the distant Manhattan skyline, which was shimmering green and luxurious behind the bulwark of its sophisticated seawall system.

Judy stood in her usual spot, sorting veggies into preordered delivery boxes with a face that suggested it was unwise to approach her.

"Hi, Shav," she said without looking up. "They're all down in the basement because, as you can see, there's nothing to do up here."

"You're harvesting now?"

"It was 115 today. I can't send my people up here any earlier, or they're gonna get fried."

"Well, do you need another hand?"

Now Judy looked up, her dark face lined and withered from countless days in the sun. "We're almost done. But thank you. Tomorrow night would be good."

There it was, an even more perfect excuse to cancel her date, one that she could mention to Jake without giving away anything and that he would understand. All she had to do was tell Judy she'd be there. "We'll be in New Jersey tomorrow," she heard herself saying instead, "so I'm not sure."

"Not sure," Judy snorted. "Well, I ain't sure how much longer I'm gonna wait for you guys to find a new base for your little operation down there."

"We know—" Shavir scrambled, too tired to offer a coherent explanation for why the operation was still there despite multiple promises to the contrary.

Judy cut her off. "As I said, they're down in the basement, so you can remind them *right now*. And tell Lenny I need to talk to him about the farm. If he can make it." Her voice was caustic. She was the only person Shavir knew who matched her mother's ability to make her feel bad, regardless of whether she had actually done something wrong. Her mom was gone, and as if Shavir didn't feel bad enough for a lifetime about the very fact of her death, Judy had somehow taken

over, making sure there was always something new to feel bad about.
Not even Lenny came remotely close, and Tara always complained
about how he had perfected the art of guilt-tripping.

"Hey, Nacho," Judy called, and behind a container of eggplants, two
rows away from them, Nacho's head popped up, adorned by the usual
bandana to keep the sweat out of his eyes. "Can you get me some more
of them crates from the basement?"

Nacho dropped his knife and came over to them, apprehension on
his broad face as he approached Judy.

"Now you're complete," she scoffed, returning her attention to the
delivery boxes. "And don't forget to tell Lenny."

"Has she been in this mood all night?" Shavir asked as she followed
Nacho into the dark staircase past the broken elevator.

Nacho shrugged. "I guess Tara told her about the new pups we got
out last night. Lenny wanted us to keep quiet about it, but you know
Tara and her theory."

Tara had many theories, but this could only be a reference to her
ground-level theory, which was that Judy was ruling Roots above
ground but had no say in things happening deep down below, which
were unrelated to the farm and thus none of her business. As a theory,
it had so many flaws it wasn't worth arguing with her, although Lenny
seemed to never miss an opportunity. Not only did no one rule Roots,
but the farm also had its cooling facilities in the basement and thus
below ground level. Plus, they all knew their illegal rescue missions
were posing an actual danger to the farm since harboring terrorists was
a crime so severe that it would end everything happening above ground
should it become known.

"Why would she tell her, then?"

"She likes to provoke her, I guess?" Nacho said as he opened the
door to their living quarters on first floor so they could drop off Sam.
He was a man of few words who strictly sought to avoid conflict with
both Tara and Judy, a wise move.

"Just what we need right now." Shavir unlocked the door to the
repurposed office cubicle that was her and Sam's home. "Angry Judy
on top of everything else."

"She's just worried about her people," Nacho said.

"You *are* one of her people."

"Yeah, that makes it worse."

Without further elaboration, Nacho walked to his own cubicle, giving her time to take care of Sam in hers.

It was a small space with a smelly old carpet, but it had a window, and its thin walls reached almost all the way to the ceiling, giving some sort of semi-privacy from Judy and the other forty people living here.

Most of them, like Nacho, were part of the West Street Project. After being homeless for years, Judy and some of her friends had started spending winter nights in what had been an abandoned office building then. This was right after the Crisis, and there had existed many such buildings in Brooklyn, emptied out by hurricanes and broken infrastructure. After getting kicked out a few times, Judy managed to locate the owner and negotiate a deal that allowed them to move permanently into the cubicles and install the farm.

For Shavir, joining shortly after, it was a place to curl up and heal after her mom had been shot during the Crisis and her life fell apart. But Nacho had been part of that original group, the West Street Project, which was why Judy gave him a particularly hard time about his illegal underground work. No one knew Nacho's full name or what he used to do before he'd washed up here, though his ability to access pretty much any building gave some pointers. Whatever he used to be, Nacho now was a dedicated farmer and activist, a crucially important member of their group who bore Judy's wrath and his own feelings of guilt with dogged stoicism.

Shavir met up with him again after feeding Sam, and they walked down to the large stuffy space of their warehouse and then to the basement, which housed the storage rooms and, hidden in another room behind those, the animals. They could hear Tara and Lenny yelling at each other as the jib door swung open and Troy stepped out with a grin on his face.

"Don't go in there. It's dangerous."

With a wry smile, Shavir walked past Troy toward the door, and then it hit her. "You're not at Buddha's tonight?" she asked, turning to him.

"Tomorrow," Troy said. "Had to swap shifts with Skyler. She's bartending for me tonight, so now I will have to work on my actual day off, lucky me."

Of course, Shavir thought. Apparently, the entire universe was conspiring to send her an unequivocal message that she'd messed up when she'd agreed to the date with Jake.

It wasn't like she hadn't known Troy bartended at Buddha's when she'd suggested they meet there. She had gotten him the job—Anil, the owner of the place, was a friend of hers. It was slightly ironic since the main purpose of Troy's joining Roots had been to get away from his posh parents in Manhattan, and Buddha's was the most upscale vegan restaurant in SoHo. But after his escape to the grit and dirt of Brooklyn, Troy had learned that for people with his education level, it was impossible to get a job here, and as much as Roots loved its volunteers, it compensated them in veggies. In Manhattan, even the bartenders had college degrees, so whether Troy liked it or not, it was his natural job market.

Why she had told Jake to meet her at Buddha's was beyond her. People like him could afford the truly fancy places in town, places like Le Déluge that still sold animal flesh—not the dogs and rabbits from the black market, but triple-certified Kobe strip steaks oozing authentic blood that ran in the veins of actual breathing cattle and wild-caught Antarctic tooth fish, the very last of them imported by airlift all the way from the Ross Sea. She wondered whether Jake ate any of it or even helped import it—yet another reason why she shouldn't have agreed to the date; they were piling up at this point. The bar was separate from Buddha's restaurant, but the bartenders could spot you through the French doors. They would dine in plain view of Troy.

"You look worried," Troy said.

"Well," she nodded toward the jib door, "you said it's dangerous."

A smile cracked across Troy's young face. He was only twenty-two, six years her junior and the rookie of the team. They were careful about adding people since everyone new was a risk, but Troy was an asset, and not only because of his ability to scout out new targets with a regularity that made them all shudder. He also had this deadpan attitude that seemed to come with growing up in Manhattan, just like his hipster haircut and the Spine addiction he shared with Finn. "Zeno's in there, too," he said with mock concern. "Don't leave him behind, okay?"

She promised she wouldn't and pushed open the door.

"You're out of your freakin' mind, girl," Lenny growled with his usual fatherly rumble, glaring at Tara like he was about to ground her. At least they were keeping their distance from the puppies, washing out crates with the brackish water that poured out of the faucets.

"Don't fucking *girl* me, okay?" Tara shot back, looking at Lenny with the defiance that marked pretty much all their exchanges, as did Lenny's next rhetorical move.

"You talk to her," he said to Shavir. "I can't do this."

Shavir ignored them both and looked at Zeno, who was coming out of one of the wooden stalls that lined the walls with microchip syringes in his hand. "What's going on?"

Zeno gently pushed back one of the older puppies that tried to follow him, emboldened enough to explore the world after six weeks in their care. "Last time I checked in," he said as he discarded the used syringes and crouched next to his medical bag to unpack two new ones, "they were fighting over the number of puppies you're taking to New Jersey tomorrow. She thinks you should take all of them at once so you're done with it. He thinks that's nuts." He threw a sideways glance at Lenny. "I hope I'm paraphrasing correctly."

"What do you think?" Shavir asked.

"I'm just playing doctor here." Zeno opened the next puppy stall. "So I can tell you that all the yelling is stressing out the dogs." With that, he closed the door behind him.

"It'll raise suspicion, that many pups," Lenny said heatedly, paying no heed to Zeno's complaint. His face was sweaty, the mass of his graying dreads heaped in a precarious lopsided tower above his head. "And that's something you can't afford. *We* can't afford."

"We can't afford to go twice!" cried Tara, her petite figure erect and proud. "Simon is expecting us tomorrow morning, and he has already arranged drop-off meetings with three of our adopters. I'm not going to jeopardize that. I don't even see what the problem is."

"The problem is," Lenny thundered, "that Frontline has seen you with puppies before, and usually, you know, they grow into *dogs* at some point. I'm against going during the day anyway."

"Right, because it's so much less suspicious at night. Oh... hi, officer." Tara looked up at some imaginary cop. "Sure, sir, I walk my puppies at two a.m., sir, because the air is so fresh at this hour." She looked at Lenny again, daring him.

"Can we take it down a notch?" As she did so often, Shavir found herself cast in the unfitting role of the voice of reason. "Lenny has a point," she said to Tara. "Frontline's all over the dogs right now. They just checked Sam again."

"And?" Tara asked. "What happened?"

"Nothing. Sam's legal. They checked his chip and let me go."

"And so are the puppies," Tara cried. "*Legal.* Zeno's chipping them right now for precisely this reason. That's the beauty of having a certified vet tech on the team. He can make them *look* legal."

"It's still a risk," Lenny said unhappily.

Shavir glanced at Tara, who stood rigidly, her neck so strained she was adding inches to her height. "I agree it's a risk," she said, weighing her words. "But Tara's right. All they can do is check their chips. If we run into them at all. Last time we didn't."

"Guess I'm overruled then." Lenny turned and headed for the door. "Do whatever the fuck you want. But if this goes wrong, Judy will throw all our asses out."

The mask of determination fell from Tara's face, revealing equal measures of defiance and guilt. This, too, was part of their routine. Catching Shavir's gaze, she rolled her eyes to assert her righteousness one more time. Then she ran after Lenny. Hopefully, she would do a better job than the last time she'd gotten him to the point of explosion. The last thing they needed was Lenny sliding into one of his darker moods with a roof full of overripe veggies and a basement full of dogs.

Zeno had moved on to taking care of the rescues from last night, ignoring the change in cast. Shavir opened the door to one of the other stalls and was immediately surrounded by a sea of puppies, so tiny compared to the ones that were ready to leave. It still amazed her how fast they grew and how resilient they were. One day they were squirming in their own poop, the next day they were happy. Injured, some of them, and hungry, all of them, but happy and eager to play. And a few weeks later, they were ready for a forever home.

Sam had been one of those squirming puppies on her very first raid when she'd been so overwhelmed by the horror of the fattening station she nearly passed out after opening the first cage. The sensory assault, combined with the sight of those babies cooped up for slaughter, were too much. Without Tara, she might not have made it outside again. But Tara had been through it before. She gave commands, cool and precise, and Shavir carried them out like a voice-controlled robot, grabbing puppies left and right. Her state of stupor had lasted until they were back down here in the basement, where she dissolved into sobs. When she finally resurfaced, one puppy was sitting right in front of her, face furrowed, looking at her like it was asking when they were going home. They'd done exactly that after a stopover in the shower.

"We've already put them on a diet, poor guys." Zeno was standing at the other side of the wood slats, nodding to the chubby little dogs surrounding her. "They looked at me like 'no way' when I fed them. Like 'that's a great appetizer, dude, but where's the main?'"

He smiled, but Shavir knew it would take him less than a minute to apologize for having told Tara about the new target Troy had found. Zeno was like that, the polar opposite of Troy, serious and unironic in a way she attributed to his day job at the Bloomsbury veterinary clinic. He was quick to take responsibility for things he hadn't actually caused, and regardless of his permanently unkempt look, he was one of the most conscientious and reliable people in the group. She knew he would have liked to be a real doctor, degree and all, but he hadn't had the money or self-confidence to put himself through vet school, so he now worked as a technician instead. Down here, it was all the same, since his medical knowledge had saved hundreds of animals.

They both knew the whole altercation just now hadn't been about tomorrow's trip at all, but about that new target, which they couldn't take on because it was a puppy mill, and there was no way they could deal with a dozen ferocious mastiffs trying to protect their babies.

These dogs were breeding machines, living in a traumatic cycle of conception, birth, and loss. Liberating them would be a suicide mission, as Lenny had put it pointedly. That was why he and Tara were in yelling mode. It helped them deal with feelings of powerlessness.

They were powerless about so many things, from the clannish remains of America's always-precarious union to the way in which those remains preyed on each other and the rest of the world, and the fact that the planet itself was turning into a place that was hostile to mammals, no matter their species or nationality. Like most people, they had accepted these things as the irrefutable reality, but there were a few things they still wanted to change. The mayor's disgusting degree of indifference toward the people living on this side of the East River. The city's food system, which was as broken as their hospitals, and the unacceptable fact that the evacuation zones of the eastern boroughs had become a major hub for the illegal meat market. As a group, Roots was fighting all these injustices, and it was when they felt powerless about those things that the yelling started.

"I'm sorry I mentioned the mill to Tara," Zeno said as expected, dropping the smile. "I just felt so bad for the dogs."

"We all do, don't beat yourself up about it." Shavir got up and joined him outside the stall. "But next time, maybe talk to Lenny first. He's the realist when it comes to what we can or can't do, even if Tara doesn't wanna hear it."

The jib door opened, and Tara came back in, looking deflated.

"How's Lenny?" Shavir asked.

"Mad. He always worries about things."

"About you."

"Problem is he thinks he's my dad. And I really don't need two of them." Tara walked to the faucet to finish the crates. "When do you want me to come over in the morning?"

"Are we taking all three of them?"

Tara nodded. "Assuming you're okay with that?"

Shavir looked at Zeno, who was watching them silently. "Are they ready to go?"

"Yeah," he said. "They're ready."

"Six-thirty then," Shavir decided. "That gives us enough time to get to the station and still have a decent cushion for... contingencies."

Tara nodded and ran the water, signaling she was done talking.

It was true that Lenny liked to play the helicopter dad, though in Tara's case that was a tempting role. She was twenty-six but didn't look much older than she had twelve years ago when she and her real dad had first set foot into the rundown apartment complex where Shavir had spent her entire life thus far, in a one-bedroom with her mom.

She still remembered that gray winter morning when the doorbell had rung and Tara and her dad were standing in the hallway, both visibly cold but smiling like they were lit by some hidden power station as Dipak introduced himself as the new facility manager and Tara as his daughter. Even then, he'd seemed miscast for the position, which came with a small salary and a reduced rent for an ill-kept apartment on the ground floor that had a view of the parking lot filled with broken cars left behind by some storm. But Dipak hadn't cared much about views. Having arrived fresh from a refugee camp in Texas that Tara's mom hadn't survived, he'd been glad to have a job and a home for his daughter. He'd asked if anything needed fixing in the building, still smiling brightly, but Shavir, only sixteen at the time, sensed the sadness and exhaustion hiding behind the smile when he added he was good with paperwork because he used to be a physicist at the University of Calcutta. Tara, standing next to him, looked tiny in an oversized sweater, black eyes large and bold. Her only words that first day were a question: did Shavir have any animals?

After that first encounter, Tara had kept coming back, ringing the doorbell every day even though Shavir couldn't offer any animals, or anything else interesting for that matter. Used as she was to spending whole days alone while her mom worked long hours as a trauma nurse at the Brooklyn Hospital Center, Tara's visits were a welcome distraction. Tara had grown up with a flock of pets she'd rescued from the streets of Kolkata and was crazy about animals in a way that seemed special to Shavir. Once the apartment became too small to contain Tara's boundless energy, they started exploring the neighborhood in direct defiance of both of their parents' orders, spending hours observing squirrels, chipmunks, birds, and all the other animals that would soon disappear, either going extinct or getting eaten.

About a year before the Crisis, they met Lenny, who had just lost tenure at a community college because of his inability to keep his mouth shut whenever he thought something needed calling out. Lenny had discovered urban community farming as an alternative way to educate and empower people. He gave them their first tour of what he even then called a farm, even though it really was just a derelict group of people drudging on the roof of a derelict building.

It was infectious, though, being among folks who had something to believe in. And once the US outlawed industrial meat production to save the last functioning antibiotics along with the climate, Tara talked about nothing else but becoming a farmer. Shavir was more hesitant since her mom didn't get paid well at the hospital, and they depended on the money she made as a server. Then the Crisis hit, followed by Shelby. The Crisis took away her mom, the hurricane their farm. It seemed like the end of everything until they met Judy and her people who needed help building Roots. And when Lenny decided to do something about the illegal meat farms springing up in the evacuation zones, Tara signed up for that, too, and Shavir followed suit.

The night of that first raid, when she'd stood down here in the basement for the very first time and exchanged that long look with Sam, that had been the night she knew she could go on living.

Sam greeted her like she'd been away for a month when Shavir returned to their cubicle an hour later after a detour to the shared bathroom and a too-short shower with cold, smelly water. She sat down on her bed and applied the healing accelerant Jake had given her to what was left of the wound on her arm. Then she took another ciprofloxacin and put the two bottles next to each other on the old file cabinet that served as her dresser, placing them between her mom's picture in its cracked frame and the rickety lamp that only worked when the cord was twisted at the right angle. The sophisticated meds looked out of place amongst this shabby collection of salvaged and scavenged things, the things she considered her own for the time being.

She knew, just like Nacho, that her actions shouldn't endanger the very thing that gave her life meaning and the only people she had in the world. She also knew that, eventually, she would do the right thing and cancel that foolish date with Jake. But it had occurred to her on her way up here that she didn't even have his number and that it might not be as easy as it was with most people to find him online. She could always ask Hector or, if everything else failed, call the restaurant and cancel their date that way, a real dick move Jake didn't deserve. But the important thing was she still had options to undo what she had done, and it wasn't like Jake would die of a broken heart once she did. People cancelled first dates all the time, for all kinds of reasons, and truth be told, he had looked more shell-shocked than anything else when she'd returned to Soma to make her grand suggestion. She contemplated the bottles for another moment and had almost convinced herself by the time she wriggled out of her jeans. A minute later, she was asleep.

It turned out to be much more difficult than expected to get three little mastiffs to behave on the steamy boardwalk along the Brooklyn seawall. They tried to look casual, just two young dog walkers headed toward the subway station with their four dogs in a borough where no one could afford dogs anymore, let alone dog walkers. It was early in the morning and the boardwalk nearly empty, but if the goal was not to draw attention to themselves, they were already failing.

Sam was leading by example, heeling perfectly at Shavir's side, but the puppies were outside for the very first time and out of control. Shavir was holding the leash of Chip, an estimated sixteen-week-old with a fawn-colored coat and a dark mask on his face just like Sam. Tara was in charge of Al and Max, who were darker in color and a little older. Together they were strong enough to pull their petite handler toward any scent that interested them, and they were interested in absolutely everything. Tara found herself quite literally drawn to the seawall that separated the boardwalk from the rising East River. She pushed her hands against the corroded steel to regain her balance, producing a low reverberation along the sheet pile.

Shavir laughed, glad that no one was around. "So much for your dog training lessons."

Tara showed her palm, covered in rust. "See that hole there? That was me. Either I have superpowers, or it's falling apart like everything else around here. The next storm surge will wash the whole thing away, and we'll have six feet of water in our basement."

Shavir shrugged, wary of an argument. "We're adapters."

"Yeah," Tara scoffed. "Like the people in Gravesend. They're now adapting to life underwater."

Shavir didn't respond. Lenny and Judy had written dozens of letters to everyone remotely responsible for Brooklyn's infrastructure, including the city council, the office of the Brooklyn Borough president, the mayor's office, and the governor's Office of Storm Recovery. Even Finn had gotten involved. But no one was investing a cent anymore in what they considered a doomed borough. Whenever a neighborhood became temporarily uninhabitable because of some disaster, the mayor took it as an opportunity to slap a permanent evacuation order onto the area, and that was that. Although no one dared admit it, Brooklyn and Queens had basically been rezoned into a giant flood zone protecting Manhattan and the other western boroughs. The place was literally shrinking, getting soggy on all sides.

"Seriously," Tara demanded. "What will we do with the animals?"

"We have to find a new place for them anyway. Judy reminds me of it every single day. She doesn't like the idea of having them on the farm."

"Yeah, it's so unusual to have animals on a farm. Judy's a freak."

"She's also the one who runs the farm. Let's not go over all that again, okay?" Shavir said. "Especially not out here."

They had reached the end of the boardwalk, and the street was busy with people going to work or getting their food carts ready. Some of them stepped off the sidewalk to keep their distance from Sam.

Shavir felt her heart sinking as she scanned the crowds for Frontline cops. "We should've taken Troy along. Or Nacho. We could have gone separately, in two groups."

"Or we could have asked Finn to take us," Tara said unhelpfully.

"I told you, I'm not going to ask him for any more favors."

"Relax, there's no one here," Tara declared, ignoring the people staring at them like they'd just stepped out of a UFO with their canine companions. "No uniforms."

The puppies were much quieter now, intimidated by the traffic and the unfamiliar scents and noises. Max, the shyest of the three, was trying to hide behind Sam. Shavir stopped to comfort him, feeling his body shaking. It was normal for him to be afraid in these surroundings, but she also felt her own hackles rising.

"This is a bad idea," she said to Tara. "Let's go back and ask Finn if he can take us with the van during the weekend. It's okay, I'll do it."

"No. We'll have others coming in, and Max's gonna be okay. We're almost there."

Shavir let go of the puppy and got up. Tara was right. It wasn't the first time they were doing this, and they had almost reached the station. She needed to relax and look normal.

"So what's the matter with Finn?" Tara asked as they crossed the street, the puppies regaining confidence and pulling forward against their harnesses.

"He gave me shit for parking Sam at his place." Talking was good, Shavir told herself. Made them look more normal. "Said I'm taking advantage of him."

Tara laughed. "He's always been great at being a dick."

They had reached the subway entrance and the edge of the stairs where Max stopped, peeked into the abyss, sat down on his behind, and instantly became immovable.

"Come on, little guy," Tara said. "You've seen those before, remember? They're just stairs. No big deal."

But Max thought otherwise. Bending his head backward, he put every one of his forty-plus pounds onto his behind and looked at her, puppy face furrowed.

With a sigh, Tara bent down and picked him up. "You're heavy!"

She started walking down the stairs, but Shavir didn't move. There were uniforms between the people walking toward them.

Two of them.

Frontline.

"What?" Tara said, turning to her.

"There." Shavir nodded toward the Frontline men who had now seen them, too, and were picking up their pace. A ring of fear closed around her throat.

"It's okay," Tara said quickly, putting Max back down. "They're legal. It's fine. Smile."

The cops came closer. People changed direction upon noticing them but Tara and Shavir kept walking downstairs, Max following hesitantly like he knew it was better to behave.

Shavir felt Sam tensing up beside her. "Easy, boy," she murmured. The cops both wore visors, but she registered the taller one was Black, the other one white. They had never stopped her before.

"Morning, ma'am," the white cop said without a hint of a smile.

Chip jumped up, ready to bark at the strange-looking men, but Shavir reached down and pressed his snout shut. If the cops heard the hoarse sounds giving away that his vocal cords had been cut, they'd know he was a rescue. She pulled a muzzle out of her bag that fit so tightly around Chip's snout he couldn't open it again. Adrenaline pulsed through her veins as she gave a warning look to Sam, who had remained silent. She glanced over at Tara, who was muzzling her puppies. Only then did she look up at the cops again.

The white cop nodded in approval. "Those your dogs?"

"Yes." Tara got up. "We're on our way to the vet."

"You got a breeder license?"

"No, sir. We acquired them from a licensed breeder in the Bronx. We're trainers with HealthDogs." She gave him a card. "They'll be service dogs once they've finished their training."

"In *Brooklyn*?"

"In Manhattan, sir."

He looked at the dogs. "Those're mastiffs. They're no service dogs."

Tara looked straight at him. "We're working with the hospitals, sir. Al and Chip will become seeing-eye dogs. And Max here will work in the psychiatric ward. We see amazing results, especially in patients with clinical depression and anxiety disorders."

The other cop turned to Sam. "And the big guy?"

"He's fully trained," Shavir said. "He helps us with the apprentices."

"The what?"

"Apprentices, sir. That's what they are called at the beginning of their training."

The cops exchanged a look that couldn't hide their bafflement. Then the white guy pulled out his reader. He walked over to Shavir and held it first to Sam's neck, then to Chip's, while she pushed the dogs' heads down. Two beeping sounds signaled code recognition. He turned the reader around, touched the display, and turned it around again. "Right hand," he said to Shavir.

She pressed her fingers against the reader. He looked at the display, waiting for it to process. "Thank you, Ms. Tayard." A curt nod, and he turned to Tara, who was already kneeling next to the other two puppies, exposing their necks. Both dogs were shivering visibly, afraid of the enormous men and their thundering voices. The cop put the reader to Max's neck and waited.

There was no beep.

He looked at the display, then bent down again, trying to get a reading. Nothing.

"He isn't chipped, ma'am," he said to Tara.

Shavir felt her adrenaline spike again. "Of course he is! They all are."

A few bystanders were observing the incident from a safe distance, some of them lifting their hands to film the scene with the inbuilt Spine cameras in their gloves. "No filming!" shouted the Black cop, his voice echoing along the bare walls. "There's nothing to see. Move on!" The people reluctantly lowered their hands but kept watching.

His partner bent down to Al and came up again. "This one is chipped." Again down to Max. "And this one isn't."

"That's impossible!" Now Tara lost her cool. "We had all of them chipped at the vet last time. They're registered to our names."

"No, they aren't. Those three are, but this one isn't."

The cop reached for Max's leash. Something inside Shavir grew cold and then scorching hot. They would take him away.

"This is a mistake," Tara said sharply. "Something's wrong with your reader."

"No, ma'am," the cop said. "Something's wrong with your dog."

"There's nothing wrong with Max." Tara's voice kept growing louder. "There must be a problem with his chip. We're on our way to the vet. They'll fix it."

"Please step away from the dog. It's illegal. I need to confiscate it."

"No!" Tara was yelling now, her voice echoing back to them. "You're gonna *kill* him!"

That was exactly what they were going to do, Shavir knew, and there was no way to stop them. Except... It was a crazy idea, but it was her only one. "Can we please call the vet, officer?" she cried, not daring to reach for her phone.

"Shut up!" The white cop glared at her through his visor. He turned to Tara again. "All illegal animals are to be destroyed. It's the law, ma'am." He grabbed the middle of the leash and yanked at it, dragging the wincing puppy a foot toward him.

But Tara didn't let go. "No!" she screamed again, furious now.

A second later, she was looking at the mouth of a Glock 18.

"Gary!" The Black cop looked alarmed at his partner, but Gary didn't care. There was a sharp clicking sound as he pointed his gun at Tara's head. "You wanna say no to me again, Brownie?" he hissed. "Let the fuck go and turn around to the wall!"

"No! You'll kill him!" Tara stared at the gun.

"Gary!" the cop shouted again, and then Tara's face hit the wall, another scream escaping her mouth as her hands were violently pulled back and handcuffed. A smudge of bright blood marked the dirty wall next to her face. But she still held the leash.

Gary pointed his gun at Max, who was cowering next to her. "Let go of the fucking dog, or I'll shoot him right here and now!"

Shavir looked on, desperately trying to figure out what to do. It took all her strength to control Sam, who wanted to throw himself at Tara's tormentor. "Sir," she called in the direction of the Black Frontline cop, whose face was darting back and forth between his rogue colleague and the crowd. "Sir," she called again.

The cop looked at the phone in her hand. "No filming!"

"No, sir. I am calling the vet. The dog is legal, it really is. And it is very valuable for the hospitals. It's a service dog. Will you please talk to the vet, sir? Please?"

The cop looked at Gary, who was pushing Tara against the wall, her hand still cramped around the leash.

Shavir dialed. "Shavir Tayard here," she said shakily when she heard the voice of Nina, the clinic's receptionist. "Can I please talk to Dr. Randers? It's an emergency."

"Mr. Randers isn't a doctor, ma'am," Nina said, bored. "Our veterinarians are—"

Shavir interrupted sharply. "It's *Shavir Tayard* speaking. I'm standing here with a Frontline patrol who wants to euthanize our service dog. I *need* to speak to Dr. Zeno Randers."

"Shavir?" Nina sounded puzzled. "I'll put you through to Zeno."

There was music for a second and then Zeno's voice. "Shavir?"

"Yes, Dr. Randers! Can you please confirm for the Frontline officer that Max is chipped and registered?" She didn't wait for Zeno's response, just held the phone out to the Black cop, looking pleadingly at where she suspected his eyes were behind the visor. Her hand was shaking. "It's Dr. Randers from the Bloomsbury Veterinary Clinic. He'll confirm the dog's legal status."

A long moment of hesitation. The world on pause. "Bloomsbury Veterinary Clinic," the cop then said in a voice that made clear he was using the voice recognition of his Spine.

"He's calling the clinic directly," Shavir whispered into her phone and hung up.

"This is Frontline," the cop said into the air. "Can I please speak to the veterinarian on duty?" An instant later, more friendly. "Good morning, Dr. Randers."

Something in Shavir gave way at hearing Zeno's name.

The cop listened. "But the reader won't recognize anything." He looked down at Max. "Mastiff, yes. Brindle. White front paw, left. That's the dog. I understand, doctor, but we can't have unregistered animals here. It's against the law. Can you please give me the chip number, so I can check it? Thank you, doctor."

He said good-bye and looked at his partner. "Given name is Max. Registered to Ms. Tara Choudhuri. All paid up."

Gary yanked up Tara's bound hands and pressed her fingers against his reader. He looked at the display and nodded at the other cop. "Your dog is free to go," he said to Tara, "but you'll be coming with us, Ms. Choudhuri. Obstructing a Frontline officer in the performance of his duties. Disobeying a Frontline officer. Violent attack against a Frontline officer. That will cost you." He let go of her hands and packed away his gun. "You may now hand the dog to your friend but make no further mistakes."

Tara turned around, a nasty wound on her forehead, blood seeping down her face. She lifted her chin and walked to Shavir, Max's leash in her handcuffed hands. The puppy hesitantly trudged behind her, terrified by the men.

"I'm okay," Tara whispered as Shavir reached for the leash. "Just get them out." Then she walked back to the cops.

Shavir took the four leashes and led the dogs down the next set of stairs, parting the people who were staring. There were Spine cameras everywhere. She lowered her head and turned her face away.

No one had been killed, so this wasn't big enough to make the news. The footage would get lost in the white noise of the Spine cloud.

SIX

JAKE WAS IN DIRE need of coffee. The usual detour to Soma had seemed pointless this morning since Shavir had taken the day off and he was going to see her tonight at the restaurant. He had chosen his old favorite route to SAFE instead, along the Manhattan seawall, for the first time in months. After climbing the steps to the boardwalk, the air clinging to him like a wet blanket, he'd stopped for a moment to bask in the glittering lights dancing on the Hudson River.

The seawall was a magical place to him, in part because he associated it with his father. Every time he stood there, he remembered that trip many years ago, when his dad had taken him to New York so he could see what *real* levees looked like. His father had spent most of their visit complaining about what was happening along their own coastline at home in Tampa, but Jake had been eleven years old and so fascinated by the enormous construction site that he'd barely listened. He still remembered the miles and miles of steel reinforcement, a giant skeleton stretched out along the shoreline, waiting to be covered in concrete and elevating the Hudson River Greenway to where it was today, towering high above the water.

That had been his one good moment this morning, looking at the river. Now he was sitting in David's ice chamber of an office, regretting that he hadn't stopped for coffee at one of the carts along the boardwalk. He was probably on as many pep pills as his boss, but the coffee was a psychological thing that helped him relax. His gaze hung on the screen wall behind David, which showed crowds of protestors with signs like "EQUALITY NOW!" and "WE'RE DYING OVER HERE" in front of a drugstore. A news ticker read: "New protests against the unfair distribution of medical supply in New York."

"Is that over in Brooklyn?"

"Queens," David said. "But you can wait for it in Brooklyn."

He had worked through the night again and had the undereye bags to prove it. The air in his office was so ridiculously cold there were goosebumps underneath the shiny layer of sweat on his arms, little droplets covering his desk. Clearly, he didn't notice any of it.

More signs were paraded across the screen wall, screaming in all-caps, "WHERE ARE OUR MEDS?" and "WHO'S SAVED BY SAFE?" Half a dozen Frontline cops stood nearby, watching.

"My cousin works at one of those." Jake nodded at the drugstore.

"I'm aware," David said dryly. "And I told you it's not an ideal environment for a young mother."

"I'll be sure to tell her," Jake scoffed. Last time he'd talked to Carrie, she'd been on her way to school with Zoe, giggling more than her seven-year-old daughter as she recounted in epic detail a T-ball game the girl had managed despite her asthma. She'd been in good spirits then, but he knew Carrie felt terrible whenever people started protesting in front of her store because it didn't have the meds they needed. By now, she was likely dealing with a version of what was transpiring on the screen wall. And the rationings hadn't even fully kicked in.

"Don't know what Frontline's doing standing around like that," David rumbled, glancing at the news feed. "They're supposed to take care of that kind of thing before people get all up in arms again."

Jake wanted to remind him that Frontline wasn't allowed to intervene in legal expressions of discontent, but David cut him off.

"Listen. About yesterday. The Cambodia thing. I wasn't—" He paused. "You're doing good work, Jake. I don't have to tell you that."

Jake nodded in muted appreciation. He had no desire to revisit yesterday's confrontation. "I wanted to talk to you, too," he said instead, "about tonight. I need—"

"What I'm saying is," David cut in, "you can't let it get to you what's happening in Cambodia. Or in LA. We're here to help the people in New York. That's what we do."

"Aren't doing much for *them*, are we?" Jake nodded to the protestors who still held up their signs behind David's back.

David turned to the screen wall and back again, puzzled.

Jake knew why. It was the kind of question Shavir would have asked. Or Carrie when she was feeling desperate and daring enough. But it wasn't a question to be asked at SAFE.

"We're doing the best we can." David's voice was flat. "You, me, everyone here. And every fucking day, it's ten new things we've got to deal with." With a swipe of his glove, he blew up one of the other news feeds on the wall, effectively replacing the images from Queens with a colorful array of animated storm track projections—the dubious art of foretelling despair, death, and devastation. "That's Tapah. Our new friend in the Luzon Strait. I'm guessing you're familiar with him?"

Jake nodded, annoyed at the sudden change of topic. He'd been observing the storm, along with five others, for the past forty-eight hours. "What's your point?"

"JTWC just upgraded our friend to a super typhoon. I don't have to tell you how fucked we are if this thing hits Hong Kong."

"Hong Kong isn't in its pathway." Jake felt the cold closing in.

"Well," David turned around to the screen wall. "I've been onto this fucker the whole night, and look at this."

The track projections still didn't indicate a direct hit to Hong Kong, but they were close enough to keep the CSR teams frantic for the next forty-eight hours. Victoria Harbor was the most important port in the region. Last time it had been hit by a storm, they'd been scrambling for weeks to find substitutes for thousands of tons of stalled or drowned critical supply from elsewhere in the world. Now the cone bottom, projecting possible points of landfall, was ridiculously wide. There was no way of knowing where it would strike.

Jake stared at Tapah's voluptuous shapes and colors, preparing for their short-lived affair. It had been stupid to tell Shavir he'd be available for dinner. Things never worked out like that for him.

A sudden movement made him shift his gaze back to David. A tremor in David's hands had come on suddenly, almost like a seizure.

"Are you alright?"

David dropped his hands below the desk. "I'm fine. Better than most people here. Go get to work now, will you? And see whether you can talk some sense into Lisa. I've tried all night, but she's even more stubborn than you can be, and this is an all-hands-on-deck situation."

Jake left the office, unsure whether he should have been more insistent since David obviously was not fine. But there was no use in provoking more lies, and, as much as he resented the thought, he needed to call Shavir now and cancel their dinner since he'd be here all night.

When he crossed the hallway, though, he saw Lisa Sanchez waiting for him in the CSR, a slight human shape against the brilliant spectacle of the screen walls. "Hey, night girl," he said as the doors slid away. "Did you have fun with Tapah?"

"Hi, day boy." Lisa stretched her back with a strained smile. "He's busy bowling toward Taiwan for now. But luckily, we got plenty of advice all night from your boss on where the storm might go next. He's just a fountain of foresight."

Jake bit his lip at the not-so-subtle reference to the fact that David had once again intruded on her territory. Lisa and David were the same rank although she was much less of a legend than he was, a fact David made sure she never forgot. At only thirty-nine, Lisa was quite young for a CSR group leader, but what she lacked in experience she made up for in dedication. She had two small children at home and no husband, so she took care of her kids during the day and worked during the nights when they were asleep. The only help she had was from her elderly mother. There was no way Lisa could keep up this brutal routine without massive amounts of pep pills, but they didn't seem to affect her health as much as they did most people. Her friendly face was usually smiling after a long night in the CSR, and she even brought in the odd bowl of cookies when she came in for the evening debrief. Now, she looked frustrated and tired. Clearly, David had made things impossible for her all night.

Jake glanced at the opposite screen wall, which was covered by path projections and a checkerboard of frantic Taiwanese news feeds.

"Are they evacuating?"

Lisa nodded. "They've issued evac orders for the southern tip, but this thing changes its path so fast you get whiplash just from watching. Perhaps they'll get lucky, and it'll swing away again. What worries us is Hong Kong."

"Yeah, David told me."

"I bet he did."

The sarcasm was too obvious to laugh away.

"What has he done this time?"

"Other than staying here all night and acting like he's my fucking boss?" Lisa caught herself, probably remembering Jake worked on David's team, not hers. "He expects a total breakdown of the infrastructure feeding Victoria Port," she continued more calmly. "I think that's nonsense. Tapah will blast the area north of Hong Kong, but I doubt he'll cut off the southern supply lines. And if that assumption is correct," her tone sharpened again, "then we should stop working to replace them because it's a fucking *waste of time*. I've tried to explain that to David, but let's just say he hasn't been very receptive."

That last part was certainly true, and Jake was tired of sugarcoating it. "He seems pretty out of it," he agreed. "He's underdoing it on sleep and overdoing it with the pills."

"Or he's taking the wrong kind," Lisa snapped.

"Meaning what?"

Lisa looked over her shoulder to make sure they were alone. "David's taking Emovia."

It took a moment for that to sink in. "You're kidding."

"I am not."

"How do you know?"

"I saw the bottle on his desk when I was in his office for the debrief."

"On his *desk*?" Jake asked, forcing his voice down to a whisper. "Jesus! That's gonna fuck him up good."

"It's already fucking him up!" Lisa hissed. "And I've got to deal with it every night. Haven't you guys noticed anything at all?"

Sure they had. Jake exhaled, struck by the revelation. He'd known David had a speed problem like pretty much everyone else in the CSR, with the exception of Masao. But this was so much worse, and it explained what he'd just witnessed in David's office.

Emovia had become wildly popular in recent years, so popular it was one of their unofficial tasks in the CSR to make dead-sure it would never run out. People were stressed and afraid, and since they could no longer do anything to improve or fix the situation, they managed their stress and anxiety instead. There was a whole array of psychotropic drugs that catered to their needs, Emovia being the cheapest and most popular. But emotion regulators weren't meant to be combined with stimulants. Drug interactions could be disastrous, ranging from mood swings and aggressive behavior to blackouts, seizures, and organ failure. It had taken a few thousand deaths for this fact to sink in, but by now the last idiot in town, let alone the head of the CSR day team, knew that if you were relying on pep pills to get through your days, you had to avoid Emovia if you wanted to stay sane. And alive.

"I have to talk to him."

Lisa frowned. "You think he'll listen?"

"I have to try." Jake said, still digesting the revelation.

David had gotten increasingly erratic over the past few months, erupting in tantrums for no good reason, torturing a team that was as dedicated to the cause as he was. Now he knew why, and he had to do something to protect both SAFE and the man who'd made it what it was today. The man who had made *him* who he was today. He had no idea why David was risking everything for a bunch of pills or what exactly they were doing for him. It was his job to make sure the city was chock-full of them, but he didn't even know because, unlike David, he'd been smart enough to stay away from them.

His more immediate problem, however, was reaching Shavir. Her change of mind had been so sudden last night, he hadn't had a chance to ask for her number. And not only was she not on any social media, but it turned out even Homeland didn't have a number or address on file for her. He couldn't believe it was possible to live in New York and be unreachable, but apparently it was for Shavir.

He decided he would call Hector later in the morning to get her number and had just opened Lisa's debrief files when a call came in on the Spine's private line. "Hey, Carrie," he said, bracing for a long list of complaints about the crowds that without doubt were protesting by now in front of the drugstore where his cousin worked part-time.

"I'm sorry to call you at work," Carrie blurted out, "but it's Zoe."

"What happened?" Jake stepped out into the quiet hallway.

Carrie was choking. She didn't have a Spine, but she had the video function enabled on her phone, so he could see she'd been crying.

"She had an attack at school."

"Her asthma?"

"She couldn't breathe suddenly."

"Is she okay now?"

"I hope so." Carrie turned to a worn couch behind her where Zoe's small figure was lying flat on her back. "She had her rescue spray with her, and someone called an ambulance, which only showed up after I'd already brought her here. They didn't take her to the hospital, can you believe it? Said she's non-essential because she could still walk." She choked up again, her face vacillating between anguish and anger.

"Did they give her anything?"

"Just one shot. And a prescription for a corticosteroid, like some cruel fucking joke! Like I'm gonna be able to do anything with that." Carrie raised the phone to her face, her watery blue eyes close now, the lines around them exaggerated. "I mean, they literally had to push a bunch of protestors out of the way to get in here, so what do they think, we're drowning in meds? We're lucky we still have Band-Aids." She pointed to the half-empty shelves surrounding her in what looked like the drugstore's medicine storeroom. "I asked them if they could leave me at least a second dose for her, but no. Apparently, they've got more precious lives to save."

"I'm sorry," Jake said, pressing against the guilt that welled up inside him. He knew Carrie wasn't accusing him, but it still felt that way like it always did when supplies were running low in the city. And it took some serious self-control to not ask her why in the world she had let her daughter play T-ball the other day. For years, even leaving the house had been a challenge for Zoe when particulate matter levels were high, which was true most of the time because the government was seeding the stratosphere with sulfate, one of its many useless attempts to engineer its way out of the changing climate. Neither Carrie nor her husband Dan had the necessary money to do much about their daughter's illness, and it was only after Zoe had nearly suffocated in her own bedroom that they had finally accepted Jake's help to get his niece proper treatment. Now, her asthma was being controlled by a complex mixture of short- and long-acting bronchodilators, and she was able to go to school again. But letting her play T-ball in this heat with the supply situation being what it was had been reckless.

"What do you need?" he asked.

"Just the corticosteroid," Carrie said, her voice small. "We still have all the other meds for her."

"Okay, scan the prescription, and I'll check my pharmacy here. I can't come to Queens, though. We've got a storm to deal with."

"Of course, not," Carrie spilled out, looking about as guilty as he felt. "Dan can come get the meds. His shift is almost over. And I'm sorry, Jake." Her eyes teared up again. "I shouldn't have let her play, I know that. But she wanted to so badly, and I can't always say no."

"It's alright," Jake heard himself saying. "We don't even know whether her attack was related to that. Could just be the crazy weather. Zoe will be okay, don't worry so much."

At the other end of the hallway, the elevator doors split open, and Masao walked out with a face that said he knew exactly what was ahead of them. Julia, Craig, and the others were behind him. The day team was ready to take over, ready for its perverse ballet with the storm.

The next few hours passed in a frenzy, Jake's mind saturated with calls, graphs, maps, messages, alerts, and bad news, barely able to separate the virtual world of his Spine feed from the people and screens layered behind it or from the coffee mug that seemed to erupt from a map of Malaysia, held out to him by Masao's left hand.

"We're gonna be here all week," Masao said from behind the Port of Penang, "won't we?"

"Looks like it." Jake sipped the hot liquid, feeling better instantly. "Thanks, man, you can read minds."

"More like bodies. Yours looked like it was gonna fall over." Masao took a sip from his own mug. "So here's the good news: our Koh Kong meds have made it to Laem Chabang."

Jake put his Spine on standby. "But?"

"They can't sail into this weather." Masao nodded to the screen wall across from them that was covered floor-to-ceiling with data on the new super typhoon.

"Any flights?"

Masao shook his head.

"Submarines? Rockets? Spaceships? Anything?"

"Not yet," Masao said. "But I'm working on it."

"Keep going, I'm handling Hong Kong. But I gotta leave now for a minute. My cousin needs some meds for Zoe. And I need to cancel something I had planned for tonight because I'm a fucking idiot."

"Yeah," Masao said. "I'm lucky this time. Ethan has this art opening in the Bronx, but it's the most generic stuff you can imagine, and he knows how I feel about that kind of thing. Said I'd be bored to death anyway." He shrugged with a grin that made him look boyish.

"Your husband is a saint."

"I'm aware."

Apart from his other considerable assets, Masao also was one of the few people in the CSR, one of the few people Jake knew, who was in a stable relationship. While surely not a saint, Ethan came pretty close to an ideal partner for someone in their business, an arts dealer with a deep appreciation for their work in the CSR and an admirable tolerance for the hours they had to invest in it. Ethan was outgoing, loud, and funny, and Masao so laconic that, reportedly, he'd said less than ten words during their entire first date—but when you saw them together, they seemed in sync with each other in ways that were hard to explain. The only other happy relationship Jake was aware of was Carrie's with Dan, and that, too, was sustained by something he couldn't name, something that was present whenever he spent time with either of them. It wasn't love, though he figured that had to be part of it; it was more like they were each simultaneously up on a tightrope while also providing the net for the other. It seemed to be the same for Masao and Ethan but how they managed to keep up this balancing act given their work in the CSR and the world they were living in was a mystery to Jake. Apparently, he couldn't even manage a date.

The sun was burning high up in the sky when Jake left SAFE ten minutes later and darted across the sweltering street. He still hadn't called Hector, though he had managed to get as far as calling up Soma's number on the Spine, only to find himself unable to dial. He'd been meaning to make the call while en route to meeting Dan, but now it was too hot to think straight, let alone formulate a coherent explanation that would leave Shavir feeling understanding enough to give him a chance to reschedule. He dove into the sparse tree shade on the other side of Hudson Street then braved the sun again for a few steps before reaching the pharmacy that kept the CSR team stocked up on the meds it needed to function, returning the favor to those who kept them in business, or so David would say.

The drug on Carrie's prescription wasn't in stock nor was any substitute for it. When he pushed open the door to the crowded deli across from SAFE, Jake was nevertheless carrying a paper bag from the pharmacy containing what he'd been told was a way of keeping Zoe functional until the next delivery of corticosteroids came in.

Dan was slumped at the counter with a can of soda, the flimsy stool beneath him looking like it might collapse any second under his weight and authority. He was wearing his Frontline uniform, the black shirt soaked with sweat despite the refrigerated air. His tense face relaxed when he saw the bag. "Thanks, man, that's—"

"They didn't have the corticoid."

The tension jumped back into Dan's face. "But this ain't fucking Queens, man!" He leaned back on his stool and looked away. Then he lowered his voice and took the bag from Jake's hand. "I thought you guys got everything over here. What about SAFE?"

"It doesn't work like that, Dan, I told you. We don't have that stuff lying around the office."

Dan peered unhappily into the paper bag. "Oh, man, Carrie's gonna kill me if I come home with that."

The counter attendant nodded at Jake, ready to take his order.

Jake shook his head and put his hand on Dan's arm. "It's a good substitute. Give Zoe this, and she'll be fine tonight."

"Seriously," Dan erupted. "What're you guys doin' over there?"

"It's just really tough right now."

"That's what you keep saying. You've seen what's happening over in Queens?" Dan vaguely pointed east. "You think we can keep that under control for much longer? Homeland says you guys make sure that stuff gets here and calms people down. So what's happening?"

There was an expression on Dan's face that Jake had never seen before. In the twelve years he'd been married to Carrie, Dan had often been mad, aggravated about all the things that went wrong in the city or angry because his daughter couldn't breathe right and he couldn't afford to get help for her. But those feelings had never been directed at Jake. When Dan had been critical of SAFE, he'd always taken pains to assert that his criticism didn't include Jake.

Now Jake didn't know what to make of the look on Dan's face but decided it was his worry about Zoe or simply the uniform that made him seem so different. He remembered what David had said earlier about it being Frontline's job to make sure the protests wouldn't escalate. And now this from Dan. It was like two of Homeland's limbs pointing fingers at each other. "I gotta go back to work," he said as he got up from his stool, "or there will be even less next week."

Dan nodded and visibly deflated, turning into his familiar self. "I'm sorry, Jake, I didn't mean for it to come out that way. I know you're doing all you can, and here you are, helping us out once again." He held up the paper bag with the meds for Zoe. "It's just a fucked-up day, and I'm feelin' it. First, we almost shoot that girl, and then my own girl almost dies. It's fucked up, I'm telling you."

"You shot a girl?" Jake asked, alarmed.

"Gary almost did. Fuckin' Gary." Dan shook his head and took a gulp from the can. "You know Gary. He gets mad fast, and it got ugly."

Jake did know Gary, a war veteran like Dan and his partner at Frontline, a man with a deep-seated anger problem he wouldn't want to meet on duty or anywhere, really.

"But the girl's alive?"

Dan nodded. "Wouldn't have been the first one killed, but this one got to me. She was so small, if you know what I'm saying, and so wild. And there were people there. Cameras everywhere. It was fucked up. But you gotta go."

"I do," Jake said, distracted by the commotion on his Spine, which had self-activated with three priority messages from Masao and a bunch of storm track projections now popping up between him and Dan in bright pulsating colors. "But we'll talk. Give those meds to Carrie, and I'll try to get the corticoid, too. Zoe will be fine, okay? Tell Carrie I'll call her."

"So see you Saturday?"

"What's Saturday?"

"Carrie didn't tell you?"

"She probably did," Jake said on his way to the door. "I'll call her."

The seventh floor was in uproar when Jake stepped out of the elevator, a mix of news feeds, cheering, and something almost akin to applause. He walked into the CSR, and there on the screen walls were the new path projections for Tapah that Masao had sent him, showing the super typhoon on a more northwestern path, missing Hong Kong.

Masao walked toward him, grinning. "Getting lucky, for once."

Jake stared at the screen walls, trying to process.

"Have you canceled yet?" Masao asked. "You said you had something planned tonight?"

Jake waited another half hour before he went to see David, who had joined them before lunch in the CSR and then left without a word in the afternoon. Stepping into the freezing office, he immediately knew why. David was hiding his hands below the desk, his face sunken. The screen walls were all dark, more than a little unusual.

"What's the news on Tapah?" David turned his unsteady gaze on him. "Is he gonna fuck us?"

Jake shook his head. "Still categorized as a super typhoon, but now on an even more northwestern path. It'll screw up our northern supply lines, but we've got it under control."

"You think that because you don't understand storms."

Jake didn't bother to respond.

"I mean it!" David barked. "You and Lisa, and the rest of you in the CSR, you believe in meteorology and forecasts and all that crap. But we're above two degrees, for fuck's sake, and what does that mean? It means no one's got a clue what will happen! I keep saying that, but for some fucking reason no one in this goddamn place ever listens to me."

"What I'm saying is," Jake said as calmly as he could manage, "we've got the northern lines covered. We've also started working on the supply from the south. Lisa's team will take care of any replacements for Macao should we need them. Landfall's expected around eleven."

"Are you gonna tell me now you wanna leave?" David asked. "I heard you this morning," he added when Jake couldn't hide his surprise. "And you got that guilty look on your face."

"Yes," Jake said slowly. "I need to leave for a couple of hours. I have this... thing I couldn't cancel." He wasn't quite clear on how he had arrived at this decision, but he still had no phone number for Shavir, and he still hadn't called Hector. Fact was, they were in a solid situation now, mostly because Lisa had shown both foresight and backbone throughout the night with her decision to focus on the area north of Hong Kong against David's advice. All new projections supported her decision, and now he could afford to leave for two hours.

"A *thing*?" David asked blankly.

"A dinner, actually."

"Just so I get this right," David leaned forward. "You just told me that this fucker is going to make landfall in about five hours from now... and you feel like going on a date?"

"Just for an hour or so. As I said, we've got it under control."

"We've got nothing under control. Absolutely *nothing*!"

"David, please." Jake forced his voice down to a level of calm. "Masao has offered to stay longer, Lisa just came in with her entire team, and I will be on standby."

"You bet you'll be on standby. Or you no longer have a job here."

Jake stared at his boss, unbelieving. In the six years he'd worked with him, David had often been unhappy about things not going the way he wanted, which was what things around here did most of the time. But he'd never insinuated Jake's job might be on the line. David's hands were still hidden underneath the desks, his pupils out of control as he seemed to be trying for a stare.

For a second, Jake considered bringing up Emovia, but he had no idea what reaction that would provoke in David's unstable state and he had other things to do. He got up and left the office.

It was a few minutes past seven when Jake pushed open the massive front door of Buddha's Kitchen, a stylish Pan-Asian restaurant with a glass mosaic water wall and dim lighting that was easy on his eyes. He'd been here once before, with Marla, a travel agent he saw sometimes who had a knack for finding new restaurants. Buddha's had just opened its doors and was all the rage among foodsters. Marla was more the carnivorous kind of girl, but the hype around the culinary magic of the restaurant's plant-based cuisine had been so enormous that she hadn't been able to resist, only to complain all evening about what meaty delicacies she could have been eating instead at Le Déluge, her favorite restaurant and one of the few places one could still legally eat parts of formerly living animals. He tried to remember what he had eaten here at Buddha's that night, but he wasn't good at noticing things even while he was eating them. The smell that filled the stylish room, however, was enticing.

The host approached to greet him, her eyes lingering disapprovingly on his creased T-shirt. Everyone around him was dressed to the extreme, elegant suits and little black dresses abounding. He, in contrast, was wearing what he'd slapped on in the morning after shooing Lucy out of his closet and popping a dress shirt into his bag. The bag sat underneath his desk in the CSR while he looked like the definition of a nerd standing in front of a counter covered in turquoise glass stones. "A table for two, Tayard?" he said. "I'm a little late."

The host couldn't find a reservation, and Shavir was nowhere to be seen. He worried for a second that she might have waited and left, but the host told him no, suggesting Shavir came here regularly. Another enigma, just like the dog she owned. While looking for her phone number, he had finally found the pet registration in her file. Three thousand dollars fully paid. It was unclear to him how she could afford that. Or afford to eat here.

At the recommendation of the host, he walked to the adjacent bar to await his party. It was nearly empty, two bartenders cleaning glasses from an earlier onslaught. He ordered a beer and sat down. It was almost half past seven, he realized when checking his Spine, and that was when it occurred to him that Shavir might not show up. For some reason, that scenario hadn't been among the ones he'd been running all day, which was ironic given how much effort and plain luck it had taken for him to get here. Disappointment creeping up on him, he took a gulp of his beer and flicked on his Spine to check on Tapah, still on its northeastern path. If he took a podcar to SAFE, he'd be back before David succumbed to a heart attack. He decided he would wait another five minutes, until he was done with his beer.

Then he saw her.

She'd somehow been in the room without him noticing, and there she was, walking toward him through the virtual storm on his Spine in sneakers and the usual jeans and tank top, looking just as out of place as he did. Her only spectacular accessory was her hair, flooding over her bare arms down to her elbows. The room's warm lights made it shine with every move she made. Once again, he was unprepared.

She smiled, almost bashful. "Hey. Here you are."

He put the Spine back on standby. "They couldn't find our table."

Shavir's eyes flew over to the bar, where one of the bartenders stood with a baffled smile and a question mark in his eyes. She lifted her hand in a half-greeting. "Should we go right over then?" she then said, glancing at Jake. "I know I'm really late."

It turned out they did have a table in the restaurant, tucked away in a dimly lit niche next to the water wall. "Thanks, Lia," Shavir said to the host, who managed a sharp nod before leaving them alone. "I'm afraid I'm not quite dressed for the occasion, so this is perfect." Shavir pointed down to her jeans that he now noticed were dirty. "I came directly from the farm. I'd have been even more late otherwise."

"That's okay." He grinned, pointing to his T-shirt.

Then the bartender came over to put a glass of beer down before Shavir, looking at her now with less surprise and more amusement.

"Thanks, Troy," she said quickly, ignoring the amusement.

"You come here often?" Jake asked since it was so very obvious.

"Not to the restaurant, but I'm friends with the owner, so I come to eat in the kitchen sometimes. The food is fantastic, but, hey, they get their veggies from Roots." She attempted a smile.

He realized he hadn't planned for this at all despite his efforts to make it happen. Now Shavir sat across from him, and he didn't know what to say. Asking about her day seemed a good choice, but it wasn't.

"Yeah," she said vaguely. "Busy. How about yours?"

The last thing he wanted to talk about was the storm that had almost wrecked their date and was still raging through the back of his mind. He also didn't want to talk about Carrie or Zoe or Dan, who had sent him a message that Zoe was feeling better. He wanted to be here, with Shavir, and that was hard enough for him already. Any mention of his day would make it impossible. What could he say that wasn't a lie?

He was still searching for an answer when Shavir spoke again.

"Are you watching stuff on your Spine?"

"Now? Of course, not."

"Why are your eyes twitching then?"

"My eyes aren't—" He paused, looking at the table to hide his confusion. "It's a habit," he then explained. "A deformation. I'm on the Spine so much my eyes have trouble finding focus."

"So your Spine's off now?"

He looked up at her again. "It's on standby."

"Meaning you can flip it on any time without me noticing."

"Why in the world would I do that?"

"Because that's what you Spine junkies do all the time." She leaned forward, an angry tinge in her voice. "I'm sorry, Jake, but if you can't ever cut the signal, what's even the point of this?"

He exhaled slowly. Then he told her about Tapah.

She stared at him. "Why didn't you cancel?"

"I don't have your number. And I didn't *want* to cancel."

She swallowed, her dark gaze still piercing him. "It's my fault," she decided. "I shouldn't have asked you point-blank like that."

"Well, I'm glad you did."

A well-dressed South Asian man with a big smile of pearly whites approached them. Shavir relaxed and returned the smile. "Jake, this is Anil, guardian over the finest vegan food in Manhattan."

"Only because we get the freshest produce from Roots," Anil replied politely before turning to Jake. "Is this your first time with us?"

Jake nodded because that seemed easiest.

Anil returned his attention to Shavir with what looked like concern. "Troy told me about your trip," he said and stopped when he saw the changed expression on Shavir's face. He flashed another smile and proceeded almost seamlessly, "And he said it went really well. Do you want me to read you today's specials?"

Jake pretended to listen and ordered the same as Shavir. After Anil left, he waited, uncertain whether he could ask about the trip.

But Shavir elaborated without prompt. "We went to New Jersey today, me and Sam." She was almost chatty now. "He loves being outside in the country, but we rarely get to go. It was great for him, running around without a leash. You aren't allowed to do that here with a big guy like him."

None of this matched up with what she had said earlier about her busy day at the farm, but he was glad they were talking at all.

"We visited the farm where Sam's from," Shavir continued, "and they asked me to help out. I was so busy cutting tomatoes that we ended up missing our train. Sorry again."

"Where is he now?"

"Sam? Upstairs in Anil's apartment. His kids love him to death."

Jake asked more questions about Sam and about Shavir's work at Roots, having finally hit a topic they both seemed comfortable with. They talked about the effects of the heat wave on the farm, about Roots's community work and the cookouts they organized up on the highest roof at a place called Prince's Garden. He was glad he had watched a Spine feature about Roots on his morning walk to SAFE. It was the reason he'd forgotten to buy himself coffee, but now it made him look like a halfway competent conversation partner. He knew so little about farming and was amazed at how much Shavir knew about the logistical challenges in the city, though she didn't seem to have an appetite tonight for blaming him for the sorry state of Brooklyn.

He eased more and more into their conversation, but when the server arrived with their appetizers, his stomach didn't feel willing to accept solid food. Misinterpreting his hesitation, Shavir explained every detail of the dish, knowing exactly which part of the arrangement of colors and textures hailed from their farm. To her own plate, she attended with great care, savoring each bite with a sensuality that left him vaguely jealous.

"Aren't you going to eat?" she finally asked.

"I'm not really hungry."

"Is that because of the amphetamines?"

He smiled wryly. "You don't beat around the bush much, do you?"

"Should I?" She raised her eyebrows. "It's pretty obvious."

"Yes, it's in part because of the amphetamines, but that's not really my problem right now."

"What is your problem right now?"

"Well, you. I'm not sure I'll ever need food again."

A surprised smile rippled across her lips, and she dropped her gaze before facing him again. "I see. What can we do about that?"

"Not much, I'm afraid." He pushed his plate to the side, relieved he no longer had to pretend to eat. "Perhaps I'll get used to it."

For the first time, her eyes had trouble meeting his. "I hope so. You really shouldn't miss this salad. Nimesh—their chef—is a genius in balancing sweet, spicy, and acidity just right."

Jake smiled. "You really like food, don't you?"

She considered the forkful of salad in front of her. "I work in an eatery and spend the rest of my waking hours on a farm, so I guess I better like food. How about you? Do you ever cook?"

"Me?" He laughed.

"Or is there someone who cooks for you sometimes?"

"Well, there's Lucy," he said lightly, "but she really is a lousy cook. It's all raw and roaches. No," he added more seriously, "not since my mom died." He'd barely finished the sentence before asking himself whether he'd said it on purpose and if so, why. He wanted to take it back, but it was too late, and it didn't fail to have an effect.

"When was that?" Shavir asked, all delight drained from her face.

"We don't have to talk about it," Jake scrambled. He knew her parents were dead, too, but he couldn't admit to the knowledge. And he never talked about his family or why they were gone.

"It's alright," Shavir said. "What happened?"

"I was twelve," was all he could get out. "We were living in Tampa."

"Hurricane Arlene."

He nodded.

"I'm sorry, Jake." She was still looking at him, features unguarded in a way he'd never seen before. "That kind of thing, losing a parent like that, it just rips you apart."

He nodded again, grateful she didn't press further.

The server arrived with two steaming bowls of curry, exchanging a look with Shavir as she left with his untouched appetizer.

"Is that why you work at Homeland?" Shavir asked when they were alone again.

"At SAFE," he corrected. "And yes, perhaps. It's a way for me... I don't know. Find meaning, I guess. I struggle with that sometimes. It helps doing something that makes sense. That's how I see it, anyway."

"What is it you really do there, can I ask?"

Jake nodded and leaned back in his chair, trying to get comfortable. He didn't want to talk about SAFE or the realities of his job, but the expression on her face told him he had little choice.

"I know you work on critical meds," she said. "Foodstuff, too?"

"When we're dealing with crop failures. But mostly meds."

"And you distribute them to the pharmacies and hospitals."

"No." He shifted his weight on the chair. They were moving into dangerous territory. "A computer system does that, making sure that everything gets spread out evenly."

"No. It doesn't." Shavir's voice had grown cold. "Nothing's spread out evenly in this town."

This would be the moment to change the topic. Or lie. But if he wanted this to go anywhere, neither was an option. This wasn't Marla, who'd learned to never ask questions about his job after she'd once compared him to a drone gunner who detonates bombs on the other side of the world. Shavir wouldn't stop asking questions, so he could either answer or walk. He felt like he was stepping out on a ledge when he mentioned the Manhattan Hospital Association.

"They're a lobbying organization that promotes the interests of Manhattan's health care providers at the mayor's office," he said, calibrating his words, "and thus at SAFE."

"I thought Homeland was run by the feds."

"It was. Still is, to some degree. But with the SAFE centers, it's more localized because the federal government is so dysfunctional. The mayor's office has some influence on what we do."

A mild way of putting it, but basically true.

"Is that the reason we don't get anything in Brooklyn and Queens?"

It was clear now where this was going. So much for her not being in the mood tonight.

"You *do* get quite a bit," Jake said slowly. "But… less than Manhattan." It probably was a first for anyone from SAFE to admit that.

"A lot less." Shavir's face was stern, her food, like his, untouched.

He inhaled. Nodded. "Look, Shavir. I grew up in Queens. And what's left of my family—my cousin—she still lives there. I know how bad it is. I told you I'm not what you think."

"How can you do it then, this job? Why?"

Against his intentions, anger rose in him. He didn't like discussing his work. He was tired of people's petty positions of moral high ground from which to judge whatever they thought SAFE was doing or not doing without reflecting on where they would be if it wasn't there. What they would eat. What they would take when they got sick. Where they would go when they needed surgery. All of these questions were conveniently omitted from the arguments against SAFE.

So why did he do it? "Probably because I'm good at it."

"Okay," she said. "But do you like doing it?"

"*Like* it?" he echoed. "This isn't about *liking* things, Shavir. It's about something needing to be done and someone needing to do it."

"Why do *you* do it then? There must be a reason."

She was like a heat-seeking rocket programmed to find her target; the intensity of her eyes impossible to bear.

Jake made himself look into them long enough to answer. "Because I've learned to focus on what's essential, not on what I like."

She considered this. "Then why are you here?"

The rocket had found its target. Jake could feel it detonating inside.

Such a simple question, but he was unable to respond. The detonation had ripped everything wide open, a bloody mess of feelings. He wished they were talking about his dead family instead.

"I'm sorry, Jake," she said, not looking sorry at all. "But I told you this would happen if we went out on a date. I've just come out of a two-year relationship that was all about lies and playing games. I can't do it anymore."

"I'm not playing any games," he said hoarsely because he couldn't say he wasn't lying.

It was in this precise moment his Spine jumped back to life, over-riding the standby mode. He froze, the bright green letters pulsating in the space between Shavir and him.

DAVID.

"I am very sorry," he squeezed out and accepted the call.

"Guess what?" bellowed David. "Turns out Tapah doesn't give a fuck about forecasts. He has decided to hit Hong Kong full on. I need you back, now." With that, he hung up.

"You have to go," Shavir said, eyes almost as black as her hair.

"I'm very sorry," Jake stumbled, still in shock.

"It's okay. It was bound to happen."

"The typhoon... it's going to hit Hong Kong."

"Jesus!" Her eyes widened. "Just go. I'll take care of the check."

"No, you won't." He signaled the server and paid for their meal while he called up the new forecasts. There it was—the projected landfall icon directly above Hong Kong.

Shavir sat in silence as he got up.

"Will you give me your number?" he spilled out.

"Homeland doesn't have it?" Her voice was caustic.

"I'm asking you."

"You know where you can find me."

"I do," he said, fed up with this, fed up with the entire world and its impossible demands on him. "But I didn't come here while a super typhoon is thrashing our supply chains because I *like* you. I came here because you are important to me. So if you're willing to put up with me one more time, I'd love to call you when this nightmare is over."

He could see her inhale, her collarbones shimmering in the glow from the water wall. "Three-four-seven-seven-nine-four-nine-seven-en-seven-two-six."

He smiled and sank back down on his chair as he activated the Spine's voice recognition feature.

"Would you mind saying that again?"

She repeated the number, each green-gleaming digit appearing in the space between them. The air felt electric.

"Thank you. I'm really sorry for this. I will make it up to you."

He got up, turned around, and kept walking until he reached the door, the street, then the next waiting podcar, the image of Shavir sitting alone in front of both of their full plates vividly on his mind.

He couldn't remember having felt this much like an asshole before, and yet, perversely, this was also the happiest he'd ever been.

SEVEN

SHAVIR SAT AT THE rear of Buddha's bar, the plate before her half empty. She'd carried it over after Jake's abrupt departure, feeling less exposed here than she had sitting at the table. Now she was drawing lines into the yellow curry with her spoon, mesmerized by the fleeting appearance of the plate's blue surface and its inevitable resubmergence.

Troy had yet to make a single comment about her date or the fact that Jake had walked out in the middle of it. He had made a point of not looking at her after she'd sat down at the bar. Instead, he had put a glass of wine in front of her and busied himself with his cocktail orders. The restaurant was still packed, but the atmosphere in the bar was relaxed and quiet, allowing her to figure out for herself how she had wound up here despite her best efforts to the contrary.

Ironically, everything had gone according to plan from the moment she'd left Tara behind with those two Frontline assholes, except she had been alone with the four dogs. She'd led them into the next incoming subway train like a sleepwalker, but the puppies were so shell-shocked from the incident that they gave her no trouble at all, not even when they got to the madhouse of Grand Central Station. They'd heeled, all four of them, like they had never done anything else in their lives, walking across the main hall in an impressive phalanx with her in the middle, the precise opposite of moving incognito.

The other passengers on the bullet train to New Jersey had stared at the dogs like they were little dragons, wings and all, but no one said a word or called the police. Aside from a conductor who just couldn't believe there wasn't a law about how many dogs could accompany a single human, the train ride would have been almost relaxing had she not been so anxious to hear from Tara.

Lenny was livid when she called him from her burner phone and told him what had happened, and then he hung up on her to take care of things. She also called Finn, who was already on his way to Brooklyn to find out where the cops had taken Tara. She felt useless sitting on that comfortable train, zipping through the swiftly changing landscape away from New York while everyone else was rushing to help the friend she'd left behind. But she did have the dogs with her, little Max sleeping on her lap the entire time.

Walking out of the station in Clinton felt like walking into a wall, unbearably hot after the cool train. As always, she was struck by the emptiness of that part of New Jersey, empty of cars and buildings, that was, and bursting with millions of trees. Most of the forests in the area were still young, the drought-resistant ashes, acacias, red oaks, and neem trees not older than two decades, all planted through the state's emergency reforestation project. She'd only seen in pictures what it had looked like before the reforestation, a checkerboard of farmland and sprawling towns, most of them demolished now and turned into a carbon-sinking kind of wilderness. The air tasted so different whenever she escorted rescues there, dry and fragrant.

On a normal trip, she'd have wondered, as she often did, what it was like living among so many trees under that big sky and at a safe distance from the Atlantic and its hurricanes, even as it meant being closer to the wildfires. She knew a few farmers around here and in upstate New York, people who had adopted dogs from them and who managed to live off the land far away from the city, dealing with the frequent crop failures. It was precarious farming all the same, but different in ways that had always interested her. This was no normal trip, though, and last thing she wanted was imagine a new way of life without Tara.

Simon stood waiting as arranged in the smoldering parking lot with his old van, inevitably wearing his farmer's hat, a permanent sunburn, and a grin. "That's a lot of dogs for one woman," he said, and then, when he saw the expression on her face, "Where's Tara?"

She told him on their way to Max's new home. Behind the windshield, an endless mass of trees was gliding by, shielding them from the sun as she explained to Simon how shitty she felt for not stopping Tara from doing what she always seemed to do—get them into trouble.

"Without you, Max would be dead now," Simon said with the usual bluntness, keeping his eyes on the road. "Tara probably, too. So I think you can feel pretty good about yourself."

She didn't though, and it made no difference when Simon told her to stop beating herself up about an unavoidable part of the job. It hadn't been unavoidable; she could have prevented it. Listening to Lenny would have been an option, talking to Finn another, one she hadn't wanted to consider for egoistic reasons.

When Simon pulled up in front of a beautiful big ranch house and asked her if she was ready, she said she would just wait in the van.

"Oh, come on, Shav! This is the best part."

"I just need to think a bit."

Simon closed the driver's door with a sigh. "I know what you're thinking. Are we stupid? Are we taking way too big of a risk? Should we stop? And the answers to that are yes, yes, and absolutely not. Because if we stop, what are we even still doing here? The planet is going to hell anyway and we can't do shit about it, so why bother surviving unless we're helping some friends who are blessed with much shorter lifespans?" He was grinning at that point. "Just a few minutes, and you'll feel better, I promise. Come on, now."

It was an easy promise to keep. Ms. Roberts, Max's new owner, led them to the large yard on the backside of her house, already populated by two other rescues, both fully grown mastiffs. They introduced all the dogs, and Simon followed Ms. Roberts inside to take care of the paperwork while Shavir stayed outside in the shade of the porch, sipping homemade lemonade. Max was shy at first, still shaken from his encounter with the cops, but he warmed up after a while and started pacing the yard with the other dogs. It was a beautiful yard, filled with brown grass and majestic old trees, surrounded by a sturdy wooden fence—a place a city dog like Sam could only dream of. She felt a pang of guilt as she watched him race little Max and his new country bumpkin buddies.

Then her phone rang with a call from Lenny, who told her that Tara was out, free to go, after Finn paid all the fees. Shavir sat down on the edge of the porch, tears running freely, overcome with relief to hear that Tara was okay—mad, but okay.

"You know what's happening on the Spine cloud right now, Shav?" Lenny asked. "It's popping up everywhere! That kind of publicity is the last thing we need. Your faces all over the cloud, together with four of our dogs and two imbecile cops. It endangers everything we do, everything we work for!"

She let him yell, figuring it was better he yelled at her than at Tara.

"You wanna talk to Finn?" Lenny asked when he'd run out of steam.

"I wanna talk to Tara."

He hesitated, but Tara grabbed his phone.

"How's Max?" she asked.

"Happy."

"You're my hero. See you tonight."

And then, after getting off the phone with Tara, she finally made herself do the right thing and called Hector. He was busy stacking cupboards at Soma, predictably ecstatic that they had coffee again, thanks to his patron saint Jake—and decidedly less ecstatic when she asked for Jake's number so she could cancel their date.

"Cancel?" he cried. "Oh, he's not gonna be happy about that."

"Well, I'm not happy about it either. Do you have his number?"

"No, Shav, he just comes here. Maybe you can call SAFE?"

Right. Why not call Homeland Security to cancel a date. "Never mind," she said to Hector before she hung up. "I'll call Buddha's."

And she had. She had actually called Buddha's Kitchen to ask Anil to somehow explain to Jake on her behalf that she couldn't meet him. But once Anil was on the phone, greeting her in his friendly voice, it seemed irresponsible to burden him with the job of fixing her mistakes. So they'd chatted for a few minutes about the complimentary crate of tomatoes he'd received with his usual delivery from Roots, and then she'd decided she simply wouldn't show that night. As a plan, it had been shitty and craven and deeply unfair to Jake, but she'd been too distraught by what had happened to Tara to come up with something better, and at least the burden of explaining herself would be with her when Jake came in for his coffee the next morning—if he ever came back to Soma at all.

It was difficult to explain even to herself how she had then ended up at Buddha's in direct defiance of her own grand master plan. She'd made a spontaneous about-face in Grand Central, debated with herself on her way over, and solidified her decision when she tossed Sam's leash into the hands of Anil's wife, Samira, in their upstairs apartment, begging her to take care of him so she could go downstairs and see Jake.

She didn't know whether Jake had believed anything she'd said to him about that trip to New Jersey, or how bad it would be if he hadn't. It probably hadn't been smart to tell him where she'd gone. But a partial lie had been easier to come up with than a more carefully calibrated one, and it also made her feel better. At least not all of what she'd said had been lies while she was demanding nothing but the truth from him. She felt embarrassed for having interrogated Jake and was still confused by the whole date—if that was even the right word.

It had gone about as badly as expected, only in very different ways. She'd come to Buddha's thinking Jake was deluding himself about the nature of his work at SAFE. Now she knew he believed he had to do it. It was a sense of duty she remembered from her mom, who could never stop raging about her badly paid job at the hospital, the fact that there were never enough meds or staff, the lack of appreciation for the taxing work she did every day, healthy or sick, ready or not. And yet she had never refused a single request to stay longer or do an extra shift. She didn't know how many times she'd tried to talk her mother into quitting her job, bringing home information on how to start a new career. But her mom would only say that times were too hard, that she was needed at the hospital.

Shavir knew what commitment was. There was no one at Roots, above or below ground, who wasn't committed. And there was plenty of complaining about how hard it was, how exhausting, how dangerous, depending on the nature of the work. She was guilty of all of the above, but the difference between her and her mother, her and Jake, was that there was no sense of duty. She didn't spend hours harvesting in the blazing sun because she felt a duty to do so. She sure as hell didn't sit on the floor of Finn's van with the others because it was her duty. She did these things because she wanted to. But her mother hadn't gone back to the hospital every day because she wanted to. She had done it because she'd felt she had to. Because her sense of duty had compelled her to do it. Maybe it was the same for Jake and SAFE, the same kind of compulsion to fulfill a duty. Whatever had happened to Jake and his family during that hurricane, he apparently needed to do this crazy job at SAFE, even as it was killing him.

"So who was that, and why did he bail on you like that?" Troy had reached the end of his patience. "What did you do?"

"I didn't do anything," Shavir said crossly. "He had to leave because of the monster typhoon that's leveling Hong Kong right now."

Troy nodded. "I saw it on the Spine. It's massive." He put down the glass he'd been wiping and picked up another one.

"See, that's why Anil wants to fire you all the time. I don't even understand how you can watch stuff while mixing drinks. How can you not drop everything?"

"Because I'm still young and capable," Troy said, grinning. "Why did your guy leave you for a storm on the other side of the world? That makes no sense."

Without doubt, telling Troy would mean dropping a bomb. But she felt like dropping bombs today for some reason. "He does supply chain management over at SAFE," she said. "I guess they have to be really quick whenever something major hits like this."

Troy forgot to polish the glass. "Your man's with Homeland?"

"He's not my man. But yes, I guess he's with Homeland, sort of."

Troy stared, his usual air of cool detachment having evaporated. "What?" she asked.

"That's an... interesting choice for a date."

"I think so, too, actually."

He still stared at her.

"Can you cut the drama?" she barked, though, really, what had she expected dropping bombs? "We went on one date that didn't work out. It's also a little paranoid to assume everyone who works for the government is out to get us. Jake has other things to do, trust me."

Now that she'd said it out loud, she realized she believed it, too. Jake was interested in her, not in what she did. It might be a bad idea to date him, but not because he was gonna get them busted. She looked down at her arm where the cut had almost healed in one day, thanks to the powerful meds he had given her. This was about her, not the group. She had no idea what Jake saw in her or why he thought she was important, but this wasn't some kind of police stunt, some covert investigation with Jake as the stooge. The thought alone was absurd.

Troy turned to put the dry glasses into the rack above the counter. "Does Finn know?" he asked over his shoulder. "Because if he doesn't, we might wanna change the subject now."

Shavir looked past Troy and saw Finn walking toward them. She tensed up, feeling caught in the act, ridiculous as that was. Suddenly she was glad Jake had left.

"Hi, Shav." Finn placed a kiss on her cheek before she could turn away and sat down next to her without asking. She could smell his aftershave, his damp hair suggesting he'd just taken a shower. His sheer physicality made her feel cornered between him and the wall. She didn't even know why he was here; it wasn't one of his regular joints.

"He didn't call me," Finn said, catching the gaze she exchanged with Troy. "Tara told me you were here, and I thought maybe you'd wanna know how she's doing." His eyes were clear and vivid, so no Emovia tonight, but that was no reason to relax. Quite the contrary.

"She sounded okay when I talked to her," Shavir said, leaning away from Finn on her stool. Tara had called when she'd been dropping off Sam upstairs. She hadn't seen the need to lie to Tara about where she was since she ate dinner here often when she was in Manhattan.

Clearly, she should have lied.

"You still mad at me?" Finn's voice had turned husky.

She knew exactly where this was going.

"Can you give me a little space, please?"

An amused smile played around Finn's lips. He stepped down from the stool, making a point of moving it away from her a few inches.

"How's Tara?" Troy asked, putting down a beer in front of Finn.

"She's alright. Mad as hell at those cops. They made me pay five thousand dollars in fines for her. Had a whole bag of offenses." Finn turned to Shavir. "Did she really punch the guy?"

She shook her head. "No. But she would have, given the chance. He was an asshole. But the other cop was okay. Without him, Max would probably be dead. And maybe Tara, too." She realized she was echoing what Simon had said about her.

"I think it was mostly people filming that prevented that," Finn said. "Anyway, they fined her for assaulting a cop. And they ordered that she chip her dog again and present it at the Greenpoint Frontline station within five days. That was my favorite part."

"Present him? How're we gonna do that? Max's in New Jersey."

Finn shrugged. "So what? Zeno chips another puppy with the same code, and we present that one. You really think they care?"

"What about the Spine footage? They can see Max on the cloud."

"Oh, come on, Shav!" Finn laughed. "We can produce a Max for them in ten minutes. Brindle mastiff, twenty weeks, white left paw. How difficult can it be?"

He was right. Frontline wouldn't care as long as there was a dog and a chip that confirmed the owner had paid three thousand dollars in municipal dog fees.

"Thanks for bailing Tara out." She forced herself to look into Finn's eyes. It was not the first time Tara had gotten herself and everyone else into trouble. And it was not the first time Finn had alleviated the consequences like it was nothing. It was amazing how dependable he could be if he wanted to, how committed. One of his many contradictions.

He shrugged in return and smiled, like he knew what she was thinking. Then he leaned toward her, just a little.

"Can I take you home?"

He laughed when he saw her face. "I don't mean home to me. I mean home to Brooklyn. I haven't picked up the veggies yet, so I can drop you off there." It sounded like a peace offering. "Where's Sam?"

"Upstairs."

"At Anil's place? Is that your... new arrangement?"

"No. I just didn't know what to do with him after coming back from New Jersey. It's some kind of emergency-super-exception. Samira allowed me to leave him with her and the kids while I was eating. Anil doesn't even know, I think. I hope Sam behaves."

"You know I didn't mean it, right, the parking thing?" Finn asked, his voice very low, his eyes very blue. "I love having Sam around, you know that."

She did know that. And she had known he would do this again. When things started out between them over two years ago, she had fallen for his act, first because she thought it was true and then because she wanted it to be true. Even then, she couldn't help noticing that Finn's feelings for her ebbed and flowed with his moods and drug use, that there were moments, many of them, when he was unreachable for her, either emotionally or entirely, his Spine switched off and his eventual explanations evasive. So she had ended it, and ended it again, but every time she'd done so, he had presented her with some version of what he was giving her now.

It was like a game, a performance scalable from the reasonable all the way up to the whispered confessions of his undying love for her, and he was excellent at calibrating it to her exact level of pissedness. Even once she'd gone through the ordeal often enough to *know* it was a performance, there was always a point at which she gave in, when it was too exhausting to keep up her anger or her distance or her commitment to not return to him. To get even, she'd started responding in kind, not picking up her phone, making herself unavailable for long stretches of time, getting up in the middle of the night to go home after he'd once asked her to do so. She couldn't remember when things had changed, when exactly she'd become fed up enough with both the breakups and the inevitable makeups to walk away for good. And she knew it was incomprehensible to Finn that she was no longer playing along.

"I'm sorry I was an ass," he said, still much too close. "I was high and totally sucked up in that garden for the Jensens. It's gigantic, and I lost so much data when the Gardener crashed this morning. I was trying to make up time, so I took something and—" His voice cracked. "It just wasn't a good moment, Shav, I'm sorry."

"Your design program crashed again?" Shavir asked. She didn't want to talk about Emovia or think about how the drug's gravitational pull directed the tidal force of Finn's feelings.

"It doesn't run well on my new Spine." He paused, searching her eyes. "Let me take you to Brooklyn, okay? You had a rough day, and I don't want you and Sam to go back on the subway at this hour when I'm driving over anyway. Can we do that? Be adults?"

She snorted. *Be adults.*

"I know." Finn smiled. "But I really wanna take you. Okay?"

It was one of those decisions she would probably regret at some point, but it did seem silly to go back on the train when he was driving that way anyway, and she dreaded taking the train at this time of night.

She slid off the stool to pick up Sam.

Anil was standing next to the kitchen entrance, printing out receipts. "Sorry about earlier with... Jake, was it?" He looked up. "I didn't realize he isn't one of your group."

"It's okay," Shavir said. "He didn't catch on." She hoped.

"You want your dog back?"

Shavir smiled. "So you do know he's up there."

"My wife tells me everything," Anil said straight-faced. He led her across the steamy kitchen, where the crew was cleaning up, scents of garlic, ginger, and lemongrass hanging in the humid air, and up the cool staircase to the apartment on the first floor.

Sam was already at the door, excited to see her.

"He's been so wonderful." Samira came out from the living room. She was a beautiful woman with soft features framed by graying black hair and a habit of wearing intricately patterned saris, no matter the occasion or weather. "The kids didn't want to go to bed."

Shavir smiled. "He's great with kids. Thanks for letting him stay here." Her stomach contracted at the vibration of the burner phone against her hipbone—a message, forwarded from her own phone. She could feel her heart rate going up, but she told herself it was probably Finn, impatient and asking her to hurry.

Anil wanted to hear more about the run-in with Frontline, but Shavir changed the subject by reminding him Finn would drop off another complimentary crate of tomatoes with Roots's normal vegetable delivery in the morning—one of the many things Finn did for the farm as if it wasn't a big deal. Then she said goodbye and walked down the stairs with Sam.

Pausing at the foot of the stairs, she pulled out the burner phone to read the message. Her stomach contracted again when she saw that it was, as she had tried not to hope, Jake.

Thank you for tonight, and sorry again for deserting you like that. I hope to make up for it on a better day if that's something you want, too. Perhaps you could show me your farm and we grab a bite in Brooklyn? I'd love to learn more... J.

The lights went off and left her standing in the darkness.

Her entire body seemed to glow alongside her phone as she leaned against the wall, her heart beating against her ribcage. He wanted to see the farm, of all places.

It was crystal clear what she had to answer and that she should do so right away to end this thing before it got out of hand. She read the message four times, reminding herself she was done with things getting out of hand and how important it was that this one didn't. Then she decided it was too risky to answer from this phone, which she would drop into the river. The lights flicked back on as she pocketed it and led Sam down the stairs to catch their ride to Brooklyn.

Eight

Lucy was relaxing in full sunlight on her favorite spot on the windowsill when Jake returned to his hot apartment just before noon. The temperature control unit had switched to her comfort zone six hours ago when, normally, he left for work and the dragon took over, hunting roaches for breakfast. She looked mildly annoyed by his intrusion before turning her face back to the sun.

Jake sat down on the bed and took off his gloves. Whatever the temperature, he was glad to be away from the chilled frenzy of the CSR. It had been overflowing with people when he'd returned from Buddha's last night, Lisa's team having pooled forces with the day team to work on replacements for the southern supply lines from Macao. By the time of landfall, the entire industrialized world had been in for the battle. They'd shared desks, using their Spines and the screen walls to secure whatever they could get their hands on for New York. The casual observer might have mistaken them for lunatics, intoxicated by the massive loads of data that surrounded, enfolded, and smothered them, all before the floor-to-ceiling spectacle of a raging typhoon.

David hadn't even looked at him when he'd returned to the CSR, guilt-ridden and repentant, knowing that this time he and everyone else deserved David's wrath. They all had disregarded David's experience because of his fragile physical state, but he'd been right all along—they were no longer able to correctly forecast a typhoon's path.

After spending the night working silently alongside Masao, he had finally walked over to David's office to apologize.

"We've all been there, Jake" had been David's laconic response. He hadn't looked any better but also not any worse given that he had added another twenty-four hours to his watch. "You need to learn from it, that's all," he'd said with what was probably a chemically induced equanimity. "We all need to learn. We need a whole new approach to this."

He had wanted to ask David what exactly he meant by *this*. And he'd wanted to ask how David could be so stupid as to take Emovia. But it hadn't been the right moment.

"Go home and get some sleep," David had told him, though he himself seemed to have plans to move permanently into his office.

The dinner hadn't been mentioned again, nor had there been any response from Shavir since then. Sitting on his bed in bright sunlight and staring at the two dancing trees on top of the building across the street, the entire night felt to Jake like a bad dream in which he had managed to both suck at his job and walk out on the most fascinating woman he'd ever met.

A call came in on his Spine, and his heart rate spiked.

He tried to conceal his disappointment when Carrie's face popped up in front of him. She looked tired, the shadows underneath her eyes exaggerated by the holographic projection. But she was smiling through the exhaustion. "I'd never even heard of the drug you gave Dan," she said, "but, boy, it works like nothing Zoe's ever had before. It's like a miracle worker, and we don't even have it listed in our Corsys pharmacy system at my store. I checked this morning."

Jake looked away. "It's brand-new, just out of trial stage."

"Yeah," Carrie said without missing a beat. "We're lucky they knew about it at *your* pharmacy."

"I wouldn't even have considered giving it to Zoe if they'd had the corticoid," Jake returned cagily. "You know with these experimental drugs there's always a risk."

"Which is why they're giving it to people in Manhattan first. There's no need to lie to me, Jake." Carrie looked at him with that cut-the-bullshit expression of hers that he had first encountered at the age of twelve, when she was barely nine.

"No," he agreed, defeated, "there isn't. I'm glad Zoe is doing so much better."

"Anyway, I'm calling because we're going to celebrate her first T-ball game with a barbecue down at the park this weekend. Will you come? It would mean so much to her."

"A barbeque?"

"I know what you're thinking," Carrie spilled out, "and I know I shouldn't have let her play that day. But she's doing so much better, and we've got these magic new pills, thanks to you, and Zoe's talking about nothing else but inviting her girlfriends. She was cooped up inside for the first six years of her life, and now she wants to go out and play. She needs a life, you know?" A steep crease had edged itself into Carrie's forehead, telling Jake to back off.

"Alright," he said, "but I'm honestly not sure I can make it." Part of him felt the need to explain why, but he knew it would be useless. Carrie made a point of never watching the news because it was all bad anyway, and her relationship to SAFE was defined by cognitive dissonance. She blamed it whenever the meds ran out at her pharmacy and yet took personal offense when he worked through the weekends instead of spending time with them. "I will try, Carrie, okay?" he said. "I want to, and I know it's important."

"Important to her, Jake. And she's only seven. You're family."

He sighed, knowing that, unless the sky fell over the next two days, he would somehow have to show up at that barbeque on Saturday. Carrie was like a sister to him and the most formative presence in his life since he'd lost his immediate family as a kid and moved to Queens to live with his aunt, a disorganized and unstable woman who had never been on good terms with his mother. His uncle had already been dead at the time, one of many lives snatched by the Second Pandemic, but his aunt had taken him in—and with him, his parents' life insurance. She'd spent the better part of that money on drugs: painkillers at first, muscle relaxers and benzos, and later the less legal stuff. By the time he was sixteen, his aunt was an opioid addict, and by the time Carrie graduated from high school, his aunt was in a digital care program that wasn't working. She'd lived just long enough to hold her grandchild, but Carrie still hadn't forgiven her mother for not having been strong or caring enough to see Zoe grow up.

Before they hung up, Carrie extracted a promise from him, and he hoped by the weekend he'd be able to honor it. Now, he needed sleep. Taking sleepers at this hour was a bad idea, so he lay down in bed and positioned his cheek over the induction field to charge his Spine before closing his eyes and wrapping himself in the cool stream from the aircon unit.

Shavir's call arrived while he was out. "Hey Jake," said her recorded voice when he checked his messages five hours later. "So how about this—" he could hear her hesitation, "you said you wanted to see the farm, and we'll all be up here this weekend, when it's supposed to be a little cooler, harvesting as much as we can before the crops start rotting on the plants. Would you like to come and help?" There was a pause. "Alright, I gotta go back to work. Let me know, okay? I hope you're feeling better when you hear this, and that you guys were able to... I don't know... get things."

He could hear her breathe, but she didn't say anything else. There was an electronic clicking sound followed by the Spine's voice asking him whether he wanted to delete or save.

"Save," he said, closing his eyes again. The rooftop farm. If the rest of the world allowed for it, he'd get some outdoor action this weekend.

Against the forecasts, Saturday promised to be even hotter than previous days, so Jake was almost grateful for the lengthy subway ride to Queens where Carrie and Dan rented a two-bedroom in a run-down apartment building in North Corona. He rarely used the city's crumbling subway system since his work rarely required or allowed him to leave Manhattan, but whenever he did, he felt like he was time-traveling back to the days when people were living lives of mindless plenitude and it all must have seemed to make sense. The subway was one of the few vestiges of twentieth-century transportation in New York, not only because it was almost one hundred and fifty years old, but because few changes had been made to it since the late 2030s when a floodgate system had been installed to protect it from the rising rivers.

He spent the entire uncomfortable ride binge-watching reports from Hong Kong and talking to Masao, who had taken over for him for the rest of the afternoon, allowing him to give in to Carrie's demands and hopefully honor Shavir's invitation. Over ten thousand people were now believed to be dead in the wake of the typhoon, and thousands more were expected to die if they couldn't contain the resulting epidemics. But the casualties were no more than a side note. The real concern was that the region's infrastructure, which affected US supply chains, would not be operational for weeks.

It was all bad news for the CSR.

Jake was drenched in sweat by the time he got off at Junction Boulevard Station. He passed two Frontline patrols before he'd left the platform and two more in the hot crowded streets on his way to Carrie's apartment. Once he got there, he had to take the steps to the fifth floor because the elevators were broken.

Carrie looked unhappy when she opened the door. "Sorry about the stairs. I've called maintenance at least ten times, but they couldn't care less. You want something to—"

Zoe darted across the room into Jake's arms, her high-pitched cry filling up the cluttered space of the apartment. The girl's face was lit up with joy when he put her down, and she immediately started recounting her T-ball game for him until Carrie told her to get her things. She truly was her mother's daughter, Jake thought, animated by the same boundless energy Carrie had had at that age, as long as she was able to breathe.

"She really seems to be doing well with the new medication," he said to Carrie when they were alone. "I wanted to bring along more, but they insisted on a prescription."

"Where can we get that? Do I take her to her normal doctor?"

"Let me handle it." Jake didn't want to think about what Zoe's pediatrician in Queens would say, given that it hadn't been possible for him to convince *his* guy at *his* pharmacy in Manhattan to give him that stuff a second time. His guy had only offered a weary smile when Jake had asked him again about the corticoid.

"So what's up with these elevators?" he asked to steer their conversation into less treacherous waters.

"It's a joke, really," Carrie snorted. "This is a six-story building, and they don't give a shit about the fact that we need to get up and down. Apparently, they think we can fly."

He glanced at his cousin, who clearly had made an effort to look nice, her face carefully made up, her blue summer dress accentuating the color of her eyes. But despite that and Carrie's bubbly nature, an air of sorrow pervaded every corner of her cramped apartment. Whenever he was in it, he felt like opening a window to let in some air.

"We've been down to one elevator for a while," she said, "but now the last one's broken. Some people can't even leave their apartments anymore. We've been taking care of Ms. Dryer across the hall because she's too frail and old to make it down and up again. Another week, and we'll start building cable winches like the people across the street."

Jake strained to see what Carrie was pointing to: an array of cords and containers along the facade of the opposite building that connected the windows on the upper floors to the ground level. "Can't you move out?" he asked, knowing he was repeating himself.

"This place is good value, actually. At least it's far enough from the river and the coast that we don't get much of the flooding."

Jake nodded, resigned. He knew they couldn't afford anything better in Queens although Dan regularly put in overtime at Frontline and Carrie worked part-time at the drugstore. He'd tried to convince them to move away, but Dan hadn't wanted to hear it.

As always, Carrie talked nonstop.

It was a strategy she had developed as a child to cheer up her depressed mother and then Jake once he'd moved in, bringing his own trauma with him. The only thing he had wanted to do back then, just a few weeks after the hurricane, was lie down somewhere and die, but Carrie wouldn't let him. At age nine, she'd been the sweetest, kindest, and most annoying thing he'd ever met. She saved his life with her never-ending presence, with that peculiar mix of neediness and devotion that made it impossible not to like her or to ever get rid of her. And once it became clear that his aunt wasn't, couldn't be responsible for them anymore, Jake took over as Carrie's big brother with what was left of himself and the insurance money. It had seemed only natural to him; he was to blame for the loss of one family, and now he had the chance to save another. In hindsight, he saw his capacities as savior had been limited, as his aunt hadn't even made it to her fiftieth birthday. But at least Carrie had pulled through, and if that was something he'd helped accomplish, he was glad he'd stayed alive.

She was still talking and had moved on to the pharmacy and patients who came in every week, some every day, in the hope that the store was restocked with whatever they needed. She seemed to know each of them by name and ailment, giving him details about their medical histories and their specific unfulfilled needs.

Carrie was blond, blue-eyed, and fairly tall, but other than that she defied every stereotype Jake had ever heard about their shared German ancestry. Not only was she loquacious and overflowing with emotion, but she had a chaotic streak and was notoriously bad at planning. When Dan called from downstairs and Zoe stood ready to go, it took Carrie half an hour to assemble all the things she wanted to take along to the barbecue, then she turned around on the stairs to get more.

Dan bore the ordeal stoically as usual. When Jake pushed open the downstairs door, overstuffed bags dangling on all sides, Dan greeted him with a smile and helped haul everything into the trunk of the waiting cab. Outside of Manhattan, traffic was still dominated by cars and buses, practically all of them electrified. But cabs were an unusually comfortable means of transportation. This one was spacious enough for them to pick up three of Zoe's cousins, and the exhilarated girls were jumping in their seats by the time they reached the park entrance. They walked into the scarred wasteland behind it, invaded by dozens of families like theirs who, for some inexplicable reason, had picked a day nearing 110 degrees for their lunchtime barbecues.

Dan was sweating profusely while he unpacked the cooler.

"So," he said, handing Jake a can of beer, "what do you say about our little hurricane?"

Jake watched Zoe running around with the other girls. "It's great to see her like this."

"It is." Dan nodded. "I just don't know where all that energy's coming from. Used to be such a quiet little angel. Always sitting on the couch, watching stuff on the pad. Then you give her those fancy meds, and it's like she wants to make up for all she's missed. I just can't keep up with that, man." He rolled his eyes in feigned desperation.

He was trying to sound comical, but there was truth to Dan's despair. He'd kept in shape with a grueling exercise routine when it had been expected of him during his time in the army. Zoe's birth had changed his perspective on life, and so he'd quit his job after his overseas assignments had gotten ever more brutal. Carrie had cried with relief the day she'd told Jake her husband was finally coming home. He'd been accepted into the VA's on-the-job training program and then hired by Frontline after the Crisis. Dan had hinted that, emotionally, that job had turned out to be just as challenging as his overseas tours, but it didn't seem to be as demanding physically.

"Zoe might actually do you some good." Jake glanced mockingly at his friend's bulging stomach. "How do you even manage to run after the bad guys?"

"We don't run, Jake, we shoot," Dan said with a crooked grin. "I thought you knew that."

"Would be so much better to start running instead."

Dan took a sip from his beer. "I'll think about it. But first I gotta make some burgers." He pulled a package of art-meat patties out of the cooler and walked to the grill.

"That stuff's gonna kill you for sure," Jake called after him.

Dan shrugged. "Sure as hell is better than eating pooches. It gets worse every day. Last week, me and Gary busted two girls with four of them big dogs. Mastiffs. Fed us some bullshit story about them being service dogs. That was their story until the smaller one lost it because we were gonna take away her pup. She was so tiny, that girl, but wild, man, and then Gary lost it, too." He looked at Jake. "Told you about that, didn't I?"

"You only said he almost shot a girl."

"Yeah, he almost did. Fucking lunatic."

"You think they stole the dogs?"

Dan shrugged. "They were all paid up and registered. But God knows where they got them from. Folks are raising and butchering them right here in the city."

"I've seen it on the Spine. Over in Brooklyn."

"Over here, too. We got tipped off a few times. Dogs all gone by the time we got there, but you wouldn't believe the whole setup they had going. If you'd seen those hellholes, you'd know why I'm sticking with our good old art-meat." Dan slabbed the first patty onto the grill. "One hundred percent lab grown and safe for human consumption. Says the fucking FDA."

Jake didn't object. He'd explained to Dan before that the New York FDA played by its own rules and that "safe for human consumption" didn't mean it was a good idea to eat it; it meant it was considered a viable option for survival. But Dan liked the idea of adhering to regulations and respecting authorities, and he was idiosyncratic in his beliefs, as evidenced by his choice to get the grill going when temperatures were nearly high enough to cook the meat on the street.

To get away from the smoke and smell, Jake watched the girls play while checking on Hong Kong and getting updates from Masao. It was an unusual day for him, away from the CSR and in the company of people who constantly demanded his attention, showering him with their own. And now he was supposed to meet Shavir at the farm, which was even more outside his comfort zone. He seriously considered going back to SAFE and asking Shavir to meet him later, in Manhattan, alone. But he helped Carrie set the table instead.

It was almost three when Jake reached the address Shavir had given him, a former office building not far from the river. An elegant e-van was parked next to it, on its side door a design of stylized trees below a set of fanned-out triangles. The vehicle stood in stark contrast to the derelict building, whose foundations were covered with fungi and brownish algae, filling the air with the scent of rot. There was no sign to indicate the farm, and the door was locked.

He wanted to text Shavir when a woman he hadn't noticed before shut the side door of the van and walked toward him with a slight limp, cursing under her breath. She was wearing work clothes and a broad-rimmed hat that was tilted to the back of her head, revealing a dark weathered face of uncertain age. She stopped when she saw him.

"Can I help you?"

"Uhm, perhaps. I'm looking for Shavir?"

The woman nodded, squinting into the sun. "They've all gone over to Prince Gardens for lunch." She rubbed her knee, scrutinizing him. "You a friend of Shavir?"

"I am, Jake Alvaro. Prince Gardens—where exactly is that?"

"Up to the roof and then three buildings over." The woman was smiling now. "Name's Judy. If you give me a minute, I'll walk you over. Just need a bandage for my knee."

She unlocked the door, gesturing for him to follow. They slowly walked up one floor since the elevator was broken, and then through another door on the landing. The space inside was enormous, divided into dozens of cubicles, their walls barely higher than he was.

The air was hot and stuffy.

He looked at Judy. "What is this?"

"It's where most of us live."

"Us—is that the Roots people?"

"Roots is all kinds of people," Judy grumbled. "Rich people. Crazy people. And poor people, like us. The people in the West Street Project. We built all this ourselves. The farm, too." She unlocked the padlock of one of the cubicles. "I'll only be a minute."

Jake wanted to look inside, but that would have been intrusive, so his gaze wandered along the opposite row of cubicles instead, all locked like Judy's. "What are the locks for if they have no ceilings?"

"There's a grille on top," Judy said. "See?" She pointed upward, and he walked over to look inside.

The space was tiny: a bed, a chair, a desk, an overstuffed shelf, and an overburdened clothes rail. There was indeed a grille, one that would have brushed his hair had he walked in.

"It does have a lot of light," he suggested, pointing to the window.

Judy chuckled. "Them big windows are a problem in the summer and in the winter. The aircon's broken, so it's either too hot or too freakin' cold in here."

"It'll get a lot hotter before it gets colder again."

"Yeah," she said. "Tell me something I don't know already."

They walked back out and up to the roof, the glaring sunlight stabbing Jake's eyes as Judy opened the door. The roof was covered from end to end with crops, sheltered from the sun by shading nets and from the wind by hedges along the parapet. At the western edge, plants seemed to melt into the green facades of Manhattan on the other side of the East River. Jake looked around and realized there were crops on the roofs of the neighboring buildings as well, all connected by wooden bridges. "You built those, too?" he asked, pointing.

"Sure, we did. And had to replace two of them this year already. Fucking storms ain't got nothing better to do but rip them apart."

They stepped onto the bridge and crossed over to the roof of the next building, then to another one of about the same size. There were crops everywhere, a few people working between the rows.

The next building was taller and older, the roof-bridge connected to an opening on the fourth floor. They walked up the staircase until they reached the top and out into what he assumed was Prince Gardens: a shockingly lush space full of bamboo, bushes, fruit trees, and what looked like thousands of flowers, much of it overarched by an enormous fanned-out tent roof that filtered the glistening light of the afternoon sun through overlapping triangles of green cloth. Several dozen people were seated in its shade around long tables, eating a late lunch. The air hummed with their conversations.

"It's quite something, ain't it?" Judy said with pride. "Welcome to our little oasis."

Jake scanned the faces at the tables, but Shavir had already seen him. She looked different as she walked toward him, more rural, wearing a long-sleeved button-down shirt and sunglasses, a broad-brimmed straw hat dangling from her neck, a pair of work gloves sticking out of her jeans pocket.

Everything inside him contracted.

"Jake." Shavir pushed up her sunglasses. "Glad you found your way over here. I meant to meet you at the farm."

It sounded oddly formal. At her table, heads were turning.

"Judy was my guide."

Shavir smiled. "Yeah, she's like that." She turned, her gaze brushing the faces at the table before she nodded to Judy then looked back to Jake. "Are you hungry?"

"Not really, no. I had to go to my cousin's barbecue."

"Well, come on then." Shavir looked relieved as she led him away from the tables and toward the staircase. "I'll show you around."

They hadn't reached the first landing when heavy galloping announced Sam. A second later, the dog was next to them.

They walked back across the bridges to the first building, Sam's claws clicking on the wood as he trailed after them. It was a familiar sound to Jake, who found himself once again transported back across decades to the same clicking, the same rhythm. But Farley would never have walked across these bridges, four stories above ground. He'd have stopped on the landing, swayed side to side, spun around, then barked his demand that Jake come back. It was usually Farley who decided where they were going.

Sam didn't seem to mind the bridges; he trotted right across.

"He's done it since he was a puppy," Shavir said. "He doesn't mind anything here and can walk, eat, and sleep absolutely everywhere. He's a real farm dog." She smiled and looked more relaxed as she led Jake through vegetable patches covered with leaves in all shades of green, overarched by the netting. If it hadn't been for Manhattan's skyline across the river, it would have felt like being in an open field in the countryside somewhere in upstate New York.

"How do you water all of this?"

"Well, we can't use tap water unless we want to contaminate it all, but we got pretty good rainwater retention systems." Shavir pointed to three large reservoirs on the western edge of the roof. "Everything up here is a problem," she added, "the water, the heat, the wind, and the cold. It's really stupid to be doing this under the real sun with real soil, not indoors like they're doing it in Manhattan. We're the dinosaurs of agriculture." She said this with conviction, but in her eyes was the same pride he'd seen earlier in Judy's.

"I think it's fantastic."

"How about some harvesting then?" Shavir pointed to a patch of shiny eggplants. "I need to cut the rest of these. Remove your gloves because you're gonna get dirty. Is your hand okay to do this?"

He peeled off his gloves and showed her his palm, a pink line all that was left of the nasty cut. She held up her healed arm and laughed. Then she took a knife and showed him how to cut the stems before putting the eggplants into crates they'd later carry to the main aisle.

Jake smiled. "Can do. I specialize in logistics."

Shavir picked up a hat from a nearby cart and gave it to him.

"Better wear this."

He eyed the hat skeptically. "I don't usually get sunstrokes."

"You don't usually work on rooftops during a heat wave," she said as she reached down her back for her own hat. "You don't want your Spine to melt into your jawbone."

He took the hat and put it on. "How do I look?"

"Like an unhappy peasant who specializes in logistics."

He bent down to the first eggplant and tried to cut it with the knife she'd given him, ashamed of his clumsiness at such a simple task. Shavir watched him, making it worse.

"Wait a sec." She reached for his hand, her touch an electric current. "Relax." Her voice was soft as she immersed both of their hands into the warm, humid topsoil. "Feel that." She smiled at his expression. "That's life."

Judging from his heartbeat, she was quite right about that, and it took all his self-restraint to keep himself from kissing her and instead do as she demanded and move his fingers against the soft resistance of the soil. "I probably wasn't born to be a farmer."

"None of us is." She let go of him. "But everyone needs to feel that once to understand where our food comes from, what we depend on for our very lives. It changed everything for me and for so many others who work here."

Jake was quite sure it wouldn't be the same for him. But he quickly developed a system that, to Shavir's surprise, allowed them to cut their trips to the central aisle in half. He found it fascinating, from a supply chain angle, what they were doing here. Local food was nothing new, nor was urban farming. But the farms in Brooklyn had all been destroyed over the years, abandoned and given up to the elements. It amazed him that they managed to keep doing this, even with the reservoirs and shading nets and solar pads and all the other things that suggested this wasn't a dinosaur but a much better adapted farm species. Like Prince Gardens, it was the result of serious planning and investment, suggesting Judy had meant it when she'd said Roots was "all kinds of people," including rich ones. This flew in the face of Shavir's claims about the neglected state of Brooklyn, but when he asked her, she told him about the West Street Project instead.

"I understand it's better than the street," he said as they were dropping off crates at the central aisle, "but I don't think I could live like that with no privacy and all the other people in there."

"It's not that bad." Shavir laughed. "Well, right now it is, because we don't have aircon, but it's a clean and safe space to spend the night."

"You *live* there?" Jake stopped walking.

She heaved her crate onto the packing table. "Many of us do. Nacho here, too."

The guy who was assembling the deliveries looked up, nodding in confirmation. He was thirtyish, his face under the red bandana burnt to a leathery brown. "We only got one open," he said, eyes hidden behind large sun glasses. "It's one of the smaller ones, but it's got decent light, and you're close to the showers. Rent's free, but—"

"Oh, no," Shavir cut in, looking flustered. "Jake's got his own place in Manhattan."

"Oh," Nacho said. "Like Finn."

"No," Shavir said sharply. "He's only visiting."

Nacho grimaced an apology. "Sorry, man," he said to Jake, grinning. "Well, you can always come back when you need it."

Shavir made a face like that wasn't funny, but Nacho only shrugged and returned his attention to the delivery boxes.

"Sorry about that," Shavir said when they were walking back to their eggplants. She looked rattled.

"No worries. Who's Finn?"

"One of our sponsors. Nacho manages our cubicles, and sometimes he's a little too eager to make sure we're at full capacity. I'm sorry he thought you were homeless."

"I guess I am, in certain ways. Were you when you came here?"

"No, but it's a good arrangement. I spend almost all I have on Sam."

Jake glanced over at Sam, who was snoring in the shade. So that was how she could afford him. "Does he even fit in there with you?"

"There's room for both of us, but we don't get a lot of visitors."

He considered her and Sam in that tiny cubicle. What a sacrifice, to live like that just to be able to keep a dog. The memory of Farley crept up on him again, but he choked it down.

"Do you leave him here when you work at Soma?"

"No. Judy doesn't like it when Sam's here without me." Shavir picked up their knives and put them back on the table. "He used to stay at my ex's," she said, still looking distraught. "But that's become... difficult. I'm looking for a new place for him right now."

Jake let that sink in.

"I think we've done enough here." Shavir took off her gloves. "For a first-timer, you're fast as lightning. Are you getting hungry?"

He wanted to ask her what "difficult" meant. And he wanted to tell her that he never got hungry. But he did feel drained, partly because he had worked so fast to avoid looking like a loser. She may have been impressed with his performance, but he was now debating whether he could make it through dinner without an extra dose of pep pills.

"We usually have a big cookout over at the garden on Saturdays," Shavir said. "We could eat dinner there, or we could walk some place where we have a little more privacy. It's not Manhattan, but there are some nice pop-ups over on Grand."

Privacy sounded great, but it was a twenty-minute walk, and he'd be lucky if he could make it back across the bridges. He opted for the cookout. After all, the point of this was to learn about the part of Shavir he didn't know yet. So far, it had been very instructive.

When they crossed the final bridge to Prince Gardens, Jake was so wiped he could barely stand. Shavir looked at him in a way that told him it was very obvious, then she suggested he relax a bit in the garden while she helped with the cooking. He was grateful since he had no idea how his system would react to an overheated kitchen or how much longer he could go without checking his Spine.

He had forced himself to keep it on standby the whole time they'd worked, and no emergency calls had come through from Masao or David. But now he needed to know. He sat down on one of the benches that lined the parapet and checked Masao's debrief messages, relieved to find nothing dramatic. Then he called David.

"Still nothing moving in Hong Kong," David growled, out of breath and apparently walking. "And still out of luck with most of the antibiotics. We're already getting heat from the hospitals in Queens because they're forced to delay surgeries. But I ain't no fucking magician, and I gotta get some sleep tonight, or I'll be the one who's dead."

David had finally left the CSR, Jake noted with relief. Two more days, and he would have beaten his own record set during the Crisis.

"Where are you?" David asked. "Are those *plants* behind you?"

Jake looked around and grinned. "Yeah, it's a garden, actually."

"A garden," David echoed. "And what are you doing there?"

"I should help with the cooking, I guess."

"You mean, like, *food*?"

"Yeah, like food." Jake laughed.

"Then maybe eat something for a change, but don't get wasted, okay? I need to talk to you in the morning. There's a chance we'll be running low on Emovia." David sounded casual, but if his tone was meant to derail Jake's suspicions, it didn't.

"How can we run low on Emovia? We get it from New Jersey."

"The problem is the capsule," David said, the underlying tension in his voice obvious. "The company producing it, Ziser, submitted two brands of capsules when they sought FDA approval. In accordance with regulations, one of them was produced domestically, in Oregon, and that place was wiped out by the fires last month. The other one used to be made at a plant north of Hong Kong. The rest you know."

It took Jake a moment to digest this. Half the city relied on Emovia to manage feelings they didn't want to have and couldn't deal with. He had no desire to find out what would happen if people could no longer do that. There were other drugs, but none as effective or affordable.

"So what do we do now?"

"Wait for Monday, so we can talk to the FDA about speed-approving another capsule. We called Kruger, but he insists Ziser go through the regular channels on a regular weekday."

The current head of the New York Food and Drug Administration was being his usual asshole-self, no surprise there.

"How bad is this going to be, David?"

"I have no idea. I gotta get some sleep now, or it'll be the end of me. I'll give you a call tomorrow morning, so don't get wasted, alright?"

"I heard you the first time. Go get your sleep."

Jake resisted the urge to take pills as he tried to think through what this latest piece of bad news would mean for the CSR. They didn't officially manage Emovia because it wasn't officially critical supply. But this would be their problem, for sure. He sent an encrypted message to Masao to get another set of brain cells working on it and got up.

Only then did he notice he wasn't alone on the roof.

It was always a risk, discussing sensitive data on the Spine. It was so immersive you forget the people around could hear you, but now he realized there was no danger since the other guy was himself on the Spine. It was the first Spine he'd seen on the farm, recognizable by the way the man was talking to the air. He was dressed in a slim dark shirt and spoke in a cool, business-like tone that could be heard on any corner of SoHo but seemed out of place here. Jake walked past the man, who noticed him and made eye contact, assessing him, before turning his back, still talking. Jake walked toward the staircase and followed the noise downstairs to the kitchen.

The room was stuffed with people and heaps of vegetables. He leaned against the wall opposite the big stove to watch the synchronized activity that, perversely, reminded him of the CSR. A Black guy in his fifties seemed to be conducting the steaming symphony of cutting and grating and bubbling and sizzling that, if anything, was the exact opposite of the cold aseptic air in the CSR. Jake recognized the man from the Spine feature about the farm. He'd been fervent then, talking into the camera with a voice oscillating between disdain and exaltation, depending on whether he was talking about the failures of the city's food system or Roots's efforts to counteract them. Now he stood next to Shavir at the stove, talking and tasting whatever was simmering in the pots in front of them. On Shavir's other side stood the energetic South Asian girl who'd been sitting at her table when Jake had first arrived; he recognized her by her slight stature and the grotesquely large bandage across her forehead.

He had never seen Shavir so at ease. At Soma, there was always restraint on her face when she interacted with customers, an invisible wall between her smile and the world. Here, there was none of that thinly veiled mockery Hector complained about sometimes. He'd always thought Roots was a second job Shavir needed to make ends meet. Now he realized she was at home in this kitchen, with these people, on these roofs.

The bandaged girl noticed him and poked Shavir.

She turned, and his adrenaline spiked as he tried to read her expression and failed. Bandage girl said something to her and giggled.

Shavir crossed the room. "Feeling better?"

He nodded and wished he'd taken some pills.

To his surprise, Jake found he was ravenous when the food was finally done, loading his plate with a selection of the delicious-looking salads, soups, and stews. They sat at the big wooden tables underneath the green awning, illuminated by lanterns equipped with LED lights.

If he had been hoping for some semi-privacy with Shavir, he wasn't getting it. Instead, he found himself in the midst of at least fifty people and sandwiched between her and the man from the Spine feature, who introduced himself as Lenny. Across from him sat bandage girl, Tara, who talked a lot and studied him like a lab rat, ignoring the beseeching looks she got from Shavir.

"You do this every Saturday?" he asked Lenny to get away from Tara's scrutiny.

"We aren't always this many," Lenny said, pausing his fork in midair, "but, yes, there's always dinner available up here for those who need it on a Saturday night."

"That's pretty cool."

Now he had Lenny's full attention. "You think so?"

Jake nodded. "And it sure is a first for me to eat eggplants I've harvested myself. I like what you made with them." Remarkably, this was true. He really did enjoy the food.

"Well, thanks for helping us with the harvest. The problem is we can't eat everything we're picking right now or sell and give it away quickly enough."

"They've got the same problems upstate and in the Midwest," Jake said then realized he shouldn't have when not only Lenny, but Tara, too, looked at him with new interest.

"What do you do?" asked Lenny.

It was one of those situations Jake hated, and he'd just brought it upon himself. From what he'd seen in the feature, he wasn't exactly among friends here.

"I work at SAFE," he said.

There was something like a collective inhale around him, and he remembered what Shavir had said to him that night at Soma—they belonged to different universes. He had a feeling he was about to be fully introduced to hers, and though he would have preferred to have been in somewhat better combat condition, he again opted for the truth. "I mostly do meds and medical equipment," he explained. "And some tech or food stuff, if it's sensitive."

The table was quiet.

"So you're part of the system that's fucking us," Lenny finally said.

"Relax, Lenny." Shavir's face was tense.

Lenny looked at her then back at Jake. "I'm sorry, since after all, you're here, which must be a first for anyone at that place. That takes some guts. But this whole scheme you guys have going over there at SAFE is just so fucked up, treating people here like we're disposable. Trash. I'd like you to acknowledge that." He got up. "Think about it, man. I need another bowl of this soup."

The eyes of the rest of the table were on Jake, including a pair of bright blue ones that belonged to the Spine man he'd noticed earlier, a good-looking guy about his own age who was scrutinizing him with unbridled hostility.

"I'm sorry," Shavir said. "Lenny can be a little intense."

The others laughed, and so did Jake, wondering whether he should have seen this coming. People started talking to each other again, giving him a break, but Lenny was going to come back at some point, and he couldn't plunge into a debate about SAFE's assorted failures and betrayals. Not in this state.

"Look," he said to Shavir, "it's not that I'm not enjoying this. I'm just so damn tired that I hardly know my name. I guess I'm not used to the hardships of farming."

She smiled. "You better go home and get some sleep then."

That was not at all what he wanted, but his strained eyes were watering, and he'd probably fall off his chair unless he took more pills. Together with the alcohol, they'd push him over the edge in a bad way, and he'd like to be able to come back here.

Shavir looked down at Sam, who had wrapped himself around her feet. "Here's a thought. You've probably had enough of Roots for tonight, and I need to take Sam for a walk. Is it okay if we walk you to the subway station?"

All Jake could do was nod, overwhelmed by relief and excitement.

Downstairs, the air was much hotter than it had been on the roof, the scent of rot more intense now. The e-van was still parked in front of the building. Jake was about to ask Shavir about it when the door to the staircase, barely closed, flew open again.

"Hey, Shav!" a voice called from behind them. It was the Spine guy, who walked toward Shavir, his right hand lifted. "You forgot this."

In the low glow of a distant streetlight, Jake recognized a phone. Its display lit when Shavir took it. She said thanks but looked mortified.

"She always forgets her phone," the man said lightly. "She actually does it on purpose, so she can't be reached. She's a very difficult woman to reach. But I guess you'll find that out."

"Jake, meet my *ex*, Finn," Shavir said, facing the man, daring him.

The scorn on Finn's face congealed into a curt nod.

He turned and walked to the van, his blond hair glowing as the light flicked on inside the cabin. Seconds later, he drove past them, his taillights leaving an angry red glow.

"I'm sorry." Shavir said. "He enjoys being an asshole."

"I noticed."

"I didn't know he'd be here today, otherwise I wouldn't have asked you to come. He hasn't been around much recently, but I guess Lenny asked because of the harvest."

Jake nodded though he had no idea what to do with the information. Clearly, his presence had rattled the guy. He remembered again Judy telling him that Roots was all kinds of people, including rich ones, and it dawned on him that he'd just met one of them.

What he couldn't fathom was Shavir and this guy being an item. That went against every idea of who he thought she was, including her theory about incompatible ends of the universe. The van's license plate had been from Manhattan, and he also remembered what that other guy, Nacho, had said, and what Shavir had answered: Finn was a sponsor. The logo on the side of the van had been an abstraction of the sophisticated tent roof overarching Prince Gardens.

He had a million questions, but it was clear Shavir didn't want to say another word. He followed her and Sam silently along the narrow path that led down to the boardwalk.

They heard voices before they saw the crowds that populated the shore. After another scorching day, half of Brooklyn was out and about in the darkness, taking advantage of the breeze along the East River. Not a single functioning streetlight had survived along the pathetic sheet-piling structure, so people carried their own LEDs. Some had brought food and music.

It was a bizarre and beautiful sight, melted into a glimmering vista of water and light by Jake's tearing eyes. "Wow," he said, grateful for the diversion. "It's like a giant party."

"Yeah, it gets pretty crazy down here when the days are hot like this."

They turned left toward Williamsburg and navigated their way through the masses. Only a few other dogs were around, making Sam a point of attraction. A little girl came running toward them, torn loose from her parents. A second later, she had her skinny arms flung around Sam's massive neck. The parents seemed remarkably relaxed.

"People around here know him," Shavir explained.

"My niece would do exactly the same. She loves dogs."

"Then you should bring her someday."

Jake nodded, imagining Zoe running around with Sam, who was now down on his front legs, tail wagging, making husky sounds instead of barking, a gross mismatch to his size.

"They cut his vocal cords when he was a puppy," Shavir said when she saw Jake's puzzled face. "It's pretty common practice to avoid complaints from neighbors."

"That's fucked up."

"Harmless compared to all the other shit they do. You said you had a dog, too, when you were a kid?"

"Farley." It was the first time in years he'd said that name out loud, and he could feel himself tensing up when he did, but he kept talking. "I used to do stuff like this with him." He nodded toward Sam and the girl. "He died with my family in the storm. My mom, my dad, and my baby brother. I'm the only one who survived."

Shavir stopped walking.

"It's alright," he said when he saw her face. "Just one of those stories everyone has. Let's not talk about it, okay? Let's walk."

He started moving again, unsure why he'd said that. Some part of him had wanted her to know because what he'd learned from her file about her mother suggested she had lived through her own trauma. They were so much more alike than she thought.

It took them nearly half an hour to cover the distance to the station, strolling side by side, talking about easier things like Zoe's love for dogs, Carrie's love for Zoe, and Lenny, who had lost tenure for yelling at his students that it was their goddamn civic duty to revolt against a system that was destroying them. Shavir laughed a lot as she recounted their early attempts at rooftop farming, and their bare arms touched whenever they rearranged their bodies to give way to oncoming people, every contact sending ripples along his nerves.

The entrance to Bedford Station emerged out of nowhere, meaning goodbye for the night. The street was much quieter at this hour, the streetlights dead or dimmed in accordance with the city's energy-saving regulations, a few people eating dinner on improvised outdoor seating near the hawker stalls. It was eerily peaceful after the madness of the boardwalk.

Jake stopped a few feet away from the entrance to the subway.

"Thanks for the day."

"I bet it wasn't what you expected."

"No." He smiled. "But I'm glad you invited me. It's great what you're doing over here. Important."

"I wanted you to see it," she said softly. "So you understand."

He wanted to say he did, but his chest had tightened.

"What are we gonna do about your eyes?" Shavir asked as she touched his face to remove a tear with her fingertip.

He hesitated another instant. Then he kissed her.

She didn't withdraw. Instead, she answered his kiss as he pulled her close, her hands on his ribcage. The world rushed away from him until he opened his eyes again and noticed Sam eying them, tail wagging.

"Your dog's a little confused, I think."

Shavir glanced down and laughed. "Poor Sam." She petted the dog's head without letting go of him. "You're gonna miss the last train to Manhattan. They no longer run all night."

"Do you wanna come with me?" Jake said. Just said it.

"To Manhattan?" She moved back a little so she could see his eyes, amusement sparkling in hers. "That's bold."

"I'm not even suggesting anything indecent." He kissed her again, feeling bolder now than he had thirty seconds ago. "I just don't want this to end, and it'll be more comfortable for you than sleeping in those cubicles. I'll probably pass out on the couch."

Shavir smiled. "Next to Lucy."

"Yes. Next to Lucy. She knows how to take me when I'm like that."

"I bet she does, your non-pet."

He checked the time. "We've got about three more minutes. Either you come with me, or I'll stay here and sleep on one of those benches along the boardwalk, probably get robbed."

"There's a free cubicle at the West Street Project."

"God, no! Come with me," he said between kisses. "I've got water... and coffee... and air conditioning."

At that, he felt her body contract in his arms, like she'd been struck.

"What's wrong?" he asked, startled.

"Okay," she said, freeing herself from his arms.

"Okay?"

"Yes." She was already turning toward the station entrance. "If Sam can come along."

"Of course he can. We'll lock Lucy in her terrarium."

"Let's go then," she called as she ran down the stairs.

A rattling in the belly of the city announced the approaching train.

NINE

A PUNGENT SMELL OF corroding metal and human sweat filled the old subway car. Together with the stored-up heat and the lack of oxygen, it was overwhelming. Shavir caught her breath as she dove in and sat down next to the door. She noticed the usual stares as Sam plopped down on the floor next to her. There had been times when stares had bothered her but not anymore.

What did bother her was whether the two Frontline men who had noticed them on the street would walk by the open door. She had placed herself strategically in the hope that they wouldn't see her and Sam. She felt certain that the cops had followed them into the station and knew from experience that they were walking alongside the train, so she waited for the doors to close, telling herself she was being unreasonable. There had been no problems with Sam's chip, plus Jake was with them. But she couldn't shake the memory of Tara's bloody face against that subway wall, the gun pointed at her and Max, and she had no idea what would happen if Jake witnessed one of those checks.

Her muscles relaxed when the doors slid shut and the train rattled into the the tunnel, the cops no more than an afterthought.

Jake looked at her across the aisle, all playful excitement drained from his face. "Do you have to be at Soma tomorrow morning?"

Only now did she realize how strange it must seem that she hadn't sat down next to him. They'd been kissing just minutes ago.

She shook her head. "We aren't done with the harvest, and Soma doesn't get much business on Sunday mornings. Just a few caffeine junkies who don't have anything better to do."

"Like me."

"Yes," she smiled. "Like you."

She moved across the aisle to join him. Sam followed her, prompting two older men wearing matching shirts and facial expressions to get up and find seats at the other end of the car.

"I actually do have coffee at home," Jake said. "Almond milk, too."

"Are you trying to hire yourself a barista?" she teased, wondering whether he had noticed the cops and that she'd been running away from them. Fuck Frontline for making her panic.

"I'm capable of making coffee myself. You'll be impressed."

"Water's fine."

Jake went quiet, and she realized she'd been brusque as she was trying to come to terms with the fact that they were headed to his apartment. It wasn't the first time she was going home with someone she didn't know very well. But Jake wasn't like Finn or any of the other men she'd known before him. She had no idea if he was really planning to sleep on the couch, but what she did know was she was supposed to be on the boardwalk right now, on her way home.

When she had invited Jake to visit Roots, she'd known that she was inviting trouble. Yet she'd needed him to see the farm, some kind of litmus test he had passed with flying colors until he'd blurted out in front of everyone that he worked for SAFE. Not that keeping it secret had been an option after she'd told Troy, but she would have preferred to have avoided him antagonizing everyone at the table. Before Jake had mentioned his work, downstairs in the kitchen, Tara had been getting a kick out of speculating about what Finn might do, and Lenny had seemed pleased that she had brought along another volunteer. Now Tara was leaving messages on her phone while Finn had apparently felt the urge to deliver his message in person, and Lenny no doubt would demand a detailed explanation of what exactly had possessed her to lead the archenemy right into their fucking headquarters. Perhaps it was a good thing she was spending the night in Manhattan.

It came almost without warning. There was a brief flicker before the lights went out, and then they were in darkness while the subway train continued on, dragged along by its own momentum until it came to a sluggish halt somewhere deep below the East River.

She heard Jake's tense voice close to her ear. "Not now."

"It's a blackout," a male voice said somewhere in the car.

"Everyone needs to stay calm," another guy added.

Jake's breath had quickened, his features illuminated by the green glow of the emergency lights as he let go of her. "Stay close, okay? Let me check how bad this is."

She could see his gaze change as he awakened his Spine. "It's just capacity overload," he announced into the car, a tremble in his voice. "We'll be moving again in a few minutes."

"I bet we'll get rolling blackouts again," someone said, sounding panicky. "And our generator's broken."

"You want your hospitals working, don't you?" someone else responded. "So maybe you'll sweat a little."

Others jumped in, debating power rationing and restrictions. Their voices grew louder, aggression rising with the temperature.

"I'm sorry," Jake said. "I bet this isn't what you bargained for."

She had no idea what exactly the bargain had been, but right now, she wished she had never set foot onto the train. She reached for Sam, who was panting, and buried her fingers in his warm fur.

"Will you still come with me?" Jake's voice was impossibly low.

She stared into the weak green light above. "Of course," she heard herself saying. "Looks like we may have to put a question mark on the air conditioning, though."

"It was the aircon that won you over, wasn't it?" he said after a while, his tone so deadpan that she decided he was teasing.

"That and the fact that Sam's never had a lizard for dinner before."

"Lucy's a dragon," Jake said, and that was when she noticed his irregular breathing.

She touched his chest; his heart was beating hard against his ribs.

"Are you okay?" she asked pointlessly since he was already slipping away, his eyes staring, his body twitching under her grip.

These were either withdrawal symptoms or signs of an oncoming panic attack. His breath was coming faster, sounding ragged.

She moved close, pressed her body against his side, her mouth to his ear. "Close your eyes, Jake," she whispered, "and breathe with me. Follow my rhythm, okay?"

He was unresponsive, so she said it again. And again. And again.

It took almost two minutes, but then his eyelids closed.

She kept breathing into his ear, slow breaths, calming him. He was still breathing too fast, but he was coming down, his right hand closed tightly around her wrist.

The lights flicked back on. There was sound and movement, excited voices, and the train started moving. Minutes later, it rattled into the bright space of 1st Avenue Station.

"Let's get off." Jake jumped up and was out the door.

They scrambled after him, her and Sam, across the station, up the escalator, and out through the doors into the night. When she caught up, Jake was leaning against the outer wall of the subway building, gulping the muggy air. He turned to her, looking haunted.

"I'm so sorry."

"It's okay. Do you need to take something?"

"I'm alright now. I don't know what went wrong in there."

"Withdrawal, I think. And a little too much of everything, probably." She couldn't help but smile. "Maybe you shouldn't have tried so hard to impress me with those eggplants."

He returned her smile. It was weak, but it was there. "Did I?"

"Very much."

"Then it was worth it." His breathing was almost normal now, his smile steadier. "Thank you," he said. "You were awesome in there. I can still feel you breathing in my ear."

"My mom was a nurse, so I learned a thing or two."

Jake studied her, his gaze unusually calm suddenly. "Was?" he said.

Shavir felt hot, like she'd crossed some line she wasn't supposed to. "She died in the riots, during the Crisis. Hit by a stray bullet. I couldn't—" She stopped, wondering how much he knew. In his position, he almost certainly had access to her Homeland file.

"It wasn't your fault," he said. "There wasn't even a functioning hospital around."

He was right, in part. There hadn't been a single hospital in Brooklyn or Queens that could have operated on her mom, not even her own hospital, where she'd just finished a twelve-hour shift taking care of injured patients lining the hallways. All surgeries cancelled, essential or not, because there had been no antibiotics left, no nothing. And thus the only way left to save her mom had been to try to get her across the bridge, to fucking Manhattan.

"Shavir," Jake said. "I know how you feel. I do. And I'm sorry. Please believe me."

"I'm not saying it's SAFE's fault," she said too fast.

"SAFE didn't exist then. The Crisis was the reason it was founded."

"But Homeland *did* exist, and it made dead sure Manhattan had everything." Her voice had grown louder. "They cut us off, all of us, everyone in Brooklyn."

"I know. My aunt died during the Crisis. In Queens. And I was living there myself at the time. I was a student. At some point you'll have to adjust your idea of me, Shavir. You don't have to like me, but can you at least do that?"

His gaze was too steady to bear. Overwhelmed, she looked down at Sam. "I'm sorry."

Jake pushed himself off the wall. "Well, I'm sorry you had to see me that way down there. And for surfing the Spine. I know how much you hate it."

"Don't worry about—"

"It's off now," he said. "The Spine. I shut it down."

"I thought you can't do that?"

"Well, I just did. Let's walk a little, okay? I'll pay a cab to get you back to Brooklyn if you like. But walk with me a little. My place isn't far."

His place was in a converted office building with a climate-controlled lobby in one of the newly naturalized streets not far from the Hudson River—not nearly as exclusive as the stately old houses in the East Village, but only affordable for people with six-figure salaries.

They hadn't spoken much on their way over here, and Jake hadn't touched her again, giving her time and space to figure things out. All that did was make her more overwhelmed. But when he pushed open the front door of the building without asking her about the cab again, she found herself relieved.

They rode up the elevator standing on opposite sides of the car and walked down the hallway on the seventh floor until Jake stopped and stuck his hands into a Delphi reader. Sam picked up a scent and focused his attention on the apartment door.

"What will he do when he sees Lucy?" Jake asked.

"I have no idea." Shavir slipped her fingers underneath Sam's collar. "Let's try."

Jake opened the door, and Sam lunged forward, nearly pulling her shoulder out its socket. Before she had a chance to grab the doorframe or anything else, he had dragged her through the half-open door several feet into the stuffy apartment.

Jake switched on the light. "Lucy's safe. She went underneath the kitchen counter."

"Good," was all Shavir could say, using her bodyweight to keep Sam in check with moderate success. "Stop it!" she finally yelled. "Down!"

Sam dropped to the floor, his nose going mad with the effort to suck in the unfamiliar air of the apartment. She dropped down next to him, both hands on his collar. "He's going to be good. He's just a little excited about the scent."

Jake frowned. "Have you told him there's been a misunderstanding about his dinner?"

"Yeah," she laughed. "He knows."

"I don't think we'll see Lucy again tonight." Jake closed the door. "She's smart enough to stay out of his way. Would you like some water? Or would you perhaps like me to help you off the floor?"

He reached out his hand, grinning, but she didn't trust Sam yet.

"Water would be great—also for Sam."

Jake walked to the kitchen and busied himself with the water, giving her time to look around. His place was smaller than expected, just a studio really, the bed in plain view in a nook to the left of the living area. It looked like a space furnished in a hurry and left in a greater one: unmade sheets on the naked bed, a few shirts in the open closet, a single glass left on an oddly shaped coffee table made of what looked like concrete, a balled-up towel on a gray couch facing the large bay window. Other than that, it was empty.

Shavir had seen a whole collection of odd living spaces over the years: the crammed one-bedroom in Brooklyn where she'd grown up with her mom, all life and joy pulled toward the magnet of its tiny kitchen; the slightly bigger place in the same building that Tara still shared with her dad, nearly empty when they'd moved in and by now home to an impressive collection of Indian knickknacks from a thousand little shops and street vendors that reminded Dipak of Kolkata; the makeshift world of the repurposed office cubicles at Roots, where people attempted to stuff entire lives into a few square feet, the in-evitable things they carried packed tightly into bags and boxes. At the other end of the spectrum were the stylish ballrooms of Finn's penthouse loft in the Village and the even larger space of her late father's bizarre mansion on the other coast in Palo Alto, pervaded by ocean breeze and smoke from the wildfires raging south and east.

Jake's place was odd but in a way that captivated her.

"When did you move in?"

"Six years ago, when I got my job at SAFE."

Jake laughed when he saw her face. "You didn't expect that answer, did you? Well, my life is mostly virtual." He handed her a glass of water and put what looked like a breakfast bowl on the floor for Sam. "I don't have anything else but, as promised, I have air conditioning." He walked over to a small unit above his bed and switched it on. Then he picked up the towel and the bed sheets and threw them into his closet. The studio looked absolutely deserted now, like a space for rent.

"Will you excuse me?" Jake said and disappeared into the bathroom.

Shavir was still sitting on the floor holding on to Sam.

With any other guy, she'd know where this was going. Finn would already have had her down on the bed. But with Jake, she had no idea. She caught herself scanning the room for signs of another woman and laughed. There weren't even signs of Jake.

Outside the bay window, the six-story brownstone across the street was glowing green. Its roof was at eye level from here, offering a premier view of the messy rooftop garden that was overgrowing solar panels and parapet in bold, unkempt cascades. Two badly managed oak trees towered above the shrubs and bushes, heat-stressed to a degree that they were shedding their leaves. Without proper care, they'd perish up there, too exposed to the elements to survive.

"Do you like my trees?" Jake had returned from the bathroom.

"They're in trouble, actually."

"I know, it's a shame." He walked over to her. "They're the reason I rented this place."

Smelling soap, she realized he'd taken a shower and probably pills. He looked at the trees while fastening a button on the black shirt he'd put on, a departure from his usual creased T-shirts and a peculiar choice given the time and circumstance.

"No one's ever up there," he said, "so I have it all to myself, my own private garden. I don't want them to die."

"Maybe you should build yourself one of those wooden bridges, like we have at Roots."

"Maybe I should. But I'm so used to seeing things from afar."

He offered his hand again, and this time she allowed him to pull her up. Again, she was struck by how calm his eyes were without the Spine, dark and steady. His entire face and demeanor had changed, he was present in a way that sent flutters to her stomach.

He let go of her and turned to the kitchen. "I need a coffee to set my system straight. You sure you don't want any?"

"I'll have some. But how about I make the coffee since, after all, I'm the pro? Is *that* your machine?" She pointed to a small designer coffeemaker tucked next to the fridge.

He nodded. "It comes with the little capsules and all."

She just rolled her eyes.

"I know," he said, grinning. "There are reasons why I'm at Soma every morning."

She went to work, making coffee for Jake as she had done so many times before.

But nothing was like before. He handed her almond milk from his fridge then leaned against the opposite counter, behind her. She could feel his gaze, direct and intense, unshielded.

"Could you make me one of those designs?" he asked.

She didn't turn around. "In the foam?"

"Please."

"Let's see what I can do for you on this little joke of a machine."

She reached up for two coffee mugs on a shelf, conscious of the fact that the hem of her tank top moved with her movement, exposing her waist. She put the mugs down.

Then Jake was right behind her, less than an inch between them.

She didn't move, just watched her own chest rising with her breath.

"I need to see how you do this," he said.

She nodded and steamed the milk before pouring the espressos into the coffee mugs while he peered over her right shoulder. She picked up the pitcher. "It's very simple. You pour the milk, and when it's almost full, you lower it and make a zigzag movement, and then you pull it back—" She painted a fern-like shape into the foam.

"I see," he murmured. "Actually, I've no idea how you just did that."

"This one's even simpler." She drew a heart into the foam of the second mug.

"Is that for me?" he asked, close to her ear.

"Yes."

"That's the first time you've given me a heart."

"Did you want one before?"

"Badly." His lips brushed her neck. "But there were nothing but ferns for me."

She turned to him.

He smiled and drew her close, and then they kissed, long, longingly.

Lowering himself, he grabbed her hips and lifted her.

Sam offered an undecided growl when they walked past him toward the bed. Shavir put a finger to her lips and told him to be a good boy.

Jake's features were so calm, it was beautiful. Once again, he had surprised her. She'd thought he would be shy, self-conscious, unsure of himself. Instead, it had been effortless, flowing, all thinking postponed until after the fact. Shavir looked at his long limbs spread out underneath the fresh bedsheets. He was even thinner than she had suspected but also more muscular. There were goose bumps on his skin where the air touched it, so she pulled up the sheet, covering him.

She sat up and looked around the empty apartment, illuminated only by the soft greenish light flowing in from the building opposite and filled with the noise of the blasting aircon.

Perhaps Jake was a stooge after all, some kind of undercover agent who had rented this place for just one night. Perhaps it was all part of his spiel—the shyness, the boldness, and even the panic attack—all meant to get her to the exact place she was now. Perhaps if she came back tomorrow, the neighbors would tell her they'd never seen the man she described, that the apartment was purchased by a young lawyer who was moving here from Boston to start her first job.

She wanted to kiss Jake again but was afraid she'd wake him, and it was time to go. She slipped her legs out from underneath the covers.

Sam woke immediately. He knew the drill.

She looked for her clothes and found a pile near the end of the bed. She checked the time on her phone. If they walked slowly, they could take the first train to Brooklyn.

Neither she nor Sam had made a sound, yet Jake stirred.

She froze.

"Hey," he said sleepily, sitting up. "What are you doing?"

She could barely make out his eyes in the dark. "Leaving."

"Now? It must be the middle of the night."

"Three-thirty. I'm sorry I woke you up."

"Where are you going?"

"Home."

"What?" He moved toward her and put his arms around her, the warmth of his body pressing through her top. "Stop, okay? You can't just disappear on me like that."

"I'm not disappearing. It's just easier this way."

"Nothing's easier. I don't want it easy. That's not what this is."

Her heart was pounding.

"Do you want it easy?" he asked.

She wound out of his arms and got up. "I need to be in Brooklyn tomorrow morning."

"Then leave tomorrow morning. But not now. Not like this." He looked up at her from the bed, naked. "Look, Shavir. If you need to go, then I'll call you a cab. But it's not what I want. I want you to spend the rest of the night with me. Wake up with me. Have coffee with me—a proper morning coffee. Made on my bizarre little machine."

"There're two full mugs on the counter."

"What is this about, Shavir? Did I do something wrong?"

"No." Her voice was small. "I'm just not used to this."

"Then come back to bed with me. Please. I'm not used to it either, but you don't have to go. I don't want you to go."

She allowed him to take her in his arms, unable to respond.

"Come back to bed," he whispered. "This place is freaking cold. I forgot to turn down the AC, and Lucy is probably so angry she'll kill us if we stay out here much longer. Let's crawl back under the covers where we're safe and warm, okay?"

"Okay."

"Okay?"

"Okay."

She could hear him smile.

"I like it when you say okay like that. Now take off those clothes before I die of exposure. Because I'm not getting back into that bed before you do."

He helped her undress and switched off the aircon before he slid back under the covers to embrace her.

Still confused, she nestled her head on his chest.

Sam was standing next to the bed, wagging his tail, probably just as confused as she was. After another minute, she heard him return to his place at the foot of the bed.

TEN

THE SHRILL SOUND GRADUALLY drifted into his consciousness. Then the insistent shaking. Jake opened his eyes and looked at Shavir's tense face. "There's someone at the door, Jake."

"Who?"

"How should I know? You live here. It seems urgent, though."

The doorbell rang again. Jake scrambled out of bed, threw on his pants, and pulled them up as he stumbled toward the front door. Sam accompanied him, spinning in circles, barking his soundless bark. Apparently, he was excited that finally someone was moving.

"Who is this?" Jake yelled into the intercom.

"For Christ's sake, open the door!" David's voice. From the hallway.

Jake unlocked the deadbolt and faced his boss, who glared first at him then at Sam standing next to him. "What the fuck's going on?" As always, he skipped the greeting.

Shavir called from behind, and Sam trotted back to her. She was mostly dressed and fussing around with her hair.

David stared at her across the room like his jaw might literally drop. "Where *are* you, Jake?" he said, returning his attention to him.

"I'm here, David. Standing right in front of you."

"What's the matter with your Spine?"

"Nothing's the matter," Jake said sharply. He still wasn't fully awake and about as stunned as David seemed to be by the sight of Shavir in the brilliant morning light, angling with one hand for her boot underneath his bed while using the other to keep Sam in check. Then it hit him. "What time is it?"

"That's a great question." David was caustic. "It's nine o'clock in the fucking morning, and I've been trying to reach you for the past three hours. I thought something happened to you."

No, Jake thought. It couldn't be nine because the Spine woke him up at five every single morning. But David's face said it was nine, and his Spine was off. Still off. "I'm sorry," he scrambled, feeling dizzy. "Why didn't you send Masao?"

"Because he's busy doing your job," David barked. "And because I thought something *happened* to you. But I see you're okay, so I'll go back to work now. Would be great if you could do the same. We've got... problems." He looked at Shavir. "I apologize for the intrusion."

Shavir nodded gracefully, and then David was gone.

"Charming, your boss." Shavir let go of Sam.

"You should see him on his bad days." Jake said. "It's my fault, actually. I forgot to switch my Spine back on last night. They probably thought I was dead."

They probably had. To show up at his doorstep like that, David must have been truly enraged or scared. The waiting emergency calls poured in the second his Spine connected to the cloud, all sent in the past four hours, accompanied by a barrage of frantic text alerts from both David and Masao. He'd slept through all that mayhem like a baby. He cursed himself for being callous and careless, so untypical for him.

Behind the projection, he saw Shavir clipping Sam's leash into his collar. "Do you want coffee?" he spilled out.

"I better go. I'm so late already."

"Please don't be mad."

"I'm not." Her smile was sudden, and then she was close, her lips brushing his. "I just think you probably should've let me go last night."

"Well, I'm glad I didn't. I had you in my arms all night."

"Yeah," she said lightly. "And you were snoring."

"I was not."

She nodded in affirmation.

"You're confusing me with your dog. That's because of the echo." He pointed vaguely around himself at the bare walls. "I do get a lot of echoing in here."

She kissed him once more. "I gotta go."

"When will I see you again?"

"Well, I'll be up on that sizzling roof the whole day again harvesting," she said as she let go of him, "because Judy thinks that compared to what's ahead of us, it will be a cool day. If I survive that, we can start thinking about our options." She paused at the door and turned to him again. "I'll text you. And you did snore at least once."

Half an hour later, Jake stepped onto the seventh floor of the SAFE building, his body buzzing from the pep pills he'd swallowed with a three-hour delay, his head humming from his attempt to catch up with the world and the unfamiliar podcar ride. His mind was still going into repeat mode whenever it saw an opportunity to relive some minute of the night he'd spent with Shavir, but the pills would help him find focus, or so he hoped.

Masao was waiting for him outside the CSR, looking upset.

"I'm really sorry, Jake. I tried to convince him to send me instead, but he wanted to go himself."

"Not your fault."

It most definitely wasn't, though Jake had rarely seen Masao this agitated. Clearly, David hadn't been the only one worrying about him. "I'm fine," he laughed, trying to calm things. "I just shut down my Spine and took too many sleepers."

Masao nodded, his eyebrows saying he didn't buy a word of it. It was understandable since, except for the two times he'd undergone a quick change of his implant processor, Jake had never shut down his Spine.

"I read everything you sent me," he said to refocus attention on the things that had been delayed while he was out. "Our antibiotics situation is starting to scare me."

"I know." Masao visibly fought down more questions and forced himself into business mode. "There's just nothing else available. The whole world is stockpiling them." He stopped. "Are you really okay, Jake? Please tell me."

"I am. It's just that I wasn't alone last night. That's why I forgot about my Spine."

If anything, Masao looked more worried now. "Ah, okay," he said. And then, slowly, the hint of a smile crept onto his face.

"So what's our stock situation with the antibiotics?" Jake asked to redirect his attention.

"Pretty bad. Look at this." With a swipe on his glove, Masao transferred data from Corsys, the medical distribution automation system that Shavir, and then Lenny, had said was screwing people in the eastern boroughs. Or, rather, they'd assumed it was SAFE that was doing the screwing, but the truth was even the CSR team knew very little about what Corsys did. It was the digital heart of SAFE's local allocation functions, operating through complicated algorithms that only its creator, Niya Taylor, fully understood. As she had demonstrated on several separate occasions, though, not even Niya could explain to them exactly how the algorithms decided who in the city got what, when, and why. It was more than questionable whether Niya was really as bad at tech communication as she seemed to be in these conversations. After all, she was perfectly lucid explaining her other brainchild, the 4Flow. The more likely explanation for her selective inarticulateness was that she'd been instructed to keep the mysteries of Corsys's moving parts to herself because information on how critical medical supply was distributed to hospitals and pharmacies in New York was considered too sensitive to share, even with the CSR staff. Especially with the CSR staff.

"Surprisingly, Manhattan's doing just fine," Masao said, voice thick with sarcasm, as he pointed to New York City's medical stockpile data on the Spine interface. "But two hospitals in Queens have run out. They're postponing or redirecting surgeries, even essential ones, and have filed an official request to share supplies with the MHA."

"The MHA's never gonna do that."

"No. But I guess they're trying anyway."

Jake tried to push to the back of his mind what Shavir had told him about her mother, the role the catastrophic lack of antibiotics had played in her personal tragedy, in Hector's, and in so many others' during the Crisis. It was everyone's nightmare in the CSR that, eventually, they might have another Crisis on their hands.

"Right now," Masao continued, "other hospitals in Queens are taking in the emergencies, but their stock's pretty low, too. The only ones drowning in meds are here in Manhattan."

Jake looked at the uneven stockpiles, remembering Shavir's face when he'd told her about the MHA during their short-lived dinner at Buddha's. As keenly aware as she was of the critical shortages in the eastern boroughs, she'd never heard of the Manhattan Hospital Association, which said a lot about how the MHA operated. For him and everyone else in the CSR, it was a pervasive presence they were told to overlook, while the rest of the city was barely aware of its machinations. There had been several motions and petitions to make all New York hospitals members of the powerful alliance, but no dice. It was a case of winner-take-all, and the way Corsys operated made sure they never stopped winning.

"When are we expecting our next deliveries?" Jake asked.

"It's hard to say because so many data feeds are down. We're still hoping for a shipment from France, but the heat wave in Europe is unbroken, killing pretty much all transportation on land or water. Our stuff from Laem Chabang is now sitting in customs, though, and one container of ciprofloxacin from Malaysia should be here on Tuesday."

"Good. We need to prioritize the hospitals in Queens then."

Masao's pale face flickered with surprise before it turned utterly blank. "Corsys does the prioritizing," he said flatly, as if unsure whether Jake was suffering from some temporary cognitive impairment due to his night off. "We have no control over that."

"You said they can no longer do surgery in Queens, right?"

"Correct. Not in those two hospitals."

"I have to talk to David."

The demonstrative blankness on Masao's face morphed into something like awe. "I guess you better talk to Gwen if you wanna try that."

"Is she in?"

Masao nodded toward the other side of the hallway. "Just walked into David's office. We must be in deep shit if she's here on a Sunday."

Gwen Hatton leaned against David's desk, looking anything but casual on a Sunday morning in her dark blue suit and high heels. She was a slim woman in her sixties with short hair, youthful-looking skin, and gray eyes that could freeze their target on contact. It was almost never a good sign when SAFE's director left her office on the eighth floor to visit the lower levels of the building and, by default, catastrophic if she came in on the weekend.

"We're waiting for Lisa," she said in a tone that suggested they hadn't been waiting for Jake.

"It's alright, Gwen." David raised his hand. "I'd like him to join us."

Lisa arrived, uncharacteristically late to the meeting and looking very tired. If she was still here, Jake realized, it meant she had stayed on after her night shift had ended—another colleague who had paid a price for his absence.

"The CSR is chronically understaffed," Gwen said as Lisa closed the door. "I'm aware that this is a serious problem with our supply situation being what it is."

"That's an understatement," David growled. "Lisa and Jake have both gone above and beyond, and so have the members of both teams. But we won't be able to keep it up for much longer. People need to sleep sometimes."

Jake exchanged a glance with Lisa. As always, David was protective of his team, regardless of what he said internally and notwithstanding the fact that, half an hour ago, he'd been seething. That he treated Lisa like she was one of his team members rather than the second group leader and therefore his equal also wasn't anything out of the ordinary. In his mind, he was the sole head of the CSR.

"I am fully aware of the situation," Gwen said. "But right now we don't have the funding for additional staff, not at that salary level. All I can offer you is a transfer of suitable people from the lower levels to the CSR."

"We'll look into that," David said impatiently. Everyone knew he didn't want anyone from the lower levels. "Most pressing now is the Emovia situation."

"That's why I'm here." Gwen paused for effect. "The FDA refuses to speed up the approval process—or, to be more precise, Frank Kruger refuses to speed up the approval process—for the new capsule. He told me he doesn't see the need for a non-critical-supply item."

"Emovia *is* critical supply," Lisa cut in. "It's on no official list but it sure as hell is critical for the survival of this city."

Gwen turned to her. "You know that, and I know it, and Frank knows it, too. The problem is he doesn't approve of it. Not that we approve of it, either, but we have to accept the fact and deal with it. Frank, on the other hand, disapproves as a matter of principle."

Kruger had made it very clear that under no circumstance could Emovia show up on the CSR's critical supply list because the drug wasn't saving lives in the way antibiotics or coagulants did. Plus, its over-the-counter availability had been approved by his predecessor, and Kruger didn't agree with that decision because he didn't consider the voluntary self-sedation of the American people a proper approach to the problem. That was why, Gwen informed them, he was insisting Ziser had to go through the regular process at the New York FDA for a new capsule. Which meant it'd be several weeks until they would have approval and another couple of weeks for production.

"That's forever!" Lisa snapped. It was highly unusual for her to be this vocal with Gwen in the room. It was either the exhaustion or she was truly fed up.

"How many times have I told you we need to build strategic reserves?" David asked, eyes on Gwen with a face like she wasn't SAFE's director but a spouse he was having an argument with. He should have turned to a pillar of ice as the recipient of one of Gwen's chilling looks.

"How many times have I told you the city's never going to do that?" she shot back. "Neither the mayor nor the FDA nor anyone else in this city are prepared to acknowledge that emotion regulation has become a necessary means of control. They will never build official reserves, and they will never allow us to make it critical supply. Are there other drugs, comparable ones, that we can get more easily?"

"They won't accept anything else!" Lisa said. "People won't accept it. They know Emovia, and they trust it with their lives, literally. The black market will explode."

"That will happen anyway." David gave her a disapproving look then turned to Gwen. "Is there any chance Kruger will change his mind? Or is there someone above Kruger who can make him change his mind? I can't believe Kruger is that powerful."

"He is that powerful," Gwen said, "unless Corsys calls a state of emergency. And there's no chance it'll do that for Emovia because it isn't critical supply. We need to get a new capsule approved, and that will take time. I'll do my best to speed it up. Until then, we need to find workable substitutes. That's what I want all of you to concentrate on."

"What about the antibiotics we need for our hospitals?" Jake asked.

Gwen looked at him coolly. "I hope you can accomplish both."

Lisa got up. "I assume we won't be communicating any of this?"

"Nothing goes out on 4Flow," Gwen confirmed. "We won't be able to contain this for very long, but for now let's keep it low-key. We don't want the city to panic."

"Good luck with that," said Lisa and was out the door.

Jake caught up with her halfway to the elevators, taken aback by the barely contained fury on her face when she turned to him.

"It's just so fucking irresponsible," she hissed, eyes on David's half-open office door. "Kruger's going to regret this. Gwen, too. Once the city explodes, regret will pour down on all of us like fucking hail." She exhaled. "I need to go home now and get some sleep. But someone needs to talk sense into Kruger. We need a new capsule, and fast."

When she paused long enough for Jake to say something, he promised her he'd talk to David before apologizing for his absence.

She nodded. "Have you talked to him about his abuse? It's serious, Jake, so don't push this off. He finally left last night, but then he was back at four in the morning. He's having some kind of adverse reaction to this stuff. You need to talk to him." With that, she hit the control panel of the elevator.

David's office door was closed when Jake returned, so he walked on to the Corsys Room instead and closed the door behind him.

It was an unassuming space packed with water-cooled banks of servers and one of the few places on the seventh floor that allowed for a calm moment to think. Its most remarkable feature was its narrow anteroom, which Niya Taylor had claimed as her freelance office since it had a window facing Abingdon Square Park, an asset she never failed to mention. She wasn't in, so Jake sat down on her chair and looked at the trees, their canopies as yellow as the ones on the roof across from his apartment. The humming of the Corsys servers filled the room, making quiet decisions about life and death.

They made such decisions every day in the CSR but always about people elsewhere in the world, or elsewhere in the no-longer-United States of America. When it came to the people in New York, an artificial intelligence was doing the deciding. He wondered if that was Corsys's true purpose—letting them off the hook at home so they could do their work abroad without feeling they were part of a system that was fucking half the city. Without a steady dose of Emovia, those abused parts of the city would explode—that was what Lisa had meant. Their approach to the problem was to find more Emovia without doing anything about the abuse.

When he stepped back into the hallway ten minutes later, he still didn't know what to say to David, but the office door was open, so he poked his head in. "Has Gwen left?"

"Gone to some charity thing. But we talked about you."

"About me?"

"Gwen thinks I need a deputy."

"She's been thinking that for a while, David. You don't *want* a deputy."

"Well, things change. We've agreed that I will ask you."

Jake processed this. Then he closed the door and just said it: "Does Gwen know you're taking Emovia? Is that what this is about?"

David's fingers slid across his glove as he put his Spine on standby. "How long have you known?" he asked without trying to deny it. His cheeks looked hollow.

"A few days." Jake sat down. "Lisa told me. She saw the bottle on your desk."

"I see." David hid his trembling hands. "No, Gwen doesn't know, or I would already be gone. But I know, and I need someone who can be in charge if something happens to me. Hence the deputy."

"I'd much rather nothing happen to you."

"So would I, but I have to take precautions."

"Just stop taking Emovia, David! We're running out of it anyway."

"Not me." David shook his head. "I won't run out, believe me." He was grinning like a madman. "So are you going to do it, the deputy thing?" he asked. "I'd really appreciate it." He was unnaturally calm, like this whole thing was just a bagatelle, a routine request.

There was only one answer possible after all David had done for him over the years. David had his sociopathic sides, but he'd also picked him, trained him, and believed in him. Jake nodded.

"Thanks, Jake." David leaned slightly forward across his desk. "One more thing, though. Whatever happened this morning, it can't happen again. Not with my best man, now my deputy. Whoever she is—and I assume she's also the reason for your tempestuous dinner the other day—she needs to play second fiddle. Your first love is SAFE. I hope we're clear on that."

For a second, Jake was too stunned to respond. "I'm gonna pretend you didn't just say that," he returned as the blood rushed to his head.

"Don't bother. I mean every word I say, and as your boss, it's my responsibility to say it. You can do whatever you want in your spare time, and I've never cared whom you're screwing. But when it interferes with your performance here, it concerns me."

He couldn't remember David ever talking to him like this before about his personal life. It had always been understood that he was fully committed to the job, willing to go above and beyond, as David had put it minutes ago when talking to Gwen. But apparently, that had been a lie, like so much in this place was lies, lies they were telling each other and themselves about what they did and who they did it for. And he, like an idiot, was playing along.

"Look," David said into the quiet room, "I see what you're trying to do with that girl. But it's not gonna work. I've tried it myself and know that it doesn't. She'll be gone before you realize it because you have nothing to offer her. And then you'll feel worse."

"You know nothing about her," Jake hissed. "And I'm not you."

"Yes, you are. Only difference is you're twenty years younger."

Jake wanted to scream that they weren't alike and that he wasn't—as David had told him so many times over so many bad drinks after so many bad days in the CSR—on the same road to hell. But he didn't scream. Instead, his rage tipped into something he didn't have a word for, something more determined, more meaningful.

"There's something I forgot to mention earlier," he said and was surprised by how calm he sounded. "I'd like us to prioritize the two hospitals in Queens that have run out of antibiotics."

There was a flash of surprise on David's face, apparently the only reaction around here to the suggestion that they help the people in their city who needed it the most. "We can't do that," he said in an equally calm voice, though now he looked wary.

"Well, actually we can. We can prioritize hospitals once they declare a state of emergency."

"Corsys makes that declaration. And it won't do so for either of those two hospitals in Queens because they're within the fifteen-minute transportation time limit. Meaning patients can safely be treated elsewhere in the area. You know all this, Jake."

Jake leaned forward, pointing to David's screen walls. "Have you watched the news? There are two other hospitals within the limit, and it's only a matter of time until both run out, too, since they're now taking in all the emergencies in Queens. They're saying that on the fucking news, and we aren't able to anticipate it?"

"We are anticipating it," David barked, losing his cool. "And once it happens, Corsys will call a state of emergency for them, and they'll be prioritized for the next shipment."

"The next shipment comes in Tuesday, and we don't know when we'll get the next!"

"I guess they better get a good deal of emergencies then, so they run out in time."

"Wow. That logic's so fucked up."

"It's the law, Jake. And the CSR isn't in the business of equal distribution. We just secure the influx of critical meds into the city. That's our job, and it's hard enough."

Jake got up. "Good thing Gwen's going to a charity thing then. It's so important to help the poor." Without another word, he left David's office, so incensed that it took real effort to greet Niya Taylor when she walked past him on his way to the CSR.

He hadn't made it back to his desk when the news broke. Three of Queens's four major hospitals were no longer able to perform essential surgeries because they didn't have enough antibiotics. Fulham was now the only sizeable medical center left in the area that could treat urgent cases. People were crowding at the entrances of the hospitals.

The CSR team stared at the screen walls, and then Masao asked aloud what everyone in the room was wondering.

"You think we're headed for a second Crisis?"

Instead of answering, Jake motioned for Masao to follow him to their desk, where he gave him the short version of what Gwen had said during their meeting—that they would treat Emovia as critical supply without admitting it, getting as many replacements as they could to tranquilize the revolution. But when Masao sat down to get to work on the substitutes, Jake walked back to the hallway. He had at best a hazy idea of what he wanted to do, but he knew there was only one person who could make it happen.

Niya greeted him with a distracted smile when he knocked at the open door of the Corsys Room. A short woman in her late twenties, she was one of the few people on SAFE's seventh floor who didn't look starved, suggesting that, like Masao, she wasn't taking stimulants on a regular basis. She was peculiar all the same, visually suffering whenever her creations weren't working due to their immense complexity and exuding happiness when they did. Her creative approach to legal

limitations was the other reason she worked here, but Jake had no idea
how far she'd be willing to go.

"Can I ask you something?" he said.

"Sure." Niya didn't take her eyes off what she was working on.

"What does Corsys do for our hospitals? What happens if one of
them calls a state of emergency and as a result moves up in the priority
chain? Is that managed by Corsys?"

"Sure," she said again. "I programmed that function."

"So how does that work?"

"Corsys is connected to the hospitals' computer systems. It receives
information about their stock and outgoing orders," Niya rattled on.
"It's not the hospitals themselves calling the state of emergency. Corsys
does that when certain parameters arise in combination. And once that
happens, the hospital is automatically prioritized and receives a delivery as soon as possible, depending on the general supply situation."

"I see." Jake closed the door. "And would you be able to *induce* that
situation so that Corsys calls a state of emergency even though not all
of the parameters are met?"

Niya turned to him, a question mark on her face.

Jake felt his pulse beating against his Spine. "Would you? Be able?"

"I've never tried, but I guess it's possible."

"And would you consider doing so if I offered you a compelling
reason?"

Niya seemed to consider this. "Does the emergency alert have to be
visible on the hospital side?"

"No. In fact, that would be a problem."

"So it would have to be asymmetric? Corsys registers and processes
the emergency alert, but the hospital's interface remains unchanged?"

"Exactly."

To his surprise, Niya smiled. "That's an interesting idea. I'm not
sure it's possible, but I could try." Her gaze returned to the screen.

"Do you want me to tell you what it's about?"

"I need to fix this first, then I'll take a look. I'm not sure I can make
it asymmetric."

"Will you let me know when you're done?" Jake asked, unsure whether it was better to pretend what he had just asked was no big deal or whether he should signal to her that he was fully aware of the potential legal consequences.

He had already opened the door when Niya spoke again.

"Hey, Jake, can you get me some chocolate from downstairs? Doesn't matter what kind. Just a lot."

Half an hour later, after raiding the vending machines on SAFE's ground floor, Jake returned with his hands full of chocolate bars.

Niya ripped open the foil of the first bar before she placed the others down on her desk. She bit into it and leaned back in her chair with a satisfied smile. "My brain burns a ton of sugar. Can we join up Spines? I don't want to run this on the control unit."

Jake closed the door, and they synchronized Spines.

"Which hospital?" she asked.

So she had already been working on this.

"I don't know. Cascades?"

"I tried it with Queens, but it should be the same." She entered the Cascades Hospital Medical Center into Corsys's input mask. "So here's the current information that you normally see. Their supply situation is pretty shitty right now."

"What does it say about their antibiotics?"

Niya called up the data. "That they don't have any."

They looked at the data sets of Trust Care Hospital, Queens Hospital, and Fulham Hospital Medical Center. The latter still had a few hundred units of antibiotics left, and, perversely, that was the problem. As long as one of them still had something left, Corsys wouldn't call a state of emergency because the other hospitals were within the transportation limit. Now came the part where they had to break the law to help all four hospitals and the patients in desperate need of surgery. Jake embarked on explaining that, but Niya interrupted him. "Do you want to activate the emergency alerts?"

"Can you do that already?" Jake asked, staggered.

She nodded.

"What about the asymmetry problem?"

"Solved." She smiled. "There's actually something really cool about the emergency alerts." She put the pointer on Fulham's supply of antibiotic suspensions. "See this?"

"They have sixty-seven units left."

"See now?" Niya moved her fingers, and the number of units changed to zero, the color of the hospital's name simultaneously changing from black to red.

"Does that signal a state of emergency?"

"Yup. See here?" She pointed to an entry on the lower left of the page. "This means that the hospital's order of antibiotics now has priority at the wholesalers. And here's the cool thing." She called up another page. "Here's Queens Hospital. Red as well. So is Trust Care Hospital, see? And Cascades. The second Fulham runs out of antibiotics, all hospitals in Queens are in a state of emergency because none of them can get their patients transported to another hospital within fifteen minutes. It's done."

"Wow," Jake said, staggered. "Is it for real? I mean, is this actually happening right now on Corsys?"

Niya nodded. "All four hospitals have been moved up in the chain, see?" She pointed into the air at what Jake assumed was her Spine projection. People got confused like this, forgetting what they saw was private. But Jake could see it on his own Spine.

"Can the hospitals see their changed status?" he asked, excited and scared that Niya had already done what he'd only imagined.

"No. They just see that they're prioritized for their outstanding antibiotics orders. And for everyone else it just looks like they've already run out."

Jake laughed. "You really are a genius, Niya. Thanks!"

"That's alright," she said with a shrug. "My brother lives in Queens."

The CSR immediately received the emergency alerts. Within hours, the MHA filed a complaint because the Manhattan hospitals would receive less than half the shipments coming in from Malaysia and Koh Kong. But there was nothing to be done. Corsys had prioritized

Queens. The MHA would have to wait and rely on its own stockpile until the next delivery came in.

"You're clearly enjoying the situation," David said edgily.

Jake didn't bother to hide his elation. "How do you expect me to react?"

"Knock yourself out, as long as you get me the additional antibiotics we now need."

"There's nothing available, David. The market's swept clean."

"Then start looking underneath the rugs," David hissed, "and while you're at it, make sure you pull out some emotion regulators, too."

Jake didn't respond, his gaze on the pulsating emergency alerts for the Queens hospitals. He was shocked at how good it felt to have broken the law. Like all troubleshooters, he had made plenty of illegal decisions over the years, but those had all been in accordance with the unspoken rules of the CSR. Now he had made a decision that directly counteracted the directives given to him, an act that instilled in him a sense of righteousness he knew was dangerous. He didn't know how likely it was that their little scheme would be discovered or what consequences they would have to face if it was. He could only hope the hospitals would receive their meds without asking questions.

What mattered to him most, though, was that he could now look into Shavir's eyes and tell the truth when he said he cared.

ELEVEN

THE DAY HAD STARTED out black. Aside from the hospital crisis, this was the big news of the day: the city was instituting rolling blackouts to avoid spontaneous power outages for the duration of the heat wave. As usual, Manhattan had received the best time slots—between two and four in the morning and two and four in the afternoon. In Queens, the blackouts were scheduled between the inopportune times of eight and ten, in Brooklyn between noon and two and midnight and two. People had started complaining immediately, and Roots was no exception. But in misery there was also opportunity.

They were sitting around the big table in the kitchen, dishes dirty from the meal the guys and Tara had eaten after a long shift in the basement. Shavir had vaguely cited dinner plans—a mistake when vagueness never worked with Lenny. He'd extracted the details from her: she was going to Queens, with Jake. Her private plans for the evening had thus become a subject for group discussion, and she was trying to refocus everyone's attention on the second hot topic of the day: to raid or not to raid during rolling blackouts.

"I just don't see why we have to rush this thing," she said to Tara, who was sitting across from her, unnaturally erect in her usual attempt to add to her height when her authority was being challenged. It was Tara's first day without a bandage around her forehead, and, apparently, she felt an urgent need to get a new one.

"Because Tara's right about this," Lenny trumpeted into the room. "People are always thrown off by the first day of blackouts, and we should take advantage of that."

"How is moving up a raid we've already planned for tomorrow night an advantage?" Shavir looked to Troy, the planner in chief.

He shrugged, suggesting he didn't have anything to add beyond what he'd already said—that doing the raid a day earlier didn't make a difference in terms of the target or their access to it.

Zeno busied himself gobbling down his fifth portion, and Nacho wasn't even there but had submitted his consent by text, as had Finn.

"Is it possible your main problem is that you're otherwise engaged?" Tara asked, a particularly low blow coming from her and in the presence of nearly everyone else.

"Alright then," Shavir said, fed up with the clumsy insinuations, "I guess we're going tonight then, if you all think it's such a brilliant idea." She grabbed the dirty dishes that weren't even hers and carried them to the sink. "Don't worry about my dinner plans. I'll be there."

"So you're still planning to go to Queens," Lenny called after her.

"Yes, I'm still planning to go to Queens." She put down the dishes with a clank. "I really don't know what all the fuss is about. There's a little girl who doesn't get to see a lot of animals, and a family who doesn't have access to fresh food if their address is any indication. You said we need to become more active in Queens, so Sam and I are going. How's this different from all the other community outreach we do?"

"Really, Shav?" Lenny thundered. "You're really asking that?"

Suddenly Jake was standing in the room.

"Am I too early?" he asked. "The door downstairs was open."

Sam jumped to his feet to greet him, as he would have done with most people, but otherwise the tension was tangible.

Shavir realized when her phone had vibrated a few minutes ago, that must have been him, but it was only a quarter past six, and she hadn't given it much thought. "Not at all," she said, having no idea how much he had heard before they'd noticed him. "We're just about done, aren't we?" She glared at Lenny. "I'll grab my things." Her bag was in the pantry, so she left Jake alone with the hyenas, hoping he would survive.

"Lenny says you're working at SAFE?" she heard Zeno asking in a tone that told her she'd better hurry with filling her bag.

But when she returned five minutes later, it was still Zeno doing the talking while Jake leaned against the wall, fondling the soft flaps of Sam's ears and looking remarkably at ease.

"Must have been terrible for them not being able to treat people," Zeno said, working Jake on the hospital situation in Queens. "I'm just a tech at a veterinary clinic, and I can't imagine turning away an animal that needs help."

She put down her heavy bag with a thud, hoping to provide Jake an out, but he didn't need her assistance.

"We're trying what we can to avoid situations like this," he said, "but sometimes the world just doesn't allow for it. Those hospitals in Queens, they're now all operational again, and we're working day and night to secure more meds."

He pushed himself off the wall. "I guess we should get going," he added, looking at her. "Carrie hates it when I'm late."

On the stairs he kissed her. "I really like your friends," he said when they came up for air. "They have such a natural curiosity about things." He reached for her bag filled with fresh vegetables from the farm: potatoes, cucumbers, tomatoes, sweet corn, bell peppers, watermelon, and the inescapable eggplants. "Oh, wow!" He laughed. "Carrie will love you."

When Carrie opened the door for them, she looked different than expected. Very blond and very blue-eyed, a sharp contrast to Jake.

"They've just cut power," she cried, "and it's not even eight yet! Can you believe—" The rest of the sentence got stuck in her throat when she noticed Sam and then Shavir.

Behind her, in the dark living room, a young girl was lighting LEDs, igniting bright little spotlights on her brown skin.

Jake started explaining, looking nervous, lacking practice. The way Carrie stared at him between glances at her and Sam told Shavir she'd had no idea, no warning, that her cousin wasn't coming alone or that one of the other dinner guests would be a dog.

Before things could get more awkward, the girl appeared, striding toward Sam as though pulled by a string.

"No, Zoe!" Carrie grabbed her daughter.

"It's okay." Shavir crouched next to Sam, hand on his collar, eyes on the girl. "He won't do anything. His name is Sam."

Zoe stepped forward and gingerly touched Sam's face. He responded by running his tongue across her face, making her giggle in delight.

Carrie relaxed. "Well, that's taken care of. What a huge dog!"

Then she finally invited them in and started scolding Jake. "You said you'd be here by seven-thirty. At seven-thirty, we had power. Now we have this." She pointed at the dark room. "But we've got LEDs for the table, and Dan got the grill going, so we're all set for dinner. Why didn't you tell me you were bringing a friend?"

Her husband came in from the balcony, wiping his hands on a greasy cloth as he waded toward them through the cluttered mess of their living room. He was both tall and big, and he looked like he had just taken a steam bath. "These bastards cut the power again," he said to Jake, "and of course we get the worst time slots over here as always. It's racism, I'm telling you, plain old racism."

He stopped short when he noticed the two hundred pounds of Sam rolling around on the floor with his daughter. "He yours?"

"Yes. I'm Shavir."

"Dan," he said and stared at her like he'd never seen a woman before. He kept it up until things got decidedly uncomfortable with Jake and his wife standing right next to him. It clearly took effort for him to redirect his attention to Sam. "That's a serious dog."

"He's very good with kids," Jake said.

Dan looked at Zoe and Sam, the dog presenting his belly, the girl rubbing it with a mix of awe and adoration. "Isn't that interesting."

Shavir was relieved when Carrie sent Dan back out to the balcony to finish the burgers and they presented her with the bag from Roots and the medical bottles Jake had brought along. Carrie admired each vegetable she extracted from the bag while talking nonstop. Jake was mostly quiet but interrupted her flood of words now and then with a tease. It was beautiful to see them together, easing into the code they must have had since childhood. It made Shavir want siblings all over again, real siblings, not the distant blood relatives she'd acquired through her father, whom she'd been excited to meet during that one trip to California after the Crisis. But the encounter had been as sobering as it had been educative, and one thing she'd learned was common genes didn't mean anything else was shared, not even language. The relationship between Carrie and Jake reminded her more of hers with Tara. She wondered if Carrie knew Jake the way Tara knew her, penetrating beneath the skin to the ugly things.

Then Zoe swept her away with her curiosity about all things related to dogs. She was a sweet little girl, utterly fearless around Sam. Shavir showed her how to get him to make his cooing sounds, and Zoe shrieked with delight. She wanted to know whether she could come visit Sam on the farm, and Shavir smiled as she nodded. In terms of community outreach, things were going well.

The meal, when it finally appeared on the table, was a veggie feast, since no one had been able to stop Carrie from preparing some of almost everything in the bag. She sat nibbling on the same cob for the better part of an hour, looking happy and asking questions about Roots. Shavir had seen this happy face before when people bought their produce or went home with full bags after helping out on the farm, and she knew Carrie would love it there—if she accepted the invitation and if Zoe could get her to follow through and visit.

Almost without exception, people accepted Roots's invitations, but only few of them showed up. There were all kinds of reasons keeping them back—busy schedules, bad backs, vague fears of the unfamiliar work or surroundings. People weren't used to dirt and crops, the smell of the leaves and the soil and the overripe veggies in the sizzling heat. They felt out of place on the farm or feared that they might.

Carrie, however, was bubbly and curious and excitable in a way that would allow her to overcome her insecurities. Plus, she had Zoe and the love of a mother for her daughter, the greatest motivator of all. By the time she was serving dessert, she knew more about Roots than Jake and half the volunteers who visited the farm while her husband had barely said anything. He seemed more interested in gobbling down his food in the dim light of the LEDs than in where it had come from, checking periodically on his daughter and Sam underneath the table.

The power was still out, and the messy room had sunk into darkness. A slight breeze drifted in from the open windows, carrying the smoke from the grill outside. The apartment building across the street was a dark presence with dozens of vaguely illuminated, staring eyes.

"Dan has a Spine now, too," Carrie announced while cutting the watermelon into miniscule pieces. "They'd have fired him otherwise."

Jake looked up. "Since when?"

"Couple of weeks," Dan mumbled, finishing off his third burger. "But I don't know how you do it with the gloves, man. I'm still using voice recognition all the time."

"Frontline really would have fired you?" Jake asked.

"Yes, sir. Bastards made me pay for it, too. Said it's standard now, and that we need to be reachable at all times and shit. As if I wasn't reachable before."

As Dan spoke, his voice and the entire room rushed away from Shavir as one thing in it became grossly expanded: Dan's face.

"So now I'm gonna have not only a cousin with a messed-up mind, but a husband, too," Carrie said in mock despair, her words drifting toward Shavir from far away.

"Ain't nobody with a messed-up mind around here," Dan said. "My mind survived three wars, it's gonna survive this little shit piece of a processor just fine."

"Are you alright?" Carrie's face was close to Shavir suddenly.

"She's fine," Dan said. "Just didn't know I'm with Frontline. And now she remembers we've met before under less pleasant circumstances." He leaned forward, his face illuminated by the LEDs. "But your dogs were legal, and Jake's family, so I suggest we relax."

So that's why he'd been staring at her like that when she first came in, Shavir thought. She hadn't recognized him then, but now it was coming back to her, his heavy breathing behind the visor, his voice echoing back from the subway walls when he'd called the clinic, how he had yelled at his colleague and talked to Zeno, believing him to be a veterinarian. She had no idea what to say to him with Jake sitting there or how to get herself out of this mess.

"I'm sorry about what happened to your friend," Dan said, making things worse.

What the hell then. "It took *six* stitches to sew her forehead up."

"Like I said, I'm sorry."

Their eyes locked across the table. It was so quiet in the room, Shavir could hear Sam's soft snoring. "Thanks for calling the vet," she said. Dan wasn't Gary. If anything, he'd been the good cop.

"Sure," Dan said. "I just knew mastiffs ain't no service dogs." He looked below the table where Zoe was asleep, using Sam as her pillow. "Guess I was wrong about that."

The power came back on, bathing them in bright light.

Pressing her hand against her lids, Shavir felt exposed, like everyone at the table would be able to see she was about to go on a raid. "I'm sorry, but I need to go," she said to Jake. "Like I mentioned earlier," she added clumsily so it wouldn't look like she was asking in response to recognizing Dan, which she absolutely was.

Jake just nodded, and Carrie was oddly quiet when she bent down to wake Zoe. But when Dan disappeared into the bedroom, she touched Shavir's arm. "Dan is a good guy, but it's hard for them, you know?" she pleaded. "There's so much anger with all the protests, and sometimes they make mistakes."

Jake still hadn't said anything. He was carrying plates to the kitchen.

Dan insisted on accompanying them to the station, his T-shirt showing a bulge when he returned from the bedroom after packing his gun. The thought sent shudders down Shavir's spine, but she reminded herself of what Dan had said: Jake was family.

They said good-bye to Carrie and a teary-eyed Zoe, who made Shavir promise three times that she would be able to see Sam again and visit Roots with her mother, perhaps her dad, too.

Shavir promised. It was all completely insane, a forceful reminder of why it wasn't a good idea for someone with her résumé to date a Homeland guy or meet his family.

The atmosphere outside felt electric. There was glass on the sidewalk from the broken window of a pharmacy, dozens of Frontline cops swarming around it.

Dan exchanged greetings with some of the cops. "It's gonna get worse," he said to Jake. "If the situation doesn't change real soon, it's only a question of what's gonna explode first, Brooklyn or Queens."

"Probably Brooklyn," Shavir said.

Dan nodded. "Probably, yes."

"I'd prefer no explosions at all," said Jake, the first time he'd said anything to her since Dan's revelation at the table. "If that's an option."

Dan looked sternly at him. "Then something needs to change. I'm telling you as someone who's literally at the frontline. You can report that to your bosses."

"We're doing everything we can, Dan," Jake said impatiently. "We have improved the antibiotics situation for the hospitals here in Queens, haven't we? It'd be nice if someone could acknowledge that."

Dan shrugged, his eyes scanning their surroundings. "I'm just saying that people are pissed, really pissed. They've been pissed before, but this time it's just too many things coming together. It's a fucking tinderbox. Just strike a match."

They had reached the station. The goodbye was brief and tense, and then Shavir, Sam, and Jake were in the half-empty train.

Shavir sat down and spent the next ten minutes staring holes into the air as she tried to come up with an answer for the question she knew Jake was formulating.

"Can I ask you what happened?" he finally asked.

Dan hadn't mentioned any numbers, so Jake didn't know it hadn't only been Sam who was with them that day. Perhaps she could buy herself some time.

"I'm sure you've seen some Frontline checks?" she asked guardedly. "When they look for the pet registration?" Jake nodded, so she continued. "This happens to me once or twice a day, and sometimes things get nasty. I know Tara doesn't look it, but she can be fierce if the cops treat her wrong. And Dan's partner, if I may say so, is an asshole."

Jake surprised her with a crooked smile. "I know Gary and concur with that assessment."

She smiled back, grateful for the deflation and hoping he wouldn't ask her to come home with him. "Were you hurt by what Dan said about SAFE?" she asked.

"No," Jake said after a long silence. "He's a good guy, and people are right to be mad."

"It's not your fault." It occurred to her that this might be true.

"Yeah, it is. Who else is gonna fix our supply situation?"

"Maybe nobody can. Not anymore."

"That's not an option."

He didn't say anything else about the matter, and he still hadn't asked her to come home with him when they approached Greenpoint.

Shavir disentangled herself from his arms.

"See you tomorrow morning?"

He nodded.

Sam looked at Jake as if expecting him to get up, too, then he followed her out of the car. She turned and lifted one hand before the departing train tore them apart.

One hour later, Shavir was sitting on her narrow bed, packing. She climbed over Sam and took the turtleneck from the clothing rack, stuffing it into her bag with the gloves and ski mask. For the umpteenth time, she was rehashing those last moments in the subway station, the expression on Jake's face as he'd looked at her through the greasy window of the train. She wasn't sure whether he had been desperate or mad or whether he'd believed a word of what she'd said.

She took off her T-shirt and grabbed her black pants. At the vibration against her hip bone, she took out her phone and read Jake's message while she wiggled out of her jeans.

Thinking of you.

She bit her lip and sat down. Then she got up again, switched off the phone, and put it on the bedside table. No more of this. Enough damage had been done already.

She slipped into her rubber boots, grabbed her bag, and led Sam across the hallway to the open door of Judy's cubicle.

"I'm leaving."

Judy looked at Sam. "Come here, boy."

Sam trotted reluctantly into the overstuffed cubicle, his head so low it seemed to graze the floor. He hated when she did this to him.

She gave Judy his leash. "Thanks for doing this again despite—"

A sharp nod. "Good luck with everything."

Down in the storehouse, the trapdoor was open. Tara was in the basement preparing, and a rumble to her left told Shavir the freight elevator was coming up. She heard Lenny's baritone before his dreads appeared at ground level. "Hi, Shav. You're late."

"I'm not. You're early as always."

"We're pretty much done. How was Queens?"

"It was nice. Anything specific you'd like to know?"

They were eyeing each other, but she felt too guilty to back down.

"I just don't think it's a clever idea to lead Homeland Security onto us," Lenny said. "That's all."

She couldn't take any more of this tonight. "Spare me another lecture, please. Jake doesn't know anything, and even if he did, it's not like he's with the FBI. His job is to get stuff from A to B."

"Right. And his work contract happens to require him to report any illegal activity he is aware of. I don't like it, Shav. It's just not safe."

"I know you don't like it," Shavir returned sharply, "but you'll simply have to live with it." She didn't want to imagine what kind of hell Lenny would give her if he knew she'd just dined with one of the guys who had smashed Tara's head against the wall. Whenever she thought about whatever was going on between her and Jake, she came to the same conclusion: it wasn't safe.

She was relieved when Nacho came up from the basement, carrying the tool bags and suggesting they open the gate to let in some air.

As if on command, the metal gate rolled up, revealing Finn's van.

The vehicle backed into the storehouse, coming to a stop as the gate closed behind it. Its headlights went out, plunging the room back into semidarkness. The driver's door opened, and Finn jumped out, clad head to toe in black like everyone else. He removed his company's magnetic tree logos from the sides of the van, moving in that overly energetic way that told her he had seen her, but he didn't look at her as he walked around the van to change the back license plate.

She was so absorbed in formulating what she might say if he dared come near her that she didn't hear Troy ask her to check the walkie-talkies. It was only when he touched her arm and asked again that she walked to the metal box on the floor next to the elevator. She crouched down and, one by one, picked up the equipment upon which their lives depended to check their functionality one more time.

Finn was suddenly crouching next to her, in his hand the aluminum-lined elastic collar that would shield his neck and thus make it impossible to trace him through his Spine processor. "Can you help me with this?" he asked, his eyes bright blue in the stray light from the elevator. She checked them for signs of whether he was clean. They had a rawness in them, so he probably was.

There was no good reason for his request other than getting her to interact with him or, just as likely, force of habit. And it might have been habit, too, that made her put down the walkie-talkie and take the collar from his hand. They both got up, and Finn leaned against the elevator gate, turning his back toward her.

She brushed his hair aside and placed the collar around his neck. It was almost weightless, a piece of equipment as outrageously expensive as it was effective in protecting them from surveillance. Spineless as she was, she didn't need one. But Finn had paid the expense not only for himself but also for Troy, the only other member of the group with a Spine. There surely were advantages to having someone among them who was absurdly rich and yet committed to their cause. Why he did it, no one really knew. She had developed her theories over the years, ranging from a deep love of animals to a deep love of her to a bored man's search for a kick and a thrill. But Finn didn't seem as dedicated to the animals as the rest of them were, nor was he particularly dedicated to her, as it turned out. And he could afford plenty of kicks and thrills that didn't involve the risk of going to prison. Maybe that was what he got out of it—the thought of what his father might say if his son should ever get arrested on charges of domestic terrorism. That was the rebel streak in him—like everything else, overdeveloped.

"Do you really have to parade him right in front of me?" he asked.

She was already regretting this. "I'm not parading anyone."

He turned to face her before she could close the latch. "Yes, you are. Why did you bring him here, to the farm, where he has no business? Are you crazy?"

"You're still hung up on that? It's a community farm, you know, not some private resort for activists. Why wouldn't I bring him here?"

"Yeah, that's right, why wouldn't you?" he parroted her. "And why wouldn't you get yourself fucked by Homeland Security?"

"Fuck off." She let go of the collar.

A hurt smile crept onto his lips. "Is he really that good, Shav? I find it hard to believe, looking at him. He must spend an awful lot of time in airless rooms staring at screen walls. And at the Spine, of course, which you love so much." He flickered his eyes with exaggeration.

Without another word, she returned her attention to the walkie-talkies, feeling Finn's stare on her back.

Then he walked back to the van.

Tara's face appeared out of the darkness. "You okay?"

"One of these days, I'm gonna kill him."

"Don't," Tara said. "He's the only one who owns a van."

Shavir closed the lid of the box, grabbed the goggles, and joined the others on the floor of the van. The vehicle whirred back to life and drove out into the night.

They were getting better every time. In and out in one minute less than Troy's projection, that was a first. Shavir peeled off her turtleneck as the van left the evacuation zone and returned to Brooklyn. As always, she felt nauseous after the raid, affected by the stench and the pervasive sense of suffering. Three of the little bodies had been cold when she'd touched them, and two of the puppies were so weak there was a chance they'd be dead by the time they got home. Zeno was squatting over their crate, giving them fluids. That it was necessary to have a quasi-vet on board for emergencies was something they'd learned after their first raid when four of the rescues had been dead on arrival because the sheer stress of it all had been too much for their little systems. As a rule, the dogs were heavily overweight, the cheapest available food shoved down their throats to ready them for slaughter. The extra weight, bad health, and overwhelming fear was a deadly combination.

"How many do we have?" Lenny asked. "Felt like a lot of them."

"Thirty-two," said Tara. "But they're really fat and definitely more than nine weeks."

"Jesus," Lenny said. "And we still have ten of the other ones left."

"Seven," Tara corrected. "I already have families for fifteen of the new ones, and that community farm in Fulton is willing to take four of the older ones if we can restore their barking."

"Which we can," Zeno said. "They're scheduled for surgery."

"Debarked, re-barked," Shavir muttered to herself, "like they have some freakin' on-off switch we can flip as we need it." She leaned against the cool metal of the van's side wall. Another night without sleep lay ahead of her.

Once they were back at the warehouse, they carried the crates to the back room in the basement. In the light, it was clear the puppies were at least twelve weeks. Back at the fattening station, they would have had another three months to live before being sold as pork chops and ground meat. They were anxious and overexcited. Shavir caressed those who allowed her to. Zeno was in the stall next to her, dressing the wounds of the two puppies who had only barely survived the trip.

"How bad does it look?" she asked.

"Their paws are bloody pulp, basically."

"I just don't get why they can't at least have them sit on proper floors. Just because you gonna kill them doesn't mean you have to torture them, too."

"Put them on bars, and you don't have to clean out their cages. Works for chicken, works for dogs, too." Zeno looked at her. "We're down to our last antibiotics. Do you think your SAFE contact—"

"He isn't a *contact*," she hissed, shocked by the idea.

Zeno frowned and resumed attending to the pup. "Well, do you think he can get us some antibiotics? We also need more for the clinic, and it's impossible to get them right now. We don't know how to do surgery without them, and, frankly, we need them for our staff as well."

Shavir swallowed, regretting her temper.

Zeno was always there for them. Without the veterinary antibiotics he brought, none of them would be alive. Still, Jake wouldn't be able to help them, nor did she plan on asking him to.

"Vet stuff isn't high priority for them," she explained. "And even if it was, it's not like he can bring home a box of meds from work." She thought of the bottles Jake had given her and Carrie and wondered if that was really true.

"Can he *make* it high priority?" Zeno wasn't one to give in easily.

"I don't think so." Shavir knew they desperately needed antibiotics, but there had to be a way to get them that didn't involve Jake. "He wouldn't see the need."

Zeno stared at her.

"What?"

"He wouldn't see the need? And that's working for you?"

She got up without responding.

"Well, we do need more antibiotics," Zeno called after her. "Tara wants to clean out that puppy mill in Gravesend."

Shavir turned around. "That's suicide."

She knew she was echoing Lenny, but if he'd ever been right about anything, it was this. Those guys ran their fucking mill right here in Brooklyn, which was unbearable for all of them, but it wouldn't do anyone any good to go out on a suicide mission.

"I guess you better talk to her then," Zeno said. "We've all told her it's too risky. But Tara's Tara. Now that we know where it is, she's set her mind on cleaning the place out."

Shavir nodded, but the thought of listening to Tara recount the suffering of the dogs in that mill was more than she could take right now. She picked up two crates. They all had to be clean before she could go to bed, and at least she wouldn't have to talk.

TWELVE

SO FAR, THE DAY had been a nightmare. Jake stared at the mosaic of news feeds covering the screen walls in the CSR, scanning the steady flow of words in his ears for key terms indicating when it was worth listening again. He forced himself to refocus on the translucent hologram of the Indian government official with whom he'd been on the Spine for the past hour, their conversation moving no longer in circles but in a slow downward vortex.

"I understand your constraints, Mr. Bhaduri, but as I said, I would need to talk to your contact first before I can make a decision."

"And as I said," the man responded without showing any signs of fatigue, "my contact doesn't speak English, so I do not see much sense in such a conversation."

Jake rubbed his eyes, trying to keep it together. It was unlikely Bhaduri was telling the truth since anyone at that level of the West Bengal administration was pretty much guaranteed to be trilingual. But it was no use calling the man a liar. If this had been an official transaction, he could have brought in an interpreter to get around the alleged language barrier, but he was using all kinds of backchannels here and couldn't risk anyone but Masao knowing the details.

Bhaduri claimed his contact had access to nearly three million standard units of certified antibiotics, enough to solve New York's most pressing supply problems. It was an opportunity almost too good to be true, one that wouldn't present itself again anytime soon. He needed to fight down his doubts and close the deal.

Bhaduri's face was as impenetrable as it had been an hour ago. Once again, he recounted all the legal and practical constraints preventing him from giving more precise information about the origin of the antibiotics and insinuated it was best to know as little as possible.

The problem was, Jake wanted to know. But they'd been at an impasse for fifty-three minutes, and he risked losing the meds if he continued insisting on more information.

"Dr. Alvaro?" Bhaduri said. "I would need to know if your institution is willing to accept the offer at the stipulated price. There are other bidders. A great many other bidders."

"I understand." Sweat trickled into Jake's burning eyes. He wanted to yell at the man, get off the Spine, walk out to the seawall, then go to sleep or otherwise lose consciousness. "I need the approval of my superior for such a large sum," he said instead.

"How long will that take?"

"Can you give me thirty minutes?"

"I can give you fifteen."

"Alright. I'll call you back."

He disconnected the call and sat for another minute, his gaze flicking along the screen walls. The upper left corner of the wall opposite him showed a group of Frontline men wading through the flooded streets out on Bergen Beach. "ILLEGAL DOG FARM RAIDED" said the news ticker. He tuned in. The farm had been raided by animal rights activists last night and reported to Frontline, the twelfth incident this year. The identity of the activists was unknown. It was also unclear what happened to the dogs. A Frontline cop said the animals had probably been moved to a location outside the city.

Jake stared at the news anchor, who moved on to the new antibiotic shortages in the Brooklyn hospitals. Last night. The fattening station had been raided *last night*.

Masao looked at him. "What did he say?"

"Nothing, really. Just took a hell of a lot of words to do it."

Jake got up, checking the time on his Spine. Less than ten minutes left to close the deal. He needed David's approval. That was where his mind needed to be.

David looked like a ghost trapped in the icy air of his office. It was impossible to ignore the emaciated body under the white shirt, the sallow skin, the shaking hands. Jake made himself look into David's sunken eyes. It still wasn't clear to him what exactly happened to the human body when pep pills were combined with Emovia, but if he needed a warning sign, it was sitting right in front of him.

"Any progress?" David asked.

"Not really. The amount is still the same."

"It's too much."

"I know. I have eight more minutes to confirm or walk away."

David nodded. "I see. Have you found out why they are selling?"

"They want the money."

"No kidding." David leaned forward. "Why is the stuff available? That's what I wanna know. Why are they offering it to us?"

"It's all legit." Jake felt like he was squeezing the words out.

"You've seen the news, right?" David pointed to the screen wall.

Jake turned to the footage he'd been staring at for hours. There was another border conflict between India and Bangladesh because the annual quota of refugees had been exceeded in late July when the Brahmaputra, the Ganges, and Meghna all flooded after heavy monsoon rainfalls. Those floods now covered three quarters of Bangladesh and had swallowed more than four hundred thousand houses. Although the waters were slowly retreating, tens of thousands of people were still trying to cross the border to India. They weren't welcome.

"Yes," Jake said. "I've watched the news."

"You think they have a surplus of meds to give away?"

"That's what my contact says."

"And you believe him."

"As I said, it all looks legit," Jake said tensely. "And you probably don't want to ask any more questions."

David frowned. "You sure you want to do this, Jake?"

"We need antibiotics, don't we?" Jake made himself look into those sunken eyes again. "And there's nothing else available. Not even under the rugs. This is it, David, and it's a lot of it."

"Then go ahead," David said. "Come back when you're done."

Three minutes left to close the deal. Masses of people were wading through knee-deep water on the screen walls. Desperate-looking Bangladeshi women in colorful saris were trying to carry their children across the border while Indian border officials pushed them back at gunpoint. After a near-complete failure in the two previous years, the monsoon had come back with a vengeance, and together with the run-off from the Himalayan glaciers, the waters had inundated most of what was left of Bangladesh. The country hadn't received much coverage from the American media in recent years, but now that its inhabitants were causing a crisis on West Bengal's border, the story was all over the place. India was a major US supplier.

"Did you get permission?" Masao asked.

Jake nodded and made the call.

Bhaduri's face was as expressionless as before when he told him they would pay the stipulated price.

They settled the modalities, and it was done.

"Congrats!" Masao said. "Two-point-eight million units while everyone else is scrambling to get their hands on a few thousand."

"We got lucky. Now we need transportation." Jake tried to feel good about the deal, but Bhaduri had said it would take them a few days to get the cargo ready for shipping because things were *complicated*. "Has Corsys called a state of emergency for Brooklyn yet?" he asked, eyes glued to the screen wall where the local newsfeeds occupying the lower left corner showed large crowds of protestors in front of hospitals.

"No," Masao said. "They're still within the transportation limit. Only three hospitals have run out so far. The media is making a big deal out of it because of what happened in Queens. They're saying that Brooklyn deserves the same treatment, to get prioritized."

Jake almost laughed. He'd have to talk to Niya then, since, apparently, they were the only ones in the city who had the guts to do anything about the situation.

It was almost 8 p.m. when Jake left the CSR to go home. He had trouble breathing as he climbed the steps to the boardwalk, and it wasn't just because of the heat. His debrief meeting with David had been deeply disturbing. David no longer remembered that he'd asked him to come back to his office or what it was he had wanted to talk about. His gaze had been out of control, and he'd seemed to have difficulty retaining information. He'd been unwilling to address any of this, and he'd refused to go home. The only way to get him to leave the CSR would have been to call an ambulance and get him dragged out, and Jake didn't want to go that far. Now he was hoping that the long walk home along the river would clear his head because he had another difficult conversation ahead of him.

Shavir had called in the late afternoon and suggested they meet at his place—a nice surprise after her sudden withdrawal last night. But even that had been ruined by the news, and as much as he dreaded it, he needed to talk to her.

She waited for him downstairs with Sam and a large, heavy bag, looking tired and sweaty in the evening heat. He resisted the urge to ask if she wanted her fingerprints registered to his apartment so she could let herself in. It was too early for that and probably also too late.

Lucy was resting on his bed when he opened the door of his apartment. She had gotten used to Sam's presence, and it was only when Shavir allowed the dog to come closer to her that the dragon lost confidence and slipped underneath the bed. Sam dropped down and crawled forward, driving his muzzle into Lucy's narrow hiding space.

"Careful, bud," Jake warned, lifting Shavir's bag onto the counter. "She might just bite off your big nosy nose."

Shavir let go of Sam. "I guess she's safe down there for now."

"Unless he manages to lift the bed. What on earth do you have in this bag?"

"Tamales, taco chips, salsa, salad, desert, and—" Shavir reached in and pulled out a bottle of red wine with the same casual affability she'd been displaying since their brief welcome kiss downstairs, "something better than water."

"Impressive," Jake said. "But now we're facing a logistical problem. I only own two plates."

"You realize you sound like a nerd."

Jake took the bottle from her hand. "Owning *one* plate sounds like a nerd. Two plates mean I'm prepared for company. And I also have the bowl we're using for Sam."

She gave him a look. "I guess we can eat from the boxes."

They ate at the kitchen table by candlelight, Jake drinking wine from a coffee mug since the number of glasses in the household had been reduced to one by Lucy. Shavir was talkative, nothing left of last night's distance, her strange silence about the dogs, and whatever had happened with Gary and Dan. It was like everything was normal, just two people sharing dinner after a busy day. Jake found himself going along, not yet ready to end the pretense. Then, after serving dessert, Shavir changed course.

"There's something I have to tell you."

"Is it related to what happened last night in Bergen Beach?"

Her eyes widened.

"I watch the news," he said. "And it is my job to make connections."

She dropped her gaze, and so it was true. She was actually doing this. It took a moment for reality to sink in. Then he said out loud what had been on his mind all day.

"You realize that under US law, what you're doing is terrorism?"

Her eyes flew up, a flare. "That's a ridiculous law. You think I'm a terrorist, saving animals from getting abused and slaughtered? *Illegally* abused and slaughtered?"

"I don't. But our laws do, and they have done so for fifty years or so. And, clearly, you're aware. Do you understand what that means if you get caught?"

"That's why we try not to get caught."

Apparently, they were good at it. Twelve fattening stations this year alone. That was what the Frontline cop had said. Jake wasn't sure what it meant for him that the woman he was having dinner with was good at terrorism. Or, rather, he did know and wished he didn't.

"Who's *we*?" he asked. "Lenny, Tara, and you?" He'd given some thought to the matter on his walk home. This was how far he'd gotten. Shavir was looking at the table, silent at first. "Troy," she then said. "You saw him at Buddha's, bartending. And at Roots yesterday."

The hipster bartender. He wouldn't have remembered, but the guy had looked familiar when he and his buddies had interrogated him about the hospital situation.

"Zeno." Shavir picked up her glass. "He was there, too. Nacho, one of the farmers who lives at the West Street Project. You met him on the farm. It's the six of us. And Finn. He drives the van." She put the glass to her lips and downed the rest of the wine.

Jake looked away. Her ex, of course. He should have known. Driving the getaway car of all things. Like in some old-fashioned heist movie.

"That's why things have been so difficult," Shavir said. "We see each other all the time, and he has trouble keeping his distance."

"Who takes the animals?" Jake asked because he didn't want to think about Finn.

"People who love them. They find homes in New Jersey, Upstate, Pennsylvania, most of them. Homes with yards where they can roam around. Some are adopted here in the city. People are lonely and afraid. They want company. And the ones we pick are animal lovers, dedicated like we are but doing a different part of the job."

"Well, you do both, don't you?" Jake asked with a glance at Sam. She nodded.

"But dogs are so expensive."

She hesitated, probably gauging how likely it was that he'd report her to Frontline. Or worse, to Homeland. The thought insulted him, but he remained quiet.

"Zeno chips them before we give them away," she said with a look like she was drowning. "Troy's good with technical stuff, and he found a way to hack the city's computer program that registers the dog licenses. He enters the information so that it looks like their license fees are paid."

"So it's *all* illegal," Jake confirmed, more for himself than for her. He remembered the satisfaction he'd felt when the Queens hospitals went to red on Corsys, when Niya and he had broken the law in the name of justice. He wondered whether Shavir felt the same. And why she was telling him all this if she was so afraid of Homeland.

"That fee is outrageous, anyhow," she snapped. "It's meant to keep people from having animals. But people don't want to be alone. And the animals need homes."

"Wouldn't it be better to stop the whole business altogether?"

"*How?*" she spat out, the tone in her voice scathing. "Can you tell me? It won't stop as long as animal meat is this profitable, and no one really cares about the animals dying for it. I've been at dozens of protests. I've signed thousands of petitions. No one cares about animals as long as they don't have to see all the suffering that's going on. When the government finally got around to outlawing factory farms, it was to save the antibiotics and, maybe, the climate, not the animals. And now, with everything that's happening on the planet, they can't be bothered at all, since, apparently, human survival is on the line. The only thing we can do is rescue the animals we find out about and allow them to have a decent life."

"How do you know they don't eat them?"

"The people who adopt?" Shavir laughed. "Because we *check* them. Plus, few people in this country are keen on eating dogs or even rabbits. They want their beef and their pork and their fucking lamb chops. As long as they think that's what they're eating, it's all good. Almost all the illegal dog meat is mislabeled because people need to believe what's on their dinner table is just like what they used to eat in the *good old days* when factory farming was legal."

"If you buy on the black market, you know the risk."

"A risk you can ignore. *That*," she pointed to the enormous mass of Sam, still lying on the floor with his nose crammed underneath the bed, "you cannot ignore."

"True," Jake said, taken aback by her fervor. "He's very difficult to ignore. And very persistent. I'm not even sure Lucy's still down there."

"She is, or he wouldn't be like this. He's persistent but not stupid."

"Do you think it would help if I fed him?" He didn't know what to do with what Shavir had just dropped in his lap, information that, by law and his contract with Homeland Security, he was required to report. But he didn't want to keep interrogating her, and the very fact that she was telling him these things made him complicit, which was perhaps why she was telling him. He pointed to a can of dog food he'd bought at a deli the day before. "I don't know whether he's supposed to eat that, but maybe he'll like it? More than Lucy, I hope."

"He doesn't want to eat her."

"You sure?"

Shavir looked at Sam and back at Jake. "Give him the food."

He got up, relieved to get away from the tension between them.

Sam was next to him before he had finished opening the can, wagging his tail in anticipation. He put the bowl on the floor, and they watched the dog gobble down the food.

"Jesus," Shavir said. "He really likes it. What's in there?"

Jake picked up the can and read. "Ground GM corn, ground GM soy, synthetic meat waste, high fructose corn syrup, ascorbic acid, propyl gallate, ethoxyquin, and butylated hydroxyanisole."

"You're ruining my dog."

Jake laughed, eager to be normal again. He stopped abruptly when an emergency call overrode the Spine's standby mode. Four bright green letters danced in front of his eyes. *LISA*.

"Accept," he said, and Lisa's voice filled his ears.

"David collapsed! He went into cardiac arrest."

"He... what?" Jake stammered. "Where?"

"Right here! He coded right in front of me, Jake! I gave him CPR. And had to shock him. Three times before his heart came back. *Three times!* He's on his way to the hospital now."

"Where to?"

"NYU Langone."

"That's good," Jake said like an automaton. "They've got everything they need."

"He looked so bad." Lisa was crying. "He was still unconscious when they carried him out. I don't know who to call. I checked his emergency contacts, but there's nothing there."

"He erased it when his wife got the divorce."

"What do I do now?"

"Nothing. You've done more than enough." Jake pressed his fingers against the surface of the kitchen counter until his nails started to hurt. He was the one who should have called the ambulance hours ago when David had still been conscious. He could have prevented this.

"I know Sandra, his ex-wife," he said. "I'll track her down."

"Will you go to Langone? Someone should."

"Don't worry about it. I'm gonna go and make the calls."

"Okay." Lisa's voice sounded small. "Thanks, Jake."

He hung up and looked into Shavir's questioning eyes.

"It's David. A heart attack."

"Oh gosh, I'm sorry, Jake."

With that one sentence, the distance between them collapsed. It was like she knew how he felt, like she could feel it. A sound escaped him, rough, ragged, something stored deep inside him breaking free and ripping the surface.

Then Shavir was next to him, holding him. "Do you want me to come with you?" she asked into his ear. "We can leave Sam here."

He knew he should say no, and not only because their identities would be checked at the hospital, and he had no idea what would happen then. He knew he should end this whole thing between them. "That'd be great," he said, and they headed for the door.

Tracking down the number of David's ex-wife posed no problem, but Sandra's voice was cold when Jake explained the reason for his call as he and Shavir walked to the brightly lit entrance of the NYU Langone Medical Center.

"Not really a surprise," Sandra said, adding that she trusted the doctors would do all they could. But when he asked for the number of their son, she lost it. "David didn't give a damn about his son when he was alive, so I don't see why Oliver should be there when he's dying."

"He isn't *dying*. I'm sure Oliver would want to—"

"You can't be sure of anything, Jake," Sandra cut in. "You have no clue what we've been through. It's nice that you're there with him, and I guess it makes sense that it's someone from SAFE who's doing that. I hope he'll make it through." With that, she ended the call.

A security guard checked their fingerprints in the entrance hall, showing no signs of alarm after reading Shavir's, who was tense and quiet while the guard explained the way to the intensive care unit.

Jake recognized the tall and elegant figure of Gwen Hatton before she turned on her high heels to face him. He asked Shavir to stay behind as he walked toward SAFE's thorny director.

"Gwen. Did Lisa call you?"

"Yes, and I was in the area." Gwen looked unusually strained as she lowered her voice. "David's heart failed as a result of the insane mix of biochemical substances in his blood. That's what the doctors said, pretty much. Did you know he was on Emovia?"

"No." Jake had no idea what it might mean if he confessed he did.

"A lot of it, apparently. And even more amphetamines. These doctors keep asking me why his Spine didn't report his condition *before* his heart failed."

Because he had the reporting function firewalled, thought Jake, like everyone else in the CSR. None of them would be working another day if they allowed their Spines to report their physical data to the MHA. Blocking that function was illegal, but what else could they do? Gwen knew this.

"I don't want an investigation," she said, "and they seem very intent on starting one. They can't believe someone had to actually *call* an ambulance. The delay almost killed him. He's lucky Lisa's certified in Basic Life Support. Otherwise, he would be dead."

"How is he doing now?"

"Still unconscious. They say we have to wait and see how it develops. The stress on his body was enormous. They don't know what happened to his brain."

Jake tried not to hear this. "I should stay. Someone should be here when he wakes up."

"I'll stay," Gwen said. "I need to know more about David's condition," she added, seeing the surprise in his eyes, "and whether they're planning to start an investigation. I need you in the CSR tomorrow morning. You're taking over for David."

Jake stared at her. "I'm not his deputy. It hasn't happened yet."

"It just happened. The day team is yours. I've already informed Lisa. Keep your Spine on standby. I might have to contact you in case there's news on David."

Jake nodded, stunned. There wasn't a ghost of a chance he'd sleep tonight. But that would at least give him time to find David's son.

It was the least he could do.

The pre-sunrise glow was the most extreme he had ever seen. Jake sat alone on his bed, mesmerized by the crazy hues of orange and red filling the bay window. The colors of the sky had been amplifying gradually for years since the government had started seeding the atmosphere with sulfur. One of the country's most ambitious geoengineering projects, it hadn't done shit to cool the climate, but at least they now got sunrises right out of a science-fiction movie.

As predicted, he hadn't slept at all. Shavir had nodded off for a bit after they'd come back from the hospital while he'd sat next to her, thinking. About Shavir and why he couldn't stop seeing her. About David and what he had done to himself. About India and what exactly Bhaduri had meant when he'd called the situation *complicated*. He hadn't come up with a single answer, and now his head hurt. It all felt wrong to him, most of all that he was the acting head of the CSR day team. He had no idea how to fill David's shoes. Or what he should say to his son. It had taken hours on the Spine to find the right Oliver Wayne. Now he needed to tell him his dad was in a coma. What if David died?

"You okay?" Shavir's voice drifted into his racing mind. She was standing next to the bed in her underwear, her hair in a loose braid down to her waist, both hands behind her back.

"What do you have there?"

She bit her lip. "Maybe this isn't such a great idea."

"What is?"

She slowly moved her hands where he could see them, in one a coffee mug, in the other a cupcake with a single lit candle. "This."

He stared at the candle, too confused to say anything.

"Happy birthday, Jake," she said with an uncertain smile.

He wanted to flip on his Spine to check the date, but she was right. It was August 7.

Shavir put down the cupcake on the bedside table, her movements awkward, her body stiff. She was clearly out of her element as her left hand lowered the coffee mug for him, so he could see the perfect heart she had drawn into the foam.

"How did you know?" he asked. "Carrie?"

She smiled. "It wasn't the man on the moon."

"I didn't know you had her number."

"We exchanged them because of Zoe and Sam. And then she called."

That was something only Carrie would do—call a woman she'd only just met and tell her it was his birthday. He took the mug and tasted the hot coffee. It helped him relax enough to manage a smile. "You're full of surprises. I had my last birthday cake when I was twelve."

"Your mom?"

He nodded. "A month before she died."

"I'm sorry."

"Don't be." He pulled her down and kissed her. "You're wonderful. I'm sorry I'm not better at this. I didn't even remember it's my birthday. Nobody does. Nobody but Carrie. And you."

"You have to make a wish."

He looked at her without understanding.

"The candle." She nodded toward the cupcake. "You need to blow it out and make a wish. That's how it's done. But you can't say it. The wish. You can't say what it is, or it won't happen."

He looked at the little flame. "How do you know?"

"*My* mom. And I didn't do it right. My wish." Her voice cracked.

He pulled her close. "Come here, that's nonsense."

Her body was limp, unresponsive. Tears wet his shoulder where she rested her face. "She got shot," she said in the same cracked voice. "It just happened. No one was shooting at her. She was just where the bullets were. And then she was bleeding. She told me how to stop it, using my clothes. But there was so much blood. I tried, but I didn't do it right. I couldn't stop it."

"You were, what, twenty?"

"Twenty-one. Old enough to save a life."

"Honey," he said softly, "it doesn't work that way."

"I know." Shavir unwound herself from his embrace, her voice stronger, more controlled. "I'm an idiot, talking about this stuff instead of celebrating with you. I actually had another surprise for you," she said abruptly, changing the topic. "A real birthday present. But now it seems like a stupid idea with all that's going on."

"A surprise, huh?"

She wiped her face with her arm, still struggling with her memories. It must have been difficult for her, going to the hospital with him. But she had done it anyway, and all he'd been thinking about was what it would mean for him if she got arrested.

"I know you're overdosing on surprises these days," she went on, "but this one you would have liked, I think. I was going to give you an address, and you'd have had to go there."

"Would you've been there, too?"

"No. It would have been just you, sitting there by yourself all night. *Surprise!*" She picked up the cupcake. "Of course, I would have been there. Blow out your candle."

"My wish is that you give me my birthday present tonight."

"You're not supposed to say it!" she scolded, but she was laughing.

"How else are you gonna know?"

She hesitated. "You sure?"

"I'm sure. I can't believe you're doing this for me in the first place, and now I sure as hell want to see it. If we wait until life gives us a break, I won't ever celebrate my birthday again. So what's the address?"

She gave it to him, and he looked up. "Vestry Street? That's right by the Hudson River."

She nodded, smiling. "I told you you'll like it."

Lisa was waiting for the debrief when Jake stepped into the CSR an hour later with a tray of coffee cups. She looked worse than last night.

"David's stable," he announced. "Still unconscious but stable. I just got a call from Gwen."

"I know. Gwen called me, too."

"That's good, right?" he asked too cheerily. "He's stable."

Lisa looked away to the screen wall across the room. "I'd never done it before, you know? I mean, you take that stupid course, and then you're certified in BLS, but I had never *done* it. And suddenly I'm here, pumping away at David's chest. And yelling at someone to get the defibrillator from the hallway, so I can shock him. *Shock* him." She exhaled, facing him. "You've seen it in a thousand movies, but you're actually sending an electric current through someone's body. And you have no idea what you're doing. I was in total panic."

"Apparently you did everything right." Jake raised the tray. "Almond latte?"

She nodded and took one of the cups. "He collapsed right in front of me, Jake."

"He's alive because of you."

"Do you know what the survival rate is after cardiac arrest?" Lisa asked sternly. "Twelve percent. That's it. Twelve percent. The vast majority don't even make it to the hospital, and half of those who do still die. The whole idea is that you get to the hospital *before* you go into cardiac arrest. That's why the death rate has gone down so dramatically. Because the Spine calls for medical support before people are coding. But, of course, we all firewall that feature because we're drugged-up freaks who sacrifice everything for the CSR. Everything. Like we have no families, no responsibilities, no one who needs or loves us. Like we're fucking alone in the world. And for what? We're not gonna be able to save this. All we ever do is kill people."

Jake put his arm around her. She was exhausted, but she was also right, and there was nothing he could say to make it better, nothing to take away the madness they were all entangled in. "You saved him," he said quietly. "That's what you should think of. You saved him."

"I don't think so." Lisa's voice was barely audible.

She leaned against him for another second then straightened up, shaking off her weak moment much like Shavir had earlier this morning. Somehow, none of them were allowed to feel pain anymore.

"We managed to unearth a few thousand units of anticoagulants," she said, in business mode now, "and also some of the cancer and HIV meds on the list. We didn't have any luck with the Emovia substitutes. And antibiotics are out of the question right now. We couldn't get anything at all. Thank God you hit that jackpot in India."

"I was lucky." He still wasn't so sure about that.

Lisa studied his face. "Gwen says you're taking over for David now?"

"Until he returns."

"Yeah," she said, "until he returns. I need to go home."

He walked her to the elevator and remained standing there after the doors had closed, uncertain what taking over for David meant for him.

David's office had been locked by security, and he had a few more minutes until Masao arrived. Without much thought, he stepped into the elevator and rode up to the eighth floor. He had been here before, but the white hallway nevertheless felt like unfamiliar territory when he stepped out and walked to the reception desk.

"I'd like to see Dr. Hatton," he said to the woman behind the counter. "Is she in?"

Gwen looked impeccable as always when he walked into the light-suffused space of her office, although she couldn't have slept more than a few hours. She was wearing the same gray suit she'd worn at the hospital last night, and Jake also recognized the blue pattern on her blouse. She hadn't gone home.

"I will ask security to open David's office for you," she said as he sat down across from her, "and they will download all relevant data from David's Spine cloud. They'll run it by me first, but you should receive everything you need this afternoon."

The thought that first Gwen and then he would be going through the contents of David's Spine was deeply disturbing. It didn't sound like she was expecting David to be back anytime soon.

She stared across the table. "I had no idea he was taking Emovia. How stupid is that with the amount of amphetamines he's on? When did he start using, do you know?"

"As I said, I didn't know he was taking it at all."

She let her gray eyes settle on him for the better part of a minute, freezing him slowly from the inside. "I just hope no one else down there is that stupid. And I hope David survives this so I can ask him what the hell he was thinking."

It sounded like the threat it was meant to be, and Jake resented the lack of empathy and sheer human decency. Sure, David had made a mistake. Sure, it had been irresponsible of him to try to hide his mistake. But he was also a CSR legend in critical condition, so a little more respect and compassion seemed in order. He wondered why Gwen was so insistent on not having known anything about the abuse. He wondered whether she was already covering her own elegant ass.

"Until David returns, you'll take his place," she said in the same flat voice, "but I want you to clear all far-reaching decisions with me. I will leave it to your good judgment which decisions fall into that category." She leaned back in her chair. "I suppose you'll have to look at David's data first, but do you have any questions right now?"

"I do. Where are we with the approval of the new Emovia capsule?"

"Stuck. That's where we are. Kruger is personally trying to mess with us, and so far, he's been very successful. The FDA has pulled this whole hygiene-concerns crap on us and thereby delayed the approval process for several weeks. We're lucky that your people found another US plant that can produce the same capsule. That leaves them no way out. They have to approve it."

"When?"

"I don't know. A few weeks if we can get them to speed-approve."

"A few weeks?" Jake echoed. "Seriously?"

It was beyond him how she could be cool like this knowing they were walking right into a homemade disaster with hundreds, probably thousands, of casualties. "We don't have a few weeks, Gwen," he said impatiently. "We had to give out an alert on 4Flow, and social media are running wild with it. The price of emotion regulators has quadrupled, and people are going insane just anticipating the shortage."

"I'm aware of that. That's why you need to get more substitutes."

"We've been busy doing that all week."

"Good. Keep me posted on your progress then." Gwen looked away. "And I've just been informed that your fingerprints are now registered to David's office. Thanks for stepping up, Jake. It's what David would have wanted." Apparently, they were done.

Below the cold surface, though, Gwen's carefully made-up face still looked tense. She'd spent all night in the hospital, and it seemed unlikely she was that worried about an MHA investigation. Perhaps all those rumors about her and David were true, Jake thought as he returned to the seventh floor. The peculiar biotope of the CSR sprouted gossip just like the next place, and there had never been a shortage of speculations about David and Gwen ever since Julia, or perhaps another member of the team, had spotted them together at a restaurant in the Bronx. It had always seemed a bizarre idea to Jake since David's manic determination had already ruined his marriage to a much more lenient woman. Imagining him with Gwen was absurd. But why, then, would she have personally gone to the hospital? Perhaps it had been security concerns after all, he decided; perhaps SAFE had much more to hide than he knew.

He was cleared immediately by the Delphi reader outside David's office and stepped inside, closing the door behind him. He sat down and started opening drawers. They weren't locked, and the Emovia bottle was in the second drawer, next to a bottle of amphetamines. *Stupid,* Gwen had said, but that was not what it was. He remembered the look in David's eyes when he'd said he wasn't going to stop.

It hadn't been a matter of stupidity. He had been afraid. Not of the drug or the MHA but of his own emotions. Gwen couldn't understand because Gwen wasn't spending her days in the CSR. But Jake could. And, he suspected, Lisa, too. When she'd told him about the abuse, she had not once wondered about David's reasons for it. As the leader of the night team, she knew.

Jake slid both bottles into his pocket. No one would find them. He'd take care of David's affairs as well as he could. He leaned back and told the Spine to call Oliver Wayne.

The cool entry hall of the NYU Langone Medical Center felt like a quiet embrace when Jake entered it hours later, trying to prepare himself for what was waiting for him in the intensive care ward. The day in the CSR had been calmer than usual because David hadn't been there to erupt all over them, but Jake was exhausted nevertheless. Being awake for over thirty-six hours took its toll, and not even an additional round of pep pills had changed anything about that.

He approached one of the nurses. "I'd like to visit David Wayne?"

The nurse checked his prints and led him down the hallway into one of the rooms. "He still isn't conscious," she said when they were standing in front of David's bed. "There's a chair if you'd like to sit down." Then David and he were alone.

He stood staring at the lifeless face. There were tubes and monitors everywhere. David's entire body seemed to be hooked up to some machine or other. "I'm sorry," he got out, and then his voice broke, and he had to collect himself. He wanted to tell David about Sandra and that he'd managed to reach his son, but he wasn't sure either was what David wanted to hear. "We're still not making much progress with the Emovia substitutes," he heard himself saying instead. "But Lisa got her hands on a few thousand units of anticoagulants and a bunch of the other stuff we're missing. Oh, yes, and Epi, too, so we can refill what they've shot into you all night." He exhaled. "Lisa was great, David. Saved your life like a pro."

There was no reaction on David's face. Gwen had said his condition was critical until he regained consciousness. She'd also said he might remain in a coma for weeks.

"Once you wake up," Jake continued, "there are a few things I need to ask you. We've been managing pretty well today, but this was a bit sudden, and you haven't really given me the rundown, you know?" He paused. It was hard to look at David's face.

The door opened behind him, and the nurse appeared again. "I'm sorry, Dr. Alvaro, but Dr. Wayne's son would like to visit his father."

Oliver Wayne stood next to her. "It's alright. He can stay."

They shook hands, but Oliver's eyes were on his father. "Jesus." He didn't look like David at all, much taller than his father with a soft face that was young and boyish. It was hard to imagine him yelling at anyone. "Thanks for calling me," he said. "My mother doesn't know I'm here. She's very... bitter about it all."

"How long since you last saw your dad?"

"I don't know. Three years?" Oliver stared at David again. "He looks so different. Not at all like my father. So small. And weak."

"It's the whole setup. All the machines. He's tough though."

Oliver nodded. "Would you mind—?"

"No, not at all. It's great you're here."

They said goodbye, and Jake left. David had almost never talked about his son, like he had almost never talked about his wife when they were together. He'd been married to SAFE all these years. Now he was lying in that room, his life depending on the very meds he'd helped secure because he had overdosed on the other meds he'd helped secure, meds that he had used to take away his loneliness.

The irony was hard to miss.

Jake took the stairs to the ground floor, unable to face the confinement of an elevator. Twenty years, David had said. That he was twenty years younger but on the same road to hell. And it *was* hell up there in the intensive care ward, though it was a hell better stocked and supplied than its counterparts in Brooklyn and Queens.

He felt dizzy when he left the staircase and stumbled toward the entrance door. He avoided a man pushing a woman in a wheelchair, and then he was outside.

Thirteen

It was hot, the range going full blast, six people stepping on each other's toes struggling to get their orders out. Half past seven, and Buddha's Kitchen had a full house. Nimesh stood at the counter, cutting vegetables with a face like he was cutting his limbs.

"I hope you aren't doing that for me?" Shavir said as she made her way toward him past bubbling pots and perfectly arranged plates of food balanced by waiters. The air was filled with the intoxicating scents of lemongrass, ginger, galangal, and kaffir lime.

Nimesh looked up from his cutting board. "My staff's busy making food for the patrons who like it, you know, *cooked*. I can hardly ask them to do this."

Shavir laughed, embarrassed that Buddha's star-decorated chef was doing the kind of menial work for her that normally fell to the lowest of his line cooks. "I can't watch this, Nimesh. Please just give me whatever goes into the dishes, and I'll slice it up myself."

Nimesh put down the knife. "What's this about? It's the first time someone asks me to give away my food as a do-it-yourself kit. Takeout, sure. But not like this."

"Because I want it to be special," Shavir said gingerly, trying to find the right form of appeasement. "A very special birthday surprise for someone very special. I have the perfect place and want the perfect dinner to go along with it. So, naturally, I had to ask you."

"I'm just saying you're enjoying some very special privileges around here." Nimesh threw the sliced vegetables into a bag on the table and started yelling at one of his cooks who had applied the sauces to a dish in the wrong order. Shavir stole a carrot and bit into it, feeling bad for the cook who bore the ordeal with a professional, "Yes, chef!"

Maybe this wasn't such a great idea.

"We'll cherish your food, Nimesh," she said, suppressing the irritation she felt whenever she witnessed this kind of abuse in the kitchen, undermining both Anil's policies and the restaurant's serene image. "I promise I will do my best and cook it to perfection."

"You think it's that easy, just throw it into a pot?" Nimesh glared, but a smile played around his mouth. He would forgive her the transgression eventually, and Jake would have the food to go with his view. If he noticed either, that was.

She felt profoundly uncertain about his decision to go through with her surprise. David's heart attack had been a shock for Jake, and what had happened before that, at Carrie's place, had given her an even more compelling reason to forget her plans for tonight. When she'd arrived at Jake's place with Sam last night, she'd been resolved to tell him the truth about the animals, only to learn that he had already figured it out. That he brought up terrorism charges right away should have been a warning sign, but, apparently, she was no longer able to heed those.

She hadn't told the others about Dan or that Jake knew about their raids. Not even Tara, with whom she had spent the entire afternoon helping Judy install long sheets of a new foil Finn had brought along, some kind of engineering masterpiece that filtered sunrays and kept crops alive. There had been barely enough for one roof, and Judy was no easy woman to be around when she feared her people might not have enough produce to sell or eat. She'd been irritated enough to complain about the dogs again, and it was only thanks to Nacho that she could be kept at a safe distance from Tara, who seemed to have only one topic of conversation these days: the horrors of the Brooklyn puppy mill and how to raid it.

Tara had tried out different rhetorical strategies, starting with the rational, moving on to the emotional, and then to a bunch of wild allegations that were meant to make them all feel guilty. By now, she had likely converted Nacho, and Lenny seemed to be wavering as well. Finn was always a wild card, so Troy and Zeno were the only ones left who might listen to the meek voice of reason.

"Is Troy working tonight?" Shavir asked, since Nimesh wouldn't give up his knife or allow her to cut her vegetables. Perhaps she could do something useful with the delay.

Nimesh nodded. "Alone at the bar and bored to death."

That was precisely what she'd been hoping for. At this time of the evening, Troy was always bored to death. The guests had moved to the tables, and all he had to do was heat up a few bottles of sake and draw beer. She offered Nimesh her help one more time before she left the kitchen and made her way to Buddha's splendid bar.

Troy wasn't bored at all, as it turned out. He was busy filling a tray with cocktails, but he was indeed alone.

"Has Tara talked to you?" Shavir got right to the point.

"About the mill? Yeah, she's been talking to everyone."

"I want that place cleaned out as much as Tara does," Shavir offered as an opening statement, "but we simply can't do it. If the breeders don't kill us, the dogs will when we reach for their puppies. They're so traumatized that we'd have to put half of them down anyway. That's why we've never taken on a mill."

Troy didn't answer, pretending the martinis he was preparing demanded his full attention. As their logistical mastermind, it would be his job to come up with a plan, and his face told her he had been working on one.

"You think we can do it?" she asked, her heart sinking.

Troy put the full glasses onto the tray. "Frankly, I don't know. It's definitely going to be hard. And complicated. For starters, we're never gonna fit all of us into the van together with all the dogs and their puppies and the bigger crates we need for them. Plus, we need more people. The seven of us is not going to be enough. We'd need someone else besides Zeno who can sedate the mother dogs."

"So we can't do it," Shavir said with finality.

"That depends."

"On what?"

"There's a subway station nearby."

Shavir laughed. "Oh, come on, Troy! You want us to catch a train after the raid? And I thought Tara was the crazy one."

"It's not without risk, but it's doable," Troy said in the cool, understated tone he used for everything. "Seems to me you're not averse to taking some pretty big risks yourself."

"What does that have to do with anything?"

Troy didn't answer immediately, as a server was approaching. "I'm just saying that if you're okay with dating this guy, you'll probably be fine on the train," he said when they were alone again. "There's another problem, though, one Zeno mentioned to me. If we get the mother dogs, too, we'll need a lot of antibiotics. He said your guy—"

"Don't," Shavir warned. "Zeno's got the wrong idea there."

Troy paused with a seriousness rarely seen in him. "Well, could you at least ask?"

"No, Troy, I couldn't." She'd thought she resented Lenny's paranoia and Tara's twisted allegations, but now she realized what was really getting to her was this brand-new strategy to instrumentalize her relationship with Jake.

"Like I said," Troy repeated, "we would need more meds from somewhere. And more people, otherwise it's going to take us too long. That's what I'm worried about."

"I'm worried about a whole bunch of things," Shavir shot back. "We've got zero experience with this kind of thing. None."

"Maybe." Troy shrugged, easing back into his usual equanimity. "But Tara's right. At some point, we've got to start. This might not be the only mill in the city, and it's right in front of our fucking noses. We can't just ignore it."

Shavir almost laughed. So much for the voice of reason and her assumption that she would somehow be able to fix this while Nimesh cut her vegetables. The only person who was fixing anything was Tara. It was amazing how she always did this. If she came up with the idea to raid the White House and unshackle the president's pooch, they'd do it, too. Apparently, madness was contagious.

"We're not done talking about this," she said as she stepped off her stool. Then she made her way back to the kitchen and on to Ian's place to embark on what would doubtlessly become yet another shipwreck.

Ian Lee was a regular at Buddha's who owned an apartment in one of the new buildings on Vestry Street, a few steps away from the Hudson River. He was a friend of Anil and put the place at his disposal when he wasn't in town. Anil used it for closed-coverage dinners that cashed in on its most appealing feature: a terrace overlooking the seawall.

Shavir opened the terrace doors and stepped out into the setting sun. She walked past oleander and citrus trees to the balustrade. Below her was a long stretch of trees and, right behind it, a million dancing lights on the dark surface of the river. It was amazing to see a bird's eye view of it, the quiet presence of the river, the reflections of the dimmed-down lights of Jersey City. The people below were disappearing into the dark spaces between the light cones of the LEDs seaming the boardwalk.

Jake would love this.

She turned back and walked through the spacious living room into the only marginally smaller kitchen. She had less than an hour left to get dinner going and change into the black dress she'd bought for the occasion. She'd felt bad about spending money on something as mundane as a dress, but after realizing all her nice clothes had been gifts from Finn, she'd taken the whole bundle of them to the second-hand store on 4th Street and got in exchange this dress along with some cash she planned on using for more sensible things.

It was the first time in six years, she realized as she unpacked her bags, that she was alone in a kitchen, cooking a meal for two. She'd helped prepare thousands of meals in between, but not alone like she used to when it was just her and her mom, her mom coming home late from her shift and grateful to have dinner waiting. Ian's kitchen was about five times the size of the one they'd had in their old apartment, where you had to move strategically, every ingredient unearthed from the depths of the crammed cupboards. Talking hadn't always been easy between her and her mom, so cooking was how they'd connected. It was a special thing between a mother and her daughter, her mom had always said, cooking things from scratch for one another.

Now Shavir was doing it for someone else who was special.

Preparing dinner took longer than expected because Ian stored his appliances in the most unexpected places. She opened five drawers for every one thing she found, and in the final spurt, she ran between the kitchen and the terrace to set the table, nearly falling twice over Sam who insisted on following her. But it was all done by the time Jake rang the doorbell downstairs, and she'd even found the time to squeeze into her new dress.

She took a gulp from the red wine that Nimesh had given her for her very special person. "To make up for all the mistakes you'll make," he'd said, still grumpy but surprising himself with a smile when she hugged him. She had allowed the bottle to air as instructed, placed it on the table outside, and now, she ascertained with one final check, everything was perfect.

"You look amazing," Jake said when she opened the door for him, but he didn't look amazing at all. Before he had set foot in the apartment, she knew with absolute certainty this was a mistake, a bad idea and the most inopportune moment.

Jake kissed her, distracted and probably overwhelmed by the setup. He'd said he wanted his birthday surprise, but now she realized he'd only been trying to be nice, appreciative of her efforts. She shouldn't have mentioned it after what had happened to David. Now, they had to go through with it.

Jake managed a smile as he stepped into the living room to greet Sam. "Smells like you imported Buddha's Kitchen."

"That's exactly right," she said, surprised he noticed. "I was hoping this time you'll be able to finish your food. And you'll see the view isn't so bad either."

She led him out to the terrace, waiting for his response, more anxious than she wanted to be.

"Wow," he said, standing at the balustrade. "Look at that view." He turned to her with a hint of relief on his face, a real smile on his lips. "Thank you, this is incredible."

"Happy birthday," she said with a pang of relief. "Are you hungry?"

"No. But I will eat."

They sat down for the cold appetizer waiting on the silvery plates she'd found in the kitchen, the table illuminated by the Asian lanterns she'd borrowed from Buddha's.

"Whose place is this?" Jake asked when she'd poured the red wine.

"A friend of Anil's, but it's ours tonight. We'll start with *som tam*."

He dug his fork into the salad and looked up after a mouthful, signaling approval.

"Green papaya, green beans, and cherry tomatoes," she couldn't stop herself from explaining, "with chilies, lime, tamarind, coconut sugar, and roasted peanuts. You had that at Buddha's, but you probably don't remember." She turned to what she knew would be the inevitable topic of the evening, birthday or not. "How's David?"

Jake's gaze darkened. "Unchanged, really." He put down his fork.

"I'm sorry." Maybe she should have waited until after dessert.

"His son was at the hospital," Jake said. "He hadn't seen his father in three years."

She remembered the man she'd seen outside Jake's apartment, features tense, peering at her suspiciously, with hostility even. "Seems like David is a very lonely man."

Jake stretched his left leg and pulled a medicine bottle out of the pocket of his pants. He offered it to her across the table, and she took it, reading the label.

Her stomach tightened when she realized it was Emovia.

"It's David's," Jake explained. "I took it from his desk so no one will find it there. We might get an investigation because David firewalled the medical functions of his Spine. This," he nodded to the Emovia bottle, "would end his career."

"He's in a coma right now," Shavir said flatly. "That might end his career, too."

Their eyes locked, and then she looked down at Sam, who had wrapped himself around her naked feet. She knew she was supposed to show more compassion for David. The man hadn't struck her as overly sympathetic that one time she'd seen him, but he was important to Jake. Like a father, perhaps, because he'd lost his real father so early in life, and fathers were important to men. Or so she'd learned from being with Finn, a man stuck in a never-ending competition with his superstar father, a repulsive vicious cycle of rebellion, approval-seeking, and rejection.

If it hadn't been for Tara's dad, who had a relationship with his daughter Shavir would have dared to call loving, she'd be wondering if it wasn't the very absence of a father that had allowed Jake to become the man he was. Then again, there had been David, and as far as she could tell, he had wreaked enough damage. She did feel sorry for the man, but she was sick of people leaving everything—their alertness, their sleep, even their fucking emotions—to a bunch of pills. There were other ways of dealing with stress, she knew that from personal experience. But that had never been a winning argument with Finn, just like it hadn't been a winning argument with David. About Jake, she didn't know, and it was something she didn't want to think about.

"Have you ever taken it?" he asked.

That was something she wanted to think even less about. "Once," she said truthfully because lying would be worse. "Finn took it after some fight we had. I thought I wanted it, too, to be like... even, you know?" She looked at Jake, uncomfortable. "It was stupid."

Jake watched her. "What does it do?"

Not a great topic for a birthday dinner, but nothing they ever spoke about was, so she tried to remember. Her memories were hazy, abstract, numb. "It kind of kills your soul. I don't know how to better describe it. It doesn't make you happy or anything, that definitely wasn't what it was like for me. Your soul kind of flatlines, and everything that happens to you happens from a million miles away. You observe it and partake in it, but you don't feel it. I found it horrifying." She paused. "What about you?"

He laughed. "With the amount of pep pills I'm on? Just look at David. I understand why he took it, though. That frightens me."

She reached across the table. "You're not him."

"I know. But I understand why he took it."

That *was* frightening.

She wanted to ask what it was he thought he understood, but she feared the answer. She got up and carried their plates to the kitchen, hers nearly empty, his nearly full. Thirty-six hours on pep pills without sleep, it was amazing he was able to sit here and have dinner at all. Visiting David probably had taken the rest out of him. It was hard seeing people in a coma. It had been hard for her mom, taking care of strangers and their distraught relatives. How much harder must it have been if it was someone you knew and cared about?

"How are your puppies?" Jake asked when she returned to the terrace, steaming bowls of green curry in her hands that smelled like the ones at Buddha's, or so she hoped.

It was a ridiculous hope since Jake barely glanced at the food when she put down his bowl. She had no idea how to respond to his question. It was an effort he was making, she told herself, so she should make an effort, too. "They're recovering," she said, calibrating her words. "It usually doesn't take very long when they're still that young."

He shook his head. "I can't believe you have forty dogs in the basement of that building."

Apparently, he'd set his mind on talking about the dogs, perhaps to distract himself from thinking about David. She felt herself tense up.

"They aren't very big yet," she said, "and they don't stay very long."

Jake put down his fork. "I don't know how to ask this, Shavir."

She waited, alarmed.

"This is probably asking a lot," he said, "but is there a chance you could stop doing this, the raids? I mean, you have the work on the farm, and that's fulfilling and important. I know you care about the animals. I know you want to save them. I understand that, but this—you're risking your own life for them, and that's just... out of proportion."

At first, she had no idea how to respond.

"It's not only my decision," she finally said. "We're doing this together, as a group. And the animals depend on us, no one else cares. But none of us are suicidal, and we've been doing this for a while now."

She felt herself getting angry and realized perhaps this was what she wanted from Jake: to challenge her and help her fight the sense of doom she felt every time she thought of the puppy mill. Though it was hardly his purpose, he'd just reminded her of why they were doing this and why chickening out wasn't an option for her. They did it to help those who couldn't help themselves, who were tortured by careless humans, killed, and gutted. Yes, it was risky. But it was what gave her life meaning, the sole reason why she was alive, why she kept going.

Perversely, she laughed.

"What?" Jake frowned.

"Well, I was actually thinking whether I could ask you to help us. I guess not."

"Help you?" he echoed. "How would I be able to help you?"

She hadn't thought of asking until just now, had refused to consider it. But it came out of her like she'd been preparing all day. "We have almost no antibiotics left. Vet antibiotics, for our animals. When we get them out, most of them are injured or otherwise sick, so we need quite a lot of that stuff. We have our contacts, but everything has run dry. Not only for us. All the veterinary clinics are running out of meds, even in Manhattan. It's a real crisis."

"I don't see how I could help."

"Could you make it critical supply?" Now it was out.

There was something like shock on Jake's face, his eyes dancing their mad little dance. "No, Shavir, I can't do that for a bunch of animals." It sounded like he was trying hard to keep it together. "We can't even get enough meds for the *people* in this city."

"They're people, too, the animals," she shot back, knowing exactly how absurd that would sound to him. It was true, though. She reached down to Sam and caressed his ears.

Jake tried to focus on her eyes. "I know that you feel that way," he said cautiously, "but it isn't a logic that will make the cut in the CSR."

"Does it make the cut with you?"

He paused, visibly searching for the right words. "We shouldn't humanize them, Shavir. And we shouldn't risk human lives for them."

Something cracked in her. She could feel it.

It wasn't the first time she'd heard this argument. It was the kind of mentality that had brought the planet to the state it was in, most animals extinct and humanity on a fast track toward its own extinction. She was actually telling Jake these things now, like she'd told many people before, at parties and protests, through pleas and petitions. She knew from experience she might as well shove the words right back down her throat for all the good they did, for all the difference they'd ever made. Either you got it, or you didn't. And in twenty-eight years, she had not been able to figure out the decisive factor.

"We're *mammals*," she yelled. "We're just another mammal, animals like them, and yet we think we can use and abuse them."

"We're using and abusing other humans, too," Jake shot back.

"And isn't that exactly the problem? Humans treating other humans like animals instead of treating *everyone* like people?"

"Stop it, Shavir!" He was glaring at her. "I can't make vet antibiotics critical supply, that's where this started, right? It's hard enough to get meds for humans, for fuck's sake! I just bought antibiotics from some super shady guy in Kolkata, knowing that something's probably off with those meds. And I did it because our hospitals—*your* hospitals in Brooklyn—can no longer operate without them. There's nothing else available in the whole fucking world!"

"What do you mean, something's off?" Shavir asked. But she already knew. This was worse than expected. No, it was exactly as expected. It was exactly the kind of shit she'd always thought SAFE was doing. "What do you mean?" she repeated since Jake hadn't answered.

"I don't know," he said. "I really don't. But when two-point-eight million standard doses of meds materialize in the middle of a global bidding scramble, usually something's off."

She inhaled, feeling sick. "You know there's a refugee crisis there, right? At the border to Bangladesh?" She knew she should stop pushing, sitting as they were on a freaking terrace where they might be overheard and it being his birthday surprise and all. But she couldn't let this go, so she lowered her voice. "If I were you and looking for the rightful owner of those meds, I'd start right there at the camps."

"I already bought them. So I'm not looking."

"Oh, great! Meaning you already know?"

"No," he returned, calm now, controlled. "There simply is no way of knowing."

"Really? I think you do know."

Her chair almost toppled as she pushed it back and picked up their full plates. Clearly, she didn't need to bother serving dessert. The living room dissolved in front of her eyes as she carried the plates back to the kitchen, Sam by her side. She put them down hard on the counter and tried to get a grip.

Sam pressed against her.

"I'm alright, boy," she murmured, still working on that grip. How the fuck had she expected this would go? And for that matter, what the fuck did she know about India? Only what was on the news, and what Tara had told her—Tara, who had firsthand experience of refugee camps, though it had been years since she'd survived one of them, and that had been here, in fucking Texas. Who knew where Jake's meds were coming from? She certainly didn't.

"I'm sorry for what I said about the animals."

Jake had come in from the terrace, looking hollowed out, very tall, and very thin. He glanced at Sam, who'd trotted over to him. "I know they're people." He petted Sam's head. "But you have to prioritize lives, Shavir. I learned that the hard way. If you don't, you lose everything. And I'm forced to prioritize all the time." He inhaled. "The reason why the hospitals in Queens have antibiotics again, for now, is that I messed with SAFE's internal distribution system. That's illegal and complicated, but I had help."

Her mind didn't immediately take in his words. She swallowed.

"I did it," Jake went on, "because you were right about what's happening in the city. How unfair it is. But we can only distribute what we have, and people here—people in Brooklyn—they will die if I don't manage to get more meds. A lot of people."

Shavir still hadn't said anything. She wanted to, but she couldn't find the words.

"I'm sorry, Shavir," Jake said. "For what I said. And for ruining your birthday surprise with my impossible life." He looked at the plates on the counter, at the terrace shimmering in the candlelight, and back at her. "It's all so... perfect. And I'm just not. I'm sorry."

"Me, too." She walked over and kissed him.

He took her in his arms, his heart racing, his back quivering.

They held on to each other like they were afraid to be torn apart by some onrushing storm, grateful they no longer had to speak, that their bodies could do the talking.

An hour later, they left the place together, holding hands but silent, and walked to Jake's apartment to spend the rest of the night.

Fourteen

Throngs of people were pressing into the picture, their furious faces half concealing the emergency entrance of the Grace Medical Center in Brooklyn, where heavily armed Frontline men kept them away from the doors. They were angry that their relatives' surgeries had been postponed and angrier that their emergencies could now only be taken in by three hospitals in Brooklyn.

What made them furious, however, was that they felt betrayed. Their disappointment erupted in caustic accusations against the indolent mayor and against SAFE, which, they said, was not only inefficient and unreliable in its provision, but also deliberately abandoning the people in Brooklyn, murdering them.

Jake stood across from the screen wall, taking it all in. He couldn't shake the feeling that David would step into the CSR at any second to yell at the news. But David wasn't going to come in or to tell him what to do or how to feel about the volley of reproaches pouring down on him like fiery rain from the goddamn screen wall.

He had visited David in the hospital every day, staring at his frozen face. Shavir hadn't found time to see him again since his birthday, and so apart from his endless work, he didn't have anything else to do. The nurses had told him he needed to engage David's mind, and the only thing that had ever done that was logistical data. So every goddamn day he stood there like an idiot and recounted for his comatose boss what he had missed: that the port of Hong Kong was still closed and Europe's infrastructure in the grip of a heat wave worse than the one in New York; that the latest hurricane in the gulf had put half of Florida under water; that the West Coast was burning, the Midwest suffocating, and Emovia still not back on the market. That everything else was as shitty as could be, and that the antibiotics he had bought from Bhaduri still hadn't made it out of Kolkata.

Yesterday, he'd reached a point where he no longer believed the meds existed at all, but this morning they had materialized at a cold storage house near Chitpur Station in the middle of Kolkata. Now they only needed to get on a train to the port, and in three days they would be here and hopefully quiet down the situation in Brooklyn. Perhaps by tonight he'd finally have some good news for David. It wouldn't be good news for Shavir, since to her mind he was stealing. But once the meds arrived and the hospital situation started improving, perhaps he could convince her there was actual good in what he did.

Masao got off his Spine and looked at him. "They say they can't guarantee the cold chain if we want to put the cargo on a train today. They've got very limited capacity. All they can offer us is normal freight cars. But given that it's antibiotics and India—"

"When can we get a freezer?"

"They don't know."

"They don't know?"

Masao shrugged. "Their infrastructure's going to hell because of the fighting. The conflict with Bangladesh is exploding like nothing they've seen before."

Jake could no longer suppress his irritation. "I don't care!" He pointed to the screen wall. "Look at that. We've got to get those hospitals back to work, or Brooklyn's gonna explode like nothing *we've* seen before!"

Masao was silent, his face expressionless.

"Sorry." Jake lowered his voice. "What about an airlift?"

"Not a chance. They're booked up for months. The parachute boat is our only option. I managed to secure a passage for tonight, but it looks like I'll have to push that back."

"No! We're taking that boat. Can't we use freezer trucks to get it to the port?"

"There's nothing available."

"For Christ's sake." Jake leaned forward. "This is a thirty-million megalopolis, are you *really* telling me there's no transportation?"

"There's plenty of transportation. The cooling is the problem." Masao was still calm.

Jake closed his eyes, his pulse in his ears. He needed to slow down. "I know. I know. Sorry. How much have you offered for a freezer truck?"

"Five times the regular price."

"Offer ten times. Or higher. I don't care. Get them to have some other guy wait."

Masao nodded, hesitating. "There's something else. This just came in from JTWC."

He transferred the data to Jake's Spine.

The hologram of an enormous storm system filled Jake's vision field, stretching from one corner of the room to the other, its giant eye transparent enough for him to see Masao's face on the other side. Another major typhoon in the Pacific. It had been a tropical depression this morning, but now it had a name and a mission to kill.

"It will impact the Philippines," Masao said from far away, "and probably also Hong Kong again. And it will delay the parachute boats. They can't sail into this weather."

Jake collapsed the hologram and erupted in a laugh. "That's just great. Is the whole fucking planet conspiring against us?"

"Looks like it."

"Feels like it, too. Go see whether you can get us those freezer trucks. And I'm gonna find out whether anyone has at least a whiff of antibiotics elsewhere in the world." He called up SAFE's supplier base on his Spine, but then he stopped.

His chest felt like it was shrinking.

He headed toward the hallway. The door to David's office was open, but he walked past it to the Corsys Room. He turned the door handle and winced when he saw Niya, who sat on her chair, looking out the window. She turned around before he could retreat.

"Did you need anything?"

"No," Jake spilled out. "I was just—"

Niya looked at the door. "Should I—?"

"No, it's fine. Keep working."

Jake wanted to leave but stood motionless. A thought had been on his mind ever since Gwen had mentioned the MHA's investigation. "What we did in Queens," he said, "with Corsys... they wouldn't be able to trace that if anyone was poking around?"

Niya looked at him plainly. "No. I did it on my Spine, and I've so many firewalls on there not even Homeland knows shit about what I do. Are you thinking about Brooklyn?"

"No, not really. That's gonna happen anyway. The next load of antibiotics will only be here in a few days. I don't think Brooklyn's hospitals are gonna make it that long."

"No." Niya shook her head. "They're pretty far down, all of them, even those who have sister hospitals here. Right now, stocks are going down even in Manhattan."

"You're following this pretty closely, huh?"

Niya shrugged. "It's a very interesting problem. And I happen to live in Brooklyn."

Jake nodded, realizing he had never asked nor cared where Niya lived, where her family was, or what she was doing in her life when she wasn't here, fixing their IT problems. He felt the urge to ask now, but that would make him look more ignorant and pathetic. "This stays between us, right?" he asked instead, ashamed. "This whole thing."

"I think so," Niya said. "I, for my part, am not too keen on losing my job and facing trial and jail time and all that. Hence the firewalls."

Jake laughed. "Thanks, Niya. I owe you a truckload of chocolate."

Niya nodded, an unreadable smile playing around her mouth. Then she turned her attention to the screen wall in front of her.

Leaving the room, Jake could breathe more easily. He walked to David's office. Closing the door behind him felt good, though it was strange to be here alone. Reporting to David, he'd always known he could be creative, as daring as he could imagine. If he was really out on a limb, he'd had to ask for David's permission. If he made mistakes, he'd had to bear David's wrath. As unpleasant as that had been, he realized now that it had given him a freedom he no longer had.

Nobody knew when David would come back. The doctors refused to give a prognosis. And Jake still didn't know what to do with the contents of David's desk or the material security had retrieved from David's Spine. He'd spent hours going over the data, feeling like he was poking around in his boss's bedroom. There was no telling how much sensitive information Gwen had deleted, but he had found a blurry snapshot of her that she must have overlooked when going through the folders: Gwen without makeup, smiling into the camera from below, an unguarded smile below large data glasses she'd never worn in public. Now he knew the rumors about her and David were true.

The other thing he had found was a list of supply items David had assembled. He called up the list on his Spine and went through its entries again. None of the items were categorized as critical, and that made him nervous. It was a long and eclectic list, including not only medical supplies, but also batteries, LEDs, some basic foods. It was all disconcerting, but what worried him most was the last item on the list: bottled water. Clearly, these were things David had considered bringing up to the CSR, and water was one of them.

The silence in the office was oppressive. A few minutes ago, he'd been longing for quiet, but the only thing it did for him was make him feel more under pressure. He flipped on the screen walls. Sight and sound flooded his brain.

BREAKING NEWS.

The letters danced in front of his eyes while the news anchor blared them into his ears, reporting another violent clash between Indian border troops and Bangladeshi refugees. Seventeen Bangladeshi were reported dead, and several dozen had been injured as they'd tried to illegally cross into West Bengal. The US media were onto this now, reporting every incident and linking it to how it would impact American supply from India. His stomach cramped. Somehow this refugee crisis was related to the antibiotics sitting in that cold store in Kolkata.

Shavir's voice was in his head, compressed and hostile as it had been when she'd sat opposite him on that exquisite terrace above the river.

You knew this, her voice said, and she was right like she had been three days ago when he had denied it. He knew 2.8 million standard doses of antibiotics didn't materialize out of thin air in the middle of a major supply crunch.

He zapped through news feeds from India and Bangladesh until he heard a thickly accented voice cursing in English. The man was a French doctor, and he looked angry. The situation in the camps was getting ever more desperate, he said to the reporter, and in the current situation it was impossible for them to help. Without medical supply, their mission was pointless. They were just watching people die. The report continued in a language Jake didn't understand. He asked the Spine to translate as he looked at UNHCR tents full of bloated bodies, oozing wounds, and swollen limbs. They were Bangladeshi refugees, and no one could say which of them were legal. The camps along the border were overflowing with hundreds of thousands of people, most of them facing deportation once their identities were verified.

"That is for the Indian government to decide," the French doctor said bluntly to the reporter. "What concerns us is that we cannot treat these people because our medical supplies magically disappear on their way from the border to the camps. How are we supposed to operate? With plastic knives? People are dying, and we cannot help them because someone is stealing our supply, and the government does nothing. This is a violation of human rights. Not only because you let people die, but also because you do not let us help. We have a right to help them, and we also have a moral obligation."

The report cut away from the enraged face of the Frenchman and back to footage from the interior of the tents showing more scenes of human injury, death, and disaster.

Jake didn't move, didn't blink. He stared at the images until they dissolved into a smear of colors. The news feed was from Bangladesh, otherwise they'd never have let the good doctor vent his frustration. Someone had diverted the international donations of medical supply for the refugees and auctioned them off to the highest bidder.

He tried to breathe, but there wasn't any air in the room.

Masao was sitting at his desk talking on the Spine to his contact in Kolkata. He paused the call when he saw Jake walking into the CSR. "Did you get my messages?"

"I have to leave for an hour. Can you take over?"

Masao looked surprised. "Sure. But I need your approval first. I sent two messages."

"What do you have?" Jake asked, like it was an imposition. He couldn't help it.

"I got the freezer trucks complete with armed guards. Our meds are on their way."

"To the port?"

"No. To Delhi."

Jake stared at his assistant. "To what?"

"Delhi. The new typhoon's gonna bring delays for all seaways, so I asked Nilay in Delhi whether he could help us out, and he found me a flight. Expensive but doable."

"Out of Delhi? When?"

"Tomorrow night. It's tight, but they can make it."

"How much?"

"Hundred-eighty thousand. I need your approval."

"But they're already on their way."

"I'm sorry. I had to act, and you didn't pick up."

Masao was right. Jake had been too distracted, too out of it, to notice the call. "Are they even gonna make it overland with only a few guards for protection?" he asked, acutely aware that he was not handling this well, that he sounded like David.

"It's a risk," Masao admitted, "but it's our best bet. We'll have our meds by Wednesday."

Jake's gaze slid to the screen wall, where the center feed showed footage of the escalating border conflict. His head felt like it was about to explode.

"Approved," he said and walked out.

"Are you okay?" Masao called after him as though there was no one else around to hear.

"No!" Jake barked. He walked back to Masao and lowered his voice. "There's something I'd like you to work on while I'm gone." He transferred David's list to Masao's Spine. "Check the supply status of each of these items."

"Now?" Masao asked. "What is that?"

"It's a list David made. Strictly confidential."

"Okay." Masao's eyes scanned the projected list between them. "Oh, man," he said quietly. "And he put water on it, too."

"There's one more thing I'd like you to check." Jake used his gloves to add another item to David's list.

"Veterinary antibiotics?" Masao read, looking confused.

"Just check it, okay? I gotta go."

"When will you be back?"

"About an hour."

"Is this about David?"

"No. Call if you need to."

The heat wave hadn't broken. At 1:30 p.m. the temperature outside was staggering, the air pervaded with the stench of rotting garbage and inadequate sewage. Jake managed to get across the sizzling asphalt of Hudson Street, and then his feet dragged through the yellowing leaves covering the paths of Abingdon Square Park. He wanted to walk, but it just wasn't possible.

A single podcar was waiting next to the deserted sidewalk at the edge of the park. He pressed his glove against its sizzling side, and the door slid open. He sank onto the smooth plastic and blurted out Soma's address, knowing only that he needed to talk to Shavir.

The biology student who worked the afternoon shift at Soma was already behind the counter, but Jake walked through the narrow opening of the kitchen door without so much as a greeting. Shavir sat next to Hector in the small back room, both staring at Hector's laptop. Surprise lit up her face when she looked up.

"Have you seen 4Flow?" Hector said, when he noticed Jake. "It's all alerts. Look at that!" His voice was shrill. "You can't have a restaurant when there's nothing to serve."

Jake looked at Hector's agitated face, unable to respond. Then Shavir's hand was in his, cool and firm against his skin. She led him to the door and kept walking until they were outside.

"What are you doing here, and why do you look like that?"

"Can I talk to you?"

"Of course you can. But we need to be inside somewhere."

They crossed the street and walked into a place that was nearly empty. The smell of bad food was overpowering, but the air was cool.

"They'll cut power in a few minutes," Shavir said when they sat down at one of the tables, "but we're good for now. What's wrong?"

"You've been avoiding me."

"No, I haven't. I was just—" She stopped. "Why are you here, Jake?"

It all came pouring out: the images he'd seen on the Bangladeshi news feed that kept replaying in his mind, paralyzing him from the inside out; the guilt he felt, the horror; and the admission that she'd been right about the refugee camps.

Shavir listened quietly, digesting. "So it's true?" she asked. "This guy, Bhaduri, he sold you antibiotics that were meant for the refugees?"

Jake nodded. "I can't know for sure, but it seems very likely. Corruption's really bad at all levels of the administration, in many places now. It's so lucrative."

"And you knew that when he made the offer."

He gave her an impatient look. "Of course, I knew about corruption. We all know."

"But you still bought them." There was disapproval in her eyes.

"Of course I did," he said, sliding back into defense mode. "Do I have to explain it again? It's my job to get us antibiotics."

"Even if you have to steal them."

"I didn't steal them," he hissed. "I bought them."

"From someone who stole them."

"I didn't know that! And I still don't know."

"Then why are you so worked up about it?" Her voice was acidic.

"Because I worry." He'd thought there was an understanding between them after their last night together, after she'd kissed him in that apartment and then gone home with him, knowing what he had done.

He'd thought this meant she understood his dilemma, the impossible situation he was in. The last thing he needed was more speeches.

She looked away as the lights went out, the aircon making one last rattling huff. "Where are they now?" she asked.

"The antibiotics? In a freezer truck on their way to Delhi."

"Can you redirect the truck?"

"Where to?"

"To the refugee camps."

He was too baffled to respond at first. "Why would I do that?"

"Because you *worry*, right? And because it sounds like you're in fact pretty sure that that's where your antibiotics belong. Just like I said."

He could feel himself losing it. "I bought them, Shavir! For a hell of a lot of money. And David approved it. They belong to New York now. They belong to those hospitals in Brooklyn that have run out. I can't just give them away to a bunch of refugees."

"So they can go to a bunch of rich guys in Manhattan."

"Not if Corsys declares a state of emergency for Brooklyn, and it will. I told you."

"That doesn't change that the meds were meant for someone else."

He put his hand down hard on the small table between them. "Stop looking at me like that. I wasn't hired to help a bunch of refugees on the other side of the world. They're not my problem, not my job. And what about the other things I've done in Queens, risking my neck? Doesn't that matter at all?"

Shavir leaned forward, her voice low. "What do you want me to say, Jake? That it's fine? That what you do is justified? I don't think it's fine. Or justified. And they aren't just a bunch of refugees. They, too, are people. People like Tara and her dad."

He looked at her, puzzled.

"Tara's parents got out of Kolkata after the big flood of 2045. Back when the US had just adopted that ambitious refugee policy it retracted two years later. Her mom didn't survive the camps, but her dad did, and so they ended up in Brooklyn."

Jake swallowed. He had assumed Tara was American, born here, but it didn't really matter. He couldn't process this anymore. He hadn't come here for this. He wasn't sure what he'd come for, but not for this. "I should probably go back," he said abruptly.

"Sure. I gotta go, too." Her voice was so cold it scared him.

"Will I see you tonight?" he asked helplessly. He knew how ridiculous it sounded, given he'd wanted to walk out a second ago, but he didn't want her to go back to Brooklyn. "It's not safe. There are protests everywhere now, not only at hospitals."

"I can't," she said as she picked up her bag. "Not tonight."

"You're going out?" he asked, alarmed. "With everything that's going on in Brooklyn? Are you crazy?"

She motioned for him to keep his voice down. "Frontline's gonna be too busy to pay much attention. That's why we're going tonight."

"Has it ever occurred to you what happens to me if you get busted?" he demanded. "They'll trace you back to me, then I'll be the one accused. I'll be the one who will have to explain why I had knowledge of this and didn't report you. It's my *duty* to report you."

"Because you work for Homeland Security," she said slowly.

"Because I work for Homeland Security."

She looked frozen, her dark eyes bottomless. "Well, the others think you're only a step away from busting us anyway. I told them you'd never do that. We'll see who's right."

She wanted to get up, but he put his hand on her arm. "Wait. This is all such a mess. I'm sorry. I won't report you. You know that. But I don't want you to go. Not tonight."

"You don't *want* me to," she repeated.

"I'm asking you not to go. I can't worry any more than I already do. Please don't go, Shavir. Not tonight. It's too dangerous."

Her face had become impenetrable, and he knew his pleas were useless. He couldn't stop her from going, couldn't make her understand or care. He'd come to her for help, and instead, she had made him feel worse. So much worse.

Her back was very straight as they walked to the door then out onto the blistering pavement. They said goodbye awkwardly, then she turned and walked away without looking back, without mentioning when they would see each other again.

FIFTEEN

THE PUPPIES PRESSED THEIR muzzles through the slits in the wooden walls of the compartments, their broken vocal cords announcing they were ready to be fed. It wasn't ten yet, and they were hungry again. They still didn't know how to eat like normal dogs.

Shavir caressed the belly of a pup that had thrown itself on its back, exposing its throat in a gesture of submission, its breath rattling from a respiratory infection, the skin scarred from the unforgiving cage wire.

"I can't believe you've found spots for so many of them this fast," she said, looking at Tara, who crouched next to her.

"It's easy right now. People wait in line to get their dog. They're so stressed and so afraid... they want comfort."

"It's a little selfish, don't you think?"

Tara shrugged. "I don't care why they do it, as long as they do it and take good care of them." She got up. "We gotta go. They'll cut power in a few minutes."

Her friend, as always, seemed at ease before the raid, even today when the stakes were so high. But it was what Tara had wanted, and, of course, she had prevailed, brushing everyone's concerns aside. After her failed attempt with Troy, Shavir had focused all her persuasive efforts on Tara, trying out every argument she could come up with to deter her from taking on the mill. She had spent half of last night at Tara's and Dipak's apartment, a place she had mostly avoided ever since she'd spent a horrific week clearing out her own apartment in that gloomy gray building after her mom's death.

Dipak had been happy to see her again after such a long time, feeding them chai and *nankhatai* cookies, their favorite sweets when they were kids. When he'd finally gone to bed, she and Tara had sat down on the bed in her room, half-whispering like they used to as kids when making secret plans, but instead hitting arguments back and forth like two deranged tennis players. When Shavir had finally gone home at half past two in the morning, it had been game, set, and match to Tara. No matter the argument, Tara had offered one response: We can't let the dogs down, they depend on us. It's what we do.

Now, Shavir didn't want to leave the basement. Her fingers traced the scars on the soft belly, the puppy's eyes fixated on her in a mixture of pleasure and anxious disbelief. She would much rather have stayed here to take care of the dogs while the others went on that fucking raid. It hadn't been a good day, and chances were it would get much worse from here. She couldn't forget the expression on Jake's face when she'd told him they would be raiding tonight. He'd meant it when he'd asked her if she was crazy.

She tried to imagine him here, in this basement full of puppies. He, who couldn't bear anyone but a lizard, who was so focused on humans, the ones he had elected to survive. What a fucked-up job that was, what a fucked-up world, forcing him to make these decisions.

She didn't know why he'd come to Soma, what he had wanted from her—some kind of absolution to make him feel better about what he did? That just wasn't fair. The veiled threat he'd made—if it had even been veiled—was lodged in her mind. It was his duty to report her. Well, he should go ahead then, but she wouldn't be stopped, not by him and not by her own fear.

"Are you coming?" Tara looked at her through the wooden slats.

"Yeah."

She got up and carefully closed the door on the disappointed faces of the little mastiffs. She followed Tara to ground level, where the others were waiting for the van, and started checking their equipment. They had decided not to invest in another set of night-vision goggles, so

Lenny had given up his since Scott would need them more urgently when he went inside to sedate the mother dogs. Scott was the new guy, a vet assistant Zeno said he trusted with his life. Hopefully, Zeno had good judgement. All their lives depended on it.

The gate rolled up, and Finn's van backed into the warehouse. Her stomach contracted. Now she would have to deal with him on top of everything else.

He jumped out and greeted the others. Then he walked over to her. She knew he was on Emovia before she looked into the graveyard of his eyes. There was no spark in them, only that chemically-induced equanimity that told her he wouldn't get emotional tonight.

The power went out with a faint click. With the van's headlights the only source of light, Finn's expression was even ghastlier.

"Are you trying to get us busted?" Shavir hissed.

"What kind of question is that?"

"You know exactly what kind of question that is."

"Relax," he said. "I've done this before."

"That doesn't make it any better, does it? We can't afford any fuck-ups tonight."

"I'll be fine." His voice was inhumanly even. "Relax."

She turned away, trying to evaluate. Maybe he was right and he'd do just fine with his magic pills. Maybe it was better than him being mad at her or otherwise worked up. It was true he'd been on pills during a raid before. It had gone okay, but it also had been a normal raid without any problems or need to react.

She walked over to Tara. "Have you seen?"

"He's high," Tara said, "isn't he?"

"He's an idiot. What are we gonna do?"

Tara shrugged. "Nothing. He'll be okay."

"How do you know?"

"He's Finn. He's always okay."

Shavir snorted. "He isn't. He just always pretends he is."

"Whatever. He's gonna drive the van and carry the crates, and he'll be fine. We don't have a plan B anyway." Tara grabbed her bag and walked to the van.

It was a twenty-minute ride to Gravesend, which Troy used to run them one more time through the details, making sure everyone, including Scott, knew exactly what to do. The puppy mill was on the ground floor, so they wouldn't have to deal with stairs this time and hopefully only one door. Zeno and Scott would go in with Tara and Shavir, hitting the mother dogs with a powerful sedative that would incapacitate them in seconds. They'd put the dogs together with their puppies into the new big crates they'd bought and carry them outside.

Finn would have to help this time because they'd need two people to carry the crates. He wouldn't go inside—he was still keeping watch for them—but he'd have to leave the van to pick up the crates at the door of the mill and load them into the vehicle with Troy. It was a risk, but it was safer than involving more new people in the raid.

Shavir tried to ignore the incessant fluttering in her stomach. They'd have a much more complicated routine this time, and they were also going earlier than usual. It was only a small mill, but it was located near the edge of a densely populated part of Gravesend, so Troy had decided it was safest to go during the scheduled blackout when the streets were dark and the people too afraid to leave their houses. But the bad feeling wouldn't go away, and it didn't help that the streets were crowded with protesters as soon as they left Ocean Parkway. Apparently, the lack of power couldn't stop people from voicing their discontent.

Gravesend was one of the most exposed and neglected neighborhoods of Brooklyn, heavily impacted by the storm surges that folded seawalls and levees like they were pieces of cardboard. Like all the communities lining the bay, it was partially flooded at high tide, a permanent evacuation zone. The streets behind the high tide lines were inhabited by thousands of people who couldn't afford anything better or were unwilling to leave. They had arranged themselves within the storms and the flooding, and no one asked questions about what their neighbors had to do to survive. But now, they were paying absurd prices for drinkable water, and the only hospital in the area was closed. They were angry and afraid, feelings they couldn't suppress anymore because the prices for Emovia were going through the roof. Shavir could see their greenish faces through the tinted window of the van.

The visual distortion of the goggles made them look ominous and hostile. Hopefully, it would be quieter around the puppy mill.

"Turn left here," Troy said to Finn, and the angry faces disappeared. The streets were desolate now, the dark houses marked by the usual flood lines. Troy led Finn into a narrow alley and told him to stop. They opened the side door of the van and stepped onto dry ground—it was too early for the tide to come in. The only sounds were the hungry lapping of waves and the shouting of protesters a few blocks away.

Troy directed them toward the back door of the house, a small brick stone that had once been a family home. It was boarded up now as these places always were and probably also soundproofed to muffle what little squeaks the puppies could make before their vocal cords were cut. A few steps led up to the door where Troy and Nacho went to work on the two old-fashioned locks blocking their way.

Two long minutes, and the door snapped open.

They stood in the remnants of a kitchen. There was an enormous fridge in one corner, dead as every other electric device in the neighborhood. A pile of dirty feeding dishes in the sink filled the air with the stench of decay. They crossed the kitchen and moved into a hallway.

There was another door, unlocked. Troy turned the doorknob, and the room behind it erupted with the dogs' broken barking. Husky sounds cut through air thick with the smell of excrement and fear. Shavir felt her stomach turn.

The dark room was filled with wire pens raised half a foot off the floor. Much bigger than the cages in the fattening stations, the pens had two openings: one door at the side and a top that could be lifted to feed the dogs or take their babies away.

Zeno and Scott put down the crate with their equipment, and Scott slipped into the protective gear they'd brought for him. Zeno loaded the jet injector and nodded to Shavir. She took out her cutter and approached the first of the pens, Scott behind her.

A large mastiff threw herself against the wire wall, her face distorted into a grimace of aggression, her bared teeth shining bright green.

Shavir jumped back and found herself in Scott's arms, taking him almost off his feet. She stepped forward again and cut the wires around the lock while the animal's teeth attacked it from the other side. The top exploded open when the dog jumped up against it, then Scott was there and pulled a hood over the head and upper body of the animal. Zeno pressed the injector gun into her fur and pulled the trigger.

The dog seemed to tumble downwards in slow motion, burying her babies as she lost consciousness. Zeno followed Scott to the next pen, where Tara was working on the lock.

Shavir stood at her cage and stared at the little bodies struggling to get free from the lifeless mass of bone and flesh that was their mother. Zeno had told them to wait forty seconds before reaching in, but the puppies were too small to bear the enormous weight, so she grabbed one and pushed against the mother's ribcage to dislodge it.

The dog whipped around with a growl, her teeth ripping through the thick material of the hood and into the flesh of Shavir's forearm.

She cried out in shock and pain. The dog let go, her head sinking back down to the floor of the pen.

"Are you hurt?" Lenny was next to her.

"No, no," Shavir stammered. "Help me!"

They bent into the pen, and Lenny lifted the mother's body an inch so Shavir could pull out the five puppies buried underneath. They were alive and able to move.

Someone tapped her on the back. Shavir turned to face Scott.

"I need your cutter."

Zeno was already standing at the next pen. She was being too slow.

"I'm coming," she said and moved to the next pen. This time, she refused to look inside after the dog had gone down. She walked to the next pen and started cutting. Tara and Troy took care of the pups that were buried underneath their mothers until Lenny and Nacho were ready to lift the dogs out of their pens and into the crates.

As the mother dogs went down one by one, the room grew quieter. All that was left was the soft squeaking of the puppies and the muffled grunts of the men as they strained their muscles to heave the unconscious dogs from the bottoms of the pens.

Shavir's arm was throbbing, drops of sweat running down from her forehead into her goggles. She used her good arm to wipe them and looked back down at the wires she was supposed to cut. They had to speed it up.

"There's fourteen of them," Zeno said when another dog sank to the floor of her pen.

"What?"

"We've given ten shots. There are four more pens. So it's fourteen."

Shavir turned her head. He was right. Troy had told them to expect twelve mother dogs, and that was what they had based their calculations on. Once again, they'd been misinformed.

Tara stood next to them. "Do we have enough shots?"

Zeno nodded. "But not enough crates."

"We're taking them."

"How?"

"Put the puppies into the crate with your equipment," whispered Tara. "And the mothers we carry as they are. On our backs."

"That's too dangerous."

"They'll be out cold."

"We can't take them, Tara."

"You wanna leave them here?" Tara glared.

"We have to."

"Bullshit," Shavir hissed. "Just put them out," she said to Zeno as she started working on the wires of the next lock. "We'll figure it out."

"Everything alright?" Finn's voice squeaked through her earphone.

"Yes," she said into her mic, giving the others a look. "We're fine."

"Everything's clear out here," Finn said. "Lovely summer night."

It was almost fifteen minutes before they started carrying out the crates. Shavir held her breath when she and Zeno lifted the first of the dogs and her puppies. They had calculated one hundred forty pounds, but it felt like two hundred. Even for two people, the weight was a challenge. Her clothes were soaked, and her forearm burned like hellfire, when they reached the back door and handed the crate to Scott and Finn. She couldn't tell whether it was sweat or blood that was seeping into her glove, but her hand was bathed in a viscous fluid.

They hurried back through the kitchen, passing Tara and Lenny with the second crate. Not being able to carry the crates alone slowed everything. Troy had calculated sixteen minutes for the entire raid, and here they were, almost twenty minutes in and only just beginning to load. She pushed the thought away and grabbed the next crate.

Twenty-four minutes had passed when they were finally done.

Scott and Nacho had already left for the subway, and Zeno and Tara were standing over the last open pen.

"This is idiotic," Zeno hissed as they yanked up the limp body of the dog and lowered it onto Lenny's shoulders. Tara didn't respond, just waited for Zeno to help her lift the second dog and place it on Troy's shoulders. From where she found the energy was beyond Shavir. She was reaching her own limits just by placing the two-week-old puppies into the last crate. Tara closed the lid, and they picked up the load and followed the men to the back door.

"So long, assholes," Tara mumbled triumphantly through her mask as she closed the door.

The air outside was a relief after the stinking heat of the house, a cool breeze from the Atlantic rustling the leaves in the only tree around.

The distant voices of the protesters were still audible.

As was the sudden sound of a rapidly approaching vehicle.

Adrenaline shot into Shavir's heart the same second Finn's warning cry exploded in her ear. Then they were running toward the van.

The headlights of the speeding car hit them when they hadn't covered half of the distance, but neither of them let go of the crate.

They ran and ran, the crate bouncing hard against their thighs.

The taillights of Finn's van flared up and came closer, the open side door beckoning.

Shavir sprinted, her lungs screaming.

Gunshots pierced the air.

She felt the impact as the bullets hit the crate.

There was a sharp cry of pain and then blood all over Troy's face.

They jumped onto what little was left of the floor of the van, someone ripping the crate out of their hands to make room for their bodies.

"Go, go, go!" Lenny yelled.

The van sped up, its side door still open.

"Help me!" Shavir screamed at Tara as she yanked at the door.

Lenny was suddenly above her, and together they managed to pull the door into its lock. Shavir sank back against the wall of crates, her pulse racing. There were no more gunshots.

"They're gone," Finn said, slowing down the van and taking a turn.

They were in the populated area of Gravesend again, amidst the protesters. Shavir heard their shouts and remembered the blood.

"How's Troy?"

"I'm okay," Troy said from behind her. "It's not me. It's the dog. It's her blood."

Shavir tried to turn around so she could see him. "Is she alive?"

"Yeah," Zeno said. "They hit her thigh. She's so out she doesn't feel a thing. We're trying to stop the bleeding."

"What about the puppies?"

"Just gimme a sec."

"Poor dog," Troy said, sounding dazed. "That bullet could have been in my neck."

He said something else, but Shavir wasn't listening. Tara hadn't moved. Hadn't responded in any way to anything they'd said.

"Tara?" she asked, ripping off her gloves and reaching for her friend's shoulder with her good hand. There was a moan in response, and then her hand was touching something wet and warm.

Shavir stared at the dark liquid covering her skin. It wasn't her own blood. For a second, the shock was so hard it paralyzed her.

"She's been hit!" she screamed, the cold recognition freezing her guts as she ripped off her goggles. "Tara's been hit! There's blood everywhere!"

She frantically tried to find the source of the bleeding, but the turtleneck covered Tara's body like a second skin. "I need a knife! Can you hear me, Tara? Can you say something?"

"How are the puppies?" Tara asked weakly. "They've been hit."

"*You've* been hit!" Shavir cut the turtleneck open with Lenny's pocketknife. "I need you to stay with me, okay?" She felt it all come back. Her clothes ripped to shreds. Her mom's wounds. The blood. The car. Williamsburg Bridge. She pushed against the memory and kept talking to Tara, trying to get her to respond.

"How bad is it?" Zeno squeezed into the tight space next to them.

"I don't know. There's so much blood."

"We need an ER now!" Zeno yelled after one quick look.

"Already going that way," was Finn's calm response.

"It's through and through." Zeno looked at the gunshot wound in Tara's shoulder. "But there's way too much blood for that. This is gonna hurt, Tara, but I have to take a look at your back." He looked at Shavir. "Can you help me move her?"

They shifted Tara's upper body so Zeno could cut open the back of her turtleneck. "There's a second entry wound in her lower back," he said. "The bullet's in her body."

Shavir squeezed her eyes shut. *Not again,* something screamed inside her. *Not again. Not again. Not again.*

"We need to stop the bleeding," she said to Zeno, but he was already working on it. "Can you check the hospitals?" she cried into the darkness from her cramped position.

"Why?" asked Finn.

"To make sure they're still doing surgery! Jake said they'll call a state of emergency for Brooklyn at some point tonight."

"Well, they haven't, and I'm not gonna uncover my Spine right now," Finn said.

"But maybe they have! Just check it, okay?"

"Calm down, Shav. It's not gonna help Tara if you're freaking out."

"She's lost consciousness," Zeno said, a tremor in his voice.

They somehow managed to reposition Tara in the confined space between the crates and the door while the van was going at least ninety miles an hour.

"Shit," Finn said, slowing down the vehicle.

"What?"

"Frontline. It's a roadblock."

Shavir could hear the sound of the Velcro as Finn and Troy ripped off the protective collars from their necks before the van came to a stop.

"Good evening, officer," Finn said to whoever was approaching the van. "I have an emergency in the back. Need to get through to the ER."

Shavir closed her eyes. The mother dogs were still out, but she could hear the muffled squeaking of the puppies through the walls of the crates. If the Frontline guy noticed or demanded to see the emergency, it would all be over.

"The ER is closed," the cop said. "You need to go to the Woodhull Medical Center. It's quickest if you go down Flatbush. All the other roads are backed up or closed."

Finn thanked the man and rolled the window back up. The van was moving again.

Shavir exhaled. "How do we know they're still doing surgery in Woodhull?"

"Because he just said so."

The equanimity in Finn's voice drove her insane.

"What if he's wrong?" she yelled.

"Shavir, I don't think—"

"I don't give a fuck about what you think!" she was yelling again into the darkness. "We need to know whether they can operate before we drive all the way to Woodhull. Call Jake."

"What?"

"I said call Jake! He'll know."

"Are you nuts?"

"Call him! Jake Alvaro. Works for goddamn SAFE, so it can't be too hard to find him. Just ask your fucking Spine!"

"Dialing their number right now." This was Troy's voice.

Shavir closed her eyes and squeezed Tara's bloody hand again. This might have been the most insane thing she'd ever done, but Jake would know.

Sixteen

Whenever you thought a day was as bad as it could get, it went ahead and got worse. Jake sat next to Lisa in the CSR, their eyes on the rapidly deteriorating situation in Brooklyn.

He had sent Masao home in the late afternoon so he could finally spend an evening with his husband. Returning from his meeting with Shavir, he hadn't wanted to be responsible for yet another failed relationship, and Ethan's patience had been tested enough in recent weeks. Masao had been unwilling to leave and had called twice since he had, the last time twelve minutes ago, right after Corsys had called a state of emergency for the hospitals in Brooklyn. For a precious moment, it had given Jake a deep sense of satisfaction, seeing Brooklyn move up in the priority chain. Then Masao had told him he'd received a call from the man who had organized the transportation deal in India, and it all seemed so senseless and nightmarish that it felt like this was some kind of Spine feature, not real life.

The man had informed Masao that the freezer trucks with their antibiotics had been stopped by the local authorities halfway to Delhi, and their cargo had been confiscated. It was now being returned to its rightful owner, who had reported it stolen. This simple piece of information had so many dreadful implications that Jake still hadn't wrapped his mind around it. Not only did it mean he had paid an outrageous price for antibiotics that had probably been sold to at least three different parties, it was also more than likely the meds would go back on the market as soon as they were back in Kolkata. And since the transaction hadn't been legal, there was nothing he could do. Worst of all, there were no antibiotics on their way to Brooklyn. The hospitals had reached a state of emergency, but there were no meds. They were fucked, just like the Bangladeshi refugees who would never see their meds. The only winners were some cunning guys in the West Bengal administration who knew how to play a frantic global market.

A green light flashed between him and the images from Brooklyn, announcing a call through SAFE's central line.

"Alvaro," Jake said with the full expectation that the receptionist would tell him Gwen wanted to speak with him.

"Sorry to bother you, Jake, but I've got a Sam Smith on the line who says he needs to talk to you urgently. It's about someone called Shavir?"

Something gripped Jake's heart and squeezed it to a standstill. "Put him through."

"Jake?" a vaguely familiar voice said. "This is Troy. We're in Brooklyn and need a functioning ER. Shavir says you can help?"

"What happened? Where is she?"

"She's right next to me and doing fine. She can't speak to you because she doesn't have a Spine. Can you please let us know where we can go? It's an emergency."

"Forget Brooklyn," Jake said. "You have to come to Manhattan."

"Manhattan? But we—"

"Where are you?"

"Flatbush, going north."

"Keep going across Manhattan Bridge and take First Avenue to Belvedere. It will be crowded because they're taking emergencies from Brooklyn now, but it's your best bet."

"Fuck," Troy spit out and repeated the information to someone who could only be Finn. "Thanks, Jake, we're on our way."

"Who's hurt?" Jake asked, but Troy had disconnected the call.

He looked at Lisa, who was watching him with alarm. "I gotta go."

"Of course. This isn't your shift anyhow."

"I'll call you about the antibiotics."

Lisa nodded. "We'll try to find something else tonight."

"Good luck with that." He hadn't intended for his words to come out sarcastically, but as he was riding the elevator down to the podcar floor, he realized that was how they had sounded.

There was a car waiting. For the first time, Jake was grateful for the flood of sight and sound that inundated him as soon as the windshield lost its transparency. *Troy said Shavir is fine*, he kept reminding himself while a female voice rhapsodized about the bliss of apathy. They hadn't stopped the Emovia ads for some unfathomable reason.

The podcar spit him out at the main entrance of the Belvedere Hospital, two blocks away from NYU Langone, where David lay unconscious in the intensive care ward. Jake walked around the corner to Belvedere's emergency entrance.

It was so much worse than he had expected. Dozens of conventional ambulances from Brooklyn were parked next to Manhattan's podcar versions, hospital personnel pushing stretchers and wheelchairs. Policemen tried to regulate the chaos, the scene eerily illuminated by the flashing lights of their cars. Jake turned, looking for Shavir. It had taken him less than ten minutes to get here, so it was possible they hadn't arrived yet. And if they had, they probably wouldn't come anywhere near the entrance with their van. Once the thought had sunk in, he started moving again, trying to anticipate where they would go.

He ran down the street and turned left into the narrow road that ran parallel to FDR Drive. Finn's van was right there, its headlights dimmed, several people crowding the open side door. Jake recognized Lenny and then Shavir, her hands upon the small dark figure in Lenny's arms. Tara. He then noticed Troy, who was closing the door from the inside. The van picked up speed and drove past him. The driver's cab was dark, but he nevertheless recognized Finn, catching his gaze for a second before the van was gone. It left behind a sight that almost knocked Jake off his feet.

They were all dressed in black, Shavir's clothes gleaming wet in the streetlights, covered in blood, as she kept both of her hands on Tara.

"Are you hurt?"

She shook her head.

"Can you help?" Lenny asked, nodding toward Tara's legs.

Together they were able to move quickly.

Lenny gasped when they turned the corner and had a free view of the emergency entrance. "She needs to get into an OR now," he said, "or she will die."

"They're doing triage, so it depends on the severity of her injuries."

"Gunshot wounds," Lenny said. "One in her shoulder, straight through, the other bullet lodged in her abdomen. She's lost so much blood she's unconscious."

Jake exchanged a look with Shavir, unable to hide his shock. "That'll do it," is all he could say, and then they were searching for a doctor.

The waiting area of the intensive care ward was crammed with miserable-looking people waiting to hear about their loved ones. The atmosphere was so different from the calm of Langone. The room was saturated with the anger, fear, and sorrow people had brought with them from Brooklyn. They looked out of place in the overdesigned environment of this hospital, some of them still carrying handwritten banners that demanded immediate treatment for all patients in every borough. They only put down their banners when approached by doctors, their faces paling as they prepared themselves for bad news.

Jake sat next to Lenny, trying to take his mind off the fact that he was coming down from pep pills. This wasn't a good moment to go into withdrawal, but Tara was in surgery, and his bag with the pills was in the CSR, so he had no choice but to deal with it.

Shavir had been in a bad way since they'd arrived. Neither he nor Lenny had realized how bad until she'd got up to get water, and Jake had touched her arm because he'd wanted to bring it to her. She screamed, and when he pulled back the sleeve of her turtleneck, he'd uncovered a bloody mess beneath: a couple serious dog bites, inflamed and swollen. They'd called a nurse, and she was being taken care of despite her protests.

"I don't get the logic of what you do."

"You don't have to," Lenny said, his voice flat. He'd told Jake it had probably been a silent alarm that had warned the breeders someone was raiding their mill. He'd also called Zeno and learned from him the injured dog had survived, but two of her puppies had been fatally hit, a fact he intended to hide from Tara once she woke up. If she woke up.

"You're liberating those dogs, right?" Jake asked. "But look at Tara. Look at Shavir. You're doing this crazy thing, risking your lives for a bunch of animals that are likely beyond fixing. Meanwhile, the whole world's going to hell. That's a little perverse, don't you think?"

"No more perverse than what you do," Lenny returned without looking at him. "We just have different priorities, that's all."

Shavir stepped through the door of the waiting room, her right forearm in a brace and bandaged all the way up to her elbow.

"How do you feel?" Jake asked once she had made her way through the crowd.

"I'm fine," she snapped. "Is there news on Tara?"

"Not yet," Lenny said. "Did they give you antibiotics?"

Shavir nodded.

"Something to take home, too, so you don't have to take dog pills?"

Another nod.

"Good." Lenny looked at Jake. "It'd be so much easier if there were enough meds for humans in this city, so we wouldn't have to take the pills that we need for our animals."

Jake hesitated. Perhaps he could offer a small piece of good news in the extended nightmare that was tonight. "There are more vet antibiotics coming in," he said, looking at Shavir. "I made them critical supply this afternoon."

She didn't say a word.

"We checked the stocks," he continued, "and saw there was almost nothing left in the city. So I prioritized them. They're under the control of the CSR now, and we've sent out a bunch of orders. I wish it was that simple for humans."

Shavir was still staring silently at him, but there was a softness in her eyes that made him feel instantly better. She'd just opened her mouth as if to reply when a doctor approached, his thin frame and starved eyes giving him away as a user of pep pills.

"How is she?" Lenny asked before the doctor could speak. The softness in Shavir's face was gone, replaced by naked fear.

"She made it through," the doctor said. "She's in critical condition, but we were able to get the bullet out and stop the bleeding. She suffered damage to part of her colon, and we had to remove that and cleanse her abdominal cavity. But there are no other vital organs affected. She was very lucky."

Shavir sat down. "Does that mean she's gonna survive this?"

"As I said, she's in critical condition," the doctor said, clearly unwilling to be the bearer of good news when bad might follow. "But the surgery went well. We've put her on antibiotics to prevent infection."

Shavir nodded, looking overwhelmed.

"Was she in that mass shooting in Borough Park?" the doctor asked.

"Walked right into it," Lenny said without a hint of hesitation. "Bullets came flying out of nowhere."

"You saved her life by bringing her here immediately," said the doctor. "They couldn't have helped her at Maimonides or anywhere else in Brooklyn. Not anymore."

Lenny nodded, looking at Jake.

"It's wrong," the doctor added grimly. "This whole situation. Look at them." He pointed to the people still holding their banners. "We can't be good doctors like that." He walked away without saying goodbye. It was clear he was beyond his limits already, and he probably had another dozen patients waiting for him.

"What shooting?" Jake asked once the doctor was out of earshot.

"The one outside Maimonides Medical Center," Lenny said. "Troy told me when I called about the dogs. Frontline shot some Black kid who was protesting, and then a whole bunch of guns went off, and several protestors got shot, some killed. It's easier if he thinks we were part of that." He looked at his watch. "I gotta call Troy and tell him Tara made it through surgery."

Jake looked around. Most of these people had probably survived the incident in Borough Park. And no antibiotics were coming because Bhaduri had blindsided him. He urgently needed some pills, or at the very least, coffee.

Shavir sat next to him, rubbing at the dark stains her clothes had left on the chair. "That's Tara's blood," she said, choking back tears.

"She's gonna make it." He wanted to put his arm around her, but she was so withdrawn. "I know all this must remind you of your mom," he added softly, "but this is a different situation, and Tara will pull through. She'll make it."

Shavir exhaled, fighting for control.

"Look." He searched for the right words, the right tone. "Don't hate me for saying this, but you're risking too much. The world's fucked up enough without you getting yourselves shot for a bunch of miserable animals. Just look." He nodded toward a woman crying into her hands, a banner lying next to her on the floor.

Shavir turned to him. "You don't give a damn about what we do. You cannot see the least bit of value in it or in those *miserable* animals."

He held her gaze. "I just prioritized vet meds in the CSR, didn't I? And I give a lot more than a damn about you. But I don't want you to put your life at risk for a bunch of dogs. I told you this afternoon. And now Tara's up there fighting for her life."

"Oh yeah, that's right," Shavir hissed. "I forgot. You tell me what's right and wrong in the world and who's worth saving."

"That's not what I'm saying."

"It's exactly what you're saying, and you've been saying it for a while. You look down on us from your precious little piece of moral high ground in the CSR because the fucked-up things you do up there are so infinitely more important than what we do."

"Moral high ground?" Jake repeated, irritation rising in him. "Who's the one that's built a whole settlement up there? You and your friends are permanent residents, judging immoral assholes like me who can't afford to live in black and white. Tara almost died because of your little stunt on a day when there aren't any meds left in Brooklyn. And the reason she's still alive is that immoral assholes like me are doing what they can to get those meds here."

"That's right," Shavir said, her voice made of ice. "Only that according to your logic, she wouldn't be here in the first place. She would have died as an infant in some refugee camp in West Bengal that lost its meds to the inhabitants of Park Avenue."

He could feel the impact of her words in his gut as his mind flashed back to Bhaduri and the antibiotics that were probably on their way to the next customer—if they existed at all, if this wasn't one big con from beginning to end.

"I lost them," he said roughly.

"What?"

"The antibiotics. They got confiscated a few hours ago."

"Well, good. Maybe they're gonna save a few lives in the camps."

"I don't think that's where they're gonna go. But there's nothing coming here."

She stared at him. "Is that why you got the vet meds instead?"

"What? No! There's no way you could get an American hospital to use vet antibiotics on patients. They're much too scared of potential damages claims, and the FDA would never—" He stopped himself. "Jesus, Shavir, can you just cut me some slack once in a while?"

"Look," she pressed out, "I'm sorry you lost your antibiotics, I really am, and it's great what you've done about the vet meds. But you really don't have to be here."

"I want to be here."

She shook her head. "No, Jake, you don't understand."

He gasped, knowing what she was about to say.

"You have this whole busy life," she continued, "saving a world that cannot be saved. And I just want to be here for Tara. Please leave."

He didn't move, uncertain what to do.

"Forget it," she said and got up. "I'll leave. I have to find Lenny."

He wanted to stop her but was still unable to move. The woman across the aisle looked at him with infinite sadness. Or perhaps he was just imagining things.

Seventeen

Three small bottles now sat next to the framed picture of her mom, the latest addition filled with antibiotics almost to the top, her going-away present from Bellevue Hospital. The second pill bottle was empty, but she'd kept it as a souvenir. The third bottle, the healing accelerant Jake had given her, was half full. She picked it up and coated the wound on her arm before covering it with a new bandage. Then she returned the bottle to its place and looked at her mom's dark eyes in the picture, the lines around them already pronounced when Tara's dad had taken the photo about a year before she'd died. She was wearing the white summer dress that had been her favorite, and there was a sparkle in her smile that had been rare at that time, a moment of happiness on a special day, arrested forever on a digital printout.

It still made her sad that her mom had never got to do what she wanted, follow her passion. In her little spare time, she would cook up a storm in her tiny kitchen, wearing her blue apron and lowering her glasses from her graying hair onto the bridge of her nose whenever she consulted the eclectic collection of plant-based recipes on her old phone. Aside from that beloved white summer dress, she'd spent her little "luxury money" on fancy spices such as cardamon, sumac, and saffron, spices ever more difficult to get. When Tara and her dad moved into the building, she would sit for hours with them, writing down whatever they could tell her about vegan Indian food.

The day the picture had been taken was the day the US government outlawed industrial meat production. The city had almost instantly erupted in protests, streets filled with screaming people who wouldn't have their freedoms curtailed unaware they were about to lose so much more. But her mom had been ecstatic. She'd left the hospital the second her shift was over and spent the entire walk home on the phone with Shavir, begging her to ask Lenny for a big bag of veggies and to invite everyone at his farm.

They'd celebrated that day together with Tara and her dad, with Lenny and whomever he could drag along from the farm, and with everyone in the apartment building who wasn't in a state of shock, devouring a four-course vegan menu and drinking copious amounts of wine. When the sun set, her mom, with that sparkling smile Dipak had captured so well in the picture, announced she would leave the hospital to become a plant-based nutritionist, helping people kick their addiction to animal parts. They'd all toasted to her resolve. Hours later, the hospital called to ask if she could cover for a nurse who'd called in sick. Off she'd gone, ignoring everyone's protests, and less than a year later, she'd been dead.

Shavir still felt guilty for failing her mom, for all the different ways in which she had failed her from the moment she'd been born to the moment her mom had died. She felt guilty for all the times she'd complained about being left alone or without the nice things she desired. For escaping the gloom of their home to be with Tara, and for not being home anymore when her mom returned from her long shifts, leaving her to cook her own dinner and eat alone. For not pushing harder after her mom's announcement about quitting her job, for not making her follow through on it. But most of all, she felt guilty for not getting her the help she needed after she got shot. For calling 911 too many times before finally accepting no one would come. For not stopping a car earlier that could have taken them to the bridge, and for not managing to keep her mom alive until they had reached the checkpoint to Manhattan.

Now new guilts layered over the old. One belonged to Tara, whom she hadn't stopped from raiding the mill. She could tell herself Tara was responsible for her own actions, as were the others. But sitting on the floor of the van, drenched in Tara's blood, had brought it all back again—the fear, the horror, and the indelible feeling of guilt. Her other new guilt belonged to Jake, whom she'd sent away after he had spared her the trauma of losing Tara, too. He had sent her a dozen messages since she'd walked out on him, and she hadn't read any of them.

After spending the night in the waiting room at the hospital, she'd dragged herself through her morning shift at Soma, figuring it was best to keep up her normal routines to not raise suspicion. Dipak had called around noon to tell her Tara was no longer in critical condition, and hearing that, for a brief happy moment, she'd come up for air. But then she'd had to explain to Dipak what had happened and ended up building a whole story around their supposed involvement in the protests in Borough Park. It had made her sick, lying to Tara's dad like that when he was so worried about his daughter, but she knew it was what Tara would have wanted and the only way to keep their story straight and everyone safe.

Upon her return to Roots, she walked right into a crisis meeting, Lenny and Judy at each other's throats, arguing about the future of Roots and what their latest raid had done to sabotage it. She'd wanted to sneak out and collapse in her cubicle, but Judy had told her to sit down next to Lenny, Nacho, Zeno, and Troy, all too shell-shocked to either protest or give in to Judy's arguments about the future of their operation. After two hours, they had postponed the meeting.

Now she was wondering if it was wise to leave Sam with Judy while she checked on the new puppies downstairs. She couldn't possibly face another guilt trip without dissolving into tears, but when she put down her mom's picture and heaved herself off the bed, Sam got up and followed her to the door out of habit, and she didn't have the strength to tell him to lie down again. Instead, she walked over to Judy's cubicle like she had done a hundred times before.

There was none of the earlier anger on Judy's face. "Come here, boy," she simply said when she saw Sam, petting his head like she always did. "Can you come in for a sec?" she added, looking up. "I got something I wanna ask you."

Resigned, Shavir stepped into the cubicle. "How can I help?"

"You can *help*," Judy said, her tone sharper, "by going online and finding yourself a new place for them bunnies, pooches, and whatever else you're collecting down there."

"We are looking for a new place, Judy." Shavir sat down on Judy's bed, accepting that she'd have to do this all over again, too weak to care. "But it's not that easy for obvious reasons, so please bear with us while we search for a better solution. Please?"

Judy eyed her suspiciously. "I'm depending on you, Shav. The others never listen to me. I know your work is important, and I know you're hurting because of what happened to Tara. I'm sorry it happened, Shav. Real sorry. But you gotta understand. Roots ain't only Lenny and you guys, it's also me and *my* people, the West Street Project." She gestured to the other cubicles surrounding them. "We fought so hard to be here, to have our place. And we've lived on the streets long enough to know we sure as hell don't wanna go back there."

"I live here, too," Shavir said, barely audibly.

"That's why I'm talking to you. I understand you guys wanna save them pooches, but this—" she again gestured around herself "—is more important."

"But Nacho—"

"Don't Nacho me!" Judy exploded. "Just because he's one of us ain't making him any smarter. Don't ask me why he don't care about getting his ass evicted or going to jail. Because that's what's gonna happen if Frontline finds out about them dogs downstairs. We can lose everything, Shav! The farm, our home, our freedom. Do you understand?" She caught herself. "I'm not saying you gotta stop," she continued more calmly. "But there needs to be more distance between Roots and that illegal stuff you're doing. I ain't gonna allow everyone to abuse my patience anymore. Those critters gotta go."

Shavir nodded. She knew Judy was right, and with Tara in intensive care, barely alive, she wasn't sure if they should go on at all. Jake's words were still on her mind, his question about whether the good they did was worth the risks they took. Right now, she wasn't sure.

"Here, this came for you." Judy pulled out a sizable package from underneath her desk. Recognition bolted through Shavir when she saw Jake's personal address. She opened the package right there, Judy frowning as she watched her retrieve the first bottles of veterinary antibiotics. "You got friends in all the right places, girl. And right on time. Zeno was complaining about not having enough meds to treat whatever you dragged out of those cages last night."

"Well," Shavir smiled, "now we do. I gotta take this downstairs."

"Sure. Maybe leave a couple for us up here?" Judy returned with her eyes on the bottles. "We haven't had any of those in a while, and it's good to have something in reserve in case, you know, something happens on the farm."

Shavir picked two bottles and gave them to Judy, who looked at the large package in a way that made her reach in and pull out three more.

"Thank you," Judy said with satisfaction. "Your friend picked well. Those all work on humans." She eyed the package again. "Fancy last name you have. Don't think I've seen it written before. First name, too. Does it mean anything, Shavir? I've been wondering about that."

"It's the Hebrew word for fragile," Shavir said as she picked up the package. "I was really small and weak when I was born, and my mom thought I might not make it."

"Hebrew." Judy looked surprised. "You Jewish?"

"I'm a lot of things. All mixed and mingled."

Judy chuckled. "An all-American girl." Her gaze was warm now, friendly in the way she could be when she wasn't miffed. "Well, this ain't no criticism of your mom or anything, but you don't look so fragile to me. Take good care of those meds, girl."

Zeno was ecstatic when Shavir told him on the phone about their package chock-full of vet meds. He asked her to give several of the dogs shots right away and texted her the details. "Thanks, Shav," he said. "Thanks for asking Jake. And please say thanks to him for me. I just checked online and saw that we can order antibiotics again for our clinic, too. That's so amazing. Thanks a lot, really. You have no idea what this means for us and for so many animals."

Tearing up, Shavir ended the call. Zeno was rarely this emotional. Perhaps she hadn't known how bad the situation had been. She had brushed him off when he first approached her about the meds, but in hindsight, it was so uncharacteristic of him, asking for favors like that. He must have been desperate. She was glad now that she had asked Jake, but she wouldn't convey Zeno's thanks to him because she had resolved she wouldn't see Jake again, not even now that he had done this unfathomable thing for her. If she talked to him, she wouldn't be able to keep her distance, and it felt so important that she did.

She opened the jib door and could tell right away that the atmosphere was different with all the big dogs here. She walked to the back room and put Jake's package on top of their emergency operation table. Then she prepared the first syringe.

Zeno had singled out nine of the puppies and only one of the mothers because the other big dogs would be too dangerous for her to handle alone. When she opened the first compartment, her heart broke open. It was the dog that had been shot during their escape.

She was lying on her side, a plastic cone around her neck, one of her hind legs bandaged. Four little ones were crawling all over her, as Zeno thought it better not to separate her from her babies. She used to have six, but two of them had succumbed to their gunshot wounds.

The dog raised her head. For a moment Shavir wondered if she was the dog who had bitten her. But that couldn't be, since she was one of the last ones they'd carried out, one that would have been left behind had Troy not carried her on his shoulders.

She crouched down next to the dog, who looked at her anxiously, ears pressed close to her head, cropped tail attempting to wag. Shavir gently touched her prickly fur.

"It's okay, girl," she whispered, "you're safe, and so are your babies."

The dog pressed her head against her and opened her massive jaws, a long pink tongue swiping her hand. Overwhelmed, Shavir sat down and caressed her. She gave her the shot, which provoked no reaction at all, then she remained sitting there, stroking the injured dog and the curious puppies that crowded her. They were so small, so much younger than the ones they usually pulled out of the fattening farms.

"I thought they're these ferocious animals," a voice said from behind the slats. The door opened, and Finn poked his head in. "Why did we bother sedating them? All we needed was a leash. May I?"

Shavir nodded though she was in no shape for an argument or anything else Finn might try, and she knew from experience that he was nearly always trying something.

He surprised her by staying on his side of the stall after closing the door, crouching down so he was at eyelevel with her, smiling. "So they're basically lap dogs?"

"This one is," Shavir said, returning the smile. "The other ones need more time." Even across the distance of the stall, she could see Finn was clean, his blue eyes vivid but tender. She used to love it when he was like this, the Dr. Jekyll to his Mr. Hyde, and she was grateful that, for now at least, this was who she was dealing with.

"I'm sorry about last night," he said. "What happened to Tara."

"We're all sorry about that. With the possible exception of Tara."

It was strange to see Finn down here in the basement, a place he avoided because he wasn't as good as they were with the dogs. That was what he always said, anyway.

"Why are you here?"

"Judy said you're down here. I wanted to see how you're doing."

She rested the back of her head against the wall. "I'm okay. At least Tara is alive, and we didn't get caught, so it wasn't a total failure. And it's so good to be here with them. Reminds you why we're doing this."

"I'm glad we got them out. I've been thinking about adopting one of them... perhaps this one?" He looked at the dog who was still resting her head on Shavir's legs. Then he got up and crossed the distance between them, petting first the puppies and then, carefully, their mother, who had tensed up when he'd approached but now was relaxing again.

"She's exhausted from everything she's gone through. But she's a good girl." Shavir looked up at Finn, who crouched close to her, indifferent, it seemed, to the fact that there was puppy poop on the floor around them, another reason why she had always thought he didn't want to be here. "You really want to adopt a dog?"

"I miss having Sam around, and I figure I have the space. Unless, of course, I can convince you and Sam to come back to me?"

She turned her head away. "Please, Finn, don't."

"I'm just telling the truth."

"Okay, but I'm... please don't." She wanted to get up, get herself out of this situation, away from the blue eyes and the vicious cycles. But she was too tired to move.

"You want me to leave?" Finn asked, his voice husky, vulnerable. "I just wanted to see if you're okay, but I can leave if you want me to."

"No," she said. "I just... I'm not okay, actually. Not at all."

Finn studied her face. "Are you still with him?"

Of course he would ask this.

"Is he the reason why we have meds for the dogs?" Finn nodded to the syringe in her chest pocket. "I wasn't able to get them, and it's not like I didn't try. But apparently, he can?"

Shavir winced. Suddenly, there was a more menacing ring to what Judy had said earlier about her having friends in all the right places. "There's no competition," she said. "That's not what this was about."

"Does that mean it's over between you two?"

"That's none of your business," she erupted. The dog looked up at her, anxious because of her raised voice, so she toned it down. "I'm really not in the mood, Finn."

"Alright," Finn said, his gaze so intense she could feel it down the back of her spine. "We don't have to talk. I just wanted to make sure you're okay, and... I miss you, Shav. I know you don't believe me, and I know you think it's some fucked-up game I'm playing, but it's the truth, and I, uhm—" He looked down at the dog before facing her again. "I know I can be an asshole sometimes, and I'm sorry if I hurt you. I really am. But you're not so easy yourself, and we've always found a way to come back and make it work again."

He still hadn't touched her, his body just close enough for her to feel its warm presence, making it easy for her to slip right back in.

And it did feel easy.

"I always came crawling back to you," she said, more to remind herself than him. "That doesn't mean it worked. Not for me."

Now he did touch her, tenderly brushing a loose strand of hair behind her ear. "I don't want you crawling, but I hope you will come back." He nodded to the dog in her lap. "You can bring her, too, if you want. Then we'll have a whole chaotic family."

Her phone vibrated audibly. A call from Jake, perhaps, and the last thing she needed. For a moment, she and Finn both waited while the phone kept humming. It could also could be Zeno, she realized, who wanted to know whether everything had gone okay with the shots. And now Finn was looking at her like he thought it was Jake, too.

She pulled out her phone. It was Carrie.

Before she knew it, she was picking up. And for once, she was lucky. Carrie didn't know anything about what had happened with Jake. She was just excited to accept the invitation to visit Roots with Zoe, who couldn't wait to see Sam again.

"That's wonderful, Carrie, I'm glad you wanna come visit the farm." Shavir gave Finn a look that made clear it was a business call and carefully freed herself from the dog. She got up and left the stall while she spoke. "This week is a bit busy, how about next?"

She wasn't at all sure it was a good idea to see Carrie again, given where things stood with Jake. But she could hardly retract her invitation to give them a tour. Carrie didn't seem to have much joy in her life, and Zoe was so keen on being outside and playing with Sam—how could she disappoint either of them? Plus, she couldn't help feeling like Carrie had saved her stupid ass just now.

She walked over to the back room and filled the next syringe while she gave Carrie directions to Prince Gardens. As always, Carrie was overly talkative, so all she had to do was let her go on and on about the latest news from Zoe and how bad things were at the pharmacy, the protests now daily and ever more furious.

She heard the jib door slam and closed her eyes in relief. Then she told Carrie how much she looked forward to showing them the farm, hung up, and returned to the dogs to confirm that Finn had left. By next week, she hoped, she would feel more confident about her decision to cut things off with Jake, and she might also find the courage to thank him for the meds he had sent her—and for everything else.

EIGHTEEN

THE COOL DARK AIR stretched out into nothingness. Jake rested his head against the kitchen wall, waiting for the sun to rise. There were no longer cranky messages from David waiting for him in the morning; now, he was inundated by a deluge of breaking news, alerts, and disasters the second he went online. Hong Kong was still dysfunctional, and many of their other providers and logistical hubs were compromised or lost. David hadn't woken up, but most of the items on his secret list were now being handled by the CSR, including bottled water. There was a pervasive sense of doom in the team that Jake knew was his job to address. But he was the wrong guy entirely to dish out optimism, caught up as he was in his personal disasters.

More than a week had gone by, and he hadn't heard from Shavir. She hadn't tried to reach him or responded to any of the messages he'd sent her. He made his own coffee at home on his silly little machine now, though he hadn't been able to stop himself from going to Soma once.

He hadn't had a plan and stood outside the front window, watching her serve a customer, wondering if it would be wrong to go in. She'd looked up suddenly, gazing directly at him through the glass. He'd felt his face glow with hope and embarrassment, but on hers had been nothing beyond her usual mask of courtesy. Then she had turned back to her customers, smiling for them. He left knowing he should never go back again. Since then, he'd spent most of his time in the

CSR, forcing himself to function. Whatever had been between him and Shavir had shattered on the floor of a crowded waiting room in the Belvedere intensive care ward.

The air was oppressive when he left his building, coffee in one hand, working the Spine with the other. The heat wave still hadn't broken, but forecasts were finally predicting a change in weather. After over six weeks above one hundred degrees, the city was so parched for rainfall people couldn't stop talking about it. Weather forecasts flickered across the obscured windshields of podcars, replacing commercials as the most pressing piece of information. Everyone was hoping for rain, but in the CSR, they were anticipating the floods that would follow, the crop failures, the delays.

They had finally managed to secure antibiotics from one of the three pharmaceutical corporations whose production sites were within the US and operational, having so far been spared by this year's disasters. Their production had been nationalized by what was left of the federal government, but that did nothing to ease the competition between the SAFE centers around the country. There was a cap on orders so that every major city could receive its fair share, but although New York was one of the biggest recipients, it would only receive a fraction of what it needed. And the local fight to the finish had only just begun.

He was talking to Masao about their strategy when he received an alert from the private part of his message center. His guts contracted violently as he moved a sweaty finger along his glove to check the sender. It took several seconds to process that it was from Marla, the first one in months. The knot in his guts unraveled, leaving numb disappointment.

"Are you still there?" Masao's voice pierced into his consciousness.

"Yes. Sorry, I was distracted."

"No problem. How much did you hear?"

"Well, nothing, actually. Can you say it again?"

"I said the army still hasn't made up its mind about making its antibiotics provisions available for the SAFE centers. They're worried that if they help the cities now, there won't be enough left in a national emergency."

"That's rich." Jake turned to the glittering surface of the Hudson. "So they'd rather watch their people die now than potentially risk their lives in the future."

"It really only affects certain people," Masao said wryly, "and they don't seem to care very much about those particular people dying."

Jake had heard everything he could stomach, so he told Masao he'd be there soon and switched back to his message center.

Haven't heard from U in ages, Marla had written, *any chance U resurface ST soon? Would love to C U + got mad cravings 4 Deluge. XX.*

He deleted the message.

It was exactly what he'd expected, and he couldn't deal with it now. He hadn't told Marla about Shavir, and she probably wouldn't care anyway. She had never asked him what he did in between their rare dinner dates, and he knew even less about her. It used to be exactly the kind of relationship he needed, a friendly face to look at while he pretended to eat and a warm body to lose himself in whenever they both had the time and stamina for it. Giving each other space was one of the unspoken agreements between them, and right now he needed that space to improve their supply situation so he could look into the eyes of his cousin when he visited her tonight.

Carrie had finally gotten desperate enough to ask him whether there was any chance he could bring new meds for Zoe. Normally, he had to divine their needs for meds then find excuses to bring them because, unless there was an emergency, Carrie was too proud and stubborn to ask for help. The fact that she was asking for them meant it was urgent, and his pharmacy had just been restocked with the corticoids Zoe needed, so he was going to jump into the subway after work and join her and Dan for dinner.

He wasn't looking forward to it. Every second word Carrie had said during their brief call had been *Shavir*, and when he'd finally told her they had broken up, there had been silence on the other line. That silence would transform into something much less agreeable when he saw her, of that he was certain.

The power hadn't yet been cut, but the elevators were still out of service when he finally arrived at Carrie's building at the end of an exhausting day. He had walked into protests the minute he left the subway in Queens and had his identity checked twice by Frontline on his way here.

People were determined not to give in this time. They wanted a more equal distribution of the few goods that were flowing into the city, or they wanted the world as a whole to change. To them, it was all the same as long as they had clean water and functioning ERs.

He knocked on the door and looked at Carrie's reproachful face three seconds later.

"For once, you're on time. And now, of course, I'm not ready."

"Frankly, it's an achievement I'm here at all and that I'm still in possession of this." He put down the two water containers he'd carried here. "The streets are crazy."

"It's getting worse every day since our guys shot that kid in Brooklyn." Dan gave him a sweaty hug. "Pretty stupid, shooting another kid like that."

"Let's not talk about it," Carrie cut in, her eyes motioning to Zoe, who was sitting on the cluttered couch, eyes glued to some kind of device. She hadn't gotten up to greet Jake or even turned her head in his direction, a stark change from her usual enthusiasm.

"What's wrong?"

"She's pouting." Carrie shrugged. "It's because we won't let her play outside with her friends because of, you know, the situation." She tried to sound encouraging as she raised her voice to reach her daughter. "Hey, sweetie. Don't you wanna say hello?"

"Where's Sam?" Zoe shot a defiant glance at her mother.

"With Shavir," Jake said as casually as he could. "You can still give me a hug."

"You stop this right here and now!" Carrie looked sternly at her daughter. "I told you, you're gonna see Sam tomorrow. I don't want no drama tonight."

"Tomorrow," Jake echoed.

"Yes." Carrie looked uncomfortable. "Shavir invited us to come to the farm, and we've been planning for this for some time. It didn't seem right to cancel."

"Of course not," Jake said. "Zoe will love it. The farm's great."

He shouldn't be so shocked, he thought as he carried the water containers to the kitchen. It was perfectly normal, Carrie and Zoe visiting the farm. Yet he felt betrayed, jealous even, that Shavir was picking up Carrie's calls and not his. He unpacked the meds while Zoe helped Carrie set the table, her mouth curling downward in a permanent pout.

"That's much more than we need," Carrie whispered when she saw the medicine bottles. "That must have been so expensive. And the water. You don't have to do this."

"I want to do this," Jake said tersely. "You're my family. And I have no idea when we'll get corticoids again. Was hard enough to get those, so put them somewhere safe."

Carrie searched his eyes, waiting for Zoe to leave with the silverware for the table. "I'm so sorry about you and Shavir. What happened?"

"Life happened. It's okay."

"Don't you think—"

"Carrie—" He gave her a warning look.

"I'm just saying, don't you think that—"

"Carrie," he said again. "Please."

"But you and Shavir—"

"*Carrie!*" His voice had been louder than intended. Zoe looked up from the arrangement she was producing on the dinner table. She spun around and joined her father on the balcony.

"I can't," Jake pleaded again with his cousin. "Can you please respect that? *Please?*"

"I just don't think it's right what you guys are doing," Carrie said, "throwing everything away like that. You seemed so good together."

"If that were true, we'd still be together. And now let's drop it."

Dinner was very different from the last time he'd been here with Shavir, both in tone and atmosphere, but also in terms of what was on their plates. Carrie was acutely aware of it, mentioning four times that it was impossible to get fresh produce. Since they had to rely on the grill again, she could only offer the usual burger and canned beans.

"You look like hell," Jake said when Dan came in from the balcony with the art-meat patties, a reddish hue in the whites of his eyes, his heavy steps shuffling in a slow slalom around the heaps of Zoe's stuff on the floor. "Have you been on the streets all week?"

"Pretty much." Dan sat down with a thud. "We can use the extra money, but it's like every single doctor's office and pharmacy wants Frontline protection now."

"And we need it, too." Carrie turned to Jake. "You wouldn't believe what's happening at our store. Customers are lining around the block, camping out in the morning before we open, and try to make their way through the protestors to get in."

"Is it about Emovia?" Jake asked, alarmed.

"You bet it's about Emovia." Carrie glared at him like it was his fault. "And about pretty much any other drug we've run out of. Again. But now we also have trouble getting simple things, like water. So much stuff is missing or crazy expensive. I could give you a whole list."

"We already have that list, trust me," Jake said. Nothing he could say would make it better, but at least this gave him the opening to ask what had been on his mind since Lenny had hurled the question at him in the hospital. "Are people still using vet antibiotics on themselves?"

"Sure," Carrie said like it was the most natural thing in the world. "If they can get their hands on them. I think by now it's mostly people using them. There's probably nothing left for all the poor critters."

"Isn't that a risk?" Jake asked. "Not all vet stuff works on humans. Or not as expected."

"Better than dying, isn't it? And it's not that big of a deal. You have to pick the right antibiotics, and you need to know how to adapt the dosage. That kind of information is all over the cloud." Carrie exchanged a glance with Dan then looked at Jake again. "The Emovia problem is so much worse, Jake, please believe me. You guys need to do something about it and fast. We've run out of pretty much every other emotion regulator we had, everything you can buy over the counter. But it's not enough, or it's not doing the trick. All I know is people are getting so frantic they'd drink bleach if someone told them it'd make them feel better."

"Well," Jake mocked, "we've already tried that."

"You need to understand how bad this is," Dan cut in, anger in his eyes. "You should come out with us sometime. There're parts of Brooklyn and Queens right now where our men refuse to go, they're that scared. We've arrested hundreds of people, of our own people, and it didn't change shit. We can't control this much longer, Jake. We keep saying that, but all that happens is they're sending us out again, more of us, with more gear. But that won't stop anyone from tossing a cocktail into a storefront or at us. Something's got to change!"

Carrie glanced at Zoe and sent her husband a silent warning across the table.

"Don't mind me, sweetie, I'm just mad about work." Dan stroked his daughter's hair.

Zoe nodded, winding away from her father's hand. "They said they're gonna close our school again," she said to Jake as if she expected him to do something about that, too.

He exchanged a look with Carrie. "That's kind of cool, isn't it?"

"No, that ain't cool at all." Zoe looked accusingly at her mother.

"You'll be outside tomorrow," Carrie said. "Which is why you'll go to bed now."

Zoe ignored that and looked at Jake again. "You gonna be at the farm, too?"

"No," he said. "You're going in the afternoon, and I have to be at work then."

"But Sam's gonna be there," Carrie interjected before Zoe could ask her next question. Jake was relieved when she got up and led his niece to her bedroom.

"Sorry about the outburst," Dan said, his gaze following his wife and daughter. "I'm so worried about them—every day I'm at work and they're out there in the city. This is no place to raise a family," he added bitterly. "Not anymore."

Dan was right, of course, and Jake had no energy left to be encouraging. The truth was he had no solution, no fix for their life or for anything else. At least Carrie would take Zoe to the farm so she could run around free and safe up on those beautiful green roofs. The subway ride to Brooklyn would be safe enough, he hoped, and Sam would ensure she had a fun day. He wanted to be there to see it, but that was another area where he had run out of fixes and solutions.

"There's something you should know," Dan said. "I know it's over between you and—"

"Shavir," Jake offered, his stomach clenching around the food he'd gotten down.

"Right. So Gary—you know when we had that little run-in with her and the dogs? Well, he still ain't buying that whole story about them being service dogs and all. He thinks it's all BS and there's some connection to that puppy mill that got raided last week. You heard about that?"

Jake nodded, trying to breathe evenly.

"Well, I don't think it's gonna go anywhere, but I couldn't talk him out of it, so I thought I'd tell you in case—," Dan frowned, "in case there's a reason why you're looking like a piece of shit these days. Just in case, you know, you still care. Gary's a bloodhound."

Carrie returned to the living room, and Dan turned his attention to his burger, leaving Jake to process the information he'd been given. While Carrie told him more about Zoe's unhappiness, Jake checked Shavir's Homeland file on his Spine. There was nothing new on it, but he wondered if he should tell Shavir, if she would listen.

Carrie stepped into the hallway with him after he'd said goodbye to Dan. "Are you sure you don't want to talk to Shavir?" she asked before he had a chance to stop her. "I know you hate me for saying this, but maybe talking would help, you know? I've been married for over fifteen years, I know these things."

"She doesn't want to talk to me, Carrie. She doesn't even respond."

"Then go there! To the farm. Or to where she works."

Jake shook his head. "I know you mean well, and I know how long you've been married. But this is very different from you and Dan, believe me. It's different ends of the universe." He tried to make his hug feel definite, and, apparently, Carrie finally got it.

"I'm sorry, Jake. I hoped so much this would work out for you."

Outside, Jake tried to make up his mind. Going home and staring at the empty walls of his apartment again was out of the question.

He could go to the CSR and help Lisa, but he couldn't face the prospect of another airless subway ride, plus he didn't want to become a copy of David entirely and risk Lisa complaining about him breathing down her neck one day. Much better to keep walking across Queens to Queensboro Bridge and then from there to Chelsea. The distance was a little insane, but he knew the area well and walking was the only thing that would help him now.

Less than an hour later, Jake stepped through the doors of the NYU Langone Medical Center. Walking through the dark streets of Queens had turned out to be a bad idea. Before even leaving the Corona neighborhood, he'd been stopped by three separate Frontline patrols, each of them making clear that it wasn't a great time for a walk, so he had finally given up and stepped into the subway at Elmhurst Avenue only to get off at Grand Central on a whim.

He didn't know why, but he needed to see David.

The nurse didn't bother to check his prints. "It's good to see you again, Dr. Alvaro. I know it's hard to believe, but comatose patients really do need the company."

"Has his son come back?"

"No. Just that one time. And Dr. Hatton was here a few times."

"No one else?"

The nurse shook her head.

Jake stepped into the dimly lit room, closing the door behind him. He studied David's face. There was no change since he'd been here two days ago.

"How did you manage to alienate all the people in your life, will you tell me that?" Only now, saying the question out loud, did Jake realize how angry he was. "How can it be that no one shows up here? How come I'm the only one who cares?"

David's waxen face didn't respond, the only sound coming from the machines keeping him alive. Jake pulled over a chair and sat down.

"How did you manage to do all that, huh? And then, when they're all gone, you turn around and kill yourself with Emovia because you can't take the loneliness. I mean, how fucking stupid is that, David?"

He stared at the motionless face, wondering whether it was indeed loneliness that had made David do this or that bigger and much more devastating feeling: hopelessness.

"Corsys broke down today," he said. "Niya couldn't do anything about it because all the data feeds are down. She was desperate. But it really doesn't matter because there's nothing available anyhow. And there's actually another storm forming in the Pacific. I mean, okay, it's almost September, but that's just—" He broke off. "The heat wave in Europe is unbroken, the situation in India is out of control, Hong Kong's worse, and don't get me started on what's left of our own country. The entire LA SAFE had to evacuate because of the wildfires. And Cristina lost her house. She's now competing with us for meds that aren't there from a motel room in San Diego. Oh, and we're nationalizing production again, like the EU, but unlike the EU, we've got no safe spots left to produce anything for very long." He looked at the floor. "What the fuck is going on, David, can you tell me? Did you know this would happen? Is that why you took the easy way out? So that I'd be stuck with your fucking list?"

He sat silently for a while, staring out the window.

Then he got up, reached into his pocket, and pulled out David's bottle of Emovia, which he had been carrying around with him every day like some perverse kind of charm.

"So does it really work?" He looked at David's empty face.

After opening and closing his fingers around the bottle for another ten minutes, he opened it and took two pills. They were big, but he swallowed them dry.

Then he waited.

The green facades of the skyscrapers outside looked beautiful and remote, like they belonged to some other world. He got up and walked to the soundproof window, resting his hands on the sill. He didn't feel any high, but he was calmer, and there was a pleasant feeling of satiation, like something that had been empty before was now filled.

He waited for another ten minutes, but there was no noticeable effect aside from the satiation, which he had to admit was pleasurable for someone who barely ate and rarely got enough of anything he craved. It occurred to him that he was looking at Belvedere Hospital a few blocks down the road, where Tara had to be hospitalized. Shavir was working all day, so she probably visited Tara in the evenings.

It was worth trying.

He said goodbye to David and walked out.

Nineteen

"I ALREADY FOUND A new home for her and her little ones," Tara said, beaming at Shavir like everything was perfectly normal when nothing was. It was uncanny how much energy she had just a week after getting shot. She bounced up in her hospital bed, turning her phone so Shavir could see the image Zeno had taken of Laika, the docile new dog from the puppy mill who now had a name. It was the dog Finn had wanted to adopt, but Tara had convinced him a traumatized female was hardly the right choice for him.

That was how Tara had put it, anyway, when she'd recounted the conversation, grinning like a madwoman. Her voice was hushed, and she was talking code because there were three other women in the room, all of them injured in the Borough Park shooting. Apparently, the hospital thought birds of a feather liked to flock together, and Lenny had told the doctor Tara had been in that shooting. While the other women were mostly asleep or taking advantage of their beds' entertainment systems, Tara had started working practically from the moment she'd regained consciousness, and she had been more efficient than ever in securing adoption spots for the new dogs. Now she was smiling, never mind she'd almost got killed.

Shavir had tried to talk with her about what happened as much as was possible in here. But Tara didn't want to talk. Her way of processing trauma was to leave it behind. Shavir couldn't help admiring it, though her mom had always said it was unhealthy. The only thing Tara wanted to talk about was the new dogs—and Jake, who had saved not only her life, but also those of at least half those dogs through his decision to make vet antibiotics critical supply. Tara was acutely aware of it, showing more gratitude for that than for her own survival.

"It's pretty amazing that he can just do that," she whispered. "Just push some kind of magic button and produce hundreds of pills."

"There's nothing magical about it," Shavir said, more irritated than she wanted to be. She still hadn't answered any of Jake's messages and didn't feel any better about it, but what was she going to say? That she was grateful? That she was sorry? That she missed him? That was all true, but none of it would bridge the chasm between them.

"Is it because of us that you called it quits with him?" Tara asked, raising her eyebrows like she was in some third-rate soap opera. "You know, I used to think he was a problem, but now that he's helped us, there's not much he can do without implicating himself."

"Can we not talk about this here?" Shavir hissed, nodding to the other women.

"They don't hear a thing. I'm just saying he's actually turned out to be quite useful."

Now that Jake was gone, everyone seemed to have found a new appreciation for him. She wondered how long it would take for them to suggest she rekindle the relationship or whether Tara was already doing that.

Then she saw the door open and someone enter the room.

Not a doctor, not a nurse. Jake.

"What are you doing here?" she asked.

"I wanted to see how Tara's doing."

He came closer. The woman in the bed next to Tara's eyed him with disapproval, but he didn't seem to notice.

Tara raised her hand in a half-waved welcome, but before he got any closer, Shavir jumped up and motioned for him to follow her outside. Her heart hammered as she waited for him in a hallway stuffed with beds and patients that gave no privacy at all.

"What do you want, Jake?" she asked, shocked at how happy she was to see him.

The elevator doors split open, and two NYPD cops stepped into the hallway followed by a woman in hospital uniform who pointed in her and Jake's direction.

Shavir's first impulse was to run. Back to Tara's room, up to the roof, anywhere. But it was too late for that, and too crowded, so she just watched as the cops came closer, her stomach cramping, her heartbeat in her ears. She looked at Jake, who looked at the cops, unperturbed. *Is he really doing this, reporting me?* she asked herself as the cops reached them, but the men barely noticed her. Instead, they turned to Jake and politely asked him to follow them.

"As I said, sir," huffed the receptionist with the air of a kindergarten teacher, "the visiting hours are over. You are welcome to come back tomorrow, but you really do need to leave now." She looked at Shavir. "You, too, ma'am, it's past eleven. Our patients need rest."

They ended up in the same elevator, riding down with a pissed hospital receptionist and two exceptionally well-behaved cops who accompanied them to the main entrance and bid them good night. The night air was hot coming out of the refrigerated Belvedere hospital, but Jake didn't seem to notice. He walked a few steps away from the entrance before stopping and turning around.

"I wanted to talk to you," he said, and it sounded like a demand.

Shavir noticed again how tall he was, but she couldn't make herself look up into his eyes. She walked past him, away from the glare of the hospital entrance into the shadows beneath a row of trees where they would have more privacy. "Thank you for saving Tara's life," she spilled out when she turned to him, still without looking him in the eye. "And thanks for sending us those vet meds. They've saved so many other lives already. Everyone wants me to thank you. They're all really grateful."

"Great," he said casually. "How about you?"

"Me, too, of course," she scrambled. "I'm sorry I didn't call, I just wasn't—" She finally looked up at him. "I wanted to call, Jake, but I didn't know what to say."

He didn't answer, and she regretted walking over here where it was too dark to read his face. She could see there were goosebumps on his arms despite the heat.

"It's all so fucking complicated," she said helplessly, resisting the urge to touch him.

"Yeah," he said.

Confused, she again tried to read his face, to understand what he wanted from her, why he was here. "What did you want to talk about?" she finally asked.

"Why you ignored me."

"I just told you—"

"At Soma."

She frowned. "Soma? You haven't been to Soma."

"I was."

"When?"

"Five days ago."

She didn't have the slightest idea what he was talking about. The last time she'd seen him at Soma had been the day of the raid when he had walked into Hector's back room in the middle of the day to tell her about India. He hadn't been back since, but she had spent every single morning feeling like she was connected to an electric current, her heart missing a beat every time someone opened the door. This had continued even when she knew it was too late, that Jake must have started his shift in the CSR after buying his coffee at one of the thousands of other coffee shops that didn't require him to make a detour on his morning walk to SAFE, places up on the High Line or on the boardwalk staffed with other baristas happy to serve him.

"Outside the window," Jake said.

"The window?"

This didn't make sense either. It was impossible to see anyone outside the window in the morning when there was not much light outside and the glare of the LEDs turned the glass into a mirror that showed her nothing but her own ghastly face waiting for Jake.

What she did know by now, however, was that something was wrong with him. If he weren't standing right in front of her, she'd have sworn it was some other guy entirely. Unless, of course, he *was* some other guy entirely, chemically speaking.

Now that recognition had finally arrived in her brain, she was certain. "What did you take?" she asked, but she knew. He didn't look at all like Finn when he was high, but she knew what this was. Jake was on Emovia.

"I wanted to talk to you," he said instead of answering her question.

"Like this?" she hissed, fighting back tears. "Why did you take it? Because of me?"

"I just want to talk to you."

She was so sick of it all, of the drugs, the drama, and the dead ends.

"That's great, Jake," she hurled back at him. "The only problem is you have no idea how to do that or what to do with me right now. Because in case you haven't noticed yet, Emovia isn't a great conversation starter. It does the opposite. It kills everything you feel and what makes you you. And it sure kills everything in me. So how are you feeling?"

"I'm a bit cold," he said, "which is weird."

"Well, great then," she said, her temples pulsing. "Maybe have some tea. But please don't ever talk to me like this again. And please stop taking that shit before you get used to it. It'll kill you, Jake. Just look at David!"

With that she walked away, knowing he felt a vague sense of serenity as he watched her go. She didn't want to turn around, yet when she did, he had already left.

She saw him walking swiftly down 1st Avenue, away from her.

The next morning started with brilliant sunshine and a significant weather alert. A thunderstorm was forecast from the west, with heavy rain and wind gusts up to fifty miles per hour. It was good news for the farm, the first promise of rain in weeks. But it was still a warning, giving Shavir the perfect excuse to cancel her afternoon with Carrie and Zoe. After last night, she dreaded the idea of showing them around and answering Carrie's questions. Shortly before noon, she called to postpone the visit.

But Carrie was undeterred. She wasn't afraid of a little rain, she said, and the significant weather in question was supposed to only graze New York in passing anyway. Apparently, she was following these things more closely than expected.

Having Carrie on the phone, with Zoe bouncing around in the background calling Sam's name, Shavir understood why postponement wasn't an option. Carrie seemed outright scared of confronting her bouncy daughter with the news that, once again, she wasn't allowed outside. Not even the prospect of using the subway seemed to put a damper on her eagerness to come, and that was saying something given that the protests in Queens were close to a boiling point.

So they were coming, and Shavir was faced with the question of what, if anything, she was going to say about Jake's Emovia use or anything related to him. She hadn't slept much after returning from Manhattan, thinking all night about whether it was her fault that Jake was taking Emovia for the first time in his life and whether it was her responsibility to do something about it. She didn't know what would have happened between them last night had he been clean, though she felt pretty certain she would have woken up next to him. Then again, it seemed unlikely that he would have shown up at all last night without the drug. Which again begged the question—should she say something to his cousin?

She hadn't made up her mind when Carrie stepped out of the staircase into the bright sunlight, Zoe behind her.

"Wow!" Carrie cried, looking around.

Shavir smiled. This was everyone's reaction when they first laid eyes on Prince Gardens, and she always enjoyed it. That was why she had suggested they meet up here rather than on the other side of the farm. "It's like... paradise." Carrie laughed. "I had no idea it was this beautiful. I thought it would be more like a big farm but up on a roof."

"That's what it is, mostly," Shavir admitted. "It's only this one that looks like some kind of rooftop oasis. It's where we recover from breaking our backs on the other roofs."

"So I guess we better stay up here, huh?" Carrie was still laughing, her features radically changed from when Shavir had last seen her in

Queens. She had been animated then but clouded. Now, joy rippled through the watery blue of her eyes. Her pale skin and long blond tresses shone in the afternoon sun. She wore a straw hat and a light blue summer dress that didn't exactly qualify as the sensible clothing Shavir had recommended on the phone.

Zoe, by contrast, looked like she was about to embark on an expedition to the Arctic Circle, wearing heavy boots and apparently anything she could find in her closet, every inch of her skin covered but her hands and her delicate face. "She wanted to be prepared," said Carrie, but before she could elaborate, Zoe let out a sharp cry and ran toward Sam, who was sleeping underneath one of the tables.

"Slow down, girl," Shavir called after her. "You're gonna scare the hell out of him."

Zoe froze mid-movement then continued, now approaching the dog like she was walking on eggshells.

Sam sleepily lifted his head and started wagging his tail.

Zoe threw another glance at Shavir, who nodded, then she wrapped her arms around the dog's massive neck. Sam made his cooing noise, signaling deep satisfaction, and Zoe looked back to them, beaming.

"Well, that's taken care of the rest of the afternoon," Carrie said.

"Looks like it. Do you want me to show you around while the weather holds up?"

Carrie turned toward Manhattan, where dark clouds were towering behind the green skyline. "Jesus! You must think I'm an idiot for wearing this." She nodded to her dress. "But I never get to wear it, so I thought today is the day. Plus," she pulled an umbrella out of her purse, followed by a transparent raincoat, "I'm ready."

Shavir laughed, suddenly glad Carrie was here. "Looks worse than it is. They sent out a weather warning for New Jersey, but it's gonna trail south from there. We're still hoping for some rain though. Do you want something to drink before we start?"

They walked down to the kitchen, where a pitcher of Judy's lemonade was waiting for them, then Shavir led them across the first bridge to the next rooftop. Zoe was wary when approaching the bridge, ignoring her mother's advice to not look down, but then Sam trotted across it in front of her, and the girl ran after him.

They walked between rows of beans, squash, tomatoes, bell peppers, lettuce, and kale, most of the plants significantly damaged by the constant heat and potent sunrays. Zoe was peeling clothes off herself like an onion, shedding layer after layer, leaving it to her mother to collect and carry everything around while she and Sam explored the farm.

Carrie was no less excited about the farm than she had been about Prince Gardens. Shavir showed her the super-foil Finn had brought them, the crops underneath looking much better than everything else around, and Carrie couldn't stop asking questions about what it was and how it worked, like she was planning to start her own farm. Zoe was fascinated to see bell peppers on the plant and in awe when Shavir showed her how to cut one for herself. She bit into it immediately, holding it like an apple.

"Careful with the seeds, sweetie," Carrie said, but Zoe didn't care about seeds. Her attention was caught by the saturated yellow of a large female squash flower, and she was off, Sam trailing behind her like her personal guardian.

"It's so good to see her like this." Carrie's eyes followed her daughter. "She gets a little lonely sometimes, being an only child and all. At least she has friends, now that we have her asthma under control thanks to Jake. She's finally able to go outside and play, but with these damn protests, she's stuck at home again and climbing the walls. Dan's so worried he won't let her go outside alone." She turned to Shavir. "I know he seems tough, and I'm really sorry you had a bad experience with him and Gary, that must have been awful. But he's also the sweetest man I know and such a good father. I can't imagine my life without him."

"It's great you feel that way about him," Shavir said, trying to find the right words and not think too much about Dan or Gary. "That makes it special."

"It does. But just because it's special doesn't mean it's always easy."

Shavir stepped onto the bridge to the next roof. She could still see Jake standing before her outside the hospital, unable to say anything meaningful to her.

"Jake thinks you're pretty special, too, you know?" Carrie said.

Shavir winced. How could she stop this?

"He does, though," Carrie insisted. "He's so different around you."

"Carrie—" Shavir stopped walking. "We really don't have to do this. It's over, as I'm sure you know, and for very good reasons."

"He's miserable, Shavir!" Carrie burst out. "I know him, and he's miserable."

"That might have to do with a lot of things. He has a lot on his plate." Shavir remembered what Jake had told her about his cousin's ability to cut through people's defenses. Apparently, she was more into dynamiting today.

"Can't you at least talk to each other?"

"We've tried that." Shavir felt her throat tightening. "It's best to just let it go."

"Yeah," Carrie snorted, "that's a fantastic strategy for both of you, isn't it? It's what everyone else in this city seems to be doing. That's why they're on the verge of battering our store windows so they can get their hands on Emovia."

Shavir looked away. Again, she saw Jake, hopelessly reduced by the pills, unable to feel his emotions or hers. "I'm worried about Jake," she heard herself saying.

She knew she was opening herself up to more questions, more beseeching, more pain, and that Jake would hate her for talking to his cousin about this. But no one had done it for David, and David might not survive that lack of care. The one thing she could still do for Jake was to say something, and Carrie was the one other human who cared.

"I honestly don't think this is just about me," she added when she had finished explaining the previous night and looked into Carrie's shocked face. "It's his work, too."

"It's his childhood and his fucking idiot of a father!"

"What do you mean?" Shavir asked, confused by the reaction. "The hurricane?"

Carrie glanced at Zoe, who was still playing with Sam. "How much do you know?"

"Not much. Jake doesn't like to talk about it. Only that his parents died. And his dog."

"That's all he said?"

"More or less. What's this about, Carrie?"

Carrie looked once more to Zoe, making sure the girl was out of earshot. Then she told Shavir about Farley.

He'd been a big dog, though not as big as Sam, some kind of mutt from the local shelter. Jake had taken that dog everywhere. It would sleep on his bed and follow him to school, his partner in crime, his friend and confidante.

Jake had been twelve when Hurricane Arlene came racing toward the west coast of Florida, and Tampa was slapped with an evacuation order. His father, as always reluctant to leave, enlisted his sons in getting the house prepared for the storm. Only when the weather was already turning did he finally start packing the car, reticent and irritable as he always was when they had to flee their home. Once they were done, Farley was missing. And without his dog, Jake wouldn't leave. There were tearful arguments shouted into gusts of wind, a raised hand, and then Jake was running. Somewhere behind him, half-lost in the storm, the voice of his father, furious. But Jake had kept running, away from him.

Shavir stood silently as Carrie told her these things, how it had been a neighbor who'd saved Jake's life, spotting him in the streets and dragging him into his car despite his desperate attempts to break free and continue the search. And how Jake didn't know how long his father had kept looking for him because he'd never seen his family again. They'd been among the hundreds of casualties left behind by Arlene.

"It was all my uncle's fault," Carrie said bitterly. "He always wanted to ride it out, every single hurricane that came up the coast. My mother was always arguing with him, and with her sister, who didn't have the guts to stand up to her husband or the power to make him leave. Most storms they rode out, and when they finally realized that this time they couldn't, it was too late." She looked at Shavir, agitated. "It wasn't Jake's fault, that's what I've been telling him for the past twenty-five years. But he doesn't wanna hear it. In his mind, he's responsible, alone, for all of it. In his mind, it's him who killed his parents and his baby brother because he ran away to look for his beloved dog. He was twelve years old, for Christ's sake, how can he have been responsible for my uncle's criminal lack of responsibility?"

Shavir had no answer. Her head was spinning. A few rows away from them, Zoe offered Sam the remains of her bell pepper, seeds and all. Nacho was harvesting beans nearby despite the heat. Behind them, the wall of clouds above Manhattan now had a greenish hue to it, towering high into a blue sky. It was very green. And very high.

"Hey, Nacho," she called, "can you check again on that storm?"

"Do you think it will come here?" Carrie asked.

The clouds filled most of the western sky. They were coming closer.

Nacho walked over, phone in hand. "They've had some serious hail and heavy rains in New Jersey, and it looks like the front is now moving toward lower Manhattan."

"Hail?" Shavir echoed.

Nacho looked up from his phone. "They just put out a severe thunderstorm warning for the southern part of Long Island."

"Let's move it then!" Shavir looked at Carrie. "Can you help?"

There was fear in Carrie's eyes, but she nodded.

"That long row of crates over there along the hedge, that's all seedlings. We need to carry them into the staircase before the hail hits. They aren't heavy, so Zoe can help. The others will harvest as much as they can."

Within minutes, the roofs were swarming with people engaged in frantic activity, cutting and carrying as quickly as they could. They all had practice at this, but normally they had more of a warning and the threat came from the Atlantic.

The dark wall from the west kept coming closer, merciless, the wind picking up steadily. They finally had to send Zoe and Sam downstairs while the rest of them kept working. Carrie was good, fast, in parallel motion with Nacho, getting as many trays of seedlings as would fit on their harvest carts, bending and turning like she'd been doing this her whole life, the blue dress aflutter around her.

Harsh gusts of wind ripped the first plants out of the crates and sent them flying across the roof. The temperature dropped minute by minute, and then the first heavy thumps on the roofs announced the assault. The windbreaker hedges bent to the ground as hailstones came shooting down like missiles, some of them the size of golf balls. Everyone sped up their efforts for one last frantic minute, and then they ran for cover, the world disappearing behind a grayish wall of water and ice, the deafening sound drowning their outcries of shock and wonder.

"Oh my God!" Carrie watched open-mouthed as the veggie beds disappeared under a thick cover of hailstones. "This is insane."

Shavir didn't say anything. She stared out into the hard world of ice.

TWENTY

JAKE STOOD NEXT TO Niya in the Corsys Room, their eyes riveted to the bizarre spectacle of Abingdon Square Park.

"It's all gone," Niya said bleakly.

Strictly speaking, that wasn't true. The yellowing foliage of Niya's beloved trees wasn't gone; it had simply relocated from the canopies to the earth, where it now covered not only the area of the park but also the surrounding streets, together with hundreds of thousands of hailstones. The trees stood almost naked, as if they had gone from summer to fall to the dead of winter in a matter of minutes.

"Will they survive this?" Niya asked, stunned. "My poor trees."

"They'll recover," Jake said absently. All he could think about was what this had done to Roots. He was keeping track of the hailstorm and knew it had moved on to the East Village from here, then to Williamsburg, Greenpoint, and some other Brooklyn neighborhoods. Right now, it was battering Queens.

His Spine dialed Shavir before he'd left the Corsys Room but reached her mailbox. He hung up and walked up to the window at end of the hallway. Below him on Hudson Street, the podcar trains rested quietly in hailstone heaps, their passengers wading across the ice-covered sidewalks in their sandals and flip flops. Others had believed the forecasters and were better equipped, some of them struggling with umbrellas against the wind and rain.

Jake leaned his forehead against the windowpane, overwhelmed by his need to talk to Shavir. He'd had a very relaxed night and a very terrible morning. He didn't know whether taking his usual two pep pills at around 6 a.m. had been his mistake, or whether he would have had a bad reaction to coming down from the Emovia regardless. Whatever it was, it had given Masao reason to ask for a private conversation in his office. Only then had he realized he'd spent the better part of the morning yelling at his team in bright outbursts of anger. Now the effects of the drugs had worn off, leaving him with a deep sense of shame and a hole in his gut that was trying to swallow him whole. Plus, he was fighting the urge to take more Emovia.

He'd apologized to Masao and the rest of the team, but he didn't know what to do with what he had done to Shavir. His memories of their interaction at Langone were dim, though he knew she'd left him standing alone. He did remember writing to her later that night, calling her, too. He also remembered writing to Marla, unfortunately, but that damage he would have to deal with later. First, he needed to talk to Shavir. He told the Spine to call Carrie.

"Oh, Jake," she cried into the phone, "I feel so sorry for them. It looks so bad."

"Are you still on the farm?"

"Yes. You wouldn't believe what's happening here."

"Is anyone hurt?"

"No, I don't think so. Zoe is fine, she's downstairs with Sam, and I don't think anyone else got injured. But look at this." She switched on her camera so he could see the devastated rooftops. "Everything is ripped apart and covered in hail."

"It's the same over here."

Carrie turned the phone, and now he could see her. "I have no idea how they're gonna be able to get their plants out of all this ice. Those hailstones even broke some of the large windows downstairs. I'm really worried about our own place. We can't afford new windows. Who pays for something like this, do you know?"

"I have no idea, Carrie, but we'll figure it out. Is Shavir there?"

"Yes." Carrie turned away from the phone and looked around. "We're taking care of the broken glass right now so no one gets hurt. Do you want me to put her on the phone?"

"Yes," he said hoarsely. "Please."

He saw shaky video of the mix of hail and glass on the ground and heard muffled voices as Carrie walked over to Shavir. Then Carrie was back on the phone. "She's just very busy right now, Jake," she said sheepishly. She'd always been a terrible liar.

Behind her, a glimpse of Shavir with a broom, turning her back.

"It's okay," Jake said. "As long as she's alright."

"She is." Carrie looked as dejected as he felt. "I'm really sorry, Jake."

"It's alright."

"I gotta go. I have to help with this mess. I'll call you later, okay?"

He dialed Shavir's number again.

"Hey," he said once he'd reached her mailbox, "I know it's over and you don't want to talk to me, and I understand. I'm just calling because I wanted to say that I'm so sorry about the hail. That must be devastating. I'm glad no one got hurt." He paused. "I'm myself again, Shavir. I wanted to tell you that, too, though I'm not even sure what that means. I'm very sorry about last night. I was... I don't know what I was. On Emovia, obviously. I was with David and I—I couldn't take it anymore." He wanted to say more, but he couldn't come up with anything. He had ruined it. They had somehow ruined it. "I'm not gonna call you again," he finally added. "I hope you'll be okay." He ended the call, his forehead still against the window. Below, a snowplow was making its way around the podcars, pushing the melting hailstones out of the way.

A green receiver lit up between him and the white streets below, making his heart stop before he identified the name of the caller. It was Gwen's secretary.

The cavernous space of Gwen's office was dim when he entered it five minutes later, rain beating against the windows. A small lamp on the shimmering surface of the desk was illuminating a bottle of bourbon and a half-filled glass in Gwen's hand. The rest of her body was outside the radius of the lamp, her face barely visible.

"David is dead."

Jake felt each word sliding down to his stomach, where it slowly exploded.

"They said it was multiple organ failure," Gwen continued, her hand with the whiskey glass disappearing into the shadow. "It's common after cardiac arrest."

"When?" Jake asked, as if it mattered.

"Half an hour ago. Do you want a drink?"

Jake shook his head and looked at the window. He should have felt more pain, but he didn't, perhaps an after-effect of the Emovia. David was dead and he didn't even know what to feel. *I don't think his son ever came back*, was the only thing coming to mind.

"No one was there." Gwen leaned forward into the glow of the lamp, enough for him to see she'd been crying. "He died alone." She paused. "I wanted to go more often, but I just couldn't bear to see him like that. You're the only one who was there for him, and I wanted to thank you."

"He was very important to me in ways that are difficult to explain."

"To me, too," Gwen said. "You've been wondering whether we were together, haven't you? You're very perceptive, that's something I value in you." She paused. "David and I were... we were close. But that was some time ago."

Jake wasn't sure he wanted to know about this or why Gwen was telling him. But it did explain certain things. Why David had been so distraught in recent months and so disinterested in his life outside the CSR. Perhaps also why he had started taking Emovia.

"I didn't leave him," Gwen said, reading his thoughts. "He left me."

Jake couldn't hide his surprise. He knew Gwen was an extremely private person, and yet she was telling him these intimate things. He wondered if she was on some kind of drug aside from the bourbon.

"We were together almost three years," Gwen continued, "but we had... problems. Two workaholics trying to have a relationship. That's not easy. He ended it because it became too much of a burden. It always seemed like he was dealing so much better with the separation than I was. I had no idea he was taking Emovia." Her voice cracked, and Jake feared she would start crying in front of him. But she pulled herself together, withdrawing back into the shadow.

For a long minute, neither of them said a word. The rain was getting harder. What remained of the grayish daylight was fading swiftly.

"Another costly disaster is all we need," Gwen said. "It's ruined the new podcar system, but hopefully it will at least damp down the situation in Brooklyn and Queens." She turned to him. "How are we doing with the antibiotics?"

The fragility in her voice was gone.

"I don't know," Jake said. "You're the one who's been in all these meetings all week. So how *are* we doing? Where are all the meds going that we've secured?"

"You know that yourself."

"To the MHA."

"Yes, most of it. The Manhattan hospitals have been taking in emergencies from Brooklyn, Queens, and the Bronx. So they haven't much left. They insist that they be able to replenish their supply in compensation before the other boroughs are served."

Jake was too drained to suppress his irritation. "Well, if the MHA wouldn't always secure the lion's share for itself, it wouldn't have to take in emergencies from the other boroughs because those hospitals could treat their patients themselves. That's why we came up with this whole state-of-emergency scheme in the first place, isn't it?"

Gwen remained unfazed. "I guess so."

"All hospitals in the city are postponing non-vital surgeries, and only a handful of ERs can still take in emergencies. You better be right about the weather calming down the protests, because if it doesn't, we're really fucked. Long Island has been on the verge of exploding for weeks now. All it takes is a spark, and then what?"

"The protests aren't just about the hospitals."

"No," Jake said, his voice rising. "They're about everything that's wrong with this city, which is a lot. But what I'd like to know is why we don't prioritize the hospitals that are in a state of emergency. Is it because they happen to be in the wrong neighborhood?"

"It's just the way things are, Jake. It's a fact of life."

"No, it isn't!" He was yelling now. "It's not a fucking fact of life. It's a decision you make. Someone makes that decision, and now I know why. They're doing *triage*, Gwen, isn't that right? They're doing triage for this whole city, only they don't base their decisions on the severity of anyone's condition. They decide whose life is worth saving and who's out of luck. And they're doing the saving by having us steal meds from people elsewhere in the world." He was glaring at Gwen, blood rushing through his veins.

"Calm down," Gwen said coolly. "You sound like David."

"Really? That's entirely possible. Because unlike you, I understand why he was feeling so desperate. I understand why he took Emovia, I really do. But I'm not David. I don't want to die like him. And I sure as hell don't wanna live like him."

Gwen frowned. "I realize you're under a lot of emotional stress because of recent events and David's passing. So I'm going to forget we had this conversation. Otherwise, I'd have to regret my decision to make you the new head of the day team, and I don't like regretting my decisions. I'd advise you, though, to acquaint yourself with the realities of the twenty-first century." She touched a screen on her desk, switching on lighting that dispelled the gloomy atmosphere of the room. "We'll talk again when you feel better."

Jake's whole body was trembling as he got up and walked toward the door. It was such an astounding contrast to how he'd felt last night, when nothing in the world had mattered much. Sitting in his apartment with a dragon and staring at his naked walls, he'd felt calm and content and satiated. Now it was all back with a vengeance: the agony, the hunger, the shame.

The doors of the elevator were open, and he stepped in. The incoming call almost escaped his attention, and when he noticed it, he picked up without registering the caller.

"Hi, Jake," Marla said in her typical bemused tone, "didn't you get my text?"

"I did." If only he knew what it had said or what he'd answered.

"So it's okay?" Her voice perked up.

"What's okay?"

"That I want to go to the Déluge instead. I know you don't like it very much, but we haven't been there in such a long time. Please say yes and make me happy. I promise I will make you happy, too." She laughed in delight at her innuendo.

The elevator split open at the door of David's office. *His* office. David would never return. "I can meet you at eight," he said to Marla, then he walked to the CSR to inform the others of David's death.

Jake's clothes were soaked through when, shortly after eight, he escaped the torrents outside and dove into the dimly lit lobby of Le Déluge. Frowning at his dripping hair, the host offered him a towel and a dry jacket to wear before reminding him to put his Spine in full 3D mode and motioning for him to follow her. Looking around, he remembered why he hadn't wanted to come here again. The walls of the lobby were lined with awards for the restaurant's exclusive animal cuisine, but what really drew those who could afford it to the Déluge was its enthralling environment. As he entered, the circular dining room was set to an African savanna, or to what African savannas had looked like before they'd all gone to hell. The continuous screen walls showed majestic baobabs and acacia trees in all directions, towering above a wide expanse of grasslands whose brilliance and visual depth were breathtaking. The illusion was completed by a chorus of bird calls, an arched ceiling that showed a darkening sky filled with a million stars, and the holograms of grazing springboks on the restaurant floor, produced by his Spine. A breeze grazed his arms, too cool to be authentic, but authenticity wasn't what this place was after.

"They've brought Africa back into rotation," Marla said when he approached their table. "Our server said it's the first time all summer because it was just too hot before. But I guess now that the rainy season has started outside, people like their restaurant a little drier."

Jake sat down without touching her, already regretting this.

"You're pretty late." Marla reached for her half-empty drink. Her dark hair was pulled back into the usual ponytail, a thick layer of mascara foregrounding gray eyes that were pretty but permanently dimmed from years of substance abuse.

"It wasn't easy to get here. And, frankly, I shouldn't be here at all."

"Charming." She looked amused. "Why are you here then?"

"Because I needed a break from disaster."

"Well, perfect." Marla defaulted to her mocking smile. "I won't give you any."

He ordered a beer, hoping it would help him relax. "How are you?" he asked while the world around them slowly changed to an Antarctic landscape teeming with penguins.

"I'm good. I'm always good when I get to see you, Jake, remember? That's why you like me. But last time you liked me was what... three months ago?"

Whatever Marla remembered was probably right, so he didn't protest and was grateful when the server returned with his beer. He took a gulp and called up the restaurant's menu on his Spine to select something he wouldn't be eating anyway. A note at the top of the page explained the offerings changed daily depending on what was available. Today they included Wagyu rib eye, Iberian Duroc cutlet, lamb chops, marinated ostrich steak, and Maine lobster. Marla ordered her usual lobster with a side of wild rice. He chose the vegetable tajine at the bottom of the menu.

"What's wrong?" Marla asked when the server left.

"Why are you asking that?"

"Because you sounded weird on the Spine last night, and you look worse now. I'm not even going to comment on your food choice. But you do seem a little off."

"David died." It didn't sound real.

"Who's David?"

"My boss."

"Oh yeah, right. When?"

"About three hours ago."

"Jeez," Marla said. "I'm sorry."

He wondered whether he should tell her more, and he wondered why the hell he was here. Certainly not to talk about David. It was one of their many unspoken rules that they never talked about work during their rare dinners, or much about their private lives, for that matter, and he didn't want to get to the point when Marla's eyes glazed over, a sure sign she was surfing her Spine. His own Spine was still on, producing not only the extinct animals that were traversing the room but also alerting him to new texts arriving in his personal message center. He'd received three messages from Carrie since he'd sat down.

Nothing from Shavir.

"How did he die?" Marla asked, so he told her. She looked shocked. "Because of Emovia?"

"It was a combination of a whole bunch of things."

"Oh, thank God," she said. "I'm taking a lot of that stuff myself, and I wouldn't really know how to stop, if you know what I mean. It's gotten so expensive though."

"Are you on it now?" It had never occurred to him that this might be the secret behind Marla's ability to make herself emotionally weightless, an ability he used to appreciate.

She laughed. "Now? What am I, stupid? We're in my favorite restaurant, and, if you'll forgive me for saying so, I'm hoping for some sex later on." She leaned forward. "You don't take Emovia during the few nice moments of your life, Jake. You take it during the many bad ones. That's the whole point of it. You'd know that if you'd ever taken any."

He stretched his left leg and pulled out David's Emovia bottle.

Marla looked confused. "You are taking it?"

He put it down on the table and pushed it toward her. "Just once. It's not for me."

Marla reached across the table. "You're the best." She packed away the bottle just before the server approached with their food.

As expected, Jake was unable to touch his plate, but at least they were finally sliding into their usual conversation mode as he nursed his third beer. Marla talked almost the entire time while the restaurant took them from Antarctica to Greenland, the Andes, Australia, New Zealand, and then, to Marla's delight, underwater to the whales, dolphins, and a bunch of other long-extinct maritime species. If he had been hoping for distraction, he didn't get it. He couldn't believe this was something he used to do, sit here and feel nothing in particular for the woman across the table. It felt like a betrayal, not so much of Shavir, but of himself, and Marla. And it didn't help that he was manically checking his message center, each time to find nothing there.

"So," Marla said when she had finished her *mousse au chocolat*, "this was delicious as always, but my question is, where do we go from here? My Spine says the podcars still aren't moving. I'm never gonna make it home to the Bronx. Are you gonna take me home with you? One really shouldn't be alone on such a sad and nasty night."

"No," he agreed voicelessly. "One really shouldn't."

He paid for their meal, and they walked from the sun of the Australian outback into the rain gusts of Manhattan. The sidewalks were covered with melting hail. Marla slipped several times in her high heels and only barely avoided hitting the pavement.

"I'm cold," she complained as they stepped into the elevator in his building. She pressed herself against him and kissed him as the cabin shot upward. She let go, laughing, when it stopped on the seventh floor, and turned to step out as the doors slid open.

"Jesus!" she shrieked and jumped back into the elevator. She turned to looked at Jake. "Do you know that dog?"

Sam stood in the hallway, fur dripping, tail wagging.

Jake didn't answer, didn't move, didn't breathe either.

"You might wanna come out, Jake," Marla said caustically, peering into the hallway. "There's someone waiting in front of your door."

He felt the urge to hit the panel, close the doors, ride down, and leave the building and his job and the city. Instead, he pushed himself off the cabin wall and stepped out into the hallway like he was in some slow-motion nightmare.

Shavir was sitting on the concrete floor, her back against the door to his apartment. Her wet hair clung to her slender frame, a puddle of water underneath her. She looked straight at him, the expression on her face impossible to decipher.

"I guess I better go now," Marla said from far away.

"No. I'll go." Shavir struggled to her feet. She walked past Marla. Then she passed him, her dark eyes as wet as her hair. "I'm sorry, Jake," she said quietly.

He watched her step into the elevator.

"Sam," she called because the dog was still standing by his side, confused. "*Sam!*" she called again, and this time, he obeyed. The elevator doors closed behind them.

Jake looked at Marla. "I'm really sorry—"

"I bet you are."

"I'm really, really sorry about this," he repeated idiotically, already walking backward. Then he opened the door to the staircase and flew down the stairs.

The only thing in sight outside was water. Other than the sheets of rain beating down onto the dead podcars and the sludge on the ground, the street was empty. She must have run to the subway station, he decided, but then she would still be on the street. Or she had walked up to the High Line instead, so he should turn left. Or she'd gone to the other side and turned onto 11th Avenue. But there was only the seawall there, and the rain was coming down too hard for that.

He stepped into the icy slush, looking again in both directions. Then he cupped his hands around his mouth and yelled, "*Sam!*" in the hope the dog would react. He waited a few seconds, then started trotting toward the High Line, cupping his hands and yelling again. He turned to check the other direction just in time to see a dog-shaped apparition below the streetlight at the corner of 11th Avenue before it disappeared into the black rain. He ran after it, the icy slush filling his shoes every time they touched the ground. He lost his footing twice, his hands, arms, legs, and chest slamming into the sludge.

11th Avenue was empty. He cupped his hands again, yelling Sam's name, but there was nothing, no one, just the broken podcars in the middle of the street. He finally ran to the seawall, stumbling up the ice-covered steps onto the boardwalk. Once he had reached the top, he stopped, his chest heaving, the rain washing over his face. The endless stretch of LED lights illuminated the mass of ice and water underneath. There was no dog and no woman.

They were gone.

TWENTY-ONE

SHAVIR RESTED HER HEAD against the grimy window of the subway train, eyes closed against the bright lights and intrusive stares. She was shivering and soaking wet, and so was Sam, whom she'd sat between her feet to protect him from the passengers crowding against them.

Her phone vibrated, but she just pressed the spot on the touchscreen to dismiss the call. It vibrated again, announcing a message. She opened her eyes, deleted it unread, and switched off the phone.

The platform at Bedford Avenue Station was crowded, voices anxious and angry. She grabbed Sam's leash tightly and walked up the stairs. Outside, the streets were thick with protestors and melting hail. Windows of cars and stores were broken, either by the hail or the people, it was impossible to tell. The rain still came down hard.

"Stay behind me," she told Sam and walked into the sludge, hoping she would notice glass shards when she stepped on them. She had crossed the street and was on her way to the East River boardwalk when a voice called out behind her, audible above the rain.

"Hey, you!"

She quickened her step and turned into an alley, seeking cover.

"You with the dog," she heard, closer now, "stop right there."

She stopped and saw two Frontline cops walking toward her, water dripping off their riot gear. Their visors were wet and misted, but before they'd reached her, she knew it was Gary. And Dan.

"Can you muzzle him?" Gary snarled.

She looked at Dan, who had given no sign of recognition, and back to Gary again. "Nothing has changed since last time you stopped me," she said. "He's still legal."

Without warning, Gary grabbed her arm, hard, and shoved her into the slush. Sam jumped up with a broken growl, and Gary's hand whipped to his holster.

"*No*," Shavir screamed, turning and tearing at Sam's collar. "*Down!*"

She scrambled up and threw her body over Sam's to protect him, frantically searching her bag for his muzzle. "Down, down, down," she kept repeating, and then she finally found the muzzle and pulled it over Sam's nose with trembling fingers, her body still covering his, a deep vibration telling her he hadn't stopped growling.

She looked up and into the barrel of Gary's gun.

"We need his neck," he said.

Shavir exposed Sam's neck, her hands shaking uncontrollably.

Dan bent down with the reader. "Thanks," he said and pressed it against Sam's wet fur until he got a beep. She held up her right hand. Another beep. "All paid up," Dan said.

But Gary didn't move, his gun still trained at Shavir. "You think we're stupid," he hissed from behind the visor, "you and your little friend, you think we're stupid, don't you? You think we buy that pile of bullshit you fed us?"

"Come on, Gary," Dan said, "she's paid up, let's move on."

"You think we don't know what's going on?" Gary snarled. "Calling us in the middle of the night, and the fucking mongrels just disappear? You think we buy that?"

"That's enough, Gary. She didn't do anything."

A long moment passed, filled with the sound of shouting, sirens, and breaking glass in the streets around them. Then Gary packed away the gun and leaned down to where she still lay on top of Sam, one hand around his collar, the other one around his muzzled nose, squeezing it.

"I'd be real careful if I were you," he said, and Sam growled so ferociously it was clearly audible despite the surrounding noise and his broken vocal cords. "I know exactly what kind of shit you're pulling, and I ain't no fucking idiot, I'm telling you."

"That's enough now," Dan said again, reaching for Gary's shoulder. "Let's go."

Gary straightened and glared at his partner.

Dan reached down to Shavir to help her up, but she didn't move. "I'm sorry," he said, barely audibly. He withdrew his hand and followed Gary back to the subway station.

Shavir pulled the muzzle off Sam's nose and kissed the flaps of his ears before burying her face in his drenched fur and erupting in long, hard sobs.

It took them almost an hour to get home, but once they'd reached the boardwalk, it was easier because there wasn't as much glass on the ground. She checked Sam's paws repeatedly in the dark, so she knew he had at least one cut by the time they arrived at Roots. She opened the door to the warehouse and led Sam down to the basement.

"He's bleeding," Tara said when they stepped through the jib door. She was sitting in a wheelchair in one of the stalls, Laika lying at her feet. Some of the other dogs were jumping against the doors of their stalls, their husky sounds filling the room. "His paws are bleeding," Tara repeated, pointing to Sam. She wore pajamas, sneakers, and a carelessly tied robe. An old towel was in her lap and, on top of it, one of Laika's puppies.

"What are you doing here?" Shavir asked, aghast.

"I needed to see them. I haven't seen them at all since the raid." Tara made it sound normal, like she was not sitting in a wheelchair in a room full of dirty dogs ten days after getting shot in the stomach. Until noon, she had been in her hospital bed in Manhattan. They had kicked her out after the hailstorm hit, telling her they needed her bed for a new patient. Finn had offered to drive her home, where she was supposed to be right now.

"How did you get here?" Shavir asked as she made sure there was a safe distance between Sam and the other dogs. "Does your dad know you're here?"

"Finn took me. It's okay, I asked him to. There was a free bed upstairs. And Dad didn't mind that I wanted to spend a night here. I'm all grown up, you know?"

That last part most certainly wasn't true. And it was hard to believe that even Finn would be irresponsible enough to drop Tara off at Roots in her condition.

"They think I'm in bed." Tara grinned. "I snuck down here."

"You gotta be fucking kidding me. What are you, five?"

"Calm down, okay, mommy?" Tara was still grinning. "I took the freight elevator down, and I'm in a top-notch wheelchair, in case you haven't noticed, courtesy of Mr. Larsen. The only thing I had to move to get down here was, like, my thumb." She pointed to the chair's joystick. "So there's been no pressure at all to my belly, if that's what you're worried about. I'm fine."

"You're not fine," Shavir said, fighting the urge to yank Tara up from her chair. "You're supposed to be in the hospital, and you would be if those assholes hadn't kicked everyone out who isn't immediately dying. You're definitely not supposed to be here. I can't even believe—" she stopped. "You know what, I can't deal with this right now. I'm gonna get something for Sam's paws. And I will call Lenny so he can get you home."

"Not Lenny—" Tara called after her, and there was something like laughter in her voice. That swanky hospital definitely had too many of those amazing painkillers she kept raving about.

Shavir walked into the back room and looked for the disinfectant, banging drawers as she did so. She heard a whirring behind her.

Tara was outside the open door in her chair. "Have you called him?"

"Not yet. But I will. How can you be so stupid? Was getting shot not enough?"

"Come on, Shav," Tara said in that voice she had reserved for moments when she knew she had truly pissed off people she didn't want to piss off. "The wound's in my back with this gigantic bandage covering it. It's all squeaky-clean, like, hermetically sealed. Look—" She pointed to the towel in her lap. "All dogs gone, and I even had a towel there. Are we good?"

"Listen to you," Shavir snorted. "No, we aren't good. Nothing's good. It's a goddamn fucked-up stinking hell of a mess."

Tara nodded in appreciation. "Where were you? Lenny was looking for you."

"In Manhattan." Shavir walked past Tara with the disinfectant and knelt next to Sam, who rolled onto his back, showing his paws.

"I had a feeling. And I happen to know you weren't with Finn."

"No. I'm not insane."

"And Soma's closed. So... Jake?"

Shavir pulled a shard out of Sam's paw and laced the wound with disinfectant. She still had some healing accelerant left. She'd use it when they were back in their cubicle.

"How did you even get there in this weather?" Tara asked.

A great question, Shavir thought. How the hell had she ended up there? "The subway's still running," she said, though that didn't even begin to answer it. She wished she could pretend to be surprised by her own actions. But this time she did know how she'd gotten there. It had started with Carrie telling her about Hurricane Arlene, then standing in that sea of broken glass with Jake on the phone. Next came his voicemail, which she hadn't wanted to hear, though she'd ended up listening to it. Twenty minutes later, her and Sam had squeezed into an overcrowded L-train before wading through the ice and water covering the streets of Chelsea. When they stood in front of Jake's building, she'd remembered her fingerprints weren't registered to his apartment, so she had no way of getting in. Then someone had opened the front door from the inside. She'd gone right up and sat down in front of Jake's apartment. She really wished it had been a spontaneous thing, irrational and out of her control. But for once, she'd had a plan: to wait for Jake to come home and spend the night with him and maybe much more than that. Then the woman stepped out the elevator in her pantsuit. End of plan.

"So did you see him?" Tara asked.

"Briefly. To say goodbye."

"I thought you'd done that already."

"Apparently, I needed to do it twice."

"Oh, Shav. How do you always get so hung up on guys?"

Shavir looked over at her. "Yeah, like women are any better."

Tara grinned. "I'm just saying. Maybe next time go at least for one from this side of the river."

" I didn't *go* for him. And he *is* from this side of the fucking river."

"I hope he'll remember that." Tara moved her wheelchair so she was right next to Sam. "Do you think he'll get us busted now, your Homeland man?"

"No," Shavir said. "But maybe Gary will."

"Gary?" Tara echoed, alarmed. "*That* Gary?"

Shavir nodded. "I just had another run-in with him."

"Fuck."

"He knows everything. Or, at least, he suspects it."

And then she told Tara. How she'd gotten shoved to the ground, staring at that fucking gun again. The other cop being married to Jake's cousin. Him recognizing her and connecting some dots. Gary connecting more dots in a way that might finish all of them, dogs and humans alike. "It's all my fault." It was a relief to say it out loud.

"No, it's not," Tara said. "Those cops would have stopped us with the puppies no matter what, and Gary would have had his ideas. That has nothing to do with you and Jake. If anything, it was my fault because I didn't listen to Lenny. I make mistakes, too, apparently." Tara couldn't stop joking even now, but this time she looked worried.

"What are we gonna do?" Shavir asked. "Tell the others? I've no idea what Gary knows."

"Let me think about it, okay?" Tara said. "Lenny's gonna freak out when he hears this, and Judy—oh my. We have to make sure she doesn't kick us out tomorrow."

"What if Gary comes here? Dan knows where I live. He knows all about Roots, his wife and daughter were here today."

"Let me think about it," Tara said again. "It's bad in a way that things are over with Jake. He could have gotten us some intel since he's with Homeland and all."

Shavir got up and carried the disinfectant to the back room.

"I'm sorry," Tara called after her. "I was just thinking out loud, and I'm a practical person. You mad at me?" she added when Shavir returned and pulled out her phone.

"I'm mad at everyone! And now I'm going to call your dad like in the old days. Because I don't believe a word of him being okay with this. I bet he's worried sick."

Despite Tara's protests, she made the call and managed to assure Dipak that his daughter was doing fine, and that, given the situation out in the streets, it was safer for her to spend the night at Roots. He thanked her like he used to do when Tara was missing, out on some youthful adventure, and Shavir had taken the time to talk to him.

They took the freight elevator up, and Shavir made sure Tara had everything she needed. Then she went to her own cubicle and told Sam he could come up on the bed. She snuggled against his big warm body and hoped for sleep so she wouldn't have to think anymore. From outside, she could hear sirens and what sounded like intermittent shots, a ghostly soundtrack to her dreams.

TWENTY-TWO

THE AIR SMELLED OF fermenting leaves when Jake stepped out the door the next morning. The pavement was covered with bits of foliage the wind had carried over from the High Line. The rain had slowed to a drizzle, rolling off the splinters of acrylic glass from the podcars' broken windshields. An army of overall-clad technicians scurried between them, repairing the damage on-site. Flowing around them was a stream of pedestrians and bikers in a futile effort to reach their destinations in time, their jackets and raincoats heralding the end of summer.

Jake climbed the steps to the seawall, past the spot where he had stood last night, drenched and desperate. He'd considered continuing his search for Shavir all the way to Brooklyn, but in the end, he had walked home and called her phone a few dozen times. Then he'd taken five sleepers and gone to bed with not much of a desire to ever wake up again, feeling unenthusiastic when he did. He'd written to Marla, too, explaining himself, and she, too, hadn't responded.

He tried to focus on his Spine as he got sucked into the human maelstrom flowing toward Lower Manhattan and called Masao to see if he'd heard anything regarding David's funeral.

"Not yet," Masao said. "But everyone is planning on going."

"Oh, great. He'll be so happy to see them."

"Yeah." Masao's voice was tinged with embarrassment. "We're all feeling really shitty. I guess we were all thinking that he'd come back."

"I know," Jake said. He, too, had been thinking that David would come back, even with all indications pointing to the contrary. "Listen," he said, trying to focus on the practical, on the things that needed to be done. "I'm head of the CSR day team now, as little as I want to even think about that, and I wanted to ask how you feel about getting promoted to troubleshooter... and I would also need a deputy."

For a few seconds, Masao was silent. "Wow," he then got out.

"I know it's kind of sudden, and kind of rough with everything that's been going on. You don't have to make a decision now, just think it over and maybe talk to Ethan. But you're doing great work, Masao."

"No... I mean I will, but... wow." Masao was smiling now.

"Good," Jake said, returning the smile. "What else is new?"

"Well, it all sucks. The hail has messed up some of our local transportation systems. The new storm in the Pacific is now another super typhoon. And there's some crazy new fungus that's destroying what was left of the corn fields in the Midwest after the drought."

"Are you telling me we'll have to bring *corn* up to the CSR?"

"No. At least I hope not. I just thought you should know because we got the new Food Pest Report."

"I have it in front of me. Looks delicious." Jake flipped through the pages of the report, using his gloves. He was about to tell Masao that he should give it to someone on their team when he walked into the guy suddenly standing in front of him.

"What the—?" he growled and moved around the man, who was transfixed, eyes on the river.

Jake followed his gaze, but there was only the shimmering surface of the water. Other people, too, had stopped walking, their engrossed faces leaving no doubt they were watching their Spines. Some of them spoke to whoever happened to be near them, voices tense and urgent.

"Hey, Jake, turn on the news," Masao said.

"Good God," was all Jake could say, and then he, too, stood arrested.

The images were on every single news feed that came up, filmed with shaky Spine cameras: groups of men looting pharmacies and confronting Frontline troops, the air filled with the smoke of explosives and tear gas. All of it was happening right now in Queens. A violent clash between a militant group of protesters and security forces had led to a shootout that had left five protesters and two Frontline men dead. The conflict was escalating quickly, spreading from Elmhurst to Corona and adjacent neighborhoods of Brooklyn and Queens. The images showed men, women, children, ambulances, and more shooting, smoke, fire, and tear gas. Jake's focus wavered out of control.

"What are they gonna do with all those injured people?" Masao asked, an uncharacteristic quiver in his voice. "Where are they gonna go, Jake? The ERs over there are as good as shut down, and they're closing off all access to Manhattan right now. There are roadblocks already on every bridge and in every tunnel."

"Get a hold of Gwen. I need to talk to her as soon as I'm in."

Jake ended the call and broke into a trot. The next stairs led him down to West Street. He called Carrie.

"Jake, have you seen?"

"Yes. Where are you?"

"I'm at work. Are you running?"

"What's happening?"

"We've closed the store and are hiding in the back. You can't imagine what's going on outside. They've all gone mad."

"Where's Zoe?"

"She's right here with me. She didn't wanna stay home, so I brought her with me. She's been so good about it, watching stuff on the pad and playing in the back room."

Zoe said something, but she was too far away for him to understand.

"Hang on a sec, Jake." He could hear Carrie talk to her daughter. "Mommy's gonna go outside real quick to talk to Uncle Jake, okay? I'll be right back."

There was a pause, and then Carrie's voice was radically changed.

"Jake, I'm so worried about Dan! He hasn't answered my calls, and I've been calling him since I heard that they shot two Frontline men."

"Calm down, Carrie." Jake slowed his pace so he could concentrate on her. "Dan's fine, okay? There are about five thousand Frontline men out there right now, and it's chaotic. Him not picking up your call doesn't mean anything."

"He has a Spine now! He can't miss calls."

"Yes, he can," Jake said as calmly as he could manage. "I have a Spine, and I've missed calls. He's probably busy as hell right now. Calm down, Carrie, okay? He's alright."

"He normally picks up my calls."

"Now is not normal, Carrie. It's not normal at all."

"I know. I need to go back to Zoe."

"Do that. I'll call again when I'm at SAFE. Don't leave the store. Don't go near the windows. Stay right there in the back room, or wherever it's safest, okay? I'll call again."

He disconnected the line and immediately dialed Shavir's number, still running toward the West Village. She didn't pick up, but at least her phone wasn't switched off. He tried to come up with the right words as he was transferred to her mailbox.

"Hey. This is not me stalking you. There was a shooting in Queens, and things are escalating. It's spreading to Brooklyn, so please be careful. I'm worried about you. And I'm sorry. Please let me know you're safe." He wanted to hang up, but he couldn't. He stopped running. "I really am sorry, Shavir. I was lonely. It was stupid. But it's not what I want. This is all wrong." He stood staring at the footage from Queens, his chest heaving. "Carrie's in the middle of this. She's at that drugstore of hers with Zoe, hiding. Manhattan has been cut off; they're sealing the bridges again. I'm so fucking scared. Please let me know you're safe, okay? I need to know you're safe." He hung up and picked up his pace.

"Gwen's waiting for you upstairs." Masao was standing in the doorway to the CSR when the elevator door opened ten minutes later.

Jake stepped right back inside.

"When are our antibiotics from Pennsylvania coming in?"

"Three days, but they can only send half—" The rest of Masao's sentence was cut off as the elevator slid upward, but Jake knew all he needed to know. He'd been thinking about this for a while.

"Good morning, Jake," Gwen said when he walked into her office. One wall was entirely covered with the images from Queens. "Masao said you need to talk to me?"

"Yes. About that." Jake pointed to the wall. "And about Brooklyn. And about the fact that Frontline and the NYPD are closing off all access to Manhattan, which means people are going to be stuck again on Long Island."

"I know. And I'm sorry for them."

"Are you? What are we gonna *do* about it, Gwen?"

Gwen looked at him unblinking. "We are going to do nothing at all about it. We, in fact, have nothing to do with it. It's a problem that Frontline is going to solve."

"Frontline?" Jake nearly laughed. "Yeah, right. They're really good at trauma surgery. We have *everything* to do with this, Gwen, because there are hundreds of emergencies in that part of our city, people with very severe injuries, and nobody knows how to help them."

"Don't be so dramatic, Jake. They know perfectly well what to do with them. They drive them to the hospitals in the area."

"Where the ERs are closed because they've got no antibiotics."

"The next delivery—"

"—is coming in three days if we're lucky, and they'll have to fight over it with the MHA. It's not working anymore, Gwen. What we've been doing isn't working anymore. David knew it, and I know it, and you know it, too. We need a new approach, we need to adapt. But until then, we'll need an ad hoc solution, or a lot of people will die."

"Ad hoc?" Gwen frowned.

"Yes." Jake finally had his breath back. "We in fact have plenty of antibiotics in the city. They just aren't certified for humans."

"Are you talking about veterinary antibiotics?"

"Yes."

"I noticed you brought them up in the CSR. I wanted to talk—"

"We'll do that later," Jake cut her off. "Right now, the thing that's important is that they are in the city, not only here in Manhattan but also in Brooklyn and Queens."

"Are you suggesting we use vet meds in our hospitals?"

"I am. We need to get Kruger to emergency-approve some of them for use in the ORs. Without the approval of the FDA, the hospitals won't touch them."

"As they shouldn't."

"Oh, please, Gwen, spare me. They're really just antibacterials that kill bacteria in whatever organism they're injected into. Half of the people in this city have been using those meds for years because they can't afford to see a doctor."

"Sure. Frank's gonna be thrilled. First, we want him to speedy-approve a non-critical-supply drug, and now we're planning to use vet meds in our hospitals." Gwen leaned forward. "He wouldn't consider such a thing, Jake."

Jake pointed to the screen wall. "Look at that. People are dying. We need a solution. And that's the only one we have right now until the next delivery comes in. Or you get the US Army to send us their stuff. It's one of the two. Unless you wanna go down in history as the SAFE director who killed the people she was supposed to save."

Gwen's face was frozen.

"Think about it," Jake said and left.

The Spine footage from Queens and Brooklyn was all over the screen walls of the CSR, supplemented with pin-sharp images from the news stations' drones hovering above the riots, zooming in so closely on the livid faces of protesters and Frontline men, you could count their pores. By now, the stations had also secured footage of the incident that had led to the fatal shooting. They replayed, in slow motion, the bodies going down again and again in an endless hail of bullets, two of them in Frontline gear, the rest in street clothing, utterly unprotected against the onslaught. The authorities had identified several of the people shot, and the news teams were trying to get statements from their families and other protesters.

"What did you tell her?" Masao asked, tearing himself away from the spectacle. "That they emergency-approve the vet meds?"

Jake gave him a look.

"I thought of it myself," Masao said with a shrug. "It just seemed a little too wacky."

"It isn't."

"Is Kruger gonna do it?"

"I don't know. I don't even know whether Gwen will ask him. She thinks I'm nuts."

"They'd have to approve the vet doxycycline and two others," Masao said plainly. "We ordered plenty of those, and they can all be used without problems in humans if you adapt the dosage. I did a little research, just in case."

Jake smiled. "Thanks. Can you send that info up to Gwen's office?"

He turned away to accept a call from Carrie. She was crying so hard he couldn't understand a word she was saying. "Please calm down," he said. "What happened?"

"*Dan!*" she screamed before her voice shattered.

His gaze returned to the screen wall, where Dan's face stared down at him. They had identified the two dead Frontline men.

"They just called me," Carrie cried into his ear. "It's him. And Gary. They shot them, Jake, they just shot them. Why? *Why?*" Her voice dissolved into sobs.

"Carrie?" Jake said. "Carrie?... Stay where you are, okay? Stay in the back room."

"I'm not," she pressed out between sobs, "in the back room. They came in."

"What? Who?"

"I don't *know!* They had guns and were tearing down stuff from the walls, and we just ran. I don't know where the others are."

"Where are you?"

"Behind our big trash cans. In the alley."

"Outside?"

"They were coming into the store, Jake! They had guns. I think they're still in there."

"Okay, okay." Jake tried to focus. "Stay where you are, alright? And stay hidden as much as you can. I'm gonna come get you. Carrie?"

"Okay," she whimpered. "Okay."

"I'm gonna hang up now so that you can take care of Zoe while I get over to Queens, but you can always reach me. Stay where you are."

"You wanna go out there?" Masao asked. "Like, *physically?*"

Jake got up.

"I don't think you can get through, Jake, really. Look at that." Masao nodded toward the screen wall. "It's like a war zone."

"I gotta try. It's just her and her little girl, and they just killed her husband. I need you to take over for me."

"Of course. But are you sure about this?"

"I mean *really* take over for me in case something happens."

Masao stared. "Okay, that's not funny, and I—"

"You'll be fine. You've done this a thousand times, and I don't know anyone who's better at it. Send that information about the antibiotics up to Gwen, okay? I'll be online when I can."

Jake stepped into the elevator, realizing he had not the slightest idea what he was going to do. There were still no podcars, so he'd have to run to the subway station on 14th Street, then change to the N line at Times Square. It was unlikely it would be going all the way to Queens, but at least it would get him to Queensboro Bridge.

He sent another message to Shavir asking where the hell she was. Then he walked out into the rain.

TWENTY-THREE

SHAVIR IGNORED THE VIBRATION against her hip bone. Another message from Jake, for sure. Likely he was worried about the news and her wellbeing. But her being hadn't been well in a while, and she needed to focus. Outside, the sound of gunshots pierced the air.

"We're still very much at the periphery of it," Lenny said grimly when he saw her flinching. "And there's nothing around here that would be attractive to anyone, not even much food anymore. The only thing you can loot here right now is a few tons of rotting mixed veggie stew and the broken junk we used to call our equipment."

They were all sitting in the kitchen below Prince Gardens, the big table covered with cutting boards, bowls, and mountains of sliced vegetables. Six big pots of tomato sauce were cooking on the stove below the open windows, rows of empty preserving jars waiting on the countertop next to it. Scattered across the floor were crates overflowing with tomatoes, eggplants, squash, cucumbers, and all the other stuff they'd picked from battered plants and pulled out of the melting hail, all of them bruised. For once in agreement, Judy and Lenny had started their emergency preservation program almost immediately after the storm had moved on to Queens, ordering everyone to harvest what was left in its aftermath in what Lenny called the reverse Cinderella way: the good ones remained on the crop, the bad ones went into the pot. Judy had been on the phone nonstop, talking restaurant buyers and community members into ordering soups, sauces, pickles, chutneys, and jams, all fresh from the roof, offering complimentary baskets of lightly damaged produce as incentive. It was a matter of hours until it would all go to waste and only a minute until Nacho would arrive with the next cartload of veggies.

"It ain't that bad," said Judy. "We saved the seedlings, and most of the crops under that new foil are just fine. If we got more foil, as I asked for, we'd be better off."

"It's pretty fucking bad," Lenny returned, stirring one of the pots with a giant ladle, "but what I'm saying is we don't need to worry about the riots. What we do need to worry about is up on our roofs. Where we gonna start?"

"We start where we always start," Judy rumbled, pouring another crate of tomatoes onto the table. "Cleaning up. Not like we're doing this shit for the first time, won't be the last either. As soon as it's done hosing down, we gonna start mopping. You're all welcome to join once you're done with your little cooking show down here."

"Okay, but what are we gonna do about the animals?" Tara asked, ignoring a warning look from Shavir. "The animals are much more urgent than whatever's left on the roof. If it keeps raining like this, our basement will flood again. When are we gonna bring them up?"

"When they're less than thirty seconds away from drowning." Judy glared at her. "You got nerve, girl, asking me that right now, to bring those crazy bitches up here."

There was another vibration in the sudden silence of the room. Shavir felt everyone's eyes on her, like it was more worrisome who was calling her than who got shot outside.

Troy leaned toward her. "You know you can block callers, right?" he asked, and there was some grinning at the table. "I think that's a really useful feature for you."

Shavir made a face, got up, and left the kitchen. She walked up to the roof where the rain had let off a little, giving her an almost clear view of Prince Gardens. It was amazing how intact it looked compared to the farm on the two middle roofs. Much of the first roof had been protected by Finn's new foil, and the garden by his patented tent roof.

She had seen that roof weather storms before, but as far as she knew, this was the first time it had been tested by extreme hail. And, boy, had it passed the test. There wasn't any damage to the sails at all, the material durable enough to bear the beating. Everything underneath looked almost unscathed because the sails had automatically tilted during the storm, protecting the leaves against the ice missiles coming in at an angle. There was some wind damage, and most of the blossoms were ruined, but other than that, the plants looked great. Apparently, Finn's own garden was the same. She hadn't talked to him since he'd visited her in the basement two nights ago, so she probably deserved Troy's mockery. She should pick up her calls or start blocking callers.

Both voice messages were from Jake as expected. She listened to the first and lowered the phone. Carrie. And Zoe. She could still see them out here, running around with Sam in the sun, eating peppers, schlepping seedlings in the wind and the hail. Carrie, who'd been undeterred by the storm, but who must be feeling so scared now, so helpless, caught in the middle of this with her daughter. How do you protect your loved ones in a riot? Shavir didn't know.

And then she dialed.

When Carrie picked up, it was like someone had suddenly pumped up the volume on the shouts and shots and sirens. "Shavir," she cried, "are you okay?"

"Yes. Jake says you're hiding in your pharmacy?"

"We were. But they started looting. We're in the back alley. I think it's okay."

Judging from the soundtrack, it wasn't okay at all. They had to be somewhere near the epicenter of the riots. "Can you get farther away from the store, away from the crowds?"

"We have to stay put," Carrie said. "Jake's gonna get us."

"Jake's in Manhattan, Carrie, that may take a while. Can't Dan come and get you?"

"No," Carrie said after a pause. "Haven't you watched the news?"

Shavir frowned. "What's wrong, Carrie?"

"He can't come right now," Carrie repeated, her voice compressed, "and I can't talk. I have Zoe with me, and she's so scared, and there's all this tear gas in the air. She can't breathe. And I didn't take her rescue puffer when we ran outside. I need to get it, but I don't know how."

"Don't go back into the store, Carrie," Shavir said while she searched her phone for the news. "Is there some building nearby that looks safe, and can you get in?"

"I don't know," Carrie said, choking. "I don't know."

Shavir stared at the display of her phone, Dan staring back at her. Dan and Gary, both shot in the riots. It was the first time she saw Gary's face without a visor, a fleshy face with ruddy skin and not much of a neck. The face of a dead man. Next to it was Dan's, posing for his official portrait with a slightly mischievous smile. She could still see those features, half-hidden by the shadows and the visor as he had reached out his hand to her last night.

"Where's the store, Carrie?" she asked as she stepped back inside and pulled the door shut behind her. Her phone said the situation was rapidly escalating in Elmhurst, and Jake was never gonna make it in time, no matter what he was planning to do or what he'd told Carrie. He wasn't even going to make it across the river because the truth was they were in the middle of a second Crisis, but she couldn't tell Carrie any of that. "Text me your address," she said instead, "and see whether you can hide a bit farther away from the street. And don't go back into the store for those meds, okay? I'm on my way."

She hung up and ran down the stairs, her mind completely devoid of a plan of how she would actually get there. She checked her phone for information on whether the subways were still running.

Tara was waiting for her in her wheelchair on the landing outside the kitchen. "Have you seen the news?" she spilled out, thrill in her voice. "About the cops? It's *them*."

"I know."

"But that's great, right? If Gary—"

Shavir cut her off as she walked past her. "Listen, can you look after Sam? I can't take him along." With that, she moved down the next flight of stairs.

"Along where?" Tara called after her. "Where are you going?"

"I need to find Jake's cousin in Elmhurst."

"In Queens?" Tara yelled. "Are you fucking insane?"

She shouted a few other things down the staircase. Shavir heard her call for Lenny by the time she pushed open the downstairs door.

Then she was running into the rain.

Her lungs burned like hellfire by the time she reached Greenpoint Station, catching the train the minute it was leaving. She collapsed on one of the seats and gulped for air. Then she called Carrie again, twice, but she didn't pick up. Hopefully that only meant it was too loud for her to hear the call.

Shavir changed trains at Court Square before finally calling Jake.

"Shavir, thank God," he breathed. "Where are you?"

His relief turned into something more like anxious rage when she told him.

"You can't go there," he yelled. "Have you seen the fucking news?"

"Homeland is locking us in again, if that's what you mean," she said, "but the thing is, bridges go both ways. You're never gonna make it across, and I'm almost there."

That latter part was a lie, but at least for now the subway was still moving, though it'd been gradually emptying out since she had changed trains. People got off, their feet hurried and their faces tense, but almost no one stepped in.

"Look, Jake," she said, "I'll call you." Then she hung up. It wasn't good for her to talk to him right now. She had no idea whether she was doing this for him, for Carrie and Zoe, or for herself. But she knew she had to do it. She felt weirdly calm though her pulse was racing. She would do this somehow.

When they approached Woodside, the driver announced the train wouldn't go any farther for security reasons. She got off and was taken aback. It was still raining, but that seemed to be doing very little for the cars and buildings burning brightly against the morning sky. If the volume had been turned up on the riots on her call with Carrie, now it was screaming. It wasn't so much the sounds that were troubling her—up close and all around her—but the smell. The smoke stung her eyes, and it carried an acrid odor of burning wood and rubber, the toxic fumes of smoldering plastic and evaporating fuel. She recoiled and wanted to turn around, run away as far as possible from the sickening smell, but she walked right into it and the memories it carried.

There had been the same smell that day she'd waited in front of the hospital because she hadn't wanted her mom to walk home alone, back in the final days of the first Crisis. Her mother could barely walk at the end of her overlong shifts, tired from attending to the unrelenting flood of patients, exhausted from witnessing the misery and bearing the fury of the relatives when she once again had to tell them that surgery had to be indefinitely postponed and that they were doing the best they could with what was available to them. That day, she'd waited a long time for her mom, and when she finally appeared, she'd looked even more drained than usual, bad enough for Shavir to wish they could stop at a restaurant on the way home so she could regain some strength and recover. But everything was closed because of the curfew, and there barely was any produce anyway, so they had walked for twenty minutes, her mom looking forward to the food she knew Shavir had cooked for her. Only they never got that far. Her mom never made it home.

Shavir stopped to catch her breath. The smoke was getting thicker, the burning in her lungs brighter. She wouldn't be able to keep this up, not in this air. She slowed to a trot, moving in the cover of parked cars and abandoned busses, ducking as low as she could. She tried not to think of her mom again, to stay focused on her surroundings.

Farther into Elmhurst, the streets were almost empty apart from small groups of retreating protesters, wounded and defeated, and the occasional Frontline car whizzing by. She was only a few blocks from the center of the riots. On the news, they'd said the patterns of resistance and attack were chaotic, impossible to predict where violence would erupt next. She tried to take smaller streets, but Carrie's drugstore was right on Broadway, not far from Elmhurst Hospital Center, smack in the middle of the battlefield.

There was no way of avoiding it.

Another Frontline patrol sped down the street, forcing her to dive behind a trash can. She waited for the car to turn the corner.

There were faces behind some of the windows on the upper levels of the worn-down house behind her, two children observing fearfully what was happening down on the streets. A boy and a girl, about Zoe's age, both staring like they were wondering what Shavir was doing down there, why she was hiding. A second later, their faces were replaced by that of a woman. Then the girl appeared again, curious or frightened or worried, Shavir couldn't tell. They locked eyes, she from her crouched position behind the trash cans and the little girl from above, facing, for the first time in her life, a world of flames and smoke and ruin. Then she was gone again, blinds falling over the window. The other apartments were all dark, their occupants either gone or hiding behind closed doors and shutters, afraid of stray bullets. Shavir got up and started to run again.

When she finally reached Broadway, the air was saturated with tear gas. She slipped out of her shirt and wrapped it around the lower part of her face as she slowed to a walk. It didn't make much of a difference, but it was enough to allow her to go on. If only she knew where to go. The four-lane street was filled with hundreds of protesters, about a dozen of Frontline's armored patrol cars standing several hundred feet away on both sides, engines running.

It all seemed suspended in time, both parties awaiting the other's first move. It looked like a bizarre game in which everyone seemed to know the rules, including the camera drones hovering above the playing field, ready to deliver the most dramatic scenes of the riot to Spine users around the world in real time.

Most of the protesters were concentrating on the Frontline cars ahead and behind them, hurling insults and Molotov cocktails. But some of them were looking up, yelling their fury at the drone cameras, waving banners with their demands above their heads. She wondered if Jake could see this right now, if he was watching live from wherever he was, if he would see her when she crossed that street, because that was what she would have to do. She needed to get across to the alley behind the building. And, looking at the Frontline cars left and right, she knew she didn't have much time before this erupted—not enough of it to move up or down the street to get behind the Frontline cars.

Even if she had the time and tried, they might stop and arrest her. The only thing she could do was walk right through it.

She waited for another eternal moment, memories toppling in her mind. She could get shot if she left her cover, just like her mom had, only there would be no one attending to her. Then again, it wasn't like having someone who cared had made any difference.

Shavir pushed herself off the wall, crossed the expanse of the sidewalk, and stepped onto the street, moving between the protesters, her eyes riveted on the Frontline cars.

It was when she had crossed the first two lanes that the cars started rolling, first on the right side, seconds later on the left. Both lines of cars were now moving toward the protestors in the middle, clamping them. People reacted immediately, a barrage of shouts, objects, and cocktails flying at the cars. A gunshot cracked above their heads, another tear gas grenade exploded, and the cars still moved forward in slow motion.

So did Shavir. The dripping faces of the men she passed betrayed anger and fear. The women, their cries sharper than the men's, carried prints showing mothers, fathers, grandparents, babies, all soaked with rain. Their free hands were raised, fists clenched. Shavir's own hands were so tightly clamped her nails pierced the skin of her palms. She kept walking, a slow slalom around the protestors, brushing their bodies and feeling their breaths when they shouted, her gaze now fixed on Carrie's drugstore. She exhaled when she reached the opposite pavement, the broken glass of the pharmacy's smashed-in windows crunching underneath her boots.

She slipped into the narrow alley to the side of the building and fell into a trot again.

"Carrie?" she called when she reached the back alley.

A blond tuft of hair appeared behind a group of trash cans. Carrie waved before immediately ducking down again. Shavir ran over and dove behind the trash cans where Carrie crouched next to Zoe, who was cowering against the wall, gasping for air.

Carrie jumped up and hugged her, her skin hot, her cheeks lined with black mascara. "Shavir's here, sweetie," she said, turning to Zoe in a voice meant to be cheerful but sounding desperate. "What about Jake?" she then asked. Zoe hadn't reacted at all.

"We don't have time," Shavir said. "Let's move."

Zoe tried to get up and collapsed in an eruption of coughs.

"She needs her meds," Carrie cried.

Shavir looked at the back door of the drugstore. Carrie's bag was somewhere inside. But before she could make one step toward the door, Broadway erupted in gunshots and screams. Within seconds, the alley flooded with running protesters trying to escape arrest.

Frontline was on the attack.

"Get up!" Shavir yelled and pulled Zoe to her feet. Then they were running, surrounded by people spitting and coughing and crying.

TWENTY-FOUR

JAKE COULD SEE THE roadblock from far away. Several old-style police cars from the Bronx were parked sideways across the lanes with flashing light bars, blocking all access to Queensboro Bridge on 2nd Avenue. About thirty NYPD cops crowded between the cars, yellow raincoats glistening in the rain.

"You can't go farther," yelled one of them. "The bridge is closed."

"I'm with Homeland," Jake said.

The cop pulled out his reader and scanned Jake's prints four times without result because he was soaked, his fingers shriveled. After changing into the N train at Times Square, he'd learned that service to Queens was suspended and the train would only run up to Lexington Avenue. Five minutes later, it was still sitting in the station. He'd decided to try his luck above ground, but the podcar system was still defunct, leaving him no choice but to walk up here.

The cop motioned Jake to sit in his car, where he gave him a towel and finally managed to get a reading of his prints. Then he started making calls. Jake got so restless that he stepped out into the rain again.

He hadn't been able to reach Carrie since she'd told him about Dan. The thought that she, Zoe, and now Shavir were in the middle of what he was seeing on the news was almost too much to bear. He didn't even know where they were or if Shavir had found them because she, too, wasn't picking up. Hopefully, they were far away from the drugstore by now since Frontline was arresting everyone in sight after the escalation on Broadway. Nine protestors were dead, and three other Frontline men had been killed, too, in the latest altercation. He didn't allow himself to think that the women or Zoe might be among the victims; even approaching that thought would paralyze him to the core. But if they weren't hiding behind Carrie's drugstore anymore, and they weren't answering their phones, how the hell was he going to find them once he made it across the bridge?

He was dialing again before he had finished the thought.

"Hey, Jake," Niya said as her hologram popped up in front of Jake. She looked tired and distraught despite her usual mask of professionalism which clearly took some effort. Towering behind her were the Corsys servers, so she was at SAFE, not at home in Brooklyn. "I was so sorry to hear about David," she said. "That was a real shock."

"Yeah, they're kind of accumulating. Are you okay?"

She paused, as if shocked by the question. "Yes, I'm okay," she then said. "I have no idea when I will be able to go home again, but other than that, I'm okay, I guess."

"What about your brother? You said he lives in Queens?"

Niya looked at him like she wasn't sure what was happening, but he truly wanted to know and there was no use being shy about it, given what was happening over there.

"He's alright," Niya finally said. "He's at our sister's house in the Bronx, and I can stay with her, too, until things calm down. Thanks for asking though—" She stopped. "Where *are* you, Jake... are those police cars behind you?" Now she looked alarmed.

"I'm at the checkpoint to Queensboro Bridge and... I need a favor."

"Of course."

Jake used his gloves to type the next words rather than saying them out loud in a place swarming with cops: *I need traces on two cell phones.*

"Okay," Niya said, looking more perplexed than before. "You have to call security for that, like you always do for your traces, and ask them—" She interrupted herself, her gaze locking with Jake's. "You don't want to call security."

"No."

"Where are the phones?"

"In Queens."

"Oh... wow." Niya's eyes widened.

"Can you do it?" Jake asked, looking over his shoulder to make sure no cop was coming closer. "I can't explain now, but it's important." She nodded.

"Thanks, Niya," he breathed, overcome with relief. "What do you need from me?"

"Just the phone numbers."

He sent her Shavir's and Carrie's numbers as the cop approached him again. "We can give you a ride across the bridge, sir," he said. "And we can inform Frontline on the other side, so they'll let you through their roadblock. But you really don't wanna go there."

"I have to. As I said, my cousin and niece are there."

"I understand, sir, but believe me, you're not gonna get very far. There's no public transportation, and there'll be a curfew before long. I understand you wanna get through to your relatives, but I advise against it. Without a vehicle, it's suicide, and neither we nor Frontline can provide you with one at this time."

"Then I'll walk."

The cop looked at him like he was seriously doubting Jake's mental abilities. "That's just... we can't do that, sir. I'm sorry."

Jake opened his mouth to respond just as Niya called him back.

"I've transferred the traces to your Spine," she said.

Jake walked away from the cop and called up the Spine's navigation system. The map showed two blinking red dots in Elmhurst, moving together. The relief was so potent this time, and so sudden, his knees buckled. He leaned against a broken podcar resting in the rain and watched the dots. Shavir's phone was leading, Carrie's falling behind, probably because of Zoe.

"Can you see them?" Niya's voice asked from far away.

"Yes."

"Great. Anything else you need?"

"Not now," Jake said as he watched Shavir's phone stop and return to Carrie's. "This is just... thanks so much, Niya. You have no idea."

He hung up and looked at the roadblock. The cops had lost interest in him, standing grimly between the cars. On his Spine, both dots were moving again in concert, slower than before, but they were going in the wrong direction, toward Carrie's apartment. He had no idea why they would risk moving into Corona, and they still wouldn't answer their phones. He needed to get to them before they walked right into the danger zone again, and there was only one stupid thing he could come up with. He switched back to his phone center and told the Spine to search for Finn Larsen, landscape architect.

"Mr. Larsen," he said when Finn picked up, "this is Jake. Alvaro."

"I know who you are. What do you want?"

"It's Shavir. She's somewhere over there in Queens."

There was silence on the other end.

"She's trying to help my cousin. I couldn't stop her."

Finn switched on his camera. "What the fuck do you want, Jake?"

"I'm trying to get to them, but the cops won't let me across Queensboro Bridge without a vehicle, and they can't give me one." He looked into Finn's hostile eyes. "I need a vehicle."

Another moment of silence.

"I'll be right there."

There was nothing left of the bullet holes in the sides of the van when Finn stopped it a few feet away from the roadblock not ten minutes later. Jake walked toward it and opened the driver door.

"Thanks for coming so fast."

Finn made no move to give up his seat. For a few seconds, they eyed each other, Jake on the street in the pouring rain and Finn in the dry cabin of his van, looking down at him.

"Can I—?" Jake said, eyes on Finn's seat. "There's not much time."

"Try the other door."

Jake stood in the rain and stared. He'd been so relieved when Finn had agreed to come that it hadn't occurred to him the man might want to join him rather than just give him his van. Who in his right mind would want to do such a thing? What was wrong with this guy?

"You're a civilian," he said. "They won't let you pass."

"Get in."

Reluctantly, Jake walked to the passenger door. "It's no problem, really, the van can drive me alone," he tried again as he climbed in.

"No fucking way," Finn said without looking at him.

Jake shut the door, wondering whether this was all about Shavir. The few things she had told him about her relationship with Finn suggested it had been a mess, but this wasn't the callous rich guy he'd pictured. The cops wouldn't let Finn across anyway, but it spoke volumes that he was crazy enough to try.

"Have you heard from her again?" Finn asked as he turned the van toward the roadblock.

"No."

"I couldn't reach her, either," Finn said, and now the tension was visible on his face. "What's our plan then? How do we find her?"

"She just found my cousin and niece at the drugstore. In Elmhurst. They're on their way to North Corona, which isn't smart, but I can't get through to either of them."

"How do you know where they are?"

"I just know, okay? How about we get moving if you're so keen on coming along?" Jake nodded toward the cops who were approaching the van. "They'll check your prints. Better make sure they like them."

"Everyone likes my prints," Finn said as he lowered his window.

He was cleared within seconds, and they were on their way to the bridge. "My father's a bigwig in the city council," he added when he saw Jake's face. "And he donates a lot to the police."

"How convenient," Jake spit out. "That will come in handy when they arrest you for domestic terrorism."

For a few seconds, the only sound was the quiet humming of the engine as the van picked up speed and entered the upper deck of the bridge. "I'm not gonna report you, so relax," Jake then added although there was no indication that his remark had rattled the man.

"We've got more pressing concerns, don't you think?" Finn was looking straight ahead like he needed to concentrate on the street, and Jake realized he was driving the van the old-fashioned way, taking control, which made sense of course.

"Why are you doing it, can I ask? I mean, with your résumé. You've got so much to lose."

"So you've checked out my résumé, huh?" Finn said, grinning as he looked over to him. "Same reason you're doing it, bro. You think you're just kissing a girl, and next thing you know, you're neck-deep involved in whatever people think is terrorism."

"I'm not involved," Jake said, looking away. "I'm just trying to save my family."

They were halfway across the bridge now, the two red dots moving steadily along the map that his Spine projected onto the watery world beyond the windshield, the low sky over Queens eerily illuminated by what had to be the fires he'd seen on the news.

The first dot stopped again and waited for the second to catch up, but this time it was Shavir's phone lagging behind. Then they were both moving again, still toward Corona. Jake was so enthralled in the virtual performance that he jumped back in his seat when the Spine lit up with a call from Shavir.

"I got them," she breathed. "We're on Britton, going northeast."

"I see where you are," Jake replied. "But you need to go east instead."

"East? But that's where I came from, and it didn't look safe."

"It's your best bet. The riots have spread to Corona, and they're also taking over the southern part of Queens Boulevard."

"But we need to go to Corona, Jake." The red dot of her phone paused again as Shavir stopped running. "Zoe is not doing well, and we don't have meds for her. We've taken turns carrying her, but we need to go to the apartment to get her rescue puffer and some other stuff she needs, then we'll wait there until it's safe again outside."

"You can't do that, Shavir. Three more Frontline cops have been killed on Broadway right in front of Carrie's store, another two in Corona, and I don't know how many protesters by now. They're all going completely berserk, you can't take Zoe there, it's too dangerous. You need to go back. Try Forty-Fifth if you can get across Broadway again, then cross over to Woodside."

"You just said they shot people there. I was in that!"

He tried not to process that information. "It's moving away from Broadway right now, north and east, and you need to get to the other side, closer to us. Please try. If you can get through to Woodside, I think we can pick you up there."

"*We?*" Shavir asked. "Where are you?"

"Not far from you. Do you need directions to Woodside?"

"No, I just *came* from there! What do you mean, you can see me?"

"Forget it. Go to Woodside, okay?" Jake stopped because Shavir was saying something indistinct, away from the phone, and then the line collapsed. The dots stopped then turned around as he had told her to. "Okay, they're doing it," he said to Finn, "we need to get to Woodside."

"What do you have?" Finn asked. "Traces?"

"Something happened, I think. They've changed course."

Finn was still looking at him.

"Yes, I put traces on their phones."

Finn nodded in appreciation. "You really are a Homeland man."

"Can we not do this?" Jake barked. He was done suppressing his irritation. "You have your connections, I have mine. So let's cut the bullshit and go find them."

Finn eyed him for another instant, the same mockery in his eyes, then he returned his attention to the street. They were approaching the roadblock on the other side of the bridge, a crisscross of Frontline cars blocking their way.

The van slowed, and Finn lowered his window, but the cops waved them through as two of the cars moved and opened a passage for them. Minutes later, they turned into Queens Boulevard toward Elmhurst.

"They've stopped again," Jake said into the silence.

He stared at the two dots, willing them to pick up their pace. But when they did, they'd changed direction again. "What are they doing?" he demanded as the dots stopped again.

"Can you call them?"

"Not picking up."

"Where are they?"

Jake zoomed in. "They've entered a building. No, just one of them ... Shavir." He looked over at Finn. "It's a pharmacy."

TWENTY-FIVE

Glass crunched under her boots as Shavir entered the gloomy interior of the pharmacy. It was a small, family-owned business, nothing like the big drugstore where Carrie worked, but it had been looted and vandalized all the same—displays knocked down, shelves overturned, packages and bottles trampled—as if people had felt the urgent need to hurt the place as much as they were hurting, as if it was all the pharmacy's fault.

She'd wrapped her shirt around her mouth and nose again, and this time it also covered her hair and the upper part of her tank top. She knew cameras were filming her as she looked around. Most of the shelves still standing were empty. Gone were over-the-counter meds, beauty products, toilet paper, vitamins, and even Band-Aids, though it was impossible to tell what the looters had taken and what the pharmacy had been missing before. She made her way to the counter where the prescription meds were stored. Hopefully, whoever had been here before had taken care of any doors and locks. And hopefully, they hadn't taken everything.

Her shoulders ached from carrying Zoe. Whenever Carrie hadn't been able to go on, she had taken over, bearing not only the weight of the seven-year-old but also her belabored, rattling breathing, a sound like something broken. The girl had been unresponsive for the past ten minutes, awake but barely able to talk. When they'd come by this place and seen the open front, a glance at Carrie had been enough to know they were going to do this.

She heard something clinking behind her and whipped around. Carrie had followed her into the store, pieces of clothing wrapped around her head and carrying Zoe.

"What are you doing?"

"I can't leave her outside alone, and you're never gonna find it without me. If anything's still here." Carrie looked around at the destroyed store. "Fucking looters."

"Go back!" Shavir hissed. "You told me."

"You don't even know where to look." Carrie walked past her, looked up into one of the security cameras, and, with one angry move, uncovered her face. "Plus, this is self-defense and first aid," she said, more to the camera than to Shavir. "A child is in mortal danger. There must be some kind of law to protect us."

There wasn't, but clearly, Carrie didn't care.

Shavir followed her through a door that was half-ajar into a room behind the counter.

"That's the narcotics cabinet." Carrie nodded to a large empty cupboard, its doors broken open, a crowbar lying on the floor. She put Zoe on a chair and told her to sit up.

The sound of the girl's breathing filled the room.

Carrie walked to a wall of drawers and began to search them so systematically it was clear just from watching that she worked at a pharmacy. Most of the drawers were either empty or sparsely filled. Carrie pushed one drawer back to get to the one below it. She looked at Shavir and held up a small box triumphantly, then she unpacked the inhaler and shook it before putting it to the lips of her daughter.

Zoe inhaled and sputtered.

"Again," Carrie said. "Hold it. And count."

This time Zoe managed to hold her breath for a few seconds before coughing again.

"That's good," Carrie said, "and again."

"Hurry up," Shavir whispered, though it was probably safer in here than it was outside.

"Can you do it alone?" Carrie asked Zoe. The girl nodded. Carrie got up and started going through the drawers again.

"What are you doing?" Shavir whispered.

"Seeing if they've left any or corticosteroids or biologics behind. Anything, really."

There was the crunching of glass, and Shavir turned toward the front room. Two figures had entered the store, ducking low. Before she'd had time to hide or utter a warning, they'd seen her, too. They both wore makeshift masks like hers. One of them carried a gun.

For a second, all three of them remained frozen while Carrie kept opening and closing drawers and Zoe sucked at her inhaler. Then the two men recovered enough to straighten up.

"We have a child in there," Shavir said. "She's very sick."

Inside the back room, Carrie stopped, on her face not panic but something like determination. She heaved her daughter onto her hip and walked to the door, facing the intruders. "There's almost nothing decent left," she said with astonishing calm. "But there's some diazepam you can use or sell. Top left drawer." With that, she walked to the broken cash counter and put money into it. "It's forty dollars for the puffer. You can take that, too, if you want," she said to the men, "but I'm not looting a pharmacy." Then she marched to the door. Shavir followed her past the looters, who stared silently.

Once they were outside, Carrie turned left and fell into a steady trot toward Broadway, still carrying her daughter. Shavir followed her, tensing up as they got closer. But they crossed Broadway without problems, and Zoe was still on Carrie's hip when they got to 45th Avenue, Carrie trotting at a superhuman pace.

It was only when they reached 79th Street that she started swaying, and Shavir realized she was going to collapse. She was there to take Zoe off her hip the moment Carrie's knees buckled, and then they were all tumbling to the sidewalk. The shock was still on Carrie's face when she looked at Shavir, but it was no longer enough to propel her forward.

She didn't have to say anything. Shavir knew what she was feeling—the sheer naked panic of realizing that no matter what she did, she no longer had the power to save the person she loved. Dan was dead, killed in the riot, and Carrie couldn't allow herself to mourn or scream, couldn't even say it out loud because she had to protect Zoe from knowledge that would be too much for her to take when she could barely breathe. Now Carrie's strength was fading in the middle of the riot zone, her gaze a silent scream.

"Jake must be real close," Shavir said as she struggled to her feet although she had no idea if that was true or how he was going to meet them. She hadn't even understood what he had meant when he'd said he was seeing them. Maybe he had eyes on them through a drone, but it wasn't like one had been following them around; maybe he could trace Carrie's phone or some other kind of shit they were pulling at Homeland. "I think we're almost there," she added, "and I can carry her again." She reached down to Carrie and pulled her up. "Should we go up here?" she asked when they were standing again.

"No," Carrie spoke for the first time since they'd left the pharmacy. "That's gonna lead us back to Broadway. We need to go all the way to Seventy-Sixth, or it won't be safe. Can you breathe, sweetie?"

Zoe hadn't gotten up. They could see her gasping for air.

"I need a moment now." Carrie revealed a small bottle and a syringe and needle in the hand she had used to balance her daughter on her hip. She ripped off the wrappings and poked the needle into the bottle, holding it up so she could see the dose.

"What is that?" Shavir asked.

"A corticosteroid I took. There weren't any pills left, and the beta agonist she's inhaling isn't cutting it. It was in one of the drawers of the desk along with a bunch of other meds. Must have been set aside for someone special, someone connected, I don't know. We haven't had that kind of stuff in our store for weeks. But my daughter is special, too, and she's goddamn essential to me." She asked Zoe to pull down the neck of her shirt to expose her upper arm. "I don't have a swab, but it should be okay," she said, sounding like a nurse as she gave the shot. "Okay. It'll take a bit to work, but we're ready."

"I'm gonna carry her, but we need to go slower." Shavir turned her back toward the girl and crouched to her knees. Zoe climbed up and wrapped her arms around Shavir's shoulders. They walked to the corner of 76th Street and turned right, but they didn't get far. There was another violent clash on the corner of Woodside, a few blocks away from them. The gusty wind carried over to them the yelling of protesters and Frontline men.

"Let's cut through the alleys again," Shavir said, and they squeezed through a small passage between two houses and then through yards and another narrow alley. Zoe was unbearably heavy, forcing her to slow down. They were walking north again, less than two hundred yards away from Woodside where they could see people running westward away from Frontline or whatever else was after them. Shavir told Carrie to call Jake because they needed a different plan.

And then the world exploded around them.

"*Tear gas*," she cried as pain shot up her nose and into her eyes. She turned, diving with Zoe on her back into the muddy backyard of a small family home. Carrie was lying next to her in the dirt and coughing when Shavir opened her eyes, barely able to see through her tears. Zoe was sobbing.

They got up again and climbed a low wooden fence into the adjacent backyard. Carrie went first, then they had to heave across Zoe, who hadn't stopped crying. God knew how long she'd have oxygen for this. Or how long they'd be able to keep this up.

They had already crossed most of the yard when Shavir heard the steps, swift and soft, a scraping of claws and clinking of chain links against the wet asphalt.

Then the dog leaped, its growl cutting through the rain as its teeth sank into Zoe's thigh. The girl shrieked as she went down.

Shavir turned to watch in horror as the Rottweiler seized Zoe's leg a second time. Then she started screaming at the top of what was left of her lungs as she grabbed the only solid object in reach and hurled it into the animal's face.

TWENTY-SIX

ONE OF THE TWO dots was no longer moving. Jake didn't notice at first because his brain was so overwhelmed by the layered visual information streaming into it as the van sped along Woodside toward the fires and the smoke. But there was no doubt, the distance between the dots was growing again. One of the signals was steadily moving toward them while the other one stayed behind.

"They've separated."

"What?" Finn barked, keeping his eyes riveted to the street. He was still driving the van himself at this breakneck speed.

"They've separated somehow. One of them is no longer moving."

"Which one?"

"Shavir." Jake's voice broke. "It's Shavir's phone."

"Call her!"

"I'm already calling! She doesn't pick up. And neither does Carrie."

Jake stared at the Spine projection. One signal kept moving, relentlessly, while the other one was stuck. Behind the projection, the street was flying toward him as Finn pushed down on the accelerator.

"I can't reach her either," Finn said. "Where's her phone?"

"No," Jake squeezed out. "We drive toward Carrie."

"*Where's Shavir's phone?* I'm not gonna leave her there."

"Carrie would never leave her behind," Jake said, his voice flat. "If she keeps running, they're either together or—" He broke off. He knew what he said was true, but the implication of the other option was so immense he couldn't finish his sentence.

He was thrown into his seat belt when Finn hit the brakes.

Another roadblock, lights reflecting off the buildings ahead of them in red, white, and blue. Armored Frontline men raised their guns.

"Turn right!" Jake yelled.

Finn yanked the van into a small street to their right, going too fast.

They skidded around a parked car and along an empty sidewalk into a narrow alley, flying by yards and fences and trash cans at a breathtaking speed only to face a dead end.

"Fuck!" Finn yelled over the screeching tires.

The van stopped two feet away from a wall.

"I'll go." Jake was out the door and over a fence to their right.

He could hear gunshots over in Elmhurst alongside sirens, drones, and helicopters as he inhaled air saturated with smoke. It was disorienting, but he ran toward the one dot moving slowly, ever more slowly. He cut through alleys and yards, his lungs almost exploding.

Another corner, and he saw them.

All three of them.

They were more stumbling than walking, moving forward conjoined like they were one single body, Zoe hanging limply over Shavir's right shoulder and Carrie leaning against Shavir, trying to support her while clinging to Zoe.

"Jake!" Tears were rolling over Carrie's face as he took Zoe from Shavir's shoulder, the dazed girl opening her eyes without seeing him.

"She got attacked by a dog."

Shavir was shaking, but he didn't dare touch her.

"Do we need a hospital?" he asked instead.

"No," Carrie said, "just get us to Roots."

He called Finn and gave him their position.

Minutes later, they met the van in an alley nearby where Finn jumped out and embraced Shavir.

Jake tried not to see her in Finn's arms as he walked past them with Zoe and lowered the girl carefully onto the van's rubber floor.

Then they slowly made their way west, away from the riots.

As the van reached Greenpoint, Jake received a call from Masao informing him that the FDA had granted SAFE's requested emergency approval for a selection of vet antibiotics. They were already being distributed, but there was a meeting scheduled with Frank Kruger and the MHA this afternoon. Gwen wanted him to be there in person.

He told Masao he would try, though he wasn't even sure whether he'd be able to cross the East River again. The riots were spreading like wildfire, Masao said, overwhelming the hospitals with hundreds of casualties. "But they're already getting antibiotics. They're all in a state of emergency, both eastern boroughs, so no matter what the MHA says, they're privileged. They're getting the lion share of the vet meds we bought, and we bought plenty." There was a quiver in Masao's voice. He paused before asking, "Did you find them?"

"Yeah," Jake said. "We found them."

Relief was mixing with exhaustion as he watched Shavir and Carrie taking care of Zoe using Finn's first-aid kit. How remote it had always been on the Spine and on the walls of the CSR. Now, the hurt and the fear and the pain were right here in this van.

Zoe was fast asleep when they reached Roots. Finn drove the van through an old metal gate into a large warehouse that was mostly empty. A group of men was working on the opposite side of the space, building something that looked like wooden stalls. They stopped as the van came in, and Jake saw Lenny walking toward them.

"The basement is flooding because of all the rain," he told Shavir as he hugged her. "We need to bring them up here." His eyes got stuck on Jake for a second, his expression unreadable, before he turned to Zoe on floor of the van. "How's she doing?"

"She can breathe again," Carrie said, "and her pants are so sturdy they prevented the worst of the attack. She'll need antibiotics though."

"No problem," Lenny glanced at Jake again. "We've got plenty."

"That won't be necessary. We'll take her along to Manhattan."

"Can we stay here?" Carrie said, more deciding than asking. "I don't want her to be driven around anymore. And I don't want her in any of those hospitals right now, not even in Manhattan."

"They wouldn't let her across the bridge anyway," said Finn.

"And I'd much rather have Zoe stay here." Carrie was still looking at Jake. "So she can see Sam when she wakes up. That's gonna do more good for her than anything else."

"But it's not safe," Jake said, vaguely shocked by the request.

"I know," Carrie returned, as if that settled it.

Perhaps she was right about Zoe, and it would be good for Carrie, too, staying here with the Roots people for a while. There was enough food, he hoped, and more company and purpose than she would find in his empty apartment with a view of two dying trees. He recognized the other men—Troy, Zeno—who had dropped their tools to come over and hug Shavir. Now that they had stopped working, he noticed there were dogs in the completed stalls, three big mastiffs, all barking the low, husky sounds he knew from Sam, their puppies weaseling around them. He stared at the dogs, realizing they had to be the rescues from the puppy mill. Then he noticed the men staring at him.

"Where's Tara?" Shavir asked, ignoring the stares.

"Upstairs, in your cubicle," the stocky guy, Nacho, said. "Judy made a deal with her that the dogs can come up if she stays away from them. I think she's for once sticking to protocol. She wanted to wait for you with Sam, but Judy said she's asleep." He turned to Carrie. "You can stay in the free cubicle if you want."

"Where we cleaned up the glass yesterday," Shavir explained. "I'll show you, then you can decide if you wanna stay here or go with Jake." She said his name without looking at him.

He carried Zoe upstairs, putting her to bed in one of those small cubicles, the one Shavir had offered in jest before coming along to Manhattan with him. That felt like another life.

Zoe hardly woke up when Judy came in and made her swallow antibiotics. "It won't hurt her," she said when Carrie picked up the bottle of veterinary doxycycline.

"I know," Carrie said. "She's had those before."

Later, Jake sat with Carrie in the small tea kitchen on the office floor. The others were gone, including Shavir, who had withdrawn at some point without saying goodbye to him and hadn't come back since then. He realized he might not see her again and that this might be what she wanted—that he left without another word. It seemed disproportional to him, his mistakes and her reaction to them. But that wasn't factoring in Finn, who had disappeared as well.

Carrie looked pale under the bright LEDs, the natural light shut out by the boarded windows. "I shouldn't have brought Zoe along to the drugstore on a day like this," she said as she poured boiling water into a tea mug. "But I didn't want to leave her at home again. She hates being alone." Her voice constricted. "Shavir was unbelievable. The way she got us out of there right when things started exploding. You can't imagine what was happening, it was like... war. But she just walked in and saved us. And then, when that monster dog attacked out of nowhere, she stood there and screamed at it. I grabbed Zoe and ran away. She didn't run, Jake. She totally didn't. She just faced it."

"I heard she also threw a phone at it."

Carrie ignored that. "She came and got us. And you, too," she added, as if only now remembering. "Thank you for getting us."

Jake nodded, feeling vaguely jealous, though he wasn't sure of what or whom or why.

"Have you talked to her?" Carrie asked.

"Shavir? Not yet, but I will at some point." Or not.

"I think she really wants to."

"What?"

"Talk."

He erupted in a laugh. "Sure."

"Why don't you ever believe me?" Carrie sounded somber, the way she used to sound as a child when he had locked himself in his room with the intention to never come out again and she—nine years old and filled with purpose and meaning—would tell him life was worth living. How she could keep that up now when her husband was dead and the world in shambles was beyond him. She hadn't mentioned Dan again, like she hadn't mentioned her beloved mother for weeks after his aunt had managed to kill herself with an overdose during the worst global supply crisis in human history.

"I'm sorry to leave you alone," he said, "but I need to go back to Manhattan for an emergency meeting with the mayor." It was true, and he couldn't possibly talk to Carrie about Shavir right now or deal with her never-ending optimism. "Finn will take me across the river. Are you sure you don't want to come along and stay in my apartment?"

"Yes." Carrie took a sip of her tea. "Zoe needs to see Sam. It will cheer her up, and she'll need that once I tell her."

He wondered if he should say something, but he used to hate it when she made him talk about what was irretrievably lost.

"What are they doing with all those dogs down there?" Carrie asked, surprising him.

"That's a long story."

"Are they breeding them? They're not—"

"No. Definitely not."

"So are they rescuing them?"

Jake looked away. "Yeah," he said. "They're rescuing them."

"Like... Sam?"

Jake nodded.

"Oh." Carrie let that sink in. "Zoe will love that."

"She can't know, Carrie. It's illegal."

"It shouldn't be."

"Well, it is, and you better forget what you saw because if anyone finds out, anyone remotely related to Frontline, they can be charged for terrorism." There was a long silence after he'd said that, and he started cursing himself almost immediately for mentioning Frontline.

"Dan knew, right?" Carrie asked.

"I don't know."

"He'd never have arrested her," she said with conviction. "Not my Dan." Her lips started quivering when she said her husband's name. "Not my Dan," she repeated, her voice cracking. Then she calmed herself again. "Maybe I'll stay here. I can't go back to that apartment, not for real, not without him. And your place is tiny. Maybe I'll stay here and work on the farm, I think I'd like that. And Zoe, too."

"Let's just wait a bit," Jake replied carefully, "process it all."

"I have no idea where else to go from here." Carrie still sounded calm, but tears were running down her cheeks. "When he was in the army, Dan always wanted me to be prepared for the worst, and of course I never was. He survived three wars, and when he came home, I thought it was over, you know? Then he gets killed in Queens, ten minutes from home. By our own people, one of our neighbors, maybe. That was always the hardest for him, that his job made him go against his own people, people who have a right to be mad, people who've been abandoned and screwed over for no good reason. People like us, you know? But we needed the money. Now it's just Zoe and me."

Jake put his arm around her. "Don't talk like that, okay? We're gonna get through this. Like we've gone through everything else."

"Dan's gone," Carrie whispered. "What am I gonna do?"

When Carrie was calm enough to look after Zoe, Jake walked across the hallway to the staircase. A wheelchair stood outside the open door to one of the cubicles, and he saw Tara sitting on the sole chair inside, across from Shavir. Shavir sat on a narrow bed, drying her hair with a towel. Sam took up the entire remaining floor space.

The women noticed him, and then Tara struggled to her feet, walking gingerly the few steps to her wheelchair. "I was just leaving," she said with that grin of hers.

"Do you have a minute?" Shavir was looking at him.

He went in, closing the door behind him, trying to breathe evenly. The cubicle was the same size as Judy's, but its window was boarded, and it wasn't nearly as stuffed with furniture and personal things. Three medical bottles sat prominently next to the framed picture of a smiling woman, her mom probably. The air smelled of shampoo.

Shavir moved a little to make room on her bed.

He carefully stepped around Sam, who wagged his tail against the floor without lifting his head. *Thump, thump, thump, thump.*

The towel was still in Shavir's hands, so Jake reached for it.

She looked at him, a question in her eyes. Then she slowly turned her back, allowing him to dry her long tresses. He went to work, his trembling fingers inches away from the curve of her neck.

"How's Carrie?" Shavir asked into the silence.

"Hurting. Thank you for getting her and Zoe out of there."

"I had to. And I'm really sorry for her, and for you, too. I know you lost a friend in Dan." She turned to him, and he nodded.

"David has died, too," he said, realizing she didn't know yet.

Something melted in her eyes. "Oh, Jake, I'm really sorry."

"Me, too. But perversely, I think it's what he wanted."

"Maybe. He didn't have much left to hang on to. But Carrie is strong, and she has Zoe. They'll both get through this. Maybe they can stay for a while. They love the farm, I saw that when they were here."

"Carrie thinks you're superwoman. I think you're just plain crazy. And I'd never have thought you'd hurl a phone at the face of a dog."

A crease shot up between Shavir's eyes. "He was dangerous," she snapped. "And it's not like I killed him. I just got him to let go of Zoe, and even that was pure luck. I feel sorry for him, actually. He was chained up and terrified by the shooting."

Jake nodded. "Are you gonna get him, too?"

"Maybe," she said, and he couldn't tell whether she was serious.

"It was amazing to see them down there, your dogs. It somehow became real for me today, seeing them for the first time. Carrie is in awe, just so you know. And she knows they're rescues, but she won't tell anyone. She talks nonstop, but she can keep a secret, too."

"She told me about Farley."

Jake inhaled. "Did she."

"I think I understand now—why you think you have to do your job, and why it's been so hard for you to understand me and what we're doing for the animals. That's why I was there last night, at your place."

"I ran after you. But you were gone."

She didn't reply to this, but he could see her collarbones move. "I always thought you didn't care about them, the animals," she said, "but I guess you feel you cared too much."

"I did. And I don't want the same to happen to you."

She took the towel from his hands. "I met Dan again last night. And Gary." She waited for him to react to that, and it didn't fail to have an effect as she told him about protecting Sam's body with her own and about what Gary had said and done to her. He could feel the rage rising in him as he imagined the scene, Shavir down in the slush and Gary threatening her, pointing his gun. And then Gary's face up there on the wall in the CSR, next to Dan's. A dead man.

"Dan warned me," he said. He swallowed, remembering how Dan had asked him if he still cared about Shavir. It had been the last time he'd seen Dan alive. "There's nothing about the raids on your Homeland file. Or on Tara's. I checked. They're both bursting at the seams with protests and petitions, and there's a report on Tara's arrest and the fines that were paid. But nothing about any raids. Perhaps Gary didn't have anything to report, or he didn't yet have time to do so."

He could see Shavir processing this and knew he'd just confirmed what she'd always suspected: that he had access to her Homeland file.

"Thanks for telling me," she finally said. "Did Homeland put a trace on my phone today?"

"No. But I did. A friend of mine, she can do these things."

"Wow," she said, studying him.

"I'm sorry."

"You got us out of there. We wouldn't have made it without you."

"And Finn," Jake couldn't stop himself from saying.

"He was there because of you."

"Yeah." His face felt hot. "I specialize in crisis logistics."

Then she kissed him.

"I'm so happy you're still alive," he whispered when he could breathe again. "Please don't make me lose you again, we've both lost so much already."

She was leaning against him, silent. Outside, the rain was beating against the boarded window, the sound mixing with the murmur emanating from some of the other cubicles on the floor.

"I know we don't see eye to eye on everything," he continued, "and I'm scared shitless just like you, but I can't do this without you."

"What?" she asked.

"This." He pointed vaguely around him. "Life."

A smile played around her lips.

"When's your birthday?" he asked.

"My birthday?"

He nodded. "You never told me."

"Homeland doesn't know?"

"I'm asking you. So we can celebrate next time."

She considered this.

"March seventh."

"It's in my calendar. And as much as I hate it, I gotta go now. We have an emergency meeting with the MHA and the FDA."

"The FDA? You think they'll emergency-approve the vet meds?"

"They already did. Thanks to you these meds are in the city, and they can save all kinds of lives. Now I wanna know how we're gonna distribute them."

She smiled. "You just never give up, do you?"

"That's never been an option available to me."

"Will you come back?"

"Tonight?"

She nodded.

"I don't know if I can. I will try."

"Okay, try then. We need help rebuilding the farm, and I've always wanted to find out if I can fit sleepovers in here."

Finn had told him to meet him on the farm, so Jake walked up to the roof, where the rain had let off a little. The plants were covered by sheets of white foil that had not been there last time he'd been up here. It didn't look nearly as bad as he'd expected, the foil still intact.

He saw Finn standing on the roof of the next building and walked over, gasping when he approached the bridge at the sight of row after row of torn and shredded plants. Manhattan's skyline was towering behind them like a menace in watery shades of gray.

"They're gonna recover," Finn said, seeing his shocked face. "That's what I've told every single one of my clients over the past twenty-four hours. And yet they all want me to rip out their plants and get them new ones so they can enjoy their view. How can you be that dumb? They want a garden but don't know the first thing about resilience."

"It looks pretty bad though. What are you gonna do?"

"What we always do," Finn said with a shrug. "Replant. Rebuild. We've seen so many storms. At least this one didn't rip out our bridges. Judy always takes that very personally."

Their ride back to Manhattan was uneventful. The Frontline men at the entrance of the Midtown tunnel were as friendly as their counterparts a few miles north, allowing them to pass without problem after scanning Finn's prints. They didn't bother to check Jake's.

"You realize she's mine," Finn said when they were underneath the East River, no other vehicle or human in sight.

Jake turned to him. "Excuse me?"

"You're not gonna walk away with my girl." Finn looked over at him, his eyes calm and cold. "That's not how this goes."

"You have a problem, man," Jake said slowly. "And she's not a girl."

"Suit yourself. But don't be delusional. You don't even understand what she's doing or why it's important to her."

"But you do."

"Yes. I do."

"I don't think so," Jake said and turned away.

Neither he nor Finn felt any desire to talk after that, so Jake woke up his Spine and prepared himself for his meeting.

"Thank you," he said when Finn stopped the van outside Grand Central. "And thank you for coming today. I'll see you at the farm."

Finn nodded and was gone.

When he left the subway on 14th Street, Jake walked up to one of the vending machines and stood there for a full ten minutes, buying every single chocolate bar it contained for Niya. There was still time left, so he shouldered his overstuffed bag and turned west to the seawall, slowly strolling toward SAFE in the pouring rain.

AUTHOR'S NOTE

My great thanks go to:

Anders Levermann for his input on various scientific matters and for coming up with the idea of an implanted communication system operated via data gloves.

Rosemary Ahern, Susannah Waters, and Federay Holmes for helping me make this a far better book than it would otherwise have been. The dedicated teams at Ebook Launch and Elzwhere for making it a physical reality.

Boris Bugla, Ursula Heise, Matthias Klestil, Salma Monani, Amara Palacios, Carina Rasse, and Kareem Tayyar for reading and commenting on various versions of the manuscript. Sylvia Mayer for many thoughtful reads and boundless support.

My husband, Michael, for absolutely everything.

Finally, Miranda from *Station Eleven* for showing me how to go about this project and for reminding me what matters most.

Parts of chapter 3 were first published in different form in the story "The Great Garden" in *The Dillydoun Review*. Parts of chapter 20 were first published in different form in the story "Le Déluge" in *Orca*.

About the Author

Alexa Weik von Mossner holds a PhD in Literature from UC San Diego and has published six scholarly books, including *Cosmopolitan Minds* and *Affective Ecologies*. On the fiction side, she has penned over 160 episodes of the German weekly TV drama series *FABRIXX*. Her short stories have appeared in American literary magazines such as *Orca*, *Delmarva Review*, and *The Dillydoun Review*. You can find her online at https://www.alexaweikvonmossner.com